Praise for New York Times bestselling author Lori Foster

"Foster's feel-good, small-town romance weaves in well-plotted story threads and complications that expose how scars from the past, if healed, can unlock more hopeful, brighter futures."
—*Shelf Awareness* on *The Summer of No Attachments*

"Full of healing, hope and, most importantly, love… An absolute delight."
—Maisey Yates, *New York Times* bestselling author, on *Cooper's Charm*

"[A] satisfying page-turner, complete with adorable animals and an idyllic summer setting."
—*Publishers Weekly* on *The Summer of No Attachments*

"A bubbly summer escape, and beyond that, a heartwarming look at the healing power of family."
—*Entertainment Weekly* on *Cooper's Charm*

"Brimming with heart, heat and humor."
—Jill Shalvis, *New York Times* bestselling author, on *Worth the Wait*

"A sexy, heartwarming, down-home tale that features two captivating love stories… Skillfully walks the line between romance and women's fiction."
—*Library Journal* on *Sisters of Summer's End*

"Storytelling at its best! Lori Foster should be on everyone's auto-buy list."
—#1 *New York Times* bestselling author Sherrilyn Kenyon on *No Limits*

LORI FOSTER

The Honeymoon Cottage

CANARY STREET PRESS

CANARY
STREET
PRESS™

Recycling programs
for this product may
not exist in your area.

ISBN-13: 978-1-335-42854-7

The Honeymoon Cottage

First published in 2022. This edition published in 2023.

For questions and comments about the quality of this book, please contact us at CustomerService@Harlequin.com.

Canary Street Press
22 Adelaide St. West, 41st Floor
Toronto, Ontario M5H 4E3, Canada
CanaryStPress.com

Printed and bound in Barcelona, Spain by CPI Black Print

The Honeymoon Cottage

1

GROANING, YARDLEY BELANGER dropped the pencil and stretched her back. She'd been at her desk too long today and her body didn't appreciate it one bit. She spent far too much time trying to find clever ways to play off the town name. Cemetery, Indiana. There was only so much she could do with that. Why couldn't it have been Bliss, Indiana? Or Romance, Indiana. Those names would have worked perfectly for a wedding planner. But no, Cemetery it was, and apparently Cemetery it would stay.

Sentiment and tradition, especially when it came to horrible old names, could really crowd out practicality.

Raising her arms high, she twisted this way and that, unkinking her muscles before attempting to focus again. She loved her work as a wedding planner, and she even enjoyed creating meals for herself, her mother and her aunt. They were tasks she'd grown into, and she took a lot of pleasure in them. She also found immense satisfaction in rehabbing their Victorian-style home.

Paying the bills, though? Not so much. And cleaning?

Ugh. She really hated that. She did it anyway because she ran the business through her home, and customers expected things to be nice. Unfortunately, her mother and aunt were messy divas who forgot a cup here, a napkin there, a pair of shoes at the bottom of the stairs… Yardley had fallen into the habit of tidying up after them.

One upside to Cemetery? She loved the area, and she loved… Oh yes, she loved the Honeymoon Cottage. Opening the email window on her computer, she again scrolled through the photos that had arrived yesterday. The owner had updated things to Yardley's suggested recommendations, and it was just so incredibly beautiful. Not that it had needed much. Nestled in mature trees with wild honeysuckle all around, within a few feet of a private cove on the lake, the cottage could be utterly bare and newly married couples would still adore it.

Yardley certainly did.

Somewhere toward the front of her house, a screen door slammed. Her mother, she thought with a grimace. Or her aunt? They were supposed to be out until dinner. Right now was not a good time for her to have to deal with their constant bickering. No one could out-insult the Belanger sisters.

Seconds later she recognized the sound of her best friend's fast footsteps. Amelia "Mimi" May never did anything leisurely, including walk. She had one speed: full go.

Like a gust of fresh air, Mimi sailed into her open office space, saying, "Oh good, you're alone." She dropped into a chair as if someone had poured her there, legs stretched out, spine slouched, elbows draped over the padded arms. Her short, curly blond hair bounced once before settling around her oval face.

Yardley grinned. "Good thing. A customer would've thought we were under attack the way you shot in here."

"Time, you know," Mimi said. "I never, ever have enough time these days."

"You always rush," Yardley countered. From grade school on, Mimi had left her breathless. She'd also befriended her, backed her up, offered defense and alibis, and once she'd even punched a boy for making Yardley cry. "That's not a complaint though. I'm glad to see you. I needed a break."

Mimi closed her big blue eyes and sighed. "Me, too."

Yardley didn't storm through life the way Mimi did, but her mouth often resembled a runaway train. For the most part, she'd learned to temper it, to slow down and think before speaking. But in moments of excitement? Few people could keep up with her.

Even fewer cared to try.

And around Mimi? She didn't need to temper anything. That's why she and Mimi were such a good fit. She loved Mimi's energy level, and Mimi never failed to mentally keep pace with her wild ramblings.

"Not enough sleep last night?" Yardley asked. "Did the baby keep you up?"

"Well, it sure wasn't Kevin." One eye peeked open. "Sammy slept fine for once. She's six months old now but Kevin hasn't yet…" Pausing, she made a face. "It's like I had a kid and became this sexless lump taking up space in the house."

Yardley sympathized—with both of them. It wasn't the first time she'd heard this complaint. "You had such a difficult birth." With two early miscarriages prior to that. "Plus, it took you a while to recover. Kevin was scared to death for you. Maybe he's just still worried."

"Not so worried that he doesn't want to fish at every available moment."

"*Every* available moment?" Yardley asked. "So that wasn't him cooking dinner the other day when I came by? Or the time before that when he was cleaning all the floors?"

"Or when he mows the lawn or does the grocery shopping or cleans my car." Blowing out a breath, Mimi groaned, "Never mind me. Kevin is great."

"He is, and so are you." Mimi could complain to her all day long and Yardley would still know the truth. Sometimes, though, a girl needed to vent. She wanted Mimi to feel free to talk to her anytime, about anything.

"The thing is, I know he *wants* to be fishing. He might not say it, but he loves being out on the boat. Probably the peace and quiet."

"If he wanted to fish, he would. A lot of guys wouldn't even ask. They'd just disappear on you. I'm betting Kevin is as busy being a parent as you are." With such an adorable baby to focus on, she doubted either of them wanted much time away.

"Right again." Mimi made a face of disgust. "I'm just horny and I have cramps."

The horniness Yardley took as a good sign. It meant Mimi was getting back to normal. But the other alarmed her. "Cramps?" she asked, sitting forward.

"My period. Since giving birth, it's like my PMS is on steroids or something. The cramps last a good seven days—before and during my period. Honest to God, I wouldn't have let Kevin touch me last night anyway." Half under her breath, she complained, "But he should have tried, damn him."

Yardley stood and snagged her friend's hand. "Come

on. We'll make that cinnamon tea you like, and I have some fresh lemon cookies that I was saving for customers."

"Customers…and best friends?"

"Exactly." With Mimi's hand held in her own, she headed to the kitchen. "Have you asked the doctor about your cramps?"

"Yup. I'm the picture of health, so no worrying."

She'd worry if she wanted to—and with Mimi's history, she had good reason for it. "Let's relax for a while. I finally got the buzzer fixed in here, so I'll hear anyone who comes in the front door—even if they don't slam the screen."

"Ha ha." Mimi dropped onto a stool at the island, close to where Yardley would heat the water for the tea.

The house, built in 1900 and updated by numerous families since then, had many challenges, but Yardley *loved* the kitchen. Little by little, when finances allowed, she'd remodeled it. Now instead of in a dinky ceramic sink, she filled the tea kettle in a copper farmhouse sink with stunning oil-rubbed bronze faucets, beneath an ornate window with cut glass panes that mimicked the glass in the upper cabinets.

Everything was fresh and new, from the cream-colored cabinets and the light fixtures to the tile and the hardware. She'd passed on updating her own bedroom at the opposite side of the entry doors to ensure she had the kitchen of her dreams.

"By the way," Mimi said, "where are Cruella and Maleficent?"

Yardley shot her friend a frown. Mimi knew she shouldn't call her mother and aunt those awful names. Not because Yardley disagreed with the comparison, but because if either of the elder women ever overheard, they'd make Mimi's life miserable.

"Shush it," Yardley said in mock warning.

Her friend shot her an impish grin full of innocence. "What? I'm always respectful to their faces."

Usually she was—except for when she took offense on Yardley's behalf. Most of the time, Yardley didn't think her mother or aunt even realized that they were insulting her. They threw not-so-subtle barbs at each other so often, there was bound to be a stray dart every now and then.

"They're out until dinner."

Sniffing the air, Mimi asked, "What are we having, anyway?"

"For dinner?" It was doubtful Mimi would get any, because she wouldn't stay away from her daughter that long. "Lasagna. That's the sauce you smell that I cooked earlier today. I'll assemble it all and have dinner on the table at six if you want to join us."

"Oh how I wish I could. No one makes lasagna like you." She sighed. Again. "Mom has Sammy, and she's great with her."

"Your mom is great in every way." Many times, Yardley had envied Mimi for her wonderful mother.

"True, true. But I'll have to get back to the little stinker before then." Mimi clasped her really impressive boobs. "I'm cutting back on the breastfeeding, but if I stayed away that long, I'd probably pop."

Yardley hurried around the island and drew Mimi in for a tight squeeze.

"Hey. What's that for?" Mimi asked, once she'd returned the embrace.

"You're just the most amazing mom. I mean, I always

knew you would be. You're so full of love and patience. Little Sammy is the luckiest girl in the world."

Snorting, Mimi said, "You only think that because I adore *you*."

The casual words hit too close to home, so Yardley smiled and turned away to retrieve the cookie tin from her new freestanding butler's pantry. "Your adoration is appreciated." So very, very much. What would her life be like without Mimi in it?

She didn't want to know.

"Adoring you was super easy and you know it. I'm weird, you're weird, it was meant to be."

"Hey," Yardley protested. "You're not weird!"

Mimi started snort-laughing and then she couldn't stop.

"Are you getting hysterical?" Her friend hadn't laughed like that in a while.

The question only made Mimi laugh harder, until Yardley reluctantly got drawn in, and soon they were both out of control cackling.

Minutes later, to the sound of the tea kettle whistling, Mimi wiped her eyes. "Ohmigod, you defended me— *from me*," Mimi explained, still wearing a huge, lopsided grin—at least until she softly asked, "Why won't you defend yourself like that?"

Rolling her eyes, Yardley turned away. "Everyone knows I *am* weird. Always have been." Growing up in Cemetery, she'd never seemed to say the right thing, do the right thing, or act the right way. Her mother was forever embarrassed by Yardley's "lack of social graces." It'd take more digits than she had on her fingers and toes to count the number of times her mother and aunt had reminded her that she was the black sheep of the Belanger line of females, which they blamed on the father she'd never known.

Not Mimi. From day one, her friend had embraced what she called "unique qualities." She admired Yardley's lack of fashion sense, and her less than classic features that were so different from her mother's and aunt's. She even liked the rapid-fire way Yardley strung together so many unnecessary, and often unwanted, words when she got going.

Thanks to Mimi, she'd stopped fighting her weirdness. For the most part.

Only with clients did Yardley attempt to settle into the staid trappings of a savvy businesswoman. She practiced a lot of "thinking before speaking," and at times it was almost painful.

She never had to do that with Mimi.

"Maybe you're the type of weirdo who can't recognize other weirdos," Mimi mused. "Did you ever think of that?"

"No." After Yardley poured the fragrant tea, she put three cookies on a plate—two for Mimi and only one for herself…because she'd eaten a few already.

Snatching a cookie even before Yardley got seated beside her, Mimi bit off half. "Mmm." Using the remaining half of the cookie to gesture, she said, "In a world full of cultured pearls, you, Yardley Belanger, are a rare abalone pearl. Exotic, colorful, and oh so beautiful."

Yardley's heart turned over in her chest. The really special part? Mimi meant it. When Yardley was with her friend, her troubles seemed less important and she felt happier, more fulfilled.

Joking her way out of an emotional stranglehold, Yardley said, "Just for that, you can have all three cookies."

"Awesome. I'd feel bad except that I know you have a bunch, and you're an amazing chef who can create more whenever you want to. I, on the other hand, make only boxed desserts."

Just like Mimi to minimize her many talents. "Are you feeling better?" Yardley asked.

"Perkier, for sure." She sipped her tea, gave another hum of pleasure, and finished off another cookie. "Over-all, you know I adore my life."

"I do know it, but that doesn't mean you can't bitch to your best friend when the mood strikes."

Mimi smiled. "Sammy's an angel. Granted, an angel who spit up all over my hair this morning, and who some-times doesn't sleep more than two hours at a stretch. An angel who likes to load her diaper thirty seconds after I've just changed her—but still an angel."

"She really is special." In more ways than one. "And so are you."

Sammy was Mimi's miracle baby. Yardley's heart still ached when she thought of how Mimi had sobbed in her arms after the first miscarriage. With the second, she'd been inconsolable—and so had Kevin. The poor man had not only mourned his lost child, but he'd suffered over his wife's pain as well. Always, every second of the way, Kevin was there with her. And when he had to work, Yardley did her best to ensure Mimi wasn't alone.

It had taken more than a year before Mimi tried again. Poor Kevin seemed to have aged ten years as they went through the pregnancy, every day a cherished milestone. When Mimi went into labor three days past her due date, Yardley had met them at the hospital…and then the night-mare began.

In the birthing room, her camera at the ready, Yardley

had waited for the first glimpse of their new baby girl. She could still recall the doctor's statement that the baby was in fetal distress. Moments later, Mimi began losing too much blood.

Kevin hadn't budged, standing stoically by the head of the bed, his hand gripping Mimi's as she'd gone terribly pale and lethargic, tears streaking down her cheeks.

Then Sammy was born and the nurses were bustling everywhere, cleaning her, checking her, and declaring her healthy. Finally, an agonizing ten minutes later that felt like hours, Mimi was stabilized as well.

It was the longest ten minutes of Yardley's life. Her vision was so blurred with tears, she'd had a heck of a time getting the promised pics of Sammy.

Kevin had broken down. Strong, reliable, stalwart Kevin. Dropping to his knees beside his wife's bed, he'd sobbed, giving broken thanks and swearing that he'd never go through that again.

With Mimi still so weak, and Kevin shattered, they'd handed Sammy to Yardley—and a bond was forged that would never be broken. Yardley had always wanted children, and six months ago Mimi had given her the next best thing. She was an unofficial aunt, an official godmother, and she loved Sammy with all her heart.

"Hey." Mimi leaned forward to see Yardley's face. "What's wrong?"

Lips trembling, Yardley shook her head, then grabbed her friend again for another fierce, almost desperate hug. "I was just thinking how close we came to losing you." If it still affected her like that, how badly did it haunt Kevin?

They both grew solemn.

"You know, I barely recall any of it," Mimi whispered,

as she always did when they discussed her daughter's birth. "Mostly I remember waking up the next day with Kevin in a chair next to the bed, his head beside my hip and his hand holding mine. The second I moved, he jumped up—and I saw his face."

Yardley knew that the tears he'd shed had been obvious in his puffy, red-rimmed eyes.

"I panicked, thinking the worst," Mimi admitted. "But he immediately reassured me that Samantha was fine. He kissed me, really fast because he knew I was ready to lose it. He lifted that little squirt from the hospital crib and handed her to me, and then I was the one sobbing."

In so many ways, Kevin and Mimi were the ideal couple—and they shored up her belief that marriage *could* be perfect...which was why she served the community and beyond as a wedding planner.

In *Cemetery*.

But hey, she sent many of those couples to the Honeymoon Cottage, where they wrapped up the memories of the very best wedding Yardley could give them.

Gah, Cemetery was a terrible name for a town. Even worse, the town council insisted that everything be named Cemetery after the founder, Henry Harrison Cemetery. Like the grocery, the florist, the bank...and her business, Cemetery Weddings.

At least that lovely little cottage had survived. It was just called "the honeymoon cottage" by most, without an official name.

Mimi nibbled on the edge of another cookie. "I still can't believe I produced such a precious little person."

"Well, you did, and Sammy will be the most loved little girl in the whole world."

Mimi picked up the last cookie and stood. "I'm suddenly anxious to see my poopy little angel again." She held up the sweet treat. "Thank you for these and the tea. Now I feel like I can face the rest of the day."

"You're welcome." Used to Mimi's quick, refreshing visits, Yardley walked with her out of the kitchen, down the hall, and to the front entry at the other side of the house. The screen door allowed in a warm, early summer breeze that carried through the open windows on both floors. Tall oak and maple trees offered shade, and numerous flowers, both in the yard and window boxes, gave the stately old home a very welcoming air.

"You've made this place stunning," Mimi said from the painted wooden porch as she looked at the new outdoor cushions on the wicker seating arrangement. "The Belanger gals are so damn lucky to have you. Do me a favor and don't ever let them forget it." She kissed Yardley's cheek and headed down the steps to her minivan.

"Come again, any time," Yardley called after her. Chatting with Mimi was always a wonderful break.

"You couldn't keep me away."

After watching Mimi back out to the main street, Yardley waved again.

Time to return to her work. Somehow she had to get her mother and aunt to spend a little less money.

She'd just gotten to her desk when her phone rang. Not her personal phone, but the one she used only for the business. Exciting. She'd love to add another wedding to her schedule so she could hopefully afford the renovations to her own bedroom and bathroom.

"Cemetery Weddings, don't let the name fool you," she practically sang—because for real, she couldn't say that seriously to save her life. "This is Yardley Belanger, the wedding planner. How may I help you?"

"My sister is getting married, and apparently she saw a country...*display* with your company name and number on it."

Wow. The deep voice sounded less than approving. "Would that be our display with the old rusty red truck? It's part of a very popular setting right now." Take that, Mr. Disapproving.

"I assume. Do you have other country displays?"

No, drat it, she didn't. The truck served as a billboard when not in use, but when necessary, it was moved to various wedding venues. "Just that one display, currently, but of course we can do any type of wedding."

"Then I must have the right place."

This time he sounded amused—at her expense. "You must." And now what? "Would your sister and her intended like to meet to discuss her wedding vision with me?"

"Her intended can't make it, so I'm stepping in, and tomorrow afternoon is the only time I have free for a few weeks. Do you have any appointments available?"

Keep it cool, Yardley. "Let me see if I can accommodate you." Knowing she had nothing at all scheduled for tomorrow, she tapped her nails on the desk for an appropriate fifteen seconds, then said cheerfully, "Good news. It seems I have a noon appointment open. Would that work?"

"That'd be great, thanks."

Well, that didn't sound as condescending. He actually seemed grateful that she could make it work. "Wonderful. You have the address?"

"Yeah, Main Street, in... Cemetery?"

Her molars locked even though she forced a smile. "That's us. A small town full of charm, history, and warmth." *With a really stupid name.* "When you spot the large cream Victorian-style house with teal-and-white trim and a rather bright pink front door, you've found me."

"Interesting. Any other features I might notice from the outside?"

An odd question, but Yardley rolled with it. "There's a lovely turret to the left when you're facing the home." She would have liked to say a *gnarly* turret, but her mother would have a cow if she used that description. "To the right there's also a balcony. Of course the house has the usual gingerbread trim and multiple brackets."

"Can't wait to see it. Noon, Ms. Belanger."

"Wait! I don't have your name."

"Sorry. I got distracted with the house."

If that was a sign of interest, it could be a bridge to win him over, since he didn't sound all that keen on the charm of a country wedding for his sis. "I understand. I'd be happy to show you around while you're here."

"That'd be great. My sister is Sheena Long, and I'm Travis. Thank you for the fast appointment."

"My pleasure, Mr. Long. See you tomorrow." As soon as she disconnected, she threw both hands in the air and jiggled in her seat.

Finally, this old house would come in handy for more than the pleasing aesthetics. It would help to win over Travis Long—such a nice name—and push her further along the road to success.

Quickly, with enthusiasm spurring her on, she assembled a fresh packet for the bride-to-be...and she'd definitely print out the photos of the Honeymoon Cottage to include.

"MOTHER, DIDN'T YOU plan to go out?" It was nearing noon, and Aurora Belanger had yet to leave. Lilith, her mother's sister, also lingered in the foyer right outside her office. It was as if they knew she had an appointment and they wanted to oversee the process. It was a fact that no matter how she succeeded, they expected her to fail, or sometimes they just disapproved of how she succeeded.

"Why the rush?" Aurora asked as she adjusted the V-neck of her sleeveless blouse to show more cleavage.

Granted, for an almost-fifty-year-old woman, her mother still had it. The problem was that she knew it, and she focused on looking sexy more than she did on making the business work. Yardley forced her mouth into a smile. "I thought you had some local honeymoon locations to scope out today."

"I don't *scope out* locations. And stop slouching."

Automatically, Yardley straightened, but damn it, she hadn't been slouching anyway. "So, what would you call it?"

"I visit, investigate, and collect valuable information that will enhance our clients' experiences." She shot Yardley a superior look. "It's a key part of the business, you know. Certainly, the locations I suggest are more appropriate than that rustic Honeymoon Cottage you always recommend."

"The cottage is amazing and you know it."

Aurora sniffed. "Most people are more interested in their honeymoon than the actual wedding."

Meaning her mother's contributions were more valuable than Yardley's efforts? Baloney. She knew one thing, though: Aurora's choices were certainly more expensive. Folding her arms, Yardley said, "Huh. I guess a lot of happy clients didn't realize that, because more than half choose the cottage, so—"

"Because it's so disgustingly cheap," Aurora insisted.

"Affordable," Yardley countered, but why she bothered, she didn't know. They'd disagreed on the point too many times to count.

"I need to leave soon for the café," Aunt Lilith interrupted. She was four years Aurora's senior, and though they shared similar features, she was more concerned with flaunting her intellect than her sex appeal. At least the niche, tea-parlor-type café Lilith owned turned a small profit, even though they'd transitioned from meeting prospective clients there to having them at the home office instead.

Lilith focused on Yardley with nerve-rattling acuity. "Whatever are you up to, Yardley? Do you have an appointment, hmm?"

"Yes, I do, and I need to prep for it. So… I'll see you both later." She took a step back. Then another. Neither of them budged. Damn.

Lilith gave her a longer look. "Don't you have something more appropriate to wear?"

Looking down at her summer dress, Yardley frowned in consternation. It was one of her favorites. She adored the way the soft, flowing material gently draped her body. The skirt ended mid-calf, and it had just enough adornment to make it professional while still being comfortable. Plus Mimi had told her that the pretty blue floral pattern matched her eyes. "I love this dress."

"It doesn't scream professionalism," said her aunt.

"I'm not sure I want my clothes to scream."

Ignoring that, her aunt said, "Yellow would be better for you, to offset your dark hair. Perhaps a business suit."

A yellow business suit? She'd look like a block of butter.

"Nonsense," said her mother. "Just the opposite is true.

It wouldn't kill you to wear something a little less matronly."

"My dress isn't matronly." Was it? *No*, no, it was comfortable, damn it.

"You have breasts. Even though they're small, you should showcase them."

Yardley started to sweat. "Look, both of you—"

Aunt Lilith cut in. "Only you, Aurora, would think she needed to be sexy to sell a wedding. If you'd furthered your education, as I did, instead of getting pregnant so young—"

"That wasn't my fault," Aurora gasped in affront—as she always did when this debate got started.

"Well, it certainly wasn't mine." Lilith scoffed. "*I* didn't have unprotected sex."

"Likely because you, dear sister, have never experienced real passion."

Lilith's face went red. "No one said passion must equal an unwanted baby—no offense, Yardley."

Yardley obligingly replied, "None taken." This whole argument was so old, she knew the lines by heart. There was always some variant of the same thing. Over and over again.

It infuriated Mimi. If her friend was here now, she'd be blasting them both.

"I did the responsible thing," Aurora specified with flair. "I raised my daughter. You'd probably have given her up."

"How dare you?" Lilith pointed one manicured finger Yardley's way. "I *love* Yardley."

"*Now* you do. But while I was carrying her?"

"I was attempting to be the reasonable one."

"You didn't want her around, but now you try to claim her as your own."

"At least I don't advise her to show off her breasts!"

Yardley lifted her phone to look at the time…and then she heard two things. A man clearing his throat, and a young woman giggling.

OMG. Awash with humiliation, she turned to face her clients…and *holy crapola*. Pretty sure her ovaries just danced.

Travis Long was a feast for the peepers. She knew because her eyes were gobbling him up from head to toe.

He wasn't the intended, thank God, just the brother. *Is he married?*

Good Lord, why did she care? But she answered herself real quick as she took him in feature by feature. Sandy-blond hair, steaked by the sun.

Dark brown eyes, fringed by ridiculous—like, *really* ridiculous—long, thick lashes.

Broad muscled shoulders.

Lean torso.

Long, strong legs.

Of course he had to be married. He'd probably had a dozen proposals by now. Some lucky woman would have snatched him up already.

Unless… Remembering her initial phone conversation, she thought maybe he was too aloof. Too unfriendly. A discerning woman wouldn't be reeled in by mere good looks. Somehow she didn't feel all that discerning right now.

Whatever this man does for a living, it works in his favor.

The young woman laughed aloud this time. "Don't worry, Ms. Belanger. He has that effect on everyone."

She nodded at Aurora and Lilith, and Yardley realized they were both gawking, too.

Appalled, Yardley loudly cleared her throat—and accomplished nothing. Her mother and aunt continued to stare.

"I've told him he could have made more money as a model," the young woman said, "but no, my brother went into construction instead."

Attempting to ignore the heat in her face, Yardley stepped forward, hand extended—toward the woman. Who would be her *client*. She was the one who mattered. "Hello. You must be Ms. Long."

"Soon to be Mrs. Borden, with your help."

"Oh, I do hope so. That I get to help, I mean. Not that you become Mrs. Borden. I'm sure that's a foregone conclusion or you wouldn't be here." *Shut up, Yardley.* "Please, just call me Yardley."

"If you'll call me Sheena."

Beside her, Travis shifted but said nothing. Compared to him, his sister looked extra petite. Her hair, lighter blond than Travis's, hung just past her shoulders. They shared the same striking dark eyes and sinful lashes.

Sheena appeared to be just out of her teens. Maybe twenty or twenty-one. Young, excited, and brimming with optimism. Total opposite of her silent, possibly brooding, brother.

What could she say with her aunt and mother still eyeballing him as if they'd never seen such a fine specimen before? Honestly, in Cemetery, they probably hadn't. "I'm thrilled for the opportunity to help plan your wedding." Reluctantly, because she wasn't yet prepared to gaze on him again, Yardley turned to Travis. It took her a second to get her lungs to work, and then she gasped, "I take it you're Travis Long, the Victorian home enthusiast?"

"I am." He briefly clasped her hand.

Very perfunctory. Not at all personal. Purely business.

But he had magic hands or something because she felt that touch radiate everywhere. With her tingling palm, she lamely gestured to the gawking duo. "My mother, Aurora Belanger, and my aunt, Lilith Belanger."

Sheena greeted them with a little less warmth than she'd shown Yardley.

Travis merely gave them a nod, then said to Yardley, "I'm relieved to see you've kept the house true to the period."

Oh goody, a safe subject, and one she was comfortable with. She could talk about the house *and* stare at him. "I've tried. Remodeling it has been a pleasure, but a slow process." She wrinkled her nose. "Matching all that trim, finding the right valance windows, the iron railings—"

"And the slate roof. That impressed me."

Oh, hey. She'd impressed him. Score one for her. "Most recently the kitchen got a facelift. I hope I did it justice."

Sheena glanced around. "It's beautiful. Can we do a tour of it later? I know it'd make this whole trip worthwhile for Travis."

She shot a warning look at her mother and aunt. "Absolutely. I'll show you everything." *What?* "I mean, every part of the house. All the rooms. And stuff." If only her mouth had a spigot she could turn off. "Even the upstairs rooms have been remodeled." Had her mother and aunt left when they were supposed to, she'd have tidied their rooms for them. Now she couldn't, meaning they were probably messy disasters.

Oh, how sweet it was to have a little payback against them. They were fanatics when it came to designing their rooms, but not so big on keeping them decluttered. Yardley knew exactly how they'd react—and they didn't disappoint her.

"Excuse me," Lilith said, exiting in a dignified, unhurried stride…until she was out of sight. Then they all heard the rushed clomping of her short heels on wood treads as she raced up the stairs.

Aurora managed a wan smile. "Yes, I should go as well. Good luck, dear. Oh, not that my daughter needs luck, of course. She's quite the talented wedding planner. Very popular here and in the neighboring towns. Why, her vintage weddings are heavily trending, or so she tells me. Personally, I prefer something a little more chic, which of course she offers."

"Mother," Yardley said, feeling her cheeks burn. "You don't want to be late."

"Oh, no. No, I don't." Aurora barely lowered her voice when she said in an aside, "Don't slouch." Then she turned and sashayed away, making a little less noise on the stairs than Lilith had. Unfortunately, they could hear them rushing around in their rooms, probably tucking away bras and shoes, clearing clutter from their desks, and hopefully tidying their beds.

It was the one thing she had in common with them: they each loved to show off the house. Since Aurora and Lilith had personally helped with the decor choices for their rooms, they were especially proud of them and loved to show them off.

Yardley pinned on her most professional smile. "We finished the upstairs as a divided living area, so both my aunt and my mother have their own private suites with bedrooms, bathrooms, and seating areas. My mother chose the side with the balcony, and Aunt Lilith has that romantic turret."

"You live here, too?" Sheena asked.

"Yes, my bedroom is off to the right of the foyer, and the kitchen is to the left." She gestured down the hall. "Only the dining room is used as my office. If you'd like to come this way, we can all get comfortable while you share your wedding ideas. Once I have a grasp of what you're thinking, I can show you my portfolio and we can go over the budget."

Travis waited for his sister and then followed along last. When she glanced back, she saw him looking around at niches in the wall, the railing that led upstairs, and the stained glass transom over the doorway to her office space.

Pride had her smiling for real. She knew she'd done an amazing job on the house.

Yardley took a seat behind her desk while Travis waited for his sister to choose one of the two padded chairs facing it. Then he took the other.

Such a good big brother—very attentive with all the earmarks of being a gentleman.

"This used to be the dining room?" he asked.

Pleased with his continued interest, she nodded. "I work from home rather than keeping a separate office space." She slid a look to Sheena. "It allows me to offer a more competitive price package than many other planners."

He nodded up at the crown molding. "I like how you added to it."

Oh, wow. He could tell that she'd done that? Smart as well as hot. "Thank you. I thought it needed a few more frills." Yardley caught his sister looking back and forth between them, and reminded herself that Sheena was the client, and she wanted to talk weddings, not old houses.

"Your brother mentioned that you'd seen my country wedding display?"

"I did," Sheena confirmed. "And I absolutely love it. That's what I'd really like. Simple but fun. Does that make sense?"

"Perfect sense."

"I have no idea where to start though." Sheena bit her lower lip. "Or what I can afford."

"That's where the wedding planner comes in," Travis said, turning to Yardley. "Suggestions?"

"How about I go over the two packages I offer, and then you can tell me just how involved I'd be?"

"That'd be perfect." This time Travis smiled at Sheena. "Don't you think?"

"I'd appreciate the help."

Oh, but Yardley loved how Travis deferred to his sister. So far he'd been terrific. "First, there's the full service, which means I'd recommend and review vendor contracts—and there are plenty right here in—" *she would not say Cemetery* "—town who are perfect, including a few who really round out the country theme if you decide on it. I'd coordinate the delivery and arrival of your vendors, plus handle the wedding day timeline. I can even be a secretary of sorts, reminding you when to order announcements, of appointments for dress fittings or parties, and I'd help you stay within your budget." Yardley beamed at her, but Sheena just glanced worriedly at Travis.

Hmm...

Yardley waited.

"And the other option?" he asked.

Clearing her throat, Yardley said, "I can serve as a consultant when you have questions, make recommendations, and assist on the actual wedding day."

Running fingers through her blond hair, Sheena admitted, "I want the dress and the fun of the country setting—because Todd, my fiancé, will love that. He's not a formal kind of guy."

Yardley tipped her head. "And you? Are you a formal kind of bride?"

"Not really. Well, other than the gorgeous white dress. The problem is that I already feel overwhelmed. I have no experience with weddings. One of my friends married, but it was just at the courthouse and we all wore our regular clothes. Travis and I don't have any family to—"

"Full service it is," Travis interrupted with an indulgent smile at his sister.

Sheena hesitated. "But you don't even know the budget yet."

Fascinated by this brother-sister relationship, and hung up on the fact that Travis wasn't married since Sheena hadn't attended a wedding, Yardley almost missed her opening. "Oh, well let me cover budgetary costs very quickly." She pulled out a pale pink linen folder embossed with the words *Making Dreams Come True*. Opening it to her standard budget breakdown, she removed two copies and placed one in front of Sheena, the other in front of Travis.

"Those are basic starting points, but things can vary depending on what you choose. Why don't you two look that over and I'll go get us some refreshments. I have flavored hot tea, or if you'd prefer coffee or water?"

"Water is fine for me," Sheena said, her wide eyes taking in the details of the budget.

"Coffee, black, would be great," Travis added.

"I'll only be a minute, but you can take all the time you need." She pressed forward a monogrammed notepad and pencil. "Feel free to jot down your thoughts or any questions you might have." Leaving them to it, she went into the kitchen, where coffee and hot water for tea already waited. Using the fancy polished silver tray she'd purchased at an antique shop, along with the delicate china cups she reserved for clients, she prepped the drinks and placed several cookies on an ornate serving plate.

Five minutes later, she was just about to lift it all when Travis asked behind her, "Need any help?"

Surprised, she jerked around and found him checking out the kitchen. "Good God, you startled me."

His dark gaze landed on her. "Sorry. Didn't mean to intrude. Todd called Sheena to ask her how it's going, so I wanted to give her some privacy. She's a little uncomfortable that I'm paying for the wedding."

The *whole* wedding? "That's, um, generous of you."

He went back to looking over her kitchen design choices. "Todd is apparently always working, so I'm glad to do it if it makes her happy." He shot her the side-eye. "Maybe from now on, you could just share costs with me, and everything else with her. Would that work?"

Whoa. That sounded an awful lot like he wanted to take over, and in the world of wedding planners, that'd be a big no-no. She'd been down this road with parents, future in-laws, and even some fiancés. "Is Sheena okay with that?"

He gave her a slow smile of approval. "I like that you're putting her first."

That sounded genuine, so she explained, "Of course. Sheena is the one who admired my country wedding display, right?"

He winced. "Yeah, that was Sheena." His pained expression made it clear it sure hadn't been his idea. Turning his attention to her sink, he ran his fingertips along the bronze. "This is stunning."

Instantly forgiving him, Yardley circled the island with enthusiasm. "I saw the design in a magazine that focuses on Victorian style. It's different, I know, but I think it works."

"Especially with these faucets."

She beamed at him.

"You obviously combined function with original design. The butler's pantry is great, by the way."

For Mimi, anyone who complimented her adorable baby girl won her over. For Yardley, it was her kitchen. She could overlook a great many flaws in a person who appreciated a really great prep space. "I do a lot of the cooking here." She did *all* the cooking. "It's a passion of mine."

The word *passion* earned her another quick glance. "Sheena told you I'm in construction. What she didn't say is that between building new houses, I renovate old ones."

Hey, common ground. "Very cool."

"It's a nice break for me." He sniffed the air. "Those cookies smell great."

See, he was winning points all over the place. "I hope they taste as good as they smell." She reached for the tray.

"Would you like me to carry that? It looks heavy."

"Sure. Knock yourself out."

He paused, one brow raised.

Yardley mentally kicked her own butt. "Didn't mean

that sarcastically, I swear. I meant, rather sincerely, that I'd appreciate it. Heck, it's not often anyone offers to… that is, most everything around here falls to me, so… Never mind." Trying to swat away the overflow of words, she suggested, "Let's see how your sister is faring," and she marched out of the room, leaving him to bring the tray.

For the next thirty minutes, around eating cookies and offering praise for their deliciousness, Sheena went over her ideal wedding while Yardley took notes.

"I already chose my fancy white dress, but I want to wear boots with it, like you had in that awesome display." Leaning forward, Sheena asked, "Want to see my dress? I have a photo of me in it."

"Of course I do." Yardley absolutely loved seeing wedding dresses, from super simple to over-the-top extravagant and everywhere in between. She adored them all.

Sheena quickly retrieved her phone and searched her photos, then turned it so Yardley could see the screen.

"Oh my." Slowly, Yardley came out of her seat and moved around the desk. She took the phone and smiled. "Wow, beautiful." The dress and the woman. It was perfect for Sheena's petite size, and the smile on her face made it all the more stunning. Sheena looked the way every bride should: thrilled, excited, and full of confidence for a love-filled future.

Genuine emotion glazed Yardley's eyes, forcing her to blink a few times. She'd seen many brides over the years, and it always hit her the same way. With happiness, and a dose of melancholy.

"I think she looks incredible," Travis said softly.

That's when Yardley realized how intently he watched

her. Forcing a big smile, she handed the phone back to Sheena. "You're going to be the prettiest bride ever."

With a short laugh, Sheena said, "I get why my big brother thinks so, but I'm sure you've seen a lot of brides."

"Dozens and dozens, and they were all special in their own way, but this—" she gestured at the phone "—and you…" She sighed. "Todd is a very lucky guy."

"That's what I keep telling her," Travis murmured.

"Hush it." Sheena gave a playful push to his shoulder, then said to Yardley, "According to Travis, no one is good enough for me."

They really were close, Yardley could see that, and it made her a little wistful. What would her life have been like with a big brother to look out for her?

But hey, she'd had Mimi, and that was even better. "Do you already have your boots?"

As if unsure of the right answer, Sheena said tentatively, "No?"

"Don't worry. We'll figure it out." Another note. "And the groom? What will he wear?"

Sheena bit her lip. "What do you suggest?"

"That depends on when you're getting married."

Hopeful, Sheena said with a question, "Mid-July?"

Hmm. They were already well into April, so that'd be cutting it close, but no way would she disappoint this lovely young woman. "I'm sure I can make that happen. Let's go over everything first so I can see what we'll need. Then we can work on an exact date depending on the venue you want. Oh, and if it does happen mid-July, then Todd and any other men in the wedding party will be more comfortable in cotton shirts than tuxes, right? So the country wedding theme will work out well. July in Indiana can be downright steamy."

Sheena clasped her hands. "I just knew you were going to say it was impossible."

"Nothing is impossible. The dress is what usually takes the longest, but you already have that done. If it needs any alterations, I can recommend a wonderful local seamstress."

"Well, the thing is… I'm four months pregnant."

Smiling, Yardley said gently, "We'll set it in mid-July, and if you need an alteration or two before then, no problem."

Travis turned to his sister. "You see? No big deal."

Giving him a fond look, Sheena said, "That wasn't his attitude when I first told him."

Feeling defensive on Sheena's behalf, Yardley narrowed her eyes at Travis. "Oh?"

He laughed. "Don't misunderstand, Ms. Belanger."

"Yardley."

Conceding with a nod, he amended, "Yardley." Then he explained, "I'm thrilled to be an uncle. My only concern was Sheena's happiness."

"My *future* happiness, because he doesn't quite know Todd well enough yet to understand how perfect he is for me."

Travis said nothing to that.

"We'll have some adjusting to do," Sheena admitted. "I dropped out of college, but my plan is to get an online degree in business."

"You seem determined enough to make it happen." Yardley thought of her own mother, who to this day insisted that she'd given up everything, all promising prospects, future plans and education, simply because she'd been a single mom. Yardley hoped Sheena would have a different attitude.

"I know as much about babies as I do weddings," Sheena admitted with a grin. "Which isn't much, right?" She placed a hand over her midriff. "But I already know I love him or her with my whole heart."

"That's a good start." Yardley found herself grinning, too. "My best friend, Mimi, has a six-month-old daughter. Like you, I had zero experience with babies, but most of it just sort of creeps up on you." She pushed out of her chair and turned to the bookcase behind her desk. Running a finger along the bottom row of books, she said, "Here it is." She withdrew the slim volume titled *What to Expect for Baby's First Year*, and reached across the desk to hand it to Sheena. "That was a good primer for me. Maybe you'll find some helpful tips, too."

"Wow." Sheena looked up at her with gratitude. "You're loaning it to me?"

"It's yours to keep."

Hugging the book to her chest, Sheena glanced at Travis. "Didn't I tell you she'd be the perfect wedding planner?"

With a long look at Yardley, Travis agreed. "She's very nice—and before we run out of time, maybe we should get back to wedding plans."

Yardley laughed. "I have my notes right here. Next on the list: flowers. Any thoughts on that?"

"Oh yes! Instead of fancy flowers I'd love something simple, like daisies, but with accent colors in soft pastels."

"Sounds lovely." Yardley scribbled away.

"I'd like to get some photos in the red truck, too, if that's possible."

"Absolutely." Because Yardley loved the people in Cemetery regardless of how she felt about the name, she started on her well-rehearsed pitch of the different vendors. "Have you been to the lake yet? If not, we can plan a day and I'll take you around to meet everyone. Most of the local vendors have storefronts there and with the warmer weather, their shops are bustling again."

"Oh, I'd love that," Sheena said. "What's the name of the lake?"

"Er…" No, Yardley refused to call it Cemetery Lake. That was just morbid. "Main Street—that is, the road we're on right now—continues on to the lake, then it intersects with Lakeshore Drive. If you're interested, there's a stunning private cottage there that's just perfect for a honeymoon." She clasped her hands to her heart. "I highly recommend it." Just mentioning it made Yardley wistful. "It's small but has everything you'd need, and the sunsets are—"

"Honeymoon in the same town where they marry, in the same state where they live?" Travis asked.

Feeling defensive over *her* dream honeymoon, she elevated her chin and suggested, "Why don't you wait to see the lake and the cottage before you pooh-pooh it?"

The corner of his mouth twitched. "Did you say 'pooh-pooh'?"

Oh God, she had. Heat seeped up her chest, up her throat, and into her face, and she just knew she looked scalded. "It's a saying. I'm sure you've heard it before."

"Maybe, but not often and not from someone so young."

"I'm thirty-one. Not that young."

He shrugged. "I'm thirty-five and usually I'd agree, but you look younger."

Yardley opened her mouth with no idea what to say. She settled on, "Thank you." Was it a compliment? Or another slight, as if she wasn't old enough or mature enough to coordinate a wedding?

Sheena jumped in. "Todd and I aren't planning to take a big honeymoon anyway. He can only get a week off work and we don't want to spend a lot of money right now, not with a baby on the way. When you have a chance, I'd appreciate seeing the cottage."

Triumphant, Yardley promised, "You're going to *love* it. I have a good feeling about you." Knowing the cottage would win Sheena over once she saw it, Yardley decided not to share the photos. It'd be better if the cottage was viewed in person. With that decided, she detailed the rest of the vendors. "If you don't already have a venue chosen, Mr. Wilson Hobert owns a huge, renovated and updated barn that's perfect for weddings and receptions. It's rustic, with some of the original features from when it was used to house animals, but now it has a small kitchen and a really pretty bathroom and changing room. There's a loft area for bands and special lights, and a wide-open floor for seating and dancing. Usually for our country wedding packages, we tow the red truck there and the photographer meets us when the wildflowers are in bloom. It's so pretty."

"I *love* it," Sheena enthused. "Yes, let's look into that!"

Travis stayed silent. Lack of enthusiasm, no doubt.

But who cared? Clearly, despite his appreciation of her home, he had no imagination. Yardley focused all her attention on Sheena. "Ms. Emily Lucretia owns a floral shop. She can order any specialty flowers you want, but of course she has all the most common flowers on hand. The best part is that she also has a variety of wildflowers in beautiful colors, including some truly luscious daisies. She grows many of them on the acreage behind her home. That's another place we could visit, by the way. You can see fields of flowers."

"I'm getting so excited!" Sheena hugged herself.

That, at least, put a smile on Travis's face.

"Mrs. Sallie Sheldrake creates the most divine wedding cakes ever. They're stunning—and delicious." Deliberately omitting the town name, she said, "We'll be sure to visit Sallie's By The Shore while we're at the lake. You can taste some samples. Oh, and speaking of tasting! Saul Culver runs his father's barbecue restaurant now. The Pit Stop does the best glazed, smoked baby back ribs in the whole state, if not the whole country."

"Ribs for a wedding?" asked Mr. Skeptical. "Won't that be too messy?"

"I don't know." Yardley gave him a sweet smile. "Are you a messy eater?"

Issuing a dare, Travis sat forward. "Let's see you eat barbecue ribs—in all white."

All white—like a bride? Unfortunately…no. Not likely to ever be her. "I'm not the one getting married, so I don't need to wear all white. Unless you're suggesting your sister can't handle it?"

Sheena snorted. "Bring on the ribs."

Man, she loved this girl with her upbeat attitude. "They have pigs in a blanket, too. Baked beans and cornbread. Or Saul can set up an old-fashioned pig roast. Steamed corn on the cob, potato salad… I'm making myself hungry."

Grabbing up another cookie, Sheena said, "Me, too."

"The photographer is also along that lakefront strip of shops. What do you say? Do you want to tour everything soon, and then you can make some final decisions?"

Sheena shot another glance at Travis. "Todd is working tons of overtime right now."

"I know, sis. It's okay. I'm free Wednesday of next week, if that works for Yardley. Say around four?" As he grinned, the gleam of challenge shone in his eyes. "Then we can finish up the tour with a dinner of ribs."

Ha! Sporting her own grin, Yardley didn't even bother to pretend-check her calendar. "Sounds great. Let's do it." She jotted the date and time on a sticky note and put it on her monitor. "Would you like to meet here and I can drive us over? Once you've seen everything and made a few decisions, I can work up a detailed budget for you."

"Perfect." Travis stood. "Do we still have time for the tour of the house?"

Oh geez, she'd forgotten all about that. "Absolutely." At least her mother and aunt were gone now. She'd heard them leave when she was getting the cookies and drinks. "Let's start in the kitchen and we'll work our way through."

2

Over an hour later, the whole-house tour complete, they meandered to the front door. Yardley had heard more compliments today than she had in her entire life. That is, if you excluded all the times Mimi gushed over her out of pure friendship.

"I'm so glad you liked the house. I've sort of put my heart and soul into it."

"It shows," Travis said with a nod.

Sheena asked, "When will you do your own room? That's the only thing undone, right? I mean, it's pretty but it's not updated like everything else."

"You know, I'm still deciding exactly what I want." What a big fat lie that was. She'd been keeping a scrapbook of ideas for two years. "No one really sees my bedroom so it didn't seem as important."

Travis lifted a brow.

Crap. *Have I just admitted that my bedroom never sees any action?* Yup, she had. But hey, it wasn't like she could bring home a boyfriend for wild, uninhibited sex when her mother and aunt lived right upstairs.

As if trying to cover for her, Sheena said, "You probably don't have a lot of privacy here."

Sometimes she had more than she wanted. "I rarely conduct business after six, so the evenings are mine alone."

"But..." Sheena tipped her head. "Your mother and aunt live here, too."

"They do, but they entertain in their rooms and pretty much leave the downstairs to me except during dinner. I mean, they'd notice if I brought a guy home. They'd be all over that." *Stop, Yardley.* "Not that I have a guy in mind or anything. I mean, not that I could bring here." By the second, her face was growing hot, so she tried a laugh. "Who'd want to be here, that is... Mostly it's just my friend Mimi."

Wearing the smallest of smiles, Travis held out his hand. "Thank you again for making time to see us. You shared a lot of great ideas, plus I enjoyed the visit, and getting to see the house was a bonus."

What does that mean, he enjoyed the visit? Now that she'd gotten to know him better, Yardley was sure she could handle touching him. Professionalism demanded it, so she clasped his hand and did her utmost not to notice the texture of his work-roughened fingertips, the warmth of his palm, and she absolutely did not make eye contact.

Damn it, she felt flushed again. *What a country bumpkin I am.*

Quickly, she turned to Sheena and shook her hand as well. She handed her the folder with all the information they'd discussed so far—minus the photos of the Honeymoon Cottage. She'd slipped those out, hopefully without being noticed. "My card is inside, too, with all my contact info. If any of you, Todd included, have any questions at all, please don't hesitate to reach out. Oh, and feel free to jot down anything further that you want to discuss on our next meeting."

Sheena hesitated only a second, and then she hugged Yardley. "Thank you so much. This could have been so awkward and embarrassing, and instead it was a blast. Like Travis said, I enjoyed our visit. I'm already looking forward to next Wednesday." She turned and went out through the screen door, then jogged down the steps and headed to a sturdy-looking truck emblazoned with TL Construction on the side.

Travis hung back a moment. "I'll second Sheena's sentiment. She's been equal parts ecstatic about the baby and wedding, and worried about how she'd pull it all together. You've reassured her."

"It's my job, one I enjoy a lot." She liked Sheena and truly wanted the best for her.

"Well, country theme aside," he teased, "you really connected, so thank you. Just do me a favor and convince her that the brother of the bride isn't wearing cowboy boots." He grinned as he, too, went out the door.

Yardley stood there, one hand on the door frame, the screen door held open, smiling like a sap until they were out of sight.

She had to call Mimi. She couldn't wait to tell her friend all about her new client…and her smokin' hot brother.

WHEN HER PHONE VIBRATED, Mimi immediately grabbed it from her pocket, answered, but didn't say anything until she'd tiptoed out of Sammy's room. Sammy had fallen asleep ten minutes ago, and Mimi had just gotten her into her crib.

Once out in the hall, she whispered, "Hello."

"Oops, bad timing?" Yardley asked.

"Nope. Just give me a sec." After clipping the baby monitor to her shorts, she silently closed the door and crept down the hall. "What's up?"

"Remember I had that appointment today?"

"Of course. I hope the excitement in your voice means it went well." Heading into the kitchen, Mimi put the phone on speaker, set it on the counter, and then opened the fridge, trying to decide what to do for dinner.

"It went great. They're coming back next Wednesday so I can show them the different vendors around the lake. Then we're having dinner at Saul's." Yardley's voice dropped. "Mimi, my client brought her brother and he's *gorgeous*."

Whoa. Dinner forgotten, Mimi shut the fridge and dropped into a chair at the small square table. "Brother?"

"He arranged the meeting. Sheena's fiancé—Sheena is my client—anyway, her guy was working so her brother came along with her. And holy guacamole, I thought my eyes would pop out of my head. Even my mother and aunt ogled him."

Mimi really wanted to see the man who'd gotten her sexually inactive friend all hot and bothered. "Tell me you got a pic of him."

"No, of course I didn't," she said, sounding scandalized. "How exactly would I have done that?"

"Hello?" Trying to sound like Yardley, Mimi said, "Dude, you're scrumptious. Let me get a pic for my bestie. *Smile*."

Yardley laughed. "You know I would never."

Opening her Facebook, Mimi asked, "What's his name?"

Full of suspicion, Yardley repeated, "His name?"

"Yeah. I'm going to look him up. I need a little zing in my life and you've convinced me he'll do the trick."

"What would Kevin say if he knew you were searching other guys on Facebook?"

Mimi snorted. "Maybe I'll tell him and we'll find out." She wouldn't mind a little jealousy from her hubs right about now. Anything would be better than the distance growing between them.

"No! You absolutely cannot tell him any of this. Promise me, Mimi."

"Babe, you're the only one who expects you to be sexually deprived. I'm sure Kevin assumes you're getting it on the regular." *Like I used to.*

"OMG, tell me you haven't been gossiping about my love life with Kevin. I'll never be able to look at him again."

"What love life? News flash, girlfriend, you don't have one."

An appalled silence stretched out. "And Kevin knows that?"

"Nah, he thinks you and Saul are banging." Judging by Yardley's loud groan, that didn't reassure her. Mimi grinned. "Teasing, hon. Just teasing. You should know everything between us is private. Not even under the threat of torture would I tell anyone you've been in a never-ending dry spell."

"It's not really a dry spell," Yardley countered. "I've just been busy working on the business."

And taking care of her annoying mother and aunt. Mimi sighed. For a while there, she'd had high hopes for Saul. He was attractive, smart, motivated and hard-working, but since Yardley never reciprocated his flirting—had in fact been sublimely unaware of it—Saul now seemed to have his sights on Emily Lucretia. "His name, Yardley."

Giving up, her friend whispered, "Travis Long."

Mimi's lip curled. "Well, that doesn't exactly inspire images of hunks." She put the name in the search bar. "Could have been Roman Fire or Hank Savage or something… Oh *hey*." Putting on the mental brakes, Mimi gazed at the vision in the profile pic. "Smoking hot" didn't do him justice. He stood outside a fire pit wearing only trunks and holding a beer. A few other guys were around him, but somehow none of them seemed important. "Wow, Yardley, how did you keep from jumping his bones?"

"Right?"

"He has just the right amount of chest hair."

"Chest hair! You can see his chest?"

Mimi heard a rush of movement and knew exactly what Yardley was doing. "Do not use your work computer! Cruella or Maleficent might stumble upon it."

"You're right. I'll use my iPad."

Mimi counted to five and then asked, "Do you have it yet?"

"Just about—wow." For a beat of five seconds, there was revered silence. "See, didn't I tell you he was mouthwatering?"

Yes, she had, and Mimi was already thinking ahead. "When do you see him again?"

"Next Wednesday, but you can forget it. He's a client and that means he's off-limits."

"You said his sister was the client."

"Close to the same thing," Yardley insisted.

"Whose rule is that?"

"The rule of professionalism."

Mimi heard the sound of a car door closing and said, "Hang on." Hustling to the front door, she got there right before Kevin did and greeted him with a whispered, "Shh… Baby napping."

He leaned in for a quick kiss and quietly stepped around her. "Yardley?" he asked, nodding at the phone.

"No, I'm setting up an illicit affair with a gigolo."

Kevin grunted a quiet laugh. "Have fun, babe." He went through the house and to the kitchen Mimi had just vacated.

"Mimi," Yardley chastised. "You shouldn't tease him like that."

"Did you hear him, though? 'Have fun, babe.' Ugh. I should strip naked and dance through the kitchen. We could see if that gets his attention."

Yardley laughed. At her. Yeah, Mimi knew she was being ridiculous, but damn it, she felt unsettled.

When she heard water running, she went to investigate and found Kevin rinsing the dishes that she hadn't yet gotten to. Deflating, she explained, "I was going to do that once I got Sammy down, but then Yardley called—"

"No problem," he said while loading the dishes into the dishwasher. "Why don't you take a break? Talk to Yardley as long as you want."

She wasn't about to tell him that her mother had been there earlier and she'd already had a break. "Fine. I'm going out to the porch, then."

He didn't reply. Grumbling to herself, Mimi carried the phone to the porch swing out front. "It's unfair that he's so wonderful." Because it made her want him and lately, he flat-out didn't seem interested.

"The bastard," Yardley said with humor. "How dare he?"

"No really. I mean it." She dropped onto the hard wooden seat, setting the swing in motion. "He's home right on time, the baby is sleeping, so it was a prime opportunity for him to make a move."

"Come off it, Mimi. You aren't shy, so why don't *you* make a move?"

Because I've gained weight and my stomach is still loose from the birth and my boobs are swollen and I don't know if he wants me. But she wasn't in the mood to admit any of that out loud. "I shouldn't have to."

"Stubborn, that's what you are. Maybe he's feeling… insecure, too."

"I'm not insecure," Mimi automatically denied. "Not much anyway." At Yardley's silence, she sighed. "Okay, so I am. Before Sammy, I couldn't move without Kevin trying to hook up. The man used every excuse under the sun to grab my ass. God forbid he caught me changing clothes. He'd act like he'd never seen me naked before. But now…" Now he was in the kitchen doing dishes. God, she was a loser. "I should go. I need to get dinner together."

"Mimi—"

"No, don't use your worried voice on me. I'm fine, I promise." To change the subject, she said, "Send Mr. Sexy a friend request."

"I couldn't!"

Yeah, she figured that'd be Yardley's reaction. She needed time, obviously, so Mimi reeled in her enthusiasm. "At least promise me you'll scour social media to see what else you can find out about him."

"Well…at this point, that's pretty much a given," Yardley admitted.

"Perfect." Even though Mimi planned to do her own snooping on the guy, she said, "Take notes and share with me tomorrow." She blew a kiss into the phone. "Love you."

"Love you, too."

Sticking her phone in her pocket, Mimi returned to the house. Kevin was still in the kitchen, but it shouldn't have taken him that long to empty the sink. As she walked in, she found him prepping hamburgers on a tray, and it stopped her in her tracks. "What are you doing?"

Without looking up, he liberally sprinkled the burgers with salt and pepper. "I thought I'd grill for dinner. It's a nice day."

When she'd gotten pregnant with Sammy, the doctor had recommended she take it easy to give her a better chance of going full-term. After the birth, they'd decided together that they didn't want to hire childcare help. They'd gone over their budget and, in the end, Mimi had permanently given up her waitressing job at Saul's restaurant.

Now cleaning the kitchen and fixing dinner was supposed to be part of her routine. "I'd have gotten dinner, you know."

He glanced up. "I know you would have, but you rarely get time to yourself these days." He set about slicing an onion.

He knew she loved grilled onions on her burgers. She liked sex too, damn it, but apparently that wasn't on the menu.

Teasing, he said, "I wouldn't mind the company while I grill, though. Want to come out with me?"

Yardley was right. He was so damn amazing, she had to cut him some slack. It wasn't his fault that his freaking perfection made her flaws worse by comparison. After all, while she *still* held too much baby weight, Kevin was leaner and more muscular from working overtime.

Whereas her boobs now had stretch marks, his chest and shoulders were tanned from yard work and the few times she'd convinced him to go fishing.

He smiled easily…and all she did was bitch.

Circling the counter, she wrapped her arms around him and squeezed him tight.

"Hey?" Holding his greasy hands out to the sides, he asked, "What's up, babe?"

Not him, obviously. "I love you, Kevin."

He tried to lean back to see her face, but she kept her cheek to his chest and held on. "You okay?"

Mimi nodded.

"You're sure? If you were having a problem, you'd tell me, right?"

And now she was scaring him. Swallowing heavily, she whispered, "I'm absolutely fine, just feeling like a slug."

"Babe." He quickly wiped his hands on a dishrag, took her shoulders and levered her back. "You're the least sluggish person I know. You get up with Sammy a few times a night, you take care of her all day long, and other than a quick trip here or there with Yardley, you never get a break."

Much more of that, she'd give in to her pity party and start bawling. "Sammy let me sleep last night, Mom was here earlier to give me a break, and now you're cleaning the kitchen and cooking."

His expression softened. "So for one measly night, you got regular sleep. Big deal. That doesn't make up for all the nights you're up and down."

He'd offered to take turns, but she had to nurse anyway. Plus he had to be up early for work. She could always try to nap when Sammy did. "Maybe."

He smoothed back her hair. "Your mom takes it as a favor when she gets to babysit, and I didn't clean the kitchen. I took five minutes to empty the sink. None of it is a big deal, okay? I just wanted to help."

"Because you're awesome like that." So what did that make her? Belatedly, she thought to ask, "How was your day?"

Returning to his vegetable chopping, he said, "The conveyor belt got jammed. Twice. I had the boss breathing down my neck because every minute it took me to fix it was another minute the line was held up."

Kevin worked at a factory just outside Cemetery as part of maintenance. For as long as she'd known him, he could fix anything. Heck, he could probably build a house from start to finish, he had so much skill. She'd fallen madly in love with him the first time she'd laid eyes on him, and every day she loved him more. "I'm sorry it was rough."

"It wasn't so bad. How about for you?"

She'd already told him the sum total of her day, minus the usual diaper changes, feedings and burping. "I got the laundry done." Why did it sound like she was bragging? "Including changing our bedding. For, oh, about an hour or so, the hamper was empty. Then Sammy had a diaper blowout and we were both covered, so…yeah. The hamper is now full of my laundry, her onesie and a few towels."

He laughed. "Have to say, I'm glad I missed that one."

The sound of his gruff amusement never failed to get her smiling, too.

"Come on. Let's get the food cooking before the pip-squeak wakes."

Mimi knew she couldn't let her sleep much longer anyway. They were finally establishing a pattern that seemed to work. Nap, then dinner, bath time, playtime, reading…and finally to bed for the night.

For now, though, she enjoyed the rare quiet time alone with Kevin. She'd missed him.

The big question was, did he miss her, too?

DESPITE HER MOTHER'S and aunt's typical complaints, Yardley walked into the town council meeting promptly at six o'clock and took a front row seat. The council met the second and fourth Thursday of each month. Citizen input was scheduled into the agenda, allowing everyone to voice concerns.

Yardley never missed a meeting.

The council gave a collective groan as she shuffled a few papers, her newest arguments ready to go. It amused her when she realized she'd sat beside the town manne-quin on the long bench. Today, Kathleen—as residents had dubbed the shapely fiberglass-and-plastic woman—was appropriately attired in a trim-fitting beige dress with matching white pumps and a clutch purse.

It was one of Yardley's favorite parts of Cemetery: the dressing up of the dummy.

Over the years, Kathleen had been seen on the street corner in fishnet hose, a miniskirt and a halter, loung-ing in a bikini at the beach, and wearing a formal as she rode a float in the annual Easter parade.

She'd been "caught" smoking behind the bleachers, climbing a fence along the cow pasture, and even perched in a tree during the annual Cemetery summer competitions.

Kathleen got around in the most interesting ways, and it was always fun to see what she'd be up to next.

It especially tickled Yardley to see Betty Cemetery's reaction. At eighty-six, the council president and great-granddaughter of the town founder wasn't amused easily. She appeared outraged that the poseable mannequin had infiltrated the sanctity of her town council, and obviously wanted to demand that it be removed. Unfortunately for Betty, the town manager gaveled in the meeting.

For the next half hour, Yardley listened to the secretary go over the minutes from the last meeting, where apparently not a single issue raised by residents had been resolved. Then the treasurer got involved for a lengthy update on the new residential units that would be opening soon, providing affordable housing for the younger set of Cemetery denizens just graduating college.

With grant funding from the state, the town had also completed some paving projects, updated public areas at the beach, and added directional signs on Lakeshore Drive so visitors would more easily find their way to food, shopping, public restrooms and golf cart rental.

The council members finally wound down, and Yardley waited to see if anyone else had an issue to raise. She didn't mind waiting to go last, because she planned to take up plenty of time.

When it was finally her turn, she stood, making a point of excusing herself from Kathleen, which made Betty lock her jaw.

"As I'm sure you're all aware, I want to raise the issue of the town name being forced on each and every business here."

"Forced?" Betty interrupted. "Young lady, my great-grandfather founded this town. We honor him by keeping his name."

"Yup," Yardley said, pretending the rudeness didn't bother her. "I'm well aware. However, knowing what a modest and honorable man your great-grandfather must have been, I have serious doubts that he envisioned seeing his name repeated everywhere." This was her newest tactic—appeal to Betty's family pride. "Surely he didn't expect Emily to name her florist shop Cemetery Florals. Or, God forbid, for M.J. to call her candy shop Cemetery Sweets and Treats. And how unfortunate does it sound for Saul to have to tack on Cemetery to his barbecue restaurant? The Pit Stop is a nice name, but the Cemetery Pit Stop sounds like he plans to feed you right before you're lowered into the ground."

Behind her, she heard Saul chuckling, but in front of her? Betty turned bright red with indignation.

"And," Yardley continued, "we don't even have a cemetery here! If we did, would it be called Cemetery Cemetery?"

Several people applauded. She didn't look back to see who they might be, but then she heard a loud whistle and knew Mimi had showed up for moral support.

Suppressing her smile, Yardley said, "I have a suggestion that I think would appropriately honor your great-grandfather and appease all the good people attempting to run successful businesses. We could add a lovely arched iron entry on the road leading into Cemetery. It could be connected to the two large stone pillars that are there now. What about, 'Welcome to Cemetery. You'll have the time of your life.'"

Betty's mouth closed.

"Or, 'Welcome to Cemetery. Perfect for a vacation.'"
As no one objected, Yardley's hope grew. "'Welcome to
Cemetery. You don't have to stay, but you'll want to.'"
On a roll, she started winging it. "'Welcome to Cemetery.
You'll love living here.' Or 'You'll live your best life.'
The possibilities are endless."

A hush fell over the room. Yardley held her breath,
waiting.

"We'll table this discussion for now." Betty's sharp
gaze cut over the audience of thirty or so residents. "I'm
sure you'll join us again at the next meeting, Miss Belanger. We can discuss it more then."

Wow. This was huge progress. Normally she was outright dismissed.

It helped that others had cheered her on this time.

"Now," Betty barked. "Someone get that absurd
dummy out of here!"

Praying that she meant Kathleen, Yardley stood and
started out of the row. Numerous smiling faces greeted
her—but it was Mimi's enormous grin that made it hard
for her to keep her triumph hidden. Twenty minutes later,
walking along the beach with Mimi, she was still dreaming of success.

"You knocked the old bird on her ass this time. It was
a glorious thing to witness."

Night and day, that's how differently she and Mimi put
things. Not that Mimi didn't nail it, it was just that Yardley
always held back. "I'll admit, it felt good." She watched
as a fish jumped out of the water, wiggled midair, and
then landed with a great splash. The warm hues of the
setting sun reflected off the lake's surface. "I love it here.
I want to stay here forever." She bent to pick up a fresh-

water mollusk shell. "The problem is that I can't see myself at Betty's age, still dancing around that awful name."

"Your suggestions were great." Sandals dangling from her fingertips, Mimi dug her toes into the sand, watching as the sky turned colorful shades of red, pink, and purple. "At this point, Betty is just hanging on out of stubbornness."

The fresh air teased Yardley's hair. As they stood there together, she closed her eyes. "Well, in case I don't win her over, I came up with a T-shirt slogan, too."

"Awesome." Also willing to linger, Mimi put her head to Yardley's shoulder. "Lay it on me."

As if showcasing a banner, Yardley fanned out her hands. "'I had a Cemetery Wedding. It's all uphill from here.'"

There was a moment of quiet, and then Mimi started snickering. "Ohmigod, that's priceless!"

Grinning, Yardley said, "Right? I mean, it'd be like a novelty item, don't you think? I could give them away to brides, and if my web address is on there, it's free publicity."

"You are such a marketing genius."

Yardley shook her head. Mimi thought everything she did was genius, which Yardley supposed was part of her job as best friend. For certain, her mother and aunt didn't agree.

She'd gone to college for a business degree because, even in her late teens, she'd recognized that her mother and aunt were running the business poorly. They were terrible at budgets, overly extravagant without a thought to cost, and often offended the clients with their too-blunt way of decreeing what was and wasn't classy.

When Yardley had gradually taken over, they'd at first been relieved—until they realized that her idea of success varied greatly from theirs.

To them, appearances were everything, but she'd been told most of her life that she didn't have the aristocratic features of other Belanger women…meaning she was flawed in some way. So what did she care about appearances? Instead of worrying about it, she'd aimed for happy over pretty, successful over sexy.

Profitable over classy.

She had that same direction for weddings. If the bride and groom had the wedding of their dreams, that's all that mattered to her. Happy clients shared with others, which grew the business.

Her mother and aunt wanted elegant weddings, and Yardley focused on making enough money to not only support them, but to renovate the beautiful Victorian home they shared, and to accommodate her mother's and aunt's expensive tastes.

"Enough about slogans. Where's my incredibly beautiful niece?"

Mimi slanted Yardley a look, then cleared her throat. "Kevin is solo-parenting tonight. He knew I was curious how it'd go at the board meeting, so he insisted on picking up baby duty." She wrinkled her nose. "I told him I'd be home by nine, though."

"The mommy genes calling to you?" Mimi was such a wonderful, loving mother. Even when she wasn't with Sammy, she was thinking about her.

"It's true. Kevin is great with her, but when I can't see her, something in me feels empty." She chewed her bottom lip. "Today I tried to take a different perspective with Kevin. Like, I'm trying to put myself in his shoes, you know?"

Keeping her expression neutral, Yardley asked, "How so?"

"Every weekday, he has to leave her." Mimi's voice

softened. "After what we went through to get her, it'd kill me to do that."

Totally understandable. "Makes you really respect moms who work outside the home, huh?"

"No kidding. I get why people refer to them as Super Moms. I'm sure some prefer working outside the home, and more power to them. But the ones who have no choice? That has to be rough."

Nodding, Yardley waited while Mimi sorted her thoughts.

"I kept wondering if it affects Kevin like that."

"Why don't you ask him?"

Groaning, Mimi watched a bird dive to the lake and fly away with a small silver fish. Her voice lowered, her tone strained. "I thought about it. The thing is, I don't know what to do if he tells me yes, that it's devastating every single day. What could I say to that?"

That could be an issue. Just as Mimi was an amazing mom, Kevin was an equally awesome dad.

Hooking her arm through Mimi's, Yardley got them meandering along the shore again. "You guys used to talk all the time."

"We still do, it's just different. More focused on other things."

And sometimes forced? Yardley didn't want to think about her ideal married couple having real issues. She wanted them happy, damn it. Like 24/7, seven days a week blissfully *happy*. Unrealistic much? Yes. Did she still want that for them? Damn right she did.

"On your right," they both heard, and together they glanced back to see Saul had lost his shirt and athletic pants and now wore only running shoes and shorts as he jogged up behind them.

"Hey," Mimi said to the guy who used to be her boss. "Lookin' good."

Grinning, he passed them, but then turned to jog backward more slowly. "What are you ladies up to? Conspiring against the town council?"

"Ha!" Mimi said. "Yardley has that all wrapped up. I'm just along for the fun."

"It was a hell of a show today." Saul slid his sunglasses to the top of his head, displaying nice green eyes. His brown hair was a bit sweaty, so he must have started his jog the second the meeting ended. It wasn't unappealing. Nothing about Saul was. "Thanks for sticking up for the Pit Stop. Your arguments were equally amusing and effective."

"That's my girl," Mimi said.

"I'm glad you stopped." Yardley shielded her eyes with a hand. "I meant to visit you, but it's been a busy couple of days."

Appearing wary, his smile slipped. "Yeah? What's up?"

Just then, Emily waved. "Wait up, Yardley!"

Ten years Yardley's senior, Emily had the kind of style that came naturally. As usual she had her long, dark blond hair in a ponytail. Wearing a white sleeveless blouse with the shirttails tied around her waist and gauzy black pants, she looked chic, cool and stylish—perfect for a warm summer day.

Without actually running, Emily hurried her pace until she reached them. Before she greeted Yardley or Mimi, she said to Saul, "Hi."

"Hi yourself," Saul replied in a tone Yardley had never heard from him before.

Fascinating. Trying to be subtle, she nudged Mimi.

Mimi looked up at the sky and started to whistle. Obviously, she felt the chemistry dancing between the Pit Stop and floral shop owners, too.

Saul and Emily stayed oblivious to them. In fact, Emily seemed to have forgotten that she'd called out to Yardley, not Saul.

Starting to feel like a voyeur, Yardley broke the silence. "I was just about to explain to Saul that I'm bringing new clients in next Wednesday. We're stopping by to see you first, Emily. I'm showing them around town, letting them see what great wedding vendors we have, and we'll end the day at the Pit Stop for dinner."

That snapped Emily out of her moony-eyed daze. "You are so good to all of us, Yardley. That's actually what I wanted to say. Just…thank you. For all you do."

Saul agreed. "Ditto from me."

"It's nothing." At least, it wasn't anything yet. But Yardley wasn't about to give up until she won the battle with Betty.

"One more thing." Emily reached out to touch her forearm. "We've been talking—"

"We?" Mimi asked.

"The different business owners. At least, the ones that were at the town council tonight—though we've all been discussing it for a while now."

Never the patient sort, Mimi pressed, "Discussing what?"

"We want Yardley to be the council president."

What? Mentally stumbling, Yardley gave a nervous laugh. "I couldn't. Betty is president." For as long as Yardley could remember, Betty Cemetery had held that position. No one would take it from her.

"She wins every year by default," Emily said.

Saul pointed out, "She never has any competition because no one will run against her."

With good reason. Betty was a force to be reckoned with.

"You could do it," Emily said.

"But…" Yardley didn't want to be council president, and she most especially did not want to usurp Betty. That wasn't her goal at all. She just wanted Betty to give on the name.

What in the world had she started?

"Please think about it." Emily turned to Saul for support. "We all agree it's a wonderful idea."

"Absolutely. You'd get my vote."

"Mine too," Mimi said, then shrugged when Yardley shot her a look of frustration. "You'd be great at it, hon, and you know it."

"Please, let's not get carried away, okay?" The last thing she needed was for the town to rally behind her for a job she didn't want. She had her hands full with her business and running the household for her mother and aunt. "We need to wait and see what Betty does with my latest proposal."

"But you're not ruling it out?" Emily pressed.

Giving her a wan smile, Yardley tried for diplomacy. She didn't want anyone to try convincing her tonight. "Not entirely—but neither am I agreeing."

"Wonderful. I'll let everyone know."

Wait—let everyone know *what*? Before Yardley could stop her, Emily hurried away with Saul falling into step beside her. At the edge of the parking lot, several business owners waited for them. Immediately they began to talk.

Oh, good grief.

"Those two are in a bad way. Saul should make his move. Ten to one Emily would be all over it."

Incredulous, Yardley turned on Mimi. "Forget those two. They'll eventually figure it out. What am I going to do, Mimi?"

"About?" her friend asked, playing obtuse.

"You know damn good and well what I mean." Done with her walk, Yardley stalked away, leaving Mimi to catch up.

"Hey." She hooked her arm through Yardley's, slowing her down. "You're their champion. Of course they want you making the decisions. You have vision, and you fight for what's right."

Was that really how the town saw her? She blew out an angry breath. "You know Aurora and Aunt Lilith will hear about this, and they're going to drive me nuts complaining that I've embarrassed them again."

"Pfft. So what? You should be used to it by now."

That was a new attitude from Mimi. Usually she immediately sided with Yardley.

"Besides, whose approval would you rather have? Theirs or the rest of the town?"

A tough question, though Mimi couldn't know it. "You have a point." Seeing another shell, Yardley picked it up.

"What do you do with those things?" She gestured at the long stretch of beach. "Every time we're here, you collect shells. It's not like there aren't dozens of them every day."

To Yardley, each shell represented a wish—and her wishes were adding up. "After I clean them, I save them in a big basket in my closet."

Baffled, Mimi turned to her with a frown. "I didn't know that, and I know everything about you."

"Maybe not *everything*." Hopefully her smile softened that reply. After all, she had a few dreams, and some awful disappointments, that were just too embarrassing to share, even with a very close friend. "You know all the important stuff."

"I do, don't I?" Appeased, Mimi turned with her, and they started walking back again.

Turning the shell over in her hand, Yardley thought of the many, many dreams she kept in that basket. The common one was a wedding of her own on this very beach. It'd be a day like today, not too hot and with a gentle breeze carried off the lake, the sounds of seagulls in the background and sweet wild honeysuckle in the air.

The best part of it all, though, would be after. For...*forever*, she'd envisioned a stay at the Honeymoon Cottage.

The Honeymoon Cottage where she and her ficti- tious-but-wonderfully-romantic husband would share the corner spa tub with only candlelight around them. Afterward they'd romp wildly—in the most romantic way, of course—on the big bed. They'd wrap up the most idyllic night ever by cuddling on the front porch in a sin- gle sturdy Adirondack chair while watching the vivid sunrise over the lake. When she sighed, Mimi gave her a funny look.

Yeah, definitely not a fairy tale she wanted to discuss out loud. With each year that passed, her odds of ever marrying grew slimmer, which made that particular fan- tasy too far-fetched, and ultimately ridiculous.

There was no fictitious-but-wonderfully-romantic hus- band. No romp. No cuddling...

Once long ago she'd mentioned her love of the Hon- eymoon Cottage to Mimi.

Mimi had immediately offered to stay there with her.

That was before she had Sammy, of course, but Yardley had asked, "What would Kevin think?"

"That we're fun-loving friends."

They'd both laughed, but Yardley had added, "And what will everyone else think?"

Never caring about things like that, Mimi had said, "We'll tell them that we're staying there to see how it is. Like a test-drive."

That had made Yardley choke. Test-drive a honeymoon? She'd been tempted, because a night there with Mimi, gossiping and laughing and sharing, would be the next best thing to her vision of honeymoon perfection. Sadly, she wasn't as daring as Mimi, so she'd passed, which meant she'd probably turned down her only chance to have firsthand knowledge of sleeping at the cottage. It didn't slow her down when recommending the place. She had a lot of amazing reviews to go by.

She would honeymoon vicariously, in the privacy of her own imagination.

The wedding part, though, that she could discuss with Mimi. It was a simple dream left over from when she had suffered her first heartbreak. "Do you remember Tommy Watkins?"

"Yeah, the little ginger creep who made you cry?"

Mimi had a real knack for colorful insults aimed at anyone who'd ever slighted her. "He was thirteen. Not really a creep, just a kid, and he didn't like me."

"He'd have been lucky to have you."

"Ha. At thirteen?" Funny that the whole thing still stuck with her. Maybe because it represented her entire love life, or rather, the lack thereof. "Before he told me to get lost, I had my whole wedding planned out."

"Did I figure into this magical ceremony with a ginger?"

Yardley laughed. "Of course you did. And we'd have had a great time, but poor Tommy would have fried. With his red hair and fair skin, it would have been cruel to put him through a beach wedding. At that age, I wasn't really thinking of him, though. Just how romantic it would be for me."

"And how great we'd look in our pretty dresses, with fresh pedicures so we could go barefoot."

"See? You get it." She shared a crooked grin. "Poor Tommy didn't. He was appalled that I was planning a wedding and honeymoon when he hadn't even kissed me. I stupidly offered to remedy that…and he ran away." Literally. After a look of revulsion.

Yardley still went hot with embarrassment when she remembered it. Her first harsh rejection had been awful. No wonder she'd waited so long to share with Mimi.

"Tommy was a coward. I'm glad he lost out on the best kiss he was ever likely to get."

"Again, *thirteen*."

"Kids kiss at thirteen," Mimi said, then added with a sly grin, "At least I did."

"You're incorrigible."

"It's why your mother always tried to warn you away from me."

"Fat lot of good it did her." From the first meeting, she and Mimi had been inseparable. Keeping that friendship was one of Yardley's few rebellions.

The sad truth was, she didn't know if her kissing had improved much over the years. She hadn't had much practice. "That next summer when his family moved away, I was so relieved that I wouldn't have to see him again."

"Speaking of heartbreakers…" Mimi not-so-smoothly changed the subject. "Have you finished going through all the photos of your stud muffin?"

"*My* stud muffin?" Trust Mimi to take her mind off the town council nonsense and storybook honeymoons that would never be. "Yes, I've looked at everything." Multiple times. It was not a hardship. "Bet you have, too."

"Heck yeah. But my viewing pleasure is altruistic because I'm thinking of you—me being married and all that."

"*Happily* married," Yardley clarified, then thought to ask, "Right?"

"Yeah, sure. You know Kevin is great."

"So much enthusiasm," Yardley quipped. "What's going on now?"

"Oh no you don't. We're talking about you and that chunk of perfect masculinity. So what are you thinking?"

Yardley banked her worry for her friend's marriage and instead indulged her. "I think he's worth dreaming about. I also think I saw a bunch of different women—" *beautiful women* "—in the pictures with him, including three that seemed serious. That means he gets around, right?"

"Ohmigod, are you kidding me? First, the man looks to be in his thirties. Of course he's gotten around. Everyone has at that age."

Except her. Yardley scowled over the reminder.

"*Anyway,*" Mimi said, dragging out the word. "You obviously didn't dive very deep into his social media. Woman number one was his sister's friend. Those hugs and shared laughs were all in fun, I'm sure."

Right. Because his sister's friend, who happened to be super sexy, wouldn't interest a guy like Travis. Baloney.

"I followed links back to her, and she's dating someone else. Obviously, she didn't really count."

"If you say so." Yardley wasn't convinced.

"Woman two was all over him, I know—"

"And he seemed to like it."

"He's a guy, so…yeah. But he wasn't totally into her."

"How in the world do you know that?" To her, he'd looked plenty interested in the pic.

"You can tell with the body language. I bet she was too high-maintenance." Mimi made a face. "Who wears that much makeup to swim in a lake?"

Yardley had wondered about that, but figured the gal had mad makeup skills or something. "Dang, Mimi. How much snooping did you do?"

"I'm thorough and that's how I know the third woman didn't make progress either, because his status says single and she's not in any recent pics, so no worries there."

"I wasn't worried. Doesn't matter to me who Travis dates because it won't be me." When Mimi opened her mouth, Yardley said, "Before you start, let me state my case. First, I'm hardly his type based on the women we saw in the pics. The women were all pretty and confident and…stacked."

"I'm calling BS on that."

"Second," she said, overriding Mimi, "he's a client. I already told you that's a no-no."

"Is he, though?" Mimi purred. "I mean sure, his sister is, but he's just a doting brother."

It would be unethical to tell Mimi that Travis was paying her fee, so she only said, "He's more involved than that. Plus," she added when Mimi started to debate it with her, "he's not a fan of my work. The man made it clear that he thinks country wedding themes are dumb."

Gasping, Mimi pulled back. "He didn't!"

"Not in those exact words, no. But he—"

The sudden applause threw her, and Yardley glanced up to see too many townsfolk still in the lot, now grinning at her and cheering.

"Well, shoot." Emily and Saul were nowhere to be seen, the sneaks.

THE SUN GLINTED off the surface of the lake, making sunglasses necessary as Yardley steered the golf cart from one strategically placed vendor to another. It fascinated Travis how Main Street and Lakeshore Drive intersected in a way to frame one section of beach.

Cemetery was overall self-sufficient with lumber mills, banks, hardware stores and such on the outskirts of town, while closer to the recreational hub—the lake—families could find everything they might need to eat, play, decorate, shop or relax.

He'd opted to sit in the rear-facing seat behind Yardley and his sister, so he caught all the curious stares from locals. Some had even hurried to set up their wares outside, as if having a new visitor was a great opportunity. Given the small size of the town, he assumed every wedding was a big deal.

Sheena would love that. In so many ways, her wedding—the wedding she'd always dreamed about—was taking a back seat to Todd's preferences.

Todd, who was too damn busy to even bother with the wedding appointments.

For once, Travis was glad. It gave him an opportunity to ensure his sister got as much of her dream realized as possible, and if Todd didn't like something, tough.

Even with his back to them and the usual sounds of a

bustling town, Travis could still hear the women talking. Sheena was full of questions, and Yardley gave plenty of reassurance.

The wedding planner had an easy way about her that was fresh and open, cheerful and knowledgeable. Everyone in Cemetery seemed to like and respect her, too. Every shop owner they visited looked at Yardley as if she held all the answers to their happiness.

His sister looked at her the same way.

Travis's gaze, however, was a bit different. He saw her, *really* saw her. Not just the wedding planner or professional woman with her own thriving business. Not just a respected member of a tight-knit community.

He saw her as a woman. A very kind woman who cared about others a great deal.

A sexy woman who seemed oblivious to her own appeal.

That's what really got to him.

Attractive women tended to know it, same as men. But Yardley? Pretty sure she had no idea that her casual vibe was straight-up hot. That her smiles seemed secretive or that her gentle heart showed in her big blue eyes.

Today she wore a long floral skirt paired with a body-hugging sleeveless shirt and flat sandals. She looked cool and comfortable, her long stride kicking up the hem of the skirt with each step she took as she showed them around town. Whenever she spoke, she gestured with her hands. She got animated when discussing all the possibilities for the wedding.

The clothes showcased a slim body with subtle curves, but more interesting was the rosy flush that often colored her lightly tanned skin. She blushed easily and often, but not necessarily from embarrassment. Enthusiasm, laughter, and the occasional insight could also send a pink tint to her cheeks.

He liked that she'd left her shoulder-length hair free. Now, as they rode along the curb, her hair blew back, sending the scent of sun-warmed vanilla to tease him.

When she stopped again, this time in front of a small cottage on the lake, Travis hopped off the golf cart and walked around to his sister.

Shading her eyes with one hand, Sheena whispered, "Wow. It's awesome."

With one of those secretive smiles curving her mouth, Yardley looked at the cabin as if she'd never seen it before—with great appreciation and a sort of awe.

Watching her, Travis said, "I'm pleasantly surprised."

Smile widening, Yardley tipped her head his way. "You were expecting…what?" She lifted her brows. "Something run-down and ramshackle?"

Too many times now, he'd accidentally insulted her. "Nothing this private." The cottage was small, but sat close to the water with a front porch that acted as a second level of the dock.

"Oh." Big, expressive eyes dominated her features; they sometimes looked smoky blue and other times, like now, were a clear gray. She wrinkled her nose. "Sorry. I love this place so much, I guess I'm defensive of it."

"Have you ever stayed here?"

Shaking her head, she said wistfully, "It's for honeymooners…" Her voice trailed off and she turned brisk again. "The trees make it seem more secluded, right? They block out the sight of the beach and help muffle the sounds of everyone playing. Plus the buoys designate this area as off-limits, so it's like you have the lake all to yourself, yet within minutes you could be on the main road to eat or shop or walk along the beach. It's small, I know, but it's so beautifully romantic, and it has everything you need."

Her passion for the cottage sounded personal, as if she described her own ideal location. Travis wondered about that. "If you were getting married—"

She shook her head. "I'm not."

So much finality, it sounded like she meant *ever*. "If you were," he insisted, "you'd stay here?"

Her gaze lovingly skimmed over the cottage, the woods around it, and then to the lake. "I've never been able to imagine anywhere better."

Huh. So not a posh resort, or international travel, not a hot spot like New York or a real beach in Hawaii. *Here*, in the town where she lived.

Her conviction had him seeing the place with new eyes. Had him seeing *her* with new eyes, too.

Sheena made her way to a stone path that skirted the deck. "I'm going to check out the shoreline first. Be right back."

Satisfaction curled Yardley's lips. "You see, your sister likes it."

"She seems to." Sitting on a tree stump, he studied Yardley's profile. Whereas her mother and aunt had thin, refined features, Yardley's cheeks were more rounded, her mouth fuller with a defined upper lip, a plump lower. It was a lush mouth made for kissing…

No. He put the brakes on that thought real fast.

There'd been that misunderstanding with Sheena's friend, Julie. When he made it clear he wasn't interested in getting involved, Julie had cut Sheena out of her life, then trash-talked them both for a while, and Sheena had been hurt.

His sister would be off-the-charts pissed if he messed up her arrangements with the wedding planner.

He'd learned his lesson on that score: avoid complications with any situation where Sheena could end up collateral damage.

Yardley turned her head to look at him. "Is there a reason you keep eyeballing me?" She tucked her hair back behind one delicate ear. "I mean, is my nose burning, or do I have cookie crumbs on my lips?"

At Cemetery Sweets and Treats, they'd indulged in a few samples. He'd eaten a small block of fudge, Sheena had tried the chocolate-covered cherries, and Yardley had nibbled on a snickerdoodle cookie.

"You're fine," he said. *Very* fine.

"Okay, well…you're sort of staring."

No "sort of" to it. She fascinated him so much that his gaze kept veering to her no matter how he fought it. "Sorry. I was just noticing that you don't look much like your mother and aunt."

"Ha! No kidding." As if this topic made her more comfortable, she moved closer. "I hear about that *all* the time. Apparently I got my common features from my father."

Common features? He had a feeling there was nothing common about Yardley Belanger. "So you look like him?"

"No idea. I've never seen him." She leaned closer and whispered behind her hand, "He was my mother's infamous indiscretion. She loves to talk about it. Makes her feel like she has a wild past or something. That is, as long as you don't refer to her as a mother. Somehow that's taboo. Makes her feel older to have a grown daughter, though really, even when I was younger she never wanted to be called Mother in public, so that excuse doesn't count." Lifting her shoulders as if it didn't matter, she added, "I guess the excitement of an indiscretion is only fun when the proof isn't standing nearby, you know?" Suddenly realizing how much she'd said, her eyes widened, and she clamped her lips together.

To Travis, her mother sounded worse than inconsiderate. If it helped her to talk about it, he was happy to listen. "You never had any interest in looking him up?"

"Him who?"

His mouth twitched as he struggled to repress a grin. She was so busy trying not to talk that she'd lost track of the conversation—and all the while, her gaze had stayed locked on him. "Your father?"

"Oh, right. I didn't mean to go on and on—"

"It's a beautiful day," he said. "I'm enjoying the company and the conversation, so feel free."

For a second there, she looked disbelieving. Then she blew out a relieved breath and visibly relaxed again. "Yeah, I've thought about it a few times, for sure. It'd be hard, though, since I don't even know his name. Mother flatly refuses to share those details. Sometimes it frustrates me," she admitted. "Every so often—actually more often than not—she and my aunt argue, and I think Lilith might spill the beans, but she never does." She shrugged again. "Makes me wonder if he was a convict or something."

Even though he sensed some anxiety behind the words, he enjoyed her teasing. "Maybe he was someone famous instead. Your mother worries that she'll lose you to him."

"There you go. I like that fairy tale." She flashed him a dimpled smile. "What about you and Sheena? She said it's just the two of you?"

"Mom and Dad died in a really stupid car accident. Dark night, one driver swerved to avoid a deer…four cars crashed." The air suddenly felt a little thicker. He looked away, saying, "Three fatalities. The driver and my parents." Damn, he still hated talking about that awful night.

"I'm so sorry."

Yardley sounded like she really meant it. It wasn't just a platitude, the thing people said when told horrific stories. It was there in her tone, how she stepped closer… she didn't know him well, but she cared anyway, and that prompted him to continue. "They were out on a date. No matter how busy they got, Dad would insist on taking Mom out at least once a month. Sometimes they'd visit friends, go to dinner and a movie, and once or twice a work party."

With a wistful note in her voice, she softly said, "Sounds like they were really in love."

Yeah, they had been. And they'd loved their kids without reserve. "I was home from college, so I volunteered to watch Sheena." He glanced at her. "She was five. I was twenty."

"I noticed the age difference."

Of course she did, and even though she said it without curiosity, he wanted to explain. "Sheena was their *happy surprise*—at least that's how my mom always put it. Dad said she was his *stop-his-heart* baby."

They both smiled.

Travis pushed off the stump to stand beside her, hands in his jeans pockets, his attention on his sister, who stood on the dock. "The cops showed up a little after eleven. Thank God Sheena was already down for the night." A butterfly flitted past his face, landed on his shoulder for a few seconds, then took flight again.

Done with the maudlin rehashing of the past, he asked, "Did you plan for the butterfly to visit, just to help sell the appeal of this place?"

She shoulder-bumped him, saying without missing a beat, "Oh, definitely. Ordered up the sunshine and gentle breeze, too. And see that puffy white cloud there?" She pointed up at the sky. "That was all me, mister. Hope you enjoy my efforts."

He enjoyed them, and her, a lot. She lightened his mood without even trying. "Come on. Let's go see what's keeping Sheena."

Yardley didn't push, didn't talk to fill the silence, or ask any questions. She just quietly kept pace with him. She was just…there. And it was nice. Really nice.

As they neared the dock, Sheena looked up and said, "Shh…"

They glanced at each other, then crept closer, each of them stepping softly so the dock vibrations wouldn't disturb whatever it was that had his sister enthralled.

At this point, Travis thought it was a good bet that even a mermaid wouldn't intrigue him more than Yardley Belanger.

3

"WHAT IS IT?" Yardley whispered, and she leaned to look over the dock close to the stacked rock retaining wall. She expected a frog or crawdad, or maybe even a few silvery little fish.

Instead, a mammoth black snake stared back at her.

"Oh, good Lord!" She leaped back so fast, she fell on her butt, causing her skirt to fly up around her thighs.

Seriously, showing her panties was the least of her concerns.

Surprised, Travis reached out a hand as if to help her, but she was already crab-crawling away on the rough-planked dock—and likely giving him one hell of a show. *Who cares because—hello—snake!*

When she felt she was a safe enough distance from that snake, she lurched to her feet, hiked her skirt up again, and ran all the way up to the house.

At first, her only thought was putting distance between her and the beady-eyed creature. Gradually she became aware of both Travis and Sheena staring after her.

Then Travis, the ass, started laughing.

OMG, what a jerk! Snakes were not a laughing matter. Before she could think better of it, Yardley snatched up a thick stick and threw it at him.

Sadly, it landed several feet short.

Grinning, Sheena joined her brother. "It wouldn't hurt you." Together they started toward the house.

"It *looked* at me," Yardley accused, then shuddered as she recalled the flick of that forked tongue.

More gently, Sheena said, "It's just a harmless rat snake."

Harmless, ha! "It's a Nope snake, and a big one." Totally creeped out and uncaring that she had an audience of two, Yardley hugged herself. "I don't do snakes. In fact, I think I'll go wait in the golf cart."

Travis caught her arm before she'd gone more than three feet. "I'm sorry I laughed."

"No, you're not," she grumbled, because he was still smiling.

"Okay, then how about I'm sorry you were scared?"

"Scared doesn't cover it. Petrified, traumatized." She glared at him. "Maybe scarred for life."

"You live here." His hand remained on her arm, loosely holding her, not to restrain but to reassure. His thumb coasted back and forth over her skin in a light caress that caused nerve endings everywhere to perk up in notice. "Surely you've seen snakes before."

All her focus did a quick redirect.

Her toes curled. Honestly, until that moment, she hadn't realized that toe-curling was a real thing. Her mouth went a little dry also, and she felt the blush climbing up her throat. Dumb. She had no reason to blush.

Pretending his warm bare flesh didn't touch her warm

bare flesh, she said, "I live here, but I avoid snakes. You never see them around the beach. It…took me by surprise." She scowled up at him. "If you saw my panties, I suggest you never admit it."

With a wicked glint in his dark eyes, he lied, "Didn't see a thing."

Yardley just rolled with it and said, *"Good."*

"Travis taught me all about snakes and bugs and stuff." Looking through a window into the house, Sheena added, "They don't scare me, but my girlfriends are like you."

"Great big cowards?"

"Yardley," he murmured, saying her name in a way no one else ever had. Sort of low and rumbly. Very guy-like. It sounded better the way he said it.

Her toes curled tighter. "Hmm?"

"Being uncomfortable with snakes doesn't make you a coward. A lot of people are uneasy around them. They're not exactly cute or cuddly."

Revulsion shuddered through her.

"But they're not cold and slimy either. They're warm, and their skin is really soft—"

Before she thought better of it, Yardley smashed her fingers against his mouth. "You're making it worse."

When she felt his lips smile beneath her touch, her stomach did a free fall down to her curled toes. Snatching her hand back, she stared at him…and realized he didn't look the least bit put off.

"Can we go in?" Sheena asked, oblivious to the life-altering situation unfolding behind her.

At least, life-altering from Yardley's perspective.

"From what I can see, it looks great," Sheena added.

When Yardley didn't immediately reply, Travis—who gazed at her with mesmerizing eyes—cocked a brow.

Reality returned in a whoosh. "Oh, yeah, the Honeymoon Cottage." The place of her dreams where she got the most magically inspired dream-time nooky.

And damn it, that made her blush again. "Of course. Sorry." She filled her starved lungs with a deep breath that didn't help enough. "I love this place so much. If I ever married, not that that's in the works or anything—nowhere close, really, since I don't even date—" *Do they need to know that, Yardley?* She pinched her mouth shut in a desperate attempt to halt the nonsensical explanations. But hey, Travis still touched her, so not babbling was difficult.

"Anyway," she continued carefully. "This is definitely where I'd stay if I was putting together my own dream wedding." There, nice wrap-up…or at least it would have been if she'd stopped talking. "The ambience is all about romance and intimacy, and the setting is so peaceful and remote. Two people in love would have all the privacy they need. I can't imagine a better place to start a marriage."

Travis said nothing, but his thumb took another gentle sweep across the oh-too-sensitive skin of her arm. And he kept watching her. It was actually kind of hot… Maybe the Honeymoon Cottage affected him too, though she doubted he needed to have imagined nooky when a guy like him could—

"Whoever built it sure is talented." Sheena trailed her fingertips over the carved wooden window frame.

Yardley agreed. "The rustic woodwork adds so much character to the overall feel of the setting." Whimsy was built into every corner and floorboard. The honeymooners wouldn't be able to avoid each other—which was how it should be as they started a life together. She could easily picture them spending a day in bed, or swimming together—*without snakes*—in between making love. "Imagine an evening here on the deck together, listening to frogs and crickets beneath a starry night." She visualized it all, far too often.

"That does sound wonderful," Sheena softly agreed.

Brought back to her guests and the task at hand, Yardley shook away the daydream. Even though she'd never enjoy the cottage, she hoped Sheena would. "Best of all, it's affordable. All the perks without the extravagant cost."

As if he'd witnessed every thought that had flitted through her brain, Travis stared down at her, like he wanted to figure her out or something.

Good luck with that, bud. Most of the time, Yardley didn't understand herself. "Wait until you see the cozy interior, then you'll know what I mean. It's perfect in every way." She nodded at the mat. "Daniel—that is, Daniel Power, who owns the cottage—put a key under there for us."

"Trusting," Travis said, finally taking his hand away… by letting his fingers graze across her forearm.

Forearms: the new erogenous zones. Who knew? Her toes, apparently, because they curled again. And maybe her lungs, given how they held up her breath.

Was that little stroke on purpose? Or did she make it out to be something it wasn't?

To distract herself, Yardley explained, "There's very little crime here in Cemetery." She rethought that and grinned. "Unless you count Kathleen. Betty considers her a crime for sure."

"Kathleen?" brother and sister asked at the same time.

"You haven't seen her yet? She's a mannequin that people dress up and prop around town."

They gave her blank stares.

Typical reaction from out-of-towners. "I don't know when Kathleen became a thing. Far as I remember, she's always been around. Everyone takes a turn putting her in some goofy situation. Like, she was in her business dress at the town council meeting, sitting right there in the front row. I thought Betty would blow a gasket. As the president of the council and the great-granddaughter of Henry Harrison Cemetery, Betty takes those meetings super seriously. Probably why someone decided to put Kathleen in there. You know, just to liven things up."

Amused, Sheena asked, "Is she still there?"

"Nah. Someone new always grabs Kathleen. Who knows where she'll turn up next. We'll watch for her, okay?"

"Wouldn't it be fun if she made it to my wedding?" Laughing, Sheena knelt down to retrieve the key, then quickly inserted it into the lock. The door opened with a squeak.

Yardley made a mental note: fix the squeak.

Sounding dubious, Travis asked his sister, "You'd like for a mannequin to be at your wedding?"

Yardley grinned. "Oh, I'm sure Kathleen would be dressed for the occasion." She peeked inside, anxious to see her suggested updates in person, even though Daniel had emailed her the images. It was funny, but she felt some ownership of the cottage, given how much she loved it and how often she recommended it. Not financial ownership, of course, but the same pride, the same affection.

"That would be such a hoot," Sheena said. "Think of the stories Todd and I could tell our kids."

Just as Sheena ventured in, Yardley's phone buzzed. She tried to ignore it, but Travis didn't. "You're getting a call?"

"A text. It's fine."

"Go ahead. We'll look around while you answer." He followed his sister. "Take your time."

"Okay, thanks." Knowing it'd be Mimi, she withdrew the phone, unlocked the screen and read the short text.

Howz it goin?

Glancing into the house, Yardley ensured neither Travis nor Sheena was paying her any attention.

He held my arm! she texted back, ridiculously excited. Tingles of awareness continued to chase up and down her spine. For a really long time!

Mimi immediately replied, Tell him u want sex.

OMG. Yardley snickered. Stop.

lol U know u want 2

Mimi was so bad. Wonderfully, wickedly bad. She was also correct. Yardley bit her lip, unsure how to answer. Will call later. That'd give her time to think about it.

[kissy-face emoji]

Kisses from Mimi. It was how she often signed off. luv u.

luv u 2

After stowing the phone, she stepped into the hand-hewn log cottage that was no more than one large sleeping and eating room, plus a tiny bathroom. A beautiful king-size bed dominated one wall with a corner-style spa tub to the left and a galley kitchen, small table and two chairs to the right. Directly across from the bed was a wood-burning stone fireplace with a television over the mantel.

Yardley knew if she ever stayed in the cabin, the television would get zero use. After all, tall windows offered a stunning view of the lake. The sunrises and sunsets would be far more interesting than anything on TV.

She'd personally chosen the handmade quilt on the bed, and the beautiful chandelier hanging over the table and chairs, both crafted by local artisans.

"The bathroom is through here." Excitedly crossing the hardwood floor, Yardley opened one of two doors to show the white pedestal sink, toilet and shower. "There's storage under the bed for your clothes." She opened the second door. "In here you have a pantry and a stack washer/dryer, plus there are hooks on the wall to hang your beach towels or swimsuits." She closed that door again. "The shower is small, but of course you'll probably want to use that spa tub together anyway, right?"

Both Travis and Sheena looked at the tub. Just as Yardley had suggested, Daniel had placed fat scented candles around the rim, along with fresh flowers. Plush towels were on a rack close at hand.

Admiring it all, Yardley breathed, "It's *so* perfect, don't you think?" When Travis gave her another discerning glance, she rushed on. "Think of the evenings you'll have sitting on the deck together with the beautiful sunset as a backdrop." She'd certainly imagined it many, many times. "The bug light and a citronella candle help keep the mosquitoes at bay so you can just relax and enjoy each other." In so many ways, the cottage paired charmingly with her country wedding plans to create the most spectacular experience.

With a shoulder against the stone fireplace, Travis watched her.

Like, intensely watched her. *Not* what she was used to. She felt her face go hot again.

With a slow smile, he said, "Great pitch. You really sell the place."

Sheena drew his attention away. "What do you think?"

"Doesn't matter what I think. You're the one who'll be staying here."

Yardley frowned over that. "I'm sure she'd like your opinion—as long as you're nice about it."

"Exactly." Sheena trailed a hand over the quilt, then approached Travis. "I think it's romantic and peaceful. Yardley's right, everything is picture-perfect."

"I think Yardley might've had a hand in that, don't you?"

Put on the spot, Yardley said, "I, um… I just tried to imagine what a new couple might appreciate." Basically, she'd given her heart free rein and made the suggestions that *she'd* love…but they didn't need to know that.

"Well, you nailed it," Sheena said. "I love it, and I know Todd will, too."

This time Travis's smile was different, full of affection instead of…whatever that was that had sparked in his dark eyes when he'd looked at Yardley. "Then I say go for it."

With a squeal, Sheena threw her arms around him. "You're the best, Travis."

"Hey." He returned his sister's hug. "As far as honeymoons go, this is a bargain, so thanks for going easy on me."

Huh. So Travis was covering the honeymoon, too? What an incredibly great guy. And apparently, he had a pretty decent cash flow—not that she wondered about that in any mercenary way or anything. As someone who often struggled with making ends meet, Yardley was always happy for the success of others.

One day, eventually, she'd get the ridiculous "Cemetery" moniker off all the businesses here and then the town could become a truly popular honeymoon destination. Would that require her to run for town council? She sincerely hoped not.

"I'm starving," Travis said, as he released Sheena. "How about we grab those ribs now?"

With one last look around at the cottage, Yardley nodded. "I gave Saul a heads-up that we'd be in, so be prepared to have your taste buds rejoice."

BECAUSE THE COTTAGE wasn't far from the Pit Stop, literally less than a mile away, it took them no time at all to get there. Finding a place to park proved a little more challenging.

Turning sideways and leaning over the seat between Yardley and Sheena, Travis asked, "Is it always this crowded?"

Wearing an expression of chagrin, Yardley shook her head. "Not on a weekday, no. Saul is always busy, but not like this." She finally wedged the golf cart into a narrow space between a car and a tree, then blew out a breath.

And sat there.

"Problem?" Travis asked, fascinated by the intent way

she stared from one vehicle to another, her mouth twisted to the side, thick lashes lowered over her eyes.

"It's just…it's a small town." She half turned to face him, then missed a beat as she first looked into his eyes, and then at his mouth at such close range.

With him leaning over the seat, and her turned toward him, they were suddenly far too close. Kissing close, actually.

Travis didn't move—and neither did she.

"Um," she murmured, still obviously distracted with his mouth. She blinked and cleared her throat. "At last count we only had eight hundred and twenty-seven citizens."

"So precise." He liked the way her gaze kept bouncing around, at his eyes, his mouth, his preoccupied sister, and his mouth again. Nice, especially since he felt the connection, too.

"Like I said, it's a small town so it's easy to…" She faded off when her gaze landed on his mouth again.

"To?"

"Keep track."

He eased back a little—to avoid temptation and to make it easier for her to concentrate. "I'm following you so far."

"Everyone knows me." Yardley gestured at the overflowing lot. "And I'm pretty sure word got out that we'd be having dinner, so…"

Sheena, who had been scoping out the crowd, turned to them with her brows up. "Everyone is that interested in your clients?"

Yardley winced. "Well, I might have told my friend, Mimi, how gorgeous your brother is."

Taken off guard, Travis straightened. And now Yardley made a point of not looking at him at all. In fact, her attention seemed desperately locked on Sheena as color flooded up her throat and into her cheeks.

"Mimi probably told anyone who would listen. She does that sometimes. So…it gets people curious, you know?"

Sheena gave a slow grin. "You and your girlfriend were gossiping about Travis?"

"Sheena," Travis warned. Yardley was already red-faced with her admission. No reason to embarrass her more.

Of course Sheena ignored the warning.

"I'm not surprised," she said to Yardley. "I mean, he really did get all the good looks in the family."

"No way," Yardley denied. "Look at you. You're fabulous with that combo of beautiful hair and dark eyes. I'd say the gorgeous looks were sprinkled around fairly."

"Uh-huh." Sheena's grin never dimmed. "So did you tell this girlfriend of yours how fabulous I am?"

"Sheena," Travis warned again, this time with exasperation.

"I'm sure I mentioned it." Yardley put both hands to her cheeks. "Oh God, and now I look scalded, don't I? If Mimi is in there, I'm going to strangle her."

Leaning closer, Sheena *loudly* whispered, "Just so you know, Travis mentioned how cute you are, too."

The hell he had! Sure, he'd thought it, but he wouldn't say anything to his sister. He had no intention of distracting from her wedding in any way. But now with Yardley staring at him wide-eyed, what could he say? If he told the truth, she'd be more embarrassed.

So maybe he'd go with Sheena's lie and let his sister deal with the repercussions.

Pasting on a smile, Travis said, "I might have mentioned your dimples. They really are cute."

Mouth dropping open, Sheena stared at him.

Yardley half smiled—which enhanced the dimples big-time. "My dimples?"

"And your eyes are really pretty. They almost take over your face, especially now with the sun reflecting in them."

"Dimples," Yardley murmured with a soft laugh.

Travis wondered why that was funny. Her dimples really were adorable.

Sheena sent him a quick glare. "Yardley, why don't you go inside and find us a table? Travis and I will be along shortly."

"Oh, sure." As if sensing the brewing conflict, Yardley escaped the golf cart at a fast clip.

The second she cleared the door, Sheena turned on him. "You—"

"Picked up where you left off." He stepped out of the back of the cart and looked around. A fresh breeze carried off the lake, stirring the scents of barbecue and freshly mown grass. The sun was bright but not too hot. Leaves rustled in mature oak and sycamore trees. He drew in a deep breath, liking it here.

Sheena gave him a push. "You led her on."

Not really. He'd only taken advantage of the opening his sister gave him. "Did you want me to tell her that you made it up? Should I have laughed at the idea of complimenting her?"

Irritation evaporated from her expression, and now her brows were pinched with guilt. "God, no. That would have been awful. I like her too much to insult her."

"Good. Because she would have been insulted, you know."

"Darn. I was trying to put her at ease since she admitted to gossiping about you. It's not like every woman who meets you doesn't go on and on."

Used to his adoring sister's skewed perception of his popularity, he replied, "Not every woman." *What exactly did Yardley tell her friend?*

Sheena snorted. "Fine. I won't force you to admit you're all that."

"Thank you," he said, deadpan.

"Answer me this, though. *Are* you interested in Yardley?"

The direct question threw him, so he hedged around it. "We're here—in Cemetery of all places—for your wedding. Why don't we just focus on that?"

Her lips curled. "You are! And that'd be cool, because I really do like her a lot. She's so easy to talk to, and she makes the whole wedding prep seem totally doable instead of overwhelming."

"I noticed."

Brows flattening again, Sheena warned, "Just don't lead her on, okay? If she gets hung up on you, then hurt, it's going to screw up everything."

"As my little sister, you might not realize it, but I don't lead on anyone." In fact, he was entirely upfront with women. For years, his main goal had been security for his sister, and that, in part, meant expanding his company. Between caring for Sheena and working as many hours as needed to get ahead, there'd been no room in his life for other involvement.

"Okay then, just... I'm not telling you who you can and can't date."

Only a little mocking, Travis said, "Appreciate that."

She rolled her eyes. "Just be extra clear with her, okay?"

Travis studied his sister, and came to a conclusion. "You're feeling protective of her, aren't you?"

Sheena didn't bother to deny it. "She has no idea how pretty she is, and her mother and aunt seemed godawful in those few minutes when we first met her."

"Obtuse, I think, more than deliberately insulting." Not that anyone should be that insensitive with family. He'd spent years making certain he was tuned in to his sister, giving her uncompromising love, showering her with attention, guiding her when he could, and anticipating what she'd need and when...

Only to have her drop out of college, give up her career goals, and pivot to being a wife and mother.

Clearly he'd missed the boat on understanding Sheena. "Whatever Yardley lacks in family support, she gets from the town instead."

"Right? Everywhere we've gone, people have been super hyped to see her. She's like a celebrity or something."

Or something. "It seems genuine." Like the woman herself.

"For sure. I mean, who wouldn't like her? She's awesome."

An apt description. "So, what do you think?" Travis nodded at the Pit Stop.

The long red-sided building looked like it could have been someone's detached garage, but it was kept in pristine condition with white shutters and a broad white porch. They could hear the laughter inside, and mouthwatering scents escaped through open windows.

"It's like the rest of the town. Nice, but also comfortable, casual and welcoming. Todd would love this place."

Did her every thought have to be about what Todd would or wouldn't like? "I want to know if *you* love it."

"Very, very much."

Travis smiled in relief, because so far, he liked it, too—the town, the vendors, the atmosphere…and the wedding planner. "You ready?" He suspected they'd be walking into a curious mob.

Sheena grinned. "Heck yeah."

They went up the two steps of the painted wooden porch. Travis reached past his sister to open the door for her. Glancing around with interest, Sheena entered. The second Travis stood in the doorway, a hush followed and everyone looked his way.

Ah, hell.

A blonde woman standing across the crowded room with Yardley sent a signal to someone, and the music abruptly changed.

Damn, but it sounded like stripper music. In fact, wait. It was David Rose's "The Stripper."

Yardley covered her face, but the guy behind the counter started cracking up.

Sheena, the goof, fell against him laughing—until she noticed the woman sitting on the end of the counter. Legs crossed, sunglasses in place, one hand raised in welcome. Her arm stayed up. And up.

"Travis," Sheena shouted over the music. "Do you suppose that's Kathleen the mannequin?"

He hoped so, otherwise something was seriously off with the gal. "She hasn't moved a muscle, so I'm guessing yes."

"How fun!" And just like that, Sheena abandoned him to investigate Kathleen.

Taking pity on him, the guy behind the counter dried his hands, turned down the music, and came out to greet Travis.

Offering his hand with a grin, Travis stepped forward. "I take it you're the owner?"

"Saul Culver." The man gave a firm but friendly handshake. "And you're Travis Long. Welcome to the Pit Stop."

"What a welcome it is." Travis glanced around at all the tables filled with laughing people.

"Done in fun, so thanks for not being offended." In an aside, Saul said, "It was Kathleen's idea."

"Ha! I bet it was." Kathleen remained perfectly perched on the corner of the bar, arm still raised. "Yardley seemed to think her friend had something to do with it."

"Yeah, and she'll give Mimi hell later, but at the moment Mimi doesn't seem to mind."

Travis studied the woman beside Yardley. Pretty in a plump, blond, casual way, she looked like the happy sort. Travis nodded to her, and she clasped her heart, staggering back a step and pretending to faint against Yardley.

He couldn't help but chuckle, too. "They've been friends a long time?"

"Yardley and Mimi? Hell, since grade school. They used to be inseparable. If you saw one, you saw the other. Since Mimi has a daughter now and Yardley runs the wedding business, things are a little different. Responsibilities and all that, but they're still like sisters."

"You have a great atmosphere here." Travis admired the black-and-white photos on the walls and the old-fashioned decor that included iron-and-wood tables and chairs. "You've owned it long?"

"My father retired fifteen years ago, so I took over." He looked around with apparent satisfaction. "I've always loved this place. Other than the occasional update, I haven't changed much."

Travis guessed him to be late thirties now, a fit guy, tall and lean. Had he and Yardley ever been a thing? "So you've known Yardley a while?"

"Most of my life." He looked toward her with a smile. "She's something, isn't she?"

Even knowing he had zero rights, that he'd only met Yardley a few days ago, that they certainly didn't have an understanding of any kind, Travis found himself feeling territorial. "Are you two…?"

"Yardley has never looked at me as anything but a friend."

Which didn't say how Saul looked at her, damn it. Was he interested? Then he followed the line of Saul's gaze and realized most of his attention was on Emily Lucretia, the pretty florist. "We met Ms. Lucretia earlier today. My sister, the one over there talking with Yardley and Mimi, is getting married. Yardley will organize everything, so she's been showing us around."

"That's Yardley for you. She's good to this town."

"And the town's good to her?"

"Everyone loves Yardley, probably more than she realizes. They look up to her, respect her, and enjoy her company. I mean, it's Yardley, you know?"

"Yeah, I do."

"C'mon. I'll walk you to your table." Since the music still played, Saul swaggered along while swinging his dish towel over his head. The show earned a wolf whistle from some of the ladies and boos from the guys.

Laughing, Travis followed him. He was keenly aware of the interest he'd drawn from men and women alike. He nodded politely, shared greetings with a few people, and then finally reached Sheena, Yardley, and her friend at the large round table.

"You," he said to Mimi, "have a wicked sense of humor."

She threw her head back, laughing. "Gotta liven things up however we can." Hooking her arm through Yardley's, she said, "I'm Amelia May, better known as Mimi to my friends."

"So, what should I call you?"

"Mimi, of course. Any friend of Yardley's is a friend of mine." She turned to Saul. "Could we get a pitcher of lemonade, hon?"

"You got it," Saul said. "And I'll bring a sampler platter to get y'all started."

"Thank you," Yardley called after him.

"So, Travis." Mimi indicated their table. "Grab a seat and tell me all about yourself."

"Mimi," Yardley growled.

Hoping to put her at ease, Travis pulled out a chair for Mimi, then Yardley, and finally his sister before taking the chair next to Yardley.

Folding his arms on the table, Travis asked, "You want the detailed version or the summary?" He liked Mimi already. She had an effervescence about her, a barely repressed energy that felt addictive.

"Summary first, and I'll let you know if I have questions."

Yardley groaned.

Sheena was busy perusing the menu and swaying to the new song on the jukebox.

Determined to let Yardley know everything was fine, Travis recited a condensed history. "Parents died in a car wreck when I was twenty. I left college, got a job in construction, and took over with Sheena since she's fifteen years younger."

Sheena looked up to say, "Isn't that amazing?"

"Very." With her chin propped on a fist, Mimi waited for him to continue.

"I did well in construction," he admitted, "and eventually started my own small business that I've built up over the years, and now..." Now, he finally had everything in line, his future secured, and soon his sister would be a married woman. "These days I enjoy rehabbing old houses more than building them, but I still do a little of both."

"And he gifts his sister with a wedding because Travis is awesome like that." Sheena gave him a nudge.

Yardley remained conspicuously quiet.

Travis tweaked a long hank of his sister's hair. "Mom and Dad left us well prepared financially."

"Many years ago," Sheena said.

He shrugged. "If they were here, they'd have done it."

"True," Sheena said. "But you weren't obligated. Todd and I would have worked it out." She said to Mimi, "I would have been satisfied going to the courthouse in a pretty dress, but Travis knew I'd always wanted more, so he's been incredibly generous."

"Most girls do," Mimi assured her, earning a searching look from Yardley.

Interesting. Some silent message had just been passed

between the women. Travis sat back in his seat. "Did Yardley plan your wedding?"

"Nah. Kevin and I did the courthouse thing. We used the cost of the wedding for a down payment on a house. Yardley was there," she said, "and that made it all special, so I have zero regrets. But I'm really glad Sheena will get her wedding. Yardley does an incredible job. She really gets it, you know? Whatever a bride describes, Yardley visualizes it and then makes it happen."

"Well, not every time," Yardley said. She snuck a peek at Travis before looking away again. "Remember that woman who wanted horses dressed up like unicorns?"

Laughing, Sheena leaned forward with glee. "Are you serious?"

"Yeah. But I had no idea where to locate ten matching white horses who would wear colorful ribbons, fake unicorn horns, and prance to the tune of the 'Wedding March.'"

Hiding his grin beneath feigned gravity, Travis mused, "Does seem like a daunting task."

"It was still a beautiful wedding," Mimi insisted. "Even with the missing unicorns."

"I'm sure she made it work."

Finally Yardley gave him her full attention. "Actually, I can do any type of wedding, and I have. Country weddings are just popular, maybe because they're so relaxed. All the vendors here can adapt. Saul's catered everything from plated prime rib to pulled pork sandwiches. The barn is great for casual settings, but we have a hall on the other side of town that's more formal. Some brides have gotten married at the gazebo on the beach with white tents set up. Some without the tents."

"Barefoot," Mimi said with a knowing glance at Yardley. "With fresh pedicures."

Yardley shot her a warning frown. "Behave."

Laughing, Mimi pretended to zip her lips.

Sheena glanced back and forth between them. "You two are like night and day."

"Right?" Yardley bumped shoulders with Mimi. "It's a wonder she puts up with me."

Mimi snorted. "She's the yin to my yang. Honestly, I couldn't get by without her."

Travis had a feeling the whole town felt that way, with good reason. "Even with different types of weddings, the other vendors are on board?"

"They're all professionals," Yardley promised. "No matter what type of flower arrangements Emily does, they're always beautiful, Sallie's wedding cakes are decadent and delicious perfection, and in my opinion, the Honeymoon Cottage is the ideal setting for everyone."

Mimi suddenly jumped, then grumbled, "Damn, it always startles me when my phone is set to vibrate." Taking it from the back pocket of her jeans, she glanced at the screen and quickly left her seat.

"Everything okay?" Yardley asked.

"Yeah, fine. It's Kevin." She winked. "I'll be right back. Save all the juicy convo for me." And with that, she hurried out of the restaurant, likely so she'd be able to hear.

Travis continued to watch Yardley, the way she tucked a silky lock of hair behind her ear, how she used her hands while telling Sheena the history behind the black-and-white photos on the restaurant's walls, and the way she laughed when they discussed Kathleen the mannequin.

All of that was nice, but he couldn't pinpoint what,

specifically, caused the driving urge to spend more time with her.

Saul came with the sampler platter, pitcher of lemonade, glasses, plates, and tableware. "Enjoy," he said, then lower to Yardley, "Just let me know when you're ready to order." After a brief squeeze of her shoulder, he moved away.

Mimi returned in time to grab the plate Yardley had put together for her. "Bless you, woman. I'm starved."

"All is well?"

"Yup. Kevin was just checking on me." She rolled her eyes, but wore a pleased smile. "You know how he is since Sammy's birth." To Sheena, she added, "Sammy is my six-month-old daughter, and FYI, nursing moms are *always* hungry." That got the two of them started on baby talk, a subject they embraced.

Casting Travis a worried frown, Yardley leaned closer to confide, "Mimi had a difficult birth and Kevin has been extra watchful over her ever since."

Just as softly, he replied, "I hope she doesn't go into detail with Sheena. She's nervous enough already."

"About being a mom?"

"About everything, really."

Yardley shook her head. "Mimi would never say anything to frighten her."

"Hey," Mimi said. "I heard my name. What are you two whispering about?"

"Weddings and babies," Travis said.

"If only I could hire Yardley to organize the birth, too." Sheena grinned. "I wanted to take one of those birthing classes, but Todd is slammed with overtime right now."

Travis looked away so his sister wouldn't see his irritation. Todd had disrupted Sheena's life in a big way, and now it seemed he didn't have time for anything. Probably would have been a good idea to wait before getting her pregnant and asking her to marry him then, right?

So often, Sheena turned things around, taking the blame for the unplanned pregnancy. Sometimes she seemed to think Todd felt pressured to marry her. But Todd was eleven years older and damn well should have—

"You're not eating," Yardley said, interrupting his dark thoughts. "Saul will be back soon to take our orders."

"I want the ribs," Sheena said. "They're incredible. And these potato skins? Ohmigod, they're so good."

Determined that his sister would enjoy every moment of her wedding adventure, Travis tried a little of everything. "I agree. It's all great."

Mimi stood. "I used to waitress here, and the crowd is my fault." She winked at Travis. "Just give me your orders and I'll let the cook know. That'll save Saul a little time."

Everyone ordered something different, with Yardley requesting the chicken tenders, Sheena the ribs, and Travis the pulled pork. There'd been enough food on the sampler to give a taste of nearly everything.

Once Mimi rushed off, Sheena pushed back her chair. "I'm going to call Todd real quick so I can tell him about the Pit Stop. He's going to love the food here, and he'll be relieved to know we're keeping a real laid-back atmosphere."

Watching her go, Travis blew out a breath.

Yardley touched his forearm. "You okay?"

"What? Oh, yeah." He briefly covered her hand with his own, and realized how right it felt to touch her. He'd noticed that at the Honeymoon Cottage, too. There'd been a connection, and neither of them could have missed it.

Maybe that's why he opened up and said, "It bugs me that her every thought is for what Todd will like, and Todd isn't even making the wedding prep a priority."

She hesitated, then retreated, sitting back in her seat, her hands folded on the table.

The warmth of her touch gradually faded, making him miss it already. "What are you thinking, Yardley?" He could see it in her eyes that she had something to say. "Come on. Don't hold back. I can take it."

Wearing a soft smile, she shook her head. "It's nothing. I just wondered if there are…issues between you and Todd."

Rubbing the back of his neck, Travis wondered how much he should say. Yardley didn't seem judgmental though, and he wouldn't mind airing his thoughts. "The thing is, Todd is always busy, so all the planning falls on Sheena. Before Todd came in and everything changed, she had a good head on her shoulders. She graduated high school at the top of her class and breezed through her first year of college." He watched a bead of condensation slowly slide down his glass of lemonade. "For as long as I can remember, she wanted to be a nurse. Not a doctor—she always specified that she wanted to spend more time with patients, not breeze in and out with diagnoses." He half smiled.

"She's not interested in that anymore?"

"I have no idea. All she talks about is what Todd wants." And it frustrated the hell out of him. "No offense, but the country wedding is for Todd because he's more comfortable in jeans. The food here is more his vibe than prime rib. I don't know if the guy's ever even worn a suit, much less a tux."

"I got the feeling that Sheena wanted those things, too. Upscale weddings can be intimidating. There's so much etiquette to follow that, to me at least, some brides lose what they want in order to have what they think is expected. Your sister is different. When she speaks of the wedding, she sounds confident about her preferences, even if some of those preferences are to make the man she loves comfortable, too."

What an incredibly astute take on things. Weddings did seem like a lot of fanfare, to the point that the meaning of the ceremony sometimes got overshadowed by all the details.

Without commenting on his silent introspection, Yardley asked, "Where does Todd work?"

When he told her the name of the factory, her brows lifted. "What?" he asked. "You look surprised."

"That's where Mimi's husband works. I wonder if they know each other."

Talk about a small world. "I'd rather you not mention it to her. If Sheena chooses to, that's fine, but I don't want her asking why I was talking about Todd."

"Okay, sure. No worries."

Taking in her guilty expression, he playfully narrowed one eye. "You said that awfully fast, especially considering you and Mimi are so close."

She winced. "Close enough that you were welcomed with that awful music."

To put her at ease, he laughed. "Saul did all the dancing. All I had to do was follow him."

After a brief hesitation, she settled her warm palm on

him again. "But that doesn't mean I repeat private conversations to her, I promise."

He believed her. "Thanks. She's touchy when it comes to Todd."

"She loves him," Yardley said with a shrug, as if that explained it.

And maybe it did. "I'm sorry if I sounded accusing."

"Pfft. I get it. I mean, look around. I goofed, telling Mimi you were…" She bit her lip, then ventured, "Gorgeous?" In a rush she added, "God, I embarrass myself so often. Anyway, you know you are, right? You have mirrors, so that wasn't a secret. It just took me by surprise when you showed up. I was expecting a bride-to-be and her ordinary brother and then, bam! *You*." She gestured up and down him, as if that explained it, before returning her small palm to his arm. "It sort of rattled me, so I told Mimi. Then she went and blabbed to everyone else and they all decided to have some fun and… I really am sorry about all this. I hope you weren't too embarrassed?"

His mouth quirked. "Actually, I'm flattered."

Sitting back again, she laughed. "Stripper music does it for you, huh? Or was it Kathleen's gusto?"

They both glanced at the mannequin, who hadn't been disturbed at all. Customers moved around her as if she were real.

"As a matter of fact, it was you, Yardley." He looked at her long enough that she couldn't misunderstand his intent. "The way you blush and how you laugh, and how you've put my sister at ease—I appreciate all of it. If a little good-natured humor follows, I don't mind." In fact, this meeting felt more like a date, possibly the most impactful first date he'd ever had.

Flustered, Yardley blinked fast, and then bypassed

his compliments to settle on the topic of Sheena. "Your sister is a doll, and I'm looking forward to working with her. That is, I assume we are?"

"We most definitely are." Confirming that gave him an idea. "You said you could put together a contract for us?"

"Of course." She moved into professional mode with ease, proving that role was an easier fit than that of an available, interesting woman. "Once Sheena gives me an idea of how many guests there'll be, her flower and menu choices, and if she wants to use the barn or not, I can write it up."

As if summoned, his sister returned with a dreamy smile. "Todd was thrilled when I told him about the food."

"Did he mention any preferences?" Yardley asked.

"He said it's up to me, but I know his family and friends would love the ribs and potato skins. Do you think those would work for the reception?"

"I think they'd be perfect." Yardley dug in her purse and produced a small binder with her wedding logo on it. Using a sparkly pink pen, she jotted down notes.

Mimi surprised him, showing up with a huge tray held aloft with all their food. She maneuvered with ease, including working around Yardley's papers, until they'd all been served.

"Wow," he said. "That took skill."

"Damn right." Mimi flexed her arm, showing off her small biceps. "That tray was light compared to some I used to carry. Now my baby girl, a pot of spaghetti, and the laundry basket are the heaviest things I lift."

Yardley glanced up. "You miss working, don't you?"

"Sometimes." She leaned over to nudge her friend

with her shoulder. "But I miss my little Sammy girl more. Soon as I chow down, I'm heading home."

"I'd love to meet your daughter sometime," Sheena said. "I don't know anything at all about babies."

"You'll learn fast," Mimi assured her. "Let me know if you ever want to visit. Sammy and I are home almost every day. Kevin doesn't get in until five, sometimes six. We could do lunch and I could—ahem—let you change a diaper or two."

Travis laughed. "There you go. Hands-on practice."

For the rest of the meal, the women made plans while he mostly observed. Yardley was subtle in the questions she asked, but she managed to get all the answers she needed, and still eat.

"Am I getting too extravagant?" Sheena asked.

Yardley paused, deferring to Travis.

"I think you're being conservative." So far, most of the wedding guests would be Todd's family and friends. "You sure you don't have anyone else you want to invite?"

"It's not like we have any close family. And since I left college, I've only really stayed in touch with ten friends." She grinned. "Though I do hope Kathleen makes it."

"I'll see to it," Mimi promised. "We'll need to claim her in advance before someone else does. I have stealth when I need it."

So far, everyone in Cemetery was so nice, they felt more like friends than new acquaintances. He turned to Yardley. "How soon will you have the contract together?"

"Not long. A few days."

Knowing his sister's schedule, he asked, "Could I come by Monday? Maybe around three?"

Yardley checked the schedule in her phone and nodded. "I should be free by one, so that works."

"I have a doctor's appointment that day," Sheena reminded him. "Todd's already arranged for the time off work."

"That's all right. You don't need to be there for that part." He'd rather she not see a final tally. If she did, she'd start worrying about money again. "I can take care of it."

Sheena bounced her gaze back and forth between him and Yardley, then stifled a smile. "Sure, if you really don't mind."

"It's not a problem."

Mimi grinned. "I hate to leave with all this interesting intrigue going on, but my maternal instincts are insisting." She stood, bent to squeeze Yardley tight and kiss her cheek, then again surprised Travis by hugging him, too. When she straightened, she said to Yardley, "Dang, have you felt him?"

"Mimi!"

While Travis laughed over Yardley's scandalized squeak, her outrageous friend patted his shoulder. "He's all firm and studly."

Sheena laughed. "I do like you, Mimi. You're extra fun."

"She's extra something," Yardley muttered.

Turning to face all the customers, Mimi held out her arms and shouted, "Bye, town. Thank you all for turning out!" She got a rousing cheer in return. Glancing back at Yardley, she said, "Call me later," and then she blew Yardley a kiss and was on her way.

"Gah," Yardley complained. "I love her, I really do, but sometimes she's like a cute, perky buffalo stampeding through."

Travis agreed with that assessment. "She has her

charm." He definitely liked how much she obviously cared for Yardley.

"You'd think so because she felt you up and called you studly."

"You could be right." Today had been fun, far more fun than he'd anticipated when he'd started this whole wedding expedition with his sister. But then, he hadn't counted on Yardley Belanger's warmth, her over-the-top friend Mimi, or the quirky awesomeness of a small town named Cemetery.

Being honest with himself, he admitted that it was mostly because of Yardley that he was already looking forward to Monday.

4

MIMI SLOUCHED LOWER on the couch, making faces with each crack that came from Yardley's aunt and mother. How the hell her friend tolerated the two of them, she couldn't imagine. She supposed Yardley loved them, regardless of their spiteful flaws. But seriously, *why*?

While her friend cooed over little Sammy, Lilith and Aurora barely spared the baby a glance—except for Lilith to say, "At least Mimi had the good sense to get married before giving birth."

"Could I help it that Yardley's father wasn't suitable?" Aurora returned.

"Wasn't suitable…and didn't ask," Lilith pointed out.

"It would have been a bigger mistake to marry the man and you know it."

"It was a mistake to get pregnant."

Here we go again, Mimi thought, noticing how Yardley very deliberately ignored the two of them.

"Of course it was," Aurora agreed. "We've been over this before, Lilith. The girl is thirty now–"

"Thirty-one," Mimi corrected.

"—so obviously it's past time to rue mistakes."

One good smack, Mimi thought vindictively. That'd knock some sense into the old bats. "Just so we're clear," she said, loud enough to interrupt the familiar squabble. "My daughter isn't a mistake. I love her with all my heart."

"Of course you do," Lilith said. "You're married."

For the love of... "That has nothing to do with it. She's *mine* and she owns my heart."

Aurora glanced over at Sammy, busy bouncing on Yardley's lap. "Yes, well, adorable as she might be, you do realize your life is over."

Damned infuriating woman. Mimi spread her arms wide. "And yet here I sit, still breathing, laughing, and loving every damned day."

Giving her the stink eye, Aurora said, "You know exactly what I meant."

"Yup, just as I know exactly how wrong you are."

Yardley cleared her throat—a nonverbal warning for Mimi to cool it. Really, she probably should. The sooner she quit engaging with them, the sooner they would leave. Yet she couldn't seem to help herself. "It's a shame you couldn't find any happiness in your life, Aurora. Must suck to have a beautiful, talented, loving daughter and still be so dissatisfied."

Totally missing the sarcasm, Aurora sighed. "Yes, I stupidly allowed myself to get distracted by a handsome face and a sexy body."

Yardley groaned.

"He was rather handsome," Lilith agreed. "I'll give you that. If only you'd been thinking about your future instead of your—"

"Lady parts?" Mimi offered helpfully, which got her narrow-eyed glares from everyone, especially Yardley. She almost laughed. "Got ya all hot and bothered, huh? You know, it's hard to imagine you that way." Like, *impossible* to imagine. In fact, Mimi didn't want to imagine it because that might make her tuna sandwich come back up on her.

"He was very exciting." Aurora sighed. "But that fleeting excitement cost me dearly."

Mimi *really* wanted to point out what she'd gained because of it—basically Yardley ran the business, cooked dinner, and kept their lives operating smoothly—but Yardley wouldn't like her saying so much. Aurora and Lilith might think they contributed, but Mimi knew the truth.

Yardley kept them busy so they wouldn't overly interfere in her plans.

"If only you'd listened to me way back then," Lilith said for, oh, the bajillionth time. "You had options, you know."

Right. She'd had the option to ditch Yardley. Why the hell did those two continue to talk about it? Like they'd said, Yardley was here and she was so damned amazing, Aurora should be thankful for the decisions she'd made.

"So, who was he?" Mimi asked, just to throw them off their continued bickering. "A guy from around here? A passing vacationer? Alien?"

Aurora cast a quick glance at Yardley, then sniffed. "It doesn't matter. He's in the past."

"Except that she resembles him," Lilith insisted with a pointed look at Yardley. "One only has to glance at Yardley to know she didn't get the classic features of the Belangers. Her cheeks are so round, they dimple when she smiles, and her nose—"

"Day-yum," Mimi interrupted. "Her dad really must've been smokin' hot, right? Yardley is so beautiful, I always wondered, because yeah, she looks *nothing* like the two of you."

This time she'd put just enough snide emphasis in the words for the insult to register.

Aurora scowled. "Why are you here, Mimi?"

"Because she's my friend," Yardley said, finally speaking up. "Mimi could visit every day, three times a day, and she'd be welcome."

Mimi really wanted to stick her tongue out at them.

Lilith waved off all the comments. "It makes no difference to me. I'm off to shop."

"Wait, what?" Bounding off the couch and holding Sammy on her hip, Yardley chased after her aunt. "What do you mean, you're shopping? For what?"

"A new outfit. Why?" Lilith looked around. "Did you need me to pick up something?"

Lowering her voice, Yardley whispered, "No, but Aunt, we talked about this."

"Yes, you said we needed to cut back on our business expenses. This isn't a business expense. It's a new outfit."

Mimi rolled her eyes. Leave it to Lilith to totally miss the point.

"We worked out a budget," Yardley insisted.

"No, you did that. I don't recall Aurora or I having any say on it."

Mostly because they'd proven long ago that they didn't know how to budget, that they were too self-indulgent to make ends meet. If it wasn't for Yardley, the biz would have gone under long ago. Mimi really wished she could point that out to them, but Yardley wouldn't like it if she did.

"The budget is there for a reason," Yardley insisted. "Once you spend what you've been allotted for incidentals, there is no more. I need you to understand that."

"It's an outfit, not a house or a car."

Knowing Lilith's taste in business chic, it'd still cost a small fortune.

"I'm serious about this, Aunt Lilith. I have bills to pay and that doesn't leave a lot of wiggle room. Not until we get more cash flow."

What Yardley meant was *enough* cash flow to counter all the many ways her mother and aunt liked to spend. Mimi knew for a fact that Yardley had a successful business. Word-of-mouth from satisfied customers brought in a lot of new people. She stayed busy, but the upkeep on the old house took a toll, even with Yardley doing as much of the yard work as she could. She cooked dinner every night to save on restaurant bills. And Yardley scrimped for herself, even knowing her aunt and mother didn't.

"Cruella and Maleficent," Mimi grumbled. She hated that they took advantage of Yardley all the time.

"You're signing that new girl, right?" Aurora lifted her designer purse strap over her shoulder. "That'll take care of the budget."

"No," Yardley said. "It won't. We need to build up our savings. We need to do more advertising. We need—"

"I'm meeting Betty for lunch," Aurora said. "We can continue this conversation when I get home tonight."

Uh-oh. Mimi sat forward.

Yardley froze. "Betty Cemetery?"

"Do you know another Betty in this town?" At the

foyer mirror, Aurora paused to apply more lipstick. Her brown hair, highlighted with red, had already been styled, but she tucked back one side, admired her reflection, and smiled. "She has a few things she wants to discuss with me."

Slipping in, Mimi took Sammy from Yardley. "I think I'll go find a cookie or something in the kitchen."

Without looking away from her mother, Yardley caught Mimi by the back of her shirt, halting her escape. "And Betty requested to see you?"

"Yes. She said it was important." Aurora glanced at Lilith. "Your aunt wasn't invited."

With a fake smile, Lilith said, "I wouldn't have gone anyway." She sailed out the door and to her small silver car.

Catching up to her, Aurora said, "Don't pretend with me. You know you feel slighted."

"That would be you—since you'll be forced to visit with her through an entire lunch."

After watching them for a moment, Yardley closed the door and turned to Mimi. "You know what this is."

Mimi winced. "Probably about the town council."

"Because *you* have been encouraging everyone in that nonsense."

Trying, but failing, to look innocent, Mimi took a stand. "You know you want to do it, Yardley. You'd finally be able to make the changes this town needs."

"But not like that." She headed off for the kitchen, so Mimi followed.

"Why not like that?" Sammy tangled a tiny fist in her hair and pulled. Ouch, ouch, ouch. "Ease up, sweetheart." Carefully, Mimi untangled her daughter's fingers, kissed her palm, and then her cheek, and ended up nuzzling her neck—which sort of smelled like the cereal she'd eaten right before they'd left to visit Yardley.

"Betty would be devastated *if* I won, and I'll look like a fool when I don't." Out of a long-standing routine, Yardley got started making tea.

Sidling around her, Mimi grabbed two paper towels, wet them in the sink, and then went about cleaning Sammy's neck. "You're a little animal, aren't you, sweetheart? You eat like your daddy, all messy but with greed. I only wish my chubby rolls were as cute as yours."

Sammy pumped her arms and legs and cooed.

"You don't have chubby rolls," Yardley said, pausing to admire the baby. "God, she just makes my heart melt."

"She's making my nose melt. I think she just loaded her diaper."

Yardley laughed, which was better than her looking all worried, and asked, "Want me to change her?"

"No, you finish our tea and then find me some munchies. I'll be right back." Mimi hurried to the living room, snagged up her diaper bag, and went into Yardley's bedroom. One-handed, she shook out a baby blanket on the top of Yardley's bedding.

Yup, that annoyed her, too. When her friend had gone about remodeling the house, she'd done every room…except her own. That's where the budget had run out, only because Yardley never made herself a priority.

Aurora had spent weeks finding just the right bedding. Lilith had tested one paint sample after another. And through it all, Yardley had supported them.

Did they return that support? No, they just acted like she was still an unplanned inconvenience. Anyone with a brain knew the two old witches would be lost without Yardley.

Pausing, Mimi stared down at Sammy, who kept trying to roll over, something she did now whenever Mimi changed her diaper, which made it a battle to get her clean. A crooked smile came with a tear, and Mimi scooped her up to cuddle her close. "Never, ever will I do that to you. I swear to you, sweetness, you will always know how much your mommy and daddy love you."

Sammy grabbed another handful of hair, this time near her scalp, which brought tears to her eyes for a new reason.

Laughing, Mimi managed to free herself. As she changed Sammy's diaper, she spoke to her about Yardley's problems. "If she wins a seat on the town council, her mother will have to respect her, right? The town will change for the better, and no way can her aunt or mother ignore that. Plus it'll give her more time away from them, you know? They won't be able to depend on her because she'll have other responsibilities. It's a win-win, don't you think?"

"Are you on the phone?" Yardley asked as she stepped into the room, making Mimi jump with guilt.

"No, just keeping Sammy entertained."

"Look at all that drool." Yardley laughed, grabbing a tissue to wipe the baby's chin.

"The joy of teething. Now she has stuff leaking from both ends."

After smoothing Sammy's cap of downy blond hair, Yardley stroked Mimi's hair, too. "The tea's ready, and I have butter cookies that'll melt in your mouth."

"Now I'm drooling." She used the baby blanket to wipe her daughter's chin once more.

Automatically, Yardley gathered up the dirty diaper and diaper bag.

Obviously, Yardley would make an amazing mom. Other than nursing, she did all the same things Mimi did, and with the same natural ease. Now if only her friend could find a guy worthy of her, one who would interest Yardley enough to put herself first for a change.

A little while later, with a cup of tea and two mouth-watering butter cookies in her stomach, Mimi yawned.

"No sleep last night?"

"It wasn't too bad, but yeah, teething is tough on everyone."

"Why don't you go crash in my bed for a bit? I'm free for another two hours."

Aw, now see. Her girl was the best. "Sleep and miss time with you?"

"Sammy's already out."

Mimi smiled at her little angel, now snuggled in her carrier. "I was going to insist that Kevin get wild with me tonight, but I swear, I think I'd prefer to sleep."

Hearing things Mimi hadn't said—which was a knack of Yardley's—she asked, "You two still aren't...back to normal?"

"I'm not even sure what normal is anymore." Feeling disloyal, Mimi made a face, peeked at Yardley, then heaved a sigh. "You know how much I love Kevin."

"Yes I do. Just as much as he loves you." She reached over for Mimi's hand. "You can tell me anything. You know that, right?"

Very true. Yardley was the one person she could always talk to. With Kevin working so much, she hated to burden him. And her mom never failed to show her love, but Mimi was a grown woman now, and she couldn't see leaning too heavily on a parent.

"Mimi? You *do* know Kevin loves you, right?"

"That's it, though. He could love me and not really want me anymore." When Yardley started to protest, Mimi hurriedly explained, "We had sex, Yardley. And it was…different. He was so damn *careful*. And quick." Feeling her cheeks burn, she said, "You know what I mean. Kevin is great in the sack, but he'd usually take his time. The other night, he acted like he was either afraid he'd hurt me, or he didn't want to tire me. He wasn't quick from lack of control, so was it disinterest?"

"No. I can't believe that. I bet it's like you said. He didn't want to get into a sexual marathon because he knew you needed sleep."

"Maybe." She bit her lip with hesitation, but this was Yardley. Nothing was taboo between them. "I've changed. I've got stretch marks on my poor boobs and my stomach still looks…*loose*." In a near wail—kept low so she wouldn't wake Sammy—she asked, "God, that sounds so gross, doesn't it?"

"No." Yardley squeezed her fingers and then released her. "It sounds like a natural occurrence for a woman who's given life to another human being. That was not only a miracle, but it was an ordeal, too. I was there every step of the way, so I should know. You went through a lot of amazing changes."

Mimi dropped her face into both hands. "I feel *really* unappealing."

Yardley immediately left her stool so she could hug Mimi close. "I swear to you, you're every bit as sexy as ever."

With a snort, Mimi let her know what she thought of that. She'd never been sexy. Cute, maybe. Or as Kevin used to say, adorable.

Bleh.

Sammy was adorable. Mimi wanted more.

"It's true," Yardley insisted. "Maybe more so now, even. Yes, you sometimes look tired, but you also have a glow. What you see as unwanted weight, I see as more curves—in all the right places, too. So what if there are a few marks on your boobs? Look at those beauties! You've gone up a whole cup size."

Mimi plumped her girls. "Yeah, there is that, I guess."

"Your butt is rounder too—and no, don't you dare roll your eyes at me. It's a stellar butt. Between that and your boobs, your waist looks really small."

Cracking a grin, Mimi asked, "You been admiring my posterior?"

"I admire *everything* about you, Mimi. You know that. And Kevin does, too. I see the way he looks at you, like he almost can't believe you're real, and even better, that you're his. Everything he feels for you is right there for the whole world to see."

Laying her head on Yardley's shoulder, Mimi asked softly, "But what if he doesn't? What if he thinks of my boobs as Sammy's now? I read that's a thing when women breastfeed."

"Nonsense." She alternately smoothed Mimi's hair and hugged her. "Even if he did—though he *doesn't*— you won't be breastfeeding much longer. It'd be a temporary thing."

With her most self-conscious issues exposed, Mimi whispered, "What if he looks at my body and only focuses on the things that are different?"

"You know what?" Yardley rubbed her back. "You need to talk to him. You need to share all these worries with him."

"How can I do that? He works all the time, then gets home and wants to help me around the house."

"Know what I think?" Yardley said. "That you're bothered by the changes in your body, and because of that, you're imagining a bunch of stuff that probably isn't even true. Maybe he's thinking the same things you are."

"That I suck?" she asked with a forced grin.

Yardley lightly smacked her shoulder. "Not the way you mean it, and I don't want to hear about any other way."

That made Mimi laugh.

"He might be worrying that he's not measuring up, that he's not doing enough to help you. You both went through a lot."

"I know." It had been a difficult birth, yet Kevin came out of it looking more scrumptious than ever, while she… didn't.

Yardley gave her a probing look. "Promise me you'll think about this, okay? If you're feeling insecure and off balance from all the changes, maybe he is, too. Maybe he's worried about providing enough for you and Sammy. Being there when you need him. Worrying that you're overworked and he doesn't want to add to your burden. Love goes both ways." With an endearing, crooked smile, Yardley added, "He might need a little reassurance, too. After all, he doesn't have me as a bestie."

"So true. Whatever would I do without you?"

"You'll never have to find out."

Since having Sammy, Mimi had been on an emotional roller coaster, and now stupid tears burned her eyes. She laughed to hide them. "Kevin might be insulted if I ask him if he's as weepy as me, but I get your drift and yes, I'll consider it, I promise."

When the landline rang, Yardley hustled to her office. After another quick glance at her sleeping daughter, Mimi went to stand in the doorway, listening in without a shred of guilt because she knew Yardley wouldn't mind.

"Hello? Oh, hey." Grinning, Yardley glanced at her, then mouthed, *It's him*, with obvious relish.

Him who? Ah, it had to be Travis. Fun! She gave Yardley a thumbs-up.

"Oh sure, that'd be fine. I have the rest of that day free. Why? What's up?" As Yardley listened, her brows went up and her smile widened. "That sounds great. Sure, I'd love it. Thanks."

Oooh, that sounded interesting. Like a legit date or something. Behind her back, Mimi crossed her fingers.

"Yup, I'm good. Today is a slow day. I'm just visiting with Mimi." She grinned. "Sure." Yardley turned to her. "Travis says hi."

"Tell Mr. Studly that I say hello."

Rolling her eyes, Yardley asked, "You heard? Yes, she's outrageous." She laughed a little, then turned to Mimi once more. "He said thank you."

Dang, but Mimi liked him. Not only was Travis easy on the eyes, but he didn't take himself too seriously either. Mimi eavesdropped while Yardley and Travis chatted for five minutes or so. Judging by Yardley's posture and expressions, she was both surprised and excited by the call and whatever offer Travis had made.

The second the call ended, Mimi demanded, "What? Tell me. Is it a date?"

Trying to suppress a grin, Yardley said, "Sort of? I mean, we're meeting Monday anyway to go over the contract, but he asked if I'd like to go with him to an antique outlet he likes where they have a lot of Victorian stuff that might interest me."

"Ohmigod, that is totally a date!" Mimi snatched her up for a hug, then caught her hand and dragged her back to the kitchen. "Soon as Sammy wakes up, we need to figure out something super stellar for you to wear. Something—" she bobbed her eyebrows "—sexy. And you have to swear to me that if even the tiniest opportunity opens up, you'll go for the gold."

"Go for the gold?"

"Sex, Yardley." She grabbed up her tea for a big swallow. Excitement worked up her thirst. If she couldn't have wild passionate sex, encouraging Yardley would be the next best thing. "I want you to sex him up."

Flustered by the possibility, Yardley shook her head. "We're going out at three o'clock!"

"So? I promise, his parts work as well in the afternoon as they do at night, guaranteed."

Red-faced and scowling, Yardley said, "I will swear no such thing."

"But you have to!" This was the most excited Mimi had been in weeks. "One of us needs to get laid right."

"You," Yardley said, pointing at Mimi, "can do that tonight if you just speak up."

"Maybe," she conceded. If she told Kevin outright what she wanted, he'd probably do his damnedest to deliver. But she shouldn't have to. The last thing she wanted was to twist his arm and get…grudging wildness. That would be awful. And humiliating.

Watching Mimi, probably reading her like a book, Yardley tightened her mouth. "I'll make you a deal," she finally said.

Cautious now, Mimi nibbled on another cookie. "What kind of deal?"

"If things move in that direction with Travis and me, if he's interested in that and if there's an actual opportunity, I'll wholeheartedly accept."

Thrusting a fist in the air, Mimi whooped. "Now you're talking."

"But only if you agree to tell Kevin what you want."

Her lips parted, but Mimi couldn't make a single sound come out.

"Promise me."

"Dirty pool, Yardley."

"That's the deal." Yardley folded her arms. "Take it or leave it."

Narrowing her eyes, Mimi studied Yardley. "I think you're bluffing." She stuffed the rest of the cookie into her mouth, then chased it with the last of her tea. "I think you're already anticipating the nasty with Travis. *I think*," she said, warming to her assumptions, "if that gorgeous hunk of testosterone gives you the slightest opening, you'll be all over it."

"Nope." Yardley lifted her nose. "You know me better than anyone, so you know how little experience I have with sex. I'm the quintessential, almost-virginal old maid."

"There is no such thing as almost-virginal."

Yardley went on. "I should have six cats. I should live in a cotton housecoat and slippers, and wear curlers in my hair around the clock."

"Clearly this is an image you saw somewhere."

"A thirty-one-year-old woman who's only had sex twice is most definitely an almost-virgin."

"Twice?" Mimi scowled. "Who was the second guy?"

Grumbling, Yardley looked away. "Same guy. I just gave him a second chance."

"Right, so back in your early twenties. Damn, girl, I know there have been opportunities since then."

With a dismissive shrug, Yardley said, "None that were worth the trouble. This is a small town, everyone knows my mother and aunt, and gossip travels faster than a golf cart. If an almost-virgin got laid, you know everyone would hear about it. Then I'd get more lectures from my mother on not allowing a baby to ruin my life."

Fury chased up Mimi's spine and curled her hands into fists. "Your mother is a—"

"Don't say it." Yardley got up to pace. "You know it doesn't bother me."

Not anymore. But when they'd been younger? For the longest time, Yardley had avoided letting Mimi visit her at home because she knew the things she'd hear. It had taken Mimi more than a few tries to prove to Yardley that it didn't matter, that even as a kid she hadn't put any stock in the ramblings of bitter old crones.

"Now I know it's more about the sisters hassling each other and has almost nothing to do with me. They enjoy arguing. What they're arguing about is usually a moot point, though my father does seem to be a major bone of contention between them."

One of these days, Mimi would tell them off. She'd vent all the years' worth of pent-up anger and frustration she felt whenever they started their callous nonsense. Whenever they'd hurt Yardley. Whenever they'd made her best friend in the whole world feel like less than she was. "That doesn't excuse them."

"No, but it is what it is."

"They would be *lost* without you."

"True enough." Yardley stepped directly in front of Mimi. "Now, about our agreement...?"

So Yardley thought to strong-arm her? Not likely. While Mimi never hesitated to speak her mind, Yardley worried endlessly about hurting someone's feelings. "Tell you what. Accomplish your end of the bargain first. Once you confirm it with me, then I'll spell things out for Kevin."

"But I'm not seeing him until tomorrow."

"So? Tonight I really do need to crash." She gave a lusty yawn—one that started out feigned and turned into the real thing. Damn, it felt like her jaws might break. "Oh, wow. Sorry about that."

Yardley tucked Mimi's hair behind her ears. "You really are beat, aren't you? You sure you don't want to go grab a nap?"

Just then, Sammy woke, and she didn't appreciate the lack of attention.

While Yardley rushed to lift the baby from her carrier, Mimi stood and stretched. "What I want is to go through your wardrobe and find you an outfit that our stud-muffin can't resist."

"*Our* stud-muffin?" Yardley asked.

"I'm claiming part ownership until I see the deed done. Then you can spread your wings and fly on your own." Arms opened wide, Mimi headed out of the kitchen at a tilt. "Fly, little bird, fly."

Laughing, Yardley fell into step behind her. "Is Sammy hungry?"

"Yeah, it's time for her to nurse. I'll prop up on your bed and see to that while you put on a fashion show. And Yardley? If you don't show me the best options, I'll be going through your closet myself." She might end up doing that anyway. Sure, she was out of shape, and in perpetual mom-mode, but deep down she still had a keen sense of style. She'd do her girl up right, and Travis Long wouldn't be able to resist her.

WITH A LAST glance at the clock, Travis finished up the work on the new faucet and started putting away his tools. He'd be seeing Yardley soon—something he'd thought about repeatedly all day. In fact, he had a hard time getting her off his mind.

So many things about her drew him in. Those big color-changing eyes that always showed her thoughts were a beautiful focal point, especially framed by feathery lashes and slightly arched brows. Yardley had expressive eyes, and he couldn't imagine anyone being immune.

She also had an incredibly appealing mouth that smiled so often, he couldn't keep his gaze off it.

Her mink-brown hair never seemed styled, which only made him want to touch it more.

And the slight crookedness of her nose made her appear more real, like a woman who had important things on her mind other than worrying about physical perfection. It was a mix of her physical appearance and her warm personality that really tugged at him.

Hearing a slight cough, Travis looked up and found Todd standing in the open doorway. As usual, his sister's fiancé wore his uniform of pale blue shirt and brown khakis. His name badge was still pinned to the front pocket of the button-up shirt. "Hey, Todd. What are you doing here?"

Running a hand over his unkempt hair, Todd glanced around, avoiding eye contact. "I wanted to talk to you. Without Sheena around, I mean."

What the hell? With a clatter, Travis closed his heavy metal toolbox. "I'm not sure that's a good idea."

"I want to repay you," Todd blurted.

Interesting. Trying to figure out the motivation, Travis straightened and folded his arms. "For?"

"Everything." His brows pinched as he explained, "The wedding stuff, I mean."

"She's my sister. It's covered." Did that statement make it clear that he did it for Sheena, not Todd? He hoped so.

"I appreciate it that you've filled in for me." Todd shifted. "And believe me, I'm damn glad Sheena's getting the wedding she wants."

"Is she?" If Todd insisted on having this conversation, then Travis would oblige him. "Seems to me most of her choices are based on what you want."

Rubbing his face, Todd muttered, "Yeah, I worried about that. My family...you know, they're loud and a little rowdy. My friends, too, I guess. Sheena wants us all to have a nice time." He tried a smile that looked uncomfortable. "Can you imagine me in a tux? Trust me, it'd be even worse for my family. But hey, they love Sheena. She's one of us now."

Good God.

"I just...man-to-man, I wanted you to know that I plan to pay you back."

"Not necessary." Travis's understanding, as far as it went, was that Todd worked overtime to make enough money to cover the expenses of the coming birth. The three of them—Sheena, Todd and the baby—would be living in a one-bedroom apartment. That sucked enough. He didn't want Sheena stressed with loans, too. "It's handled."

"Damn it." Todd swallowed hard. "Can't we discuss this?"

Travis drew a breath for patience. This man would be his sister's husband; he didn't want there to be a strain between them. "If that's what you want, but we'll have to make it quick. I have an appointment with the wedding planner."

"To sign the contract, I know. And I have to hurry to make the appointment with Sheena. They're doing an ultrasound today."

Todd seemed genuinely excited for that. Relaxing a little, Travis leaned back on the new granite countertop. "Will they be able to tell if she's having a boy or girl?"

"Maybe. They said it depends on the position of the baby." He rushed on to say, "We don't have a preference though." He rubbed his hands on his thighs. "I'm nervous about it, to tell you the truth. Sheena is so small and my mom said we were all big babies…" In a near croak, he whispered, "Actually, it scares me to death."

Yeah, it scared Travis a little too—and just like that, he and Todd found some common ground.

"Sheena's small, but strong." A little warrior, more often than not. Travis had done everything in his power to make it so while raising her. He'd had a different perspective in it all, being her brother instead of a parent. He'd done his fair share of coddling, but he'd also pushed her to overcome fears, and he'd done his utmost to make things like bugs and snakes, home repairs, car and yard work as ordinary to her as they were to him. Her independence had been important to him. He'd wanted her to be self-sufficient so she'd never have to rely on anyone.

He'd even ensured she knew some self-defense moves. Until she'd hooked up with Todd, gotten pregnant and dropped out of school, Travis had been congratulating himself on a job well done. He almost laughed at the irony. "She's seeing the doctor regularly, right? She has good insurance." Travis had seen to that.

"Yeah, and once we marry, she'll be covered under my employee plan. It's great. That's one of the reasons I work there. Good pension, good insurance, decent pay."

Decent was a subjective term, but he liked Todd's sincerity.

"Glad to hear it." Lifting the heavy toolbox, Travis started forward. "Sounds like we're both on a timeline."

"Right." Todd fell into step beside him. "But we didn't really settle anything." With new determination, he said, "I'm a hard worker. I love Sheena. I'll make sure she has everything she needs. I swear it."

It was an odd position to be in, Travis decided as he locked up the house. Todd was thirty-one, same age as Yardley, but eleven years older than Sheena. Right now, having this heart-to-heart, Travis felt like he was speaking with a much younger man.

Sheena claimed he intimidated Todd. Could be true, though it wasn't deliberate on Travis's part.

With the house secured, Travis spoke as he headed for his truck. "Why don't we table this discussion for now? We're both in a hurry, and—"

"I don't want Sheena holding back." With the statement out there, Todd met his gaze. "She feels bad, letting you take care of things."

No way. He and Sheena were close. He'd reassured her many times. "I've told her—"

"I know, man. She brags on you all the time. She's crazy about her big bro, right? But she thinks you've already done too much, so she's constantly trying to figure out the cheaper way to get things done." Todd rubbed his ear. "This is her big day. Everything needs to be perfect for her."

Well damn. "Here's the thing, Todd. I know my little sister. She goes after what she wants, but she's sensible about life. I can almost guarantee you that she's thinking about the future—" a future with Todd "—and that includes a new baby, a new life as a wife and mother. Kids aren't cheap."

"Don't I know it." Todd looked a little ill as he said it. "I've been looking into that."

Knowing he needed to tread softly here, Travis said, "Eventually you guys will want a bigger place, maybe even a house, right?"

Flushing, Todd glanced away.

Something to hide? Or just discomfort over the topic? With no way to know, Travis continued. "Sheena is already weighing the fun of a wedding against the practicality. She doesn't want to start married life with a mountain of debt." Todd shouldn't want that either, in his opinion.

"It's because I've shortchanged her." Todd blew out a breath, then met his gaze with defiance. "I wouldn't do anything differently. I love her, I already love our baby, but the timing sucks, I know."

The timing was no longer relevant. "Sheena's in it for the long haul. She may be only twenty, but the girl has a streak of determination a mile wide. She'll do her part to make it all work."

Reassured by that, Todd nodded. "I'll be doing my part too. Making her happy is important to me."

Happiness wasn't the only component involved, though. There was financial security. Physical comfort.

Trust and love. All things Travis wasn't comfortable discussing with Todd. "I believe you, so let's move past the cost of the wedding, okay? I'll talk to Sheena, without mentioning our conversation. I'll make sure she's not scrimping for my sake."

Rather than agree, Todd glanced up at the sun, then out at the street. "This is a really great area. Nice house, too."

"I've enjoyed fixing it up."

"I'm still going to repay you." Twisting his mouth to the side, Todd admitted, "It might not be right away though."

Giving up, at least for now, Travis said, "No problem."

"Thanks." He held out his hand. "I mean it, man. Thank you for always being there for her."

"She's my sister," Travis stated, because for him, it was that simple. "She's all the family I have."

With a crooked grin, Todd shook his hand. "Soon we'll be brothers-in-law, and then my family will be yours." He actually laughed. "Not sure if that's a good thing or a bad thing, but either way, I will never give Sheena up, so you'll be stuck with the lot of us."

Not exactly an uplifting thought…but overall, it gave Travis something to think about.

5

LINGERING IN HER room until the last possible moment helped Yardley avoid yet another argument. Her mother had come home yesterday livid over the idea of her challenging Betty. Didn't matter that she stated, repeatedly, her disinterest in a town council position, and her actual refusal to run for president of said council. Her mother harped on.

Soon as Lilith got home, she'd joined in, appalled by the idea of Yardley "rocking the boat."

With a last glance in the mirror, Yardley questioned Mimi's idea of a perfect outfit. As she'd promised, Yardley had left open the top *three* buttons of the white sleeveless blouse. She could see her meager cleavage, which meant Travis would see it too.

Her boobs struggled to be average size. She saw absolutely no reason to show them off, especially when it seemed so…obvious. If she could do up just one more button, that'd make the outfit fine. She actually liked the fitted capri jeans, strappy sandals, and even the hoop earrings and—she glanced down at her foot—the ankle bracelet. The last was a gift from Mimi, and she hadn't worn it often. For some reason, it felt decadent.

Silly. After all, it was only her ankle. Like her boobs, her ankles were pretty average. Everyone had them. Wasn't like hers drew much attention.

Hearing a sound, she glanced out the window and saw Travis pull up to the curb. His hair looked damp, as if he'd recently showered. Wearing a T-shirt and tan cargo shorts with sneakers, he looked amazing. Fit, strong, *hot*.

And if she stood there much longer, he'd be at the door and her mother or aunt would answer and then… Rushing, Yardley grabbed her purse and left the room.

Immediately, Aurora spotted her and launched right into her usual complaints. "I hope you've been thinking about the trouble you could cause us. Betty said she's going to ban us from the town directory."

"And I told you she wouldn't dare." Yardley wasn't the only one who would pitch a fit about that. Many of the other businesses relied on her referrals.

"But if she does?" Lilith asked, falling into line with Aurora.

Pivoting from her path to the front door, Yardley asked, "What's this? You two are on the same side?" She put a hand to her heart. "I'm feeling faint."

"I'm not agreeing with her," Lilith insisted. "But she has a point, Yardley. Betty has always been the town council president."

"So? She can't keep the seat through intimidation." She turned to Aurora. "And no, Mother, for the hundredth time, I don't want it. But if she starts playing those games, someone else will."

"Someone else, but not you," Lilith said.

"Oh, Yardley," her mother lamented. "Please don't set yourself up for disappointment. You'll embarrass us all."

Through the screen door, Travis said, "Knock, knock."

Oh, great. He'd heard her and her family carrying on again. Glaring at her mother and aunt, who were now wide-eyed, Yardley turned with a smile. "Hey, Travis. Right on time." She managed one step forward, determined to get them on their way—but blast it, Aurora beat her to the door.

"How nice to see you again… Mr. Long, is it?"

"That's right."

She held the door open. "Come on in."

"I'm actually ready to go," Yardley said.

Lilith smiled at Travis. "Go? I assumed you were here on business, Mr. Long."

"Call me Travis." Looking not the least discomfited, he smiled. "Actually, it's a combined trip. I have a contract to sign, but then Yardley and I are going to look at—"

"We're going out," Yardley interrupted, moving to the door. "I have the contract with me. We can go over it during the ride."

Without missing a beat, Travis said, "That sounds perfect."

"Wait," Lilith protested, a suspicious glower in place. "Where did you say you're going?"

Since he'd obviously caught on, Travis looked at Yardley for direction.

Well, shoot. "I'll be looking at things for the house. No biggie."

"So a *date*?" Aurora said with smooth satisfaction. "Oh, and Yardley, I just realized how nice you look."

"It's a very different outfit for you, Yardley."

Aurora elbowed Lilith. "My daughter always looks nice."

"Of course," Lilith agreed, "even with her father's features. But this style…" In a voice not nearly low enough, she said to her sister, "It's almost sexy."

"Hmm," Aurora said while toying with the long chain of her necklace. "Yardley, if I could just have a moment—"

To undo another button? *Not happening.* "Sorry," she said, sliding her arm through Travis's and urging him along. "We don't want to be late."

"Late to shop?" Lilith asked.

"It's a special sale at an antique shop," Travis said smoothly as she practically dragged him out the door. "Sorry to rush off."

"Keep walking," Yardley muttered low. "No matter what they say, even if they follow us."

"Uh…" He glanced back. "Yeah, they're right behind us."

She groaned. "Don't stop."

He gave a short, strangled laugh. "Are we planning to outrun them?"

"If necessary." Hoping Travis would continue on to his truck, she turned to her mother and aunt and shot them a smile…that included a warning look. "No reason to walk us out."

That stymied them for only a moment. Aurora rallied first. "What time will you be home?"

"I'm thirty-one, Mother. I'll be home when I'm home."

"So…no dinner?" Lilith asked.

Was that her main concern? Well, *good.* Easy enough. "I'll probably be home before then."

"Or not," Travis said from right behind her.

She jumped, but her mother smiled with sly pleasure. "Take all the time you need," Aurora said.

"I suppose we could have something delivered," Lilith decided.

Great. Now they'd put another dent in the meal budget.

"Ready?" Travis asked, taking her arm and gently turning her. This time he was the one who said low, "Keep walking."

Her mouth curled. "Should I thank you for the rescue?"

"Is that what it was?" He opened the passenger door, waited until she'd climbed up to the seat, then closed it again and gave a final wave to Aurora and Lilith, who still stood in the driveway staring after them.

Soon as he was behind the wheel, she picked up their conversation again. "I'm sorry they're being so weird."

"It's a *little* weird," he agreed with a grin. "But I don't mind."

"I had hoped they'd be out until after we'd gone, but as you heard, they're annoyed with me, so they came home early." She glanced around the inside of his truck. It was big, clean, but clearly a work truck. Nothing fancy, and obviously functional.

"Why are they annoyed?"

"You know all that talk about— Ohmigod."

Travis spotted it at almost the same time she did. Kathleen the mannequin, dressed in a very patriotic red, white and blue halter with red sequin shorts, sat on the curb at the busiest four-way stop, holding a sign that said, "Elect Yardley Belanger as Town Council President. Be the change you want to see in Cemetery."

Her heart dropped into her stomach.

Travis, the jerk, cracked up.

Without thinking about it, she punched his shoulder. "Stop the truck. We can throw her in the back."

Still chuckling, he glanced at her. "You serious? You want me to steal a mannequin?"

"Someone had to have just put her there. Mother and Aunt Lilith only arrived home an hour ago, and this is the route they'd have taken. I'd still be hearing about it if they'd seen it."

"I'm not stealing a mannequin," he said, reaching over to give her hand a squeeze. "Relax. It's just a prank, right?"

"I'm seriously thinking about punching you again." She craned her head around, staring at the mannequin as they drove away. Then what she'd said registered, and she winced. "By the way, I'm sorry I hit you."

"Not sure I'd call that a hit, but you weren't really mad anyway, so don't worry about it."

"I was too mad." Or…maybe more like shocked. "This is awful."

"Tell me why."

"Why?" Since he didn't live in Cemetery, maybe he didn't get the repercussions. "Remember, Betty Cemetery is the great-granddaughter of the town founder. She's served as president of the council for as long as I can remember. Apparently people have been talking about me running for president, and Betty's furious. She told Aurora—"

"You call your mother by her first name?"

Yardley snorted. "Until she hit forty-five, I was forbidden from calling her Mother in public. She said she was too young to be a mother." Seeing the tension on his face, she added, "I called her Mother at home, though. Now referring to her as Aurora while in public is just a habit that sometimes slips through."

He gave one brief, somewhat stiff nod. "Sorry I interrupted. You said Betty Cemetery told your mother something?"

Odd that he appeared offended on her behalf. She should explain that she didn't mind—but no. That'd require way too much family history. "Betty told my mother that if I tried running for town council, she'd remove our wedding service from the website directory and the printed pamphlets at the welcome center. A lot of our clients come from people who visit, see all the listings in the directory and how nicely they function together—food, flowers, activities and ceremonies—and then decide they want to use us. If we're removed, we'd stand to lose a lot of business."

"Not just for you though, right? Seems to me that you pull in those other vendors. They depend on you."

Wow, he really got it. Impressed, she said, "We depend on each other. I'm in my groove working with them. I know what to expect, I can easily estimate the cost, and they're reliable."

"So Betty would be hurting the whole town in her effort to hurt you."

Yardley shrugged. She didn't think Betty would actually go through with it. "I won't be blackmailed. I told Aurora, and I meant it, that if Betty tries something like that, I'll retaliate. It could get ugly fast."

"Wow. Lots of drama for such a small town."

Her tensed shoulders dropped when she released a big breath. "It's mostly my fault. Every time the council meets, I bring up new reasons why every single service in Cemetery shouldn't have to carry the town name. Betty insists, and so far, I'm the only one to fight her on it." Warming to that topic, Yardley half turned in her seat.

"It's ridiculous and everyone knows it, but they go along to get along and probably lose business because of it."

"I have to admit, when Sheena first told me she wanted to marry in Cemetery, I was…taken by surprise."

Yardley snorted again. "I bet you laughed. It's absurd enough to be funny." Enjoying how easily they conversed, she stopped feeling self-conscious about her family and just relaxed. "I've been coming up with T-shirt slogans. My newest one is, 'If I die in Cemetery, I'll have to be buried in Allbee.' What do you think?"

"Why wouldn't you be buried here?"

Throwing up her hands, she said, "Because Cemetery doesn't *have* a cemetery! Isn't that the goofiest thing ever? All our funeral services are in Allbee, the next town over."

"Huh. In that case, the T-shirt slogan is great."

She dropped back in her seat. "Only insiders will get it, though. Still, it could be a conversation starter."

"I have a conversation starter. Want to hear it?"

Hmm. The way he turned so serious, she said, "I don't know. Do I?"

"Let's find out." He flashed her a reassuring smile. "Is it so strange for you to go out with a guy?"

Immediately feeling foolish, she said, "Well, this isn't really going out. I know that, so—"

"It is." Then he shook his head. "I mean, to me it is. I like you, Yardley. I'd enjoy seeing you more."

Slamming on the mental brakes and concentrating on not showing her shock, Yardley peered at him. He'd just said that so easily, as if it wasn't a big deal. But holy smokes, *look at him*. And then yeah, look at *her*.

There had to be a catch. "Why?"

He glanced at her again. "Why what?"

"Why do you like me?"

Laughing softly, he shook his head. "So I see your mother and aunt aren't the only ones with a unique approach."

"Oh no, don't you dare compare me to them."

"No?"

So much for her skipping the family history. "Look, I'm the black sheep. Nothing at all like the *classically beautiful Belangers*, you know." She rolled her eyes. "I've heard that my whole life. I'm the odd duck, and I like it that way. It's a point of pride, now." She sent him a mock frown. "So I'm serious, bud, no comparisons."

"Got it." He fought another smile. "Though I'd call you unique, not an odd duck, and while you're not classically beautiful—whatever the hell that is—you are pretty."

Oh, how nice. "You think?"

"Pretty doesn't quite cover it, actually. I'd say super cute, but also warm, with your own brand of sex appeal."

Sex appeal? "Huh. I have my own brand." She pretended to primp—since this was all in fun. "Now I'm glad I let Mimi talk me into leaving that extra button undone."

Lower, he said, "Yeah, I'm glad about that too. Remind me to thank her."

A slow heat went from her exposed chest up her neck and then seeped into her face. She cleared her throat— such a clichéd thing to do!—and out of sheer preservation, moved on to a different topic. "Would you like to go over the contract?"

"How about you answer my question first. That is, unless I'm being too nosy? If I am, feel free to tell me to back off."

That'd never happen, since she didn't want him to, but it brought up a curious question. "Would you? Back off, I mean?"

"I wouldn't ask any more personal questions, and yeah, I'd keep things more professional. Is that what you want?"

Already shaking her head, she said, "Heck no. So far, this has been fun. You're easy company."

The corner of his mouth lifted. "That's me, easy. Except I'm going to point out that you're still not answering the question."

"Remind me what it is again."

"Yardley." The look he sent her was both tender and amused. "You don't go out much?"

"If like, *never*, isn't much, then yeah, I don't go out much." That sounded pathetic, so she started explaining. "You met my family, so you saw what prospective dates would have to deal with. And it's a ridiculously small town. Everyone knows me, and they're all used to me *not* hooking up. If I even glanced at a guy, it'd be the hottest gossip for days. You met Saul, so you know he's a nice guy. Well, for a short time he was a little…friendlier, if you know what I mean. Like maybe interested, but not coming right out and saying so. Sort of testing the waters, I guess. And oh my God, you'd have thought we were found having sex on the beach." Catching herself, she gasped, "Not that we did! Not that I *would*."

This explanation was going on and on, and now she was dying a little trying to find a good stopping point.

Didn't help that Travis looked really interested.

She did that stupid throat-clearing thing again. "I like Saul. He's great. But my friend, Emily—the flower lady?—I think she has a big-time thing for him. Since he's the only obvious choice for those of us under fifty, and since I would never even think of doing that to Emily—that is, if I even could, because I'm pretty sure

Saul has a big thing for her too, but yeah. Without Saul, there's no one." She tossed up her hands in finality.

Without missing a beat, Travis asked, "But Emily is interested so you aren't?"

"She's a friend."

He nodded as if that made sense. "There's no one else your own age?"

Good grief, that's all he said? After all her verbal vomit, he had two measly questions. She was kind of impressed that he'd managed to keep up. "Not in Cemetery, not really. I mean, there are a few guys, but I've never gotten over them being dicks in elementary school—pardon my French, but they really were."

"Pretty sure the 'dick' insult is universal, not exclusive to France."

"Ha ha." Travis was quick with the comebacks, something she admired. "Mimi used to whip up on the boys when they were mean to me, so dating them now would be really weird."

"There are other towns close by."

She wrinkled her nose. "Heading out of town just to find a date seems so desperate—and time-consuming. How does that work, anyway? Do people hang in bars? I'm not much of a drinker, so that wouldn't work for me. Mimi says I'm a lightweight, but she can't drink more than two glasses of wine, either. Now, since she's nursing Sammy, she can't drink at all, and I don't think she misses it."

"There are other places you could meet men."

"Right. Not like I'd find someone at the grocery store. Most of the men I meet are in the process of getting married, you know. You're the exception…" Running out of options, Yardley slapped a hand over her mouth. It was the only way to ensure her thoughts wouldn't start running again. Through her fingers, she mumbled, "Not that I was suggesting—"

Travis smiled. "Stop that. I like hearing all your explanations. I'm getting the fast rundown, and that makes things easier."

"Easier?" she asked around her fingers. No one ever thought her rambling explanations made things *easier*.

"To get to know you."

Well, what do you know? He didn't turn the truck around to take her back, and in fact, he said he liked her spewing of nonsense. Usually it was only Mimi who felt that way.

And maybe Saul, for that very brief time when he'd been considering her. She'd kept things as friendly as possible, while also making sure it didn't go beyond friendship. Her reward was that now Saul and Emily seemed to be getting closer.

"So." She dropped her hand and blew out a breath. "Contract. Let's go over that before I spill more of my guts."

"Spill away, but sure, we can cover the contract first."

"I'd planned to do this at home, at my desk, but with Aurora and Lilith there—"

"Say no more. I get it, and I'm glad you opted to bring it with you."

Better and better. Just wait until she told Mimi that Travis wasn't at all put off by an extremely awkward, almost-virginal, over-thirty woman who had verbal fits without endings. She grinned as she retrieved the contract from her big purse. Mimi would be even more excited than she was.

Spreading the paperwork out across her thighs, Yardley asked, "Want me to go over it item by item?"

"Is that what you usually do?"

Usually she handed it to the person and they read it at their leisure. Being the driver, he couldn't do that. "Sometimes," she fibbed, because she'd never done it before.

"Go for it."

"So, we'll start with the venue." At least with this, she could stay on task. No more crazy convos that led nowhere.

Yardley went through each item, sharing the expected expense, until she finished and gave the total of the budget. "I know I can do a really awesome wedding for Sheena with that price, but there's wiggle room in some of the options if it's too much. Like fewer flowers, less expensive options on the photo package, other drinks, or a cash bar." Biting her lip, she studied his profile. He didn't look flummoxed by the price tag, but he hadn't said anything yet either. "What do you think?"

As he pulled up to a stoplight, he reached for the paper, then looked it over. "You can tailor it to Sheena's preferences for that?"

"Yup, absolutely."

"Okay, how about this." He took her pen, wrote on the contract, and handed it back to her. "Can you add that in for incidentals?"

"But…" He'd just added a really nice cushion. "Those are handled as they come up."

"It's been brought to my attention that Sheena is holding back because she doesn't want to overburden me."

"I know, and it makes sense."

He did a double take. "You know?"

"Your sister is pretty transparent, and she appreciates you so much. Of course she wouldn't want to go overboard." Yardley tipped her head. "I'm surprised she'd mention it to you, though. She seemed determined to just go as low as possible."

"Sheena didn't say anything. Todd came by to see me."

"Oh?" More than once she'd felt Travis's...disapproval? Disappointment? Something less than a wholehearted endorsement of Todd as a mate to his sister. "So," she said cautiously. "How'd that go?"

"He wants to repay me for the wedding. He said that way, Sheena can go out and get whatever she really wants, but I thought she was already doing that."

Smiling, Yardley imagined how uncomfortable that conversation might have been for Travis. She hadn't known him long, but she already knew he was a take-charge guy, and that he enjoyed indulging his sister. "Todd sounds like a considerate man."

"He's growing on me." Turning onto another road, he accelerated to keep up with traffic. "I like that he was actually paying attention enough to know what Sheena didn't say. I also don't want them to start out with the debt of a wedding. I meant it when I told Sheena I didn't mind. Guess I need to explain to her again that there's money set aside for stuff like this."

"Stuff like weddings?"

"And her college, though she might not use that now."

"You never know. A lot of women put their education on pause to handle other priorities. Once the baby is a little older, she might want to go back to her original plan to be a nurse."

"I wouldn't be at all surprised. In so many ways, she amazes me." He pulled into the parking lot of a big, warehouse-type building and found an empty spot to park the truck. After turning off the ignition, he shifted to face her. "Until then, I don't want her cutting corners on her wedding. God willing, it'll be her one and only, so it should be memorable."

"I will make that happen," she vowed.

His mouth curved. "I believe you."

"Well, I hope so." Sure, she might fudge things a little here and there, but she wasn't a liar. She always tried to be straight with clients so there wouldn't be any disappointment in the end result.

"It's not a small thing, Yardley. When you say something, I know you really mean it. I appreciate that." Before she could think better of grinning, which she did, or come up with a reply, which she didn't, he said, "Add the incidentals, I'll sign, and if you end up needing more, let me know."

Seriously, he was a dream client. Also a dream man. Maybe none of this was real? Oh hell, *what if I am dreaming*?

"Yardley?"

That sounded real enough. And hey, with indrawn breath, she filled her head with the most wonderful scent, like subtle spices, sun-warmed flesh and…earthy man. So it wasn't a dream, just an aberration.

She gave him a sunny smile. "Incidentals. You bet. And thank you."

Once they finished up the contract, she gave him his copy and stored her own. Then they headed in.

And of course, the smile stayed on her face.

TRAVIS WATCHED YARDLEY browse through row after row of drawer pulls, a basket on her arm. Every so often, she examined one more closely, smiled and put it into her basket. Each pull was colorful, and different from the others.

Finally he asked, "What are you going to do with those?"

"Aren't they pretty?" She picked up a round knob with

blue-and-white flowers. "They'll look great on the drawers in my walk-in closet."

"A different one for each drawer?"

"Yup. They complement each other, don't you think?"

He studied them again—and had to agree. Each was unique, and yet they all coordinated. Yardley Belanger had a great eye for design. Enjoying the insight, he said, "You like a lot of color."

"In my personal space, yes. I went more neutral in the rest of the house, but in my room? I want only bright and cheery. Oh, look at these!"

On a shelf higher up were three knobs in bright turquoise with yellow-and-red designs. Yardley reached up before he could offer to get them for her.

Suddenly she stilled, then whispered, "Oh, no."

Her horrified tone alarmed him. "What's wrong?"

Keeping her back to him, she slowly lowered her arm, wrapped it across her chest, and glanced around.

"Yardley?"

"I, um, have a problem."

He didn't see a problem. "Are you hurt?" Maybe she'd pulled a muscle, though he didn't know how.

"The thing is…" Over her shoulder, her fretful gaze met his. "It's an, um, *delicate situation.*"

Lost, Travis waited.

"I swear," she grumbled. "This could only happen to me." After glancing around again, she breathed low, "I'm wearing this stupid demi-bra that Mimi lent me. She received it as a gift, but hasn't been able to wear it because now that she's nursing, her girls are too big for it. But apparently mine aren't big enough because one just completely…*popped* out."

"You don't say." And damn it, he'd missed it.

Setting the basket aside, she crossed both arms over her chest and finally turned to him with big eyes and red cheeks. "It's even worse than that, though."

The things this one woman said... She was forever taking him by surprise, and he found that he liked it. A lot. "Worse?" Keeping his gaze on her face wasn't easy, when his eyes really wanted to check out her chest and her "popped free" breast. "How do we fix it?"

"We?" she croaked, looking shocked by the possibility.

Caught between wanting to laugh, and needing to kiss her, Travis opened his arms. "I'll assist however I can."

Her arms tightened. "Part of the problem is that I used these dumb cutlets."

"Cutlets?" He had no idea what that might be, especially in relationship to breasts.

"Like I said, I wasn't big enough to fill out the bra." As if confessing a sin, she said, "I have small boobs. Since I get my looks from my dad, whoever he may be, I guess I can assume he wasn't very busty either."

This time he gave in to a chuckle. "Take it from a connoisseur of breasts, you're perfect."

"You haven't even seen them yet, so how would you know?"

Yet? She made it sound like a foregone conclusion that he'd see her eventually, and honest to God, he wished that moment was now. "So...you mentioned cutlets?"

"Yeah, you know. Those silicone push-up pads women use to enhance things?" When he stared, she said, "For added cleavage and stuff."

"Okay." Never in his thirty-five years had he shared a conversation like this one. With Yardley, it seemed anything was possible.

"Never mind. You've probably only dated busty women."

"No, I..." How was he supposed to have this conversation with her, here in the middle of the warehouse? "You said that's worse somehow?"

"The cutlet is *loose*. If I uncross my arms, it might fall through my blouse and hit the floor, and wouldn't that just be the most humiliating thing ever?"

He supposed that could be pretty embarrassing. Luckily, she didn't want for a reply.

"I mean, even worse than standing here with an escaped boob while trying to explain all this to *you*."

He couldn't help it; his gaze dipped to her chest.

She gasped, "Don't you dare!"

Both his brows went up. "So... I'm not supposed to look?" Even though she kept talking about it? "Because I really want to look."

She half laughed, half groaned. "No, you can't. I don't want to draw more attention than I already am. If I stand here like this much longer, someone's going to think I'm stuffing drawer pulls into my bra to steal them or something."

He hadn't considered that, but yeah, they were starting to look suspicious. "You want to just go out to my truck and I'll buy them for you?"

She shook her head. "I think I might have a plan. You're big enough to block me while I *situate* things back where they belong."

He hesitated, and he tried to resist, but finally the words just left his mouth. "I could help with that."

Yardley stared at him, then her expression softened. "Oh, that low sexy voice," she breathed. "If we weren't standing in the middle of the aisle, I might be tempted."

He'd only whispered so others wouldn't overhear. Nothing sexy about that—he didn't think. But Yardley looked like she meant it. He'd have to remember to whisper to her more often. Then what she said registered. "*Might* be tempted?"

"For real? Okay then, I'm totally tempted. Heck, I've been tempted from the moment I laid eyes on you. Getting to know you has only made it worse. You're like a double-whammy. Totally hot and a great personality."

"Thank you." He felt the same about her.

She made a point of checking out the area. "Not really the right place for anything fun, I'm afraid. Now turn around and try to look inconspicuous."

He grinned. "Yes, ma'am." Picking up the basket, he stepped in front of her, his back to her front. "Arrange away. Just know that I'm going to be imagining it all."

"If anything hits the floor, do *not* look."

He laughed as he heard her rustling around behind him. She was fast, he'd give her that.

In no time at all, she said, "Whew. That's done. Clearly, showing cleavage is not my forte."

Slowly, Travis turned back to her. She'd buttoned the blouse nearly to her chin. "Mind if I tell you something?"

"I hope nothing is showing through?" She quickly looked down at herself again.

Touching her chin, Travis lifted her face. "You don't need to show more cleavage. You don't need…cutlets." What a stupid idea. "Whether you realized it or not, I've been tempted from the time we first met, too. And I don't need to see you naked to know you don't need enhancements."

She gave him the prettiest smile. "Thank you."

"From now on, how about you just do whatever you want and let the rest of the world deal with it?"

For the longest time, she stared up at him. "I think that's the nicest thing anyone has ever said to me."

How sad was that? He'd given her a simple compliment, a *sincere* compliment, and it moved her. From what he'd seen so far, she should be receiving accolades every day. In fact, he'd already heard several people in Cemetery singing her praises. Maybe they didn't share with her. Or maybe…she meant it was a nice compliment coming from a man. He had to wonder just how much experience she'd had with personal relationships. Despite what she'd said earlier, the idea of her not dating at all seemed too far-fetched for a woman like her.

On impulse, he bent and put his mouth to hers in a brief, soft kiss. "I really like you, Yardley."

Surprise widened her eyes. "I like you, too."

Things were moving faster than he'd expected, but then he hadn't counted on Yardley's wholehearted participation. He'd anticipated working harder, winning her friendship, and going from there. He figured by then, the wedding would almost be there and afterward, they could finally get together—in all the ways he wanted.

"Come on," he said, needing a minute to chart his course. "I'll show you some stained glass wall hangings." Taking her small, soft hand in his, he led her out to the main aisle.

Silence dragged on—his fault. He'd jumped the gun, and now she didn't know what to say when the woman was usually talking a mile a minute. Obviously he'd confused her when that had never been his intent.

"So, Travis…" she said quietly. "What are we doing?"

Good question. "I'm *trying* not to think about making a move."

"On me?"

Or her cutlets, her escaped breast…that sweet mouth. "Yes."

She went silent again for a heartbeat, then offered, "If you did, I'd be okay with it."

He gave an inward groan. Pure temptation, that's what she was. Red-hot, wholesome, sexy temptation. What a dynamic combo. "Here's the thing."

"God," she groaned, trying to tug her hand free. "I knew there would be a thing."

"Not that kind of thing." Holding on to her, he led her into a small alcove of bathroom fixtures, sinks, and even a big copper tub.

"Wow." Immediately diverted, Yardley pulled away to examine it with excited awe. "Will you look at this magnificent thing?"

He was looking—at Yardley.

"Have you ever seen a more beautiful tub anywhere? I mean, the tub at the Honeymoon Cottage is amazing, too." She slid him a look. "It has jets, you know."

"I noticed." He didn't want to think about his sister and Todd enjoying that tub together.

Luckily, Yardley let that line of conversation go. "But second to that? *This* tub."

The woman was a true Victorian fan. Even while enjoying her distraction, he did his best to get them back on track. "Sheena is getting married in just a few months."

"Mid-July. I haven't forgotten. I'll have everything arranged." She ran delicate fingers along the rim of the double-slipper tub. "Two could fit in this thing, it's so big." Her eyes flared and she shot him a sideways glance. "Not that I was hinting or anything."

Yardley tended to say exactly what she meant, no hinting to it. He stepped forward, determined to have this conversation. "I like you, Yardley. You like me. My only hesitation is that I don't want to cause a potential conflict that could make Sheena uneasy before her wedding. She's stressed enough."

"Conflict?" Giving up her examination of the tub, she straightened. "You mean with *me*?"

She acted like it was most unheard of thing ever. He asked, "What if I said or did something that pissed you off?"

"I don't get pissed off."

Skeptical, he said, "You sounded pretty pissed at Betty."

"Ha. Yeah." Marginally contrite, she shrugged. "I wasn't, not really. I think I understand her. Maybe. I was a little irked, though."

Would her version of "a little irked" be enough to screw up his sister's wedding plans? He didn't know, and he didn't want to take the chance. "I thought we could take it slow." But he definitely wanted to keep seeing her. "We could use the time until the wedding to get to know each other better. That way, if something happens, it won't put Sheena in the middle."

"This almost sounds like you're going to stop being nice and get all obnoxious and creepy or something."

"I wouldn't—at least I hope you don't think that of me." He sought a way to explain his concern. "It's just that a conflict has happened before, and Sheena lost a friend."

"Sheena blamed you?"

"Not really, but she was still hurt by it." Not wanting to look like a bastard, he said, "Her friend was interested, I made the mistake of joking around with her, and she took it for more than it was. We never..." He shook his head. "She kissed me once, but I ended that real fast because I had other priorities at the time, and fooling around with my kid sister's friend wasn't on the agenda. But the girl blew up all over social media anyway, it got ugly, and she didn't only slam me, but Sheena, too."

Slender brows knitting in a frown, Yardley said, "Doesn't sound to me like she was much of a friend." She looked at the tub with longing. "*And* I'm not a jerk like that."

His mouth twitched. "I already know that."

"Other than advertising the business, and seeing the stuff Mimi posts, I don't do much on social media." She wrinkled her nose. "I mean, I did look you up. That's not too stalkerish, is it?"

"No." It pleased him to know she'd been interested right from the start. "I looked you up, too. Okay if I send you a friend request?"

She was already nodding before he finished. "Like I said though, I'm not on there much. It's one of those things that can be fun, or it can be totally evil, and it changes so quickly that I dodge it overall." Then she rushed out, "Not that I'll dodge you, I promise."

He couldn't help but grin. "Thanks."

Brightening, she asked, "You really looked me up?"

"Of course."

"Now I wish I'd had something interesting on there." With a shrug, she went back to admiring the tub.

Funny Yardley. He had a feeling her thoughts didn't rest very often, not when she cared about so many people. But since none of this was about social media, he again tried to get them back on track. "The point is that I think it'd be best if we took it slow."

Without appearing the least bit offended, Yardley asked, "How slow is slow?"

At least for this he had an answer. "More visits like today. Sometimes dinner or a movie." Hell, he was already frustrated with the limitations he was putting in place. "Dating. What do you think?"

"A few kisses?"

"I vote yes." That brief taste he'd had of her only made him want more.

She eyed him. "But…no sex?"

Holding back a groan wasn't easy. The way she said it, with explicit disappointment, made it really difficult for him to say, "Stop tempting me."

"Ha! You started it with that kiss." Her gaze moved over him. "Or maybe it's just looking like you look. And being so nice to your sister." She followed that observation with a frown. "But you did refuse to stop and get Kathleen, so by now Betty has seen her. I hope you know that means I'll be going home to two grumpy women."

Seemed to him her mother and aunt were always disagreeable. Setting aside the basket again, Travis cupped her face. "What do you say, Yardley? Want to grab dinner after we're done here? Next week, I could show you the house I'm working on." At least there wasn't any furniture in there yet. Without a bed or couch, they couldn't—shouldn't—do much more than kiss.

Though the idea of taking Yardley up against a wall had serious merit. He had a feeling she'd enthusiastically endorse the idea.

"Right," she said, interrupting the detailed image now

plaguing his brain. "No sex." She sighed. "I sort of had a deal with Mimi though, so this is going to be tough."

She should try it from his end. "What kind of deal?"

Gesturing at him, or more precisely, his body, Yardley said, "She wanted me to jump at any opportunity."

"I'm liking Mimi more and more." He especially liked knowing that Yardley had Mimi in her corner.

"But I wanted something from her too, so we made a deal that if I took advantage of you, she'd have to do as I requested. Only you're not willing, so—"

"Whoa, hold up right there." He edged closer, close enough for their bodies to touch. "I'm beyond willing to the point of impatient." She needed to know that. "I'm just cautious when it comes to Sheena's big day." His sister had been his number one priority for a very long time. It was now an ingrained habit.

"Right. I'll tell Mimi we're going to take months to think about it."

When she put it that way... "That does sound disturbingly slow, doesn't it?" Especially since Yardley made it clear that she didn't need time to get to know him better. As he considered things, he noticed the way the overhead fluorescent lighting glinted on her dark brown hair, making some of the strands appear red, and others golden. That lighting put a sparkle in her eyes, turning the hue more blue than gray. He noted the thickness of her lashes and how they curled. And her incredibly sexy mouth... currently twitching at one corner, as if she fought against a grin—and then, the grin won.

Leaning closer, she whispered, "Mixed signals, Travis. I mean, you're saying one thing, but your eyes are saying something *very* different."

Of course she was right. Kissing her again seemed the

only reasonable option, so he pressed his mouth to her soft lips. She stepped against him.

One second, two...

Moving back a pace, Yardley fanned her face. "I'd seriously love to try that when we don't have a warehouse full of people watching us."

The things she said... Would she ever stop surprising him? He hoped not. "I can make that happen." Kissing, he reminded himself. Only that, for now.

But two months for the rest? Could he even hold out that long?

Not with the way she teased his senses. Hell, he wasn't sure he'd last a week—but he was going to try. Rubbing a hand over his neck, he said, "I mucked this up, didn't I?"

She gave him a quick hug.

That turned into a stroke up his back.

Followed by a long sigh. "Good gravy, Mimi's right. You're solid."

He let his own hands do a little stroking. "And you're soft."

Shivering, she looked up at him. "You haven't mucked up anything. Guess I'm just more impatient than you."

With her saying it like that, it was difficult to find any real importance in waiting.

After patting his left pec, she reluctantly withdrew her hand. "I've had a lot of fun today. So yes, I'd love to do dinner and whatever else you might have in mind. I'll just work on Mimi so she's not waiting on me."

Travis had a feeling the two women got into a lot of entertaining mischief.

She gave the bathtub a last, lingering look, then took his hand while mumbling, "It'd never fit."

"Excuse me?"

"That tub." She led him out of the alcove and toward the front, where registers waited. "My bedroom and bathroom are the last to be remodeled, but I'm still deciding on what I want—and of course, what I can afford. I think that tub would be a few inches too big, which sucks because it'd sure be grand. Worth the financial indulgence." Glancing at him, she asked, "Are you a bath or shower person?"

He could count on one hand the number of times he'd had an actual bath. "Shower. Quick in, quick out."

"I guess that's most people. Aurora and Lilith prefer quick showers too. Mimi likes a bath, but she doesn't linger as long as I do. I like bath bombs and lots of steam and a good book to keep me company. I lock the door, turn off the phone, and make it my alone time."

Picturing that—and liking the picture a lot—he asked, "You think that big copper tub would make it even better?"

"It sure couldn't hurt, right?" With a comically lofty expression, she said, "I could soak in style."

He laughed. "If you want a copper tub, I can probably find you a similar one that's more affordable."

Stepping into line to check out, she pressed a hand to her heart. "My hero. Are there any times when you aren't wonderful?"

Too many to count, but what she thought mattered. "See me often enough, and you can judge for yourself."

After a few seconds, she held out her hand. "Sounds like a good deal to me."

As they shook on it, Travis had the feeling that his entire life had just changed—and he didn't have a single complaint.

6

IN THE HIGH chair that Yardley had found at a yard sale, Sammy worked at eating small pieces of fruit.

"She's getting good at that," Yardley noted.

Mimi watched her daughter stuff a piece of pear into her mouth, then happily gum it—with a lot of drool escaping down her chin. Content, Mimi sipped her tea. No one made tea like Yardley. Or maybe it was just being with Yardley that made the tea taste better. "The high chair looks great. Fess up. How much time did you spend cleaning it?"

"I'd lie and say it just needed to be wiped off, but you know me."

"Indeed I do. An hour? Two?"

Yardley smiled. "Probably closer to three. It wasn't dirty, but I wanted to make sure it was sanitized top to bottom. I had to use a tiny scrub brush to get in around rivets, and I took off the straps to run them through a hot wash, then had to put them back together again."

That knack for cleanliness wasn't something they had in common. "Sammy probably gets exposed to ten times the germs at home than she ever gets here." Mimi would have cleaned a used high chair, but no way would she have gone to that much trouble.

"I have to keep things clean since clients come in here."

"Don't give me that. You'd keep things immaculate either way—just as I'll always be a little messy."

"You're not messy," Yardley protested. "You're wonderfully comfortable. Big difference."

They both heard the screen door close, then the rhythmic tapping of high heels on hardwood. Mimi winced theatrically. "The witches are home."

Yardley shot her a cross frown for that comment, but it was all bluster. Since…well, *forever*, Mimi had complained about the abysmal way they treated Yardley, and Yardley had staunchly defended them out of some misguided family loyalty that, as far as Mimi could see, only went one way.

Lilith reached the kitchen first. "Lord, what a day," she said as she set her purse on the counter. "Betty came to the café again. As usual, customers gravitated to her. This is not going to turn out well."

"Why not?" Yardley asked, pretending she didn't know why Betty was currently haunting her mother and aunt. "You said her visits have business booming."

"No, I said she sits there and gossips about us where I'm sure to see it."

"Either way." Yardley waved a dismissive hand. "They're all paying customers so let Betty do her thing. Pretend you don't notice."

Lilith scowled.

Her mother, Aurora, entered with a scathing glance at Yardley and Mimi. "While Lilith and I are trying to avoid a catastrophe, you two are here gobbling cookies again." She eyed Mimi, specifically from her neck to her knees and back up again. "Perhaps you should cut back on that just a bit, dear."

Without having seemed to move, Yardley landed in front of Mimi, her shoulders stiff and her attitude bristling. Keeping her voice low and uncharacteristically mean, she said, "You will not insult Mimi. Not now, not ever."

Aurora managed a tight smile. "I wasn't, exactly."

Ha. Mimi—and everyone else—knew that she *exactly* was. "No worries. I'm not easily insulted." *Not by either of you.*

"Good." Lifting her chin a notch, Aurora played with the chain of her necklace, teasing a small gold medallion back and forth over the upper swells of her still impressive breasts. "It's just that you look like the epitome of a happy housewife."

Meaning a dowdy housewife? "I am that," Mimi replied coolly. "I'm also a proud, loving mother. Being so content makes it easy to ignore insults that don't matter." *Boom*, she thought. *Direct hit.*

Lilith redirected the animosity to Yardley. "It's been a week. You need to smooth things over with Betty. She won't be patient much longer."

"There's nothing to smooth."

"More signs are showing up," Aurora stated after losing the staring contest with Mimi. "Instead of gallivanting around town with a *client*, maybe you could attend to your business here."

Mimi shot to her feet, but again, Yardley stepped in front of her.

In an utterly calm voice—one Yardley had cultivated

for everyone except Mimi—she said, "Travis is not a client. His sister is."

"But he's paying us."

That stymied Yardley, but only for a moment. "True, but he's leaving all the decisions to his sister. On the two occasions I've been out with him, we've discussed the wedding, so I don't see how that's much different from what the two of you do."

"We," Lilith said, obviously put out, "don't do it with hot men."

"Got ya a little jealous, doesn't it?" Mimi snuck in.

Taking a deliberate step back, Yardley bumped into her, then sent her a look that clearly said, *Don't help.* Getting the hint, Mimi pretended to lock her lips, but she still grinned, and finally Yardley rolled her eyes, her own mouth twitching.

Aurora glanced at Sammy, who blew a spit bubble at her. The awful woman appeared repulsed at first, but then she surprised Mimi by touching two fingers to Sammy's cheek in a soft caress.

Straightening again, she said, "The point is that you need to concentrate on business right now, at least until this mess with Betty is cleared up."

"Most of the time, it seems I'm the only one concentrating on our business." And with that jab, Yardley calmly took a sip of her tea.

Gliding forward, Lilith frowned. "How dare you say that? I'm the one who's had to conduct business with potential clients while Betty-freaking-Cemetery continues to give me the evil eye."

Both Yardley and Mimi froze. Almost as one, they snickered. Mimi forgot her lips were locked and asked, "*Freaking*-Cemetery? Did you really say that?"

"She did," Yardley confirmed. "I heard it too."

"You're both ridiculous." Pointing at Yardley, Lilith said, "You should worry more about improving your education so that you can better understand these delicate situations. It would be time better spent than mimicking your mother's foolish past."

"My *what*?" Aurora demanded.

Only half under her breath, Mimi muttered, "And they're off."

"If the girl is experiencing some passion, I'm glad!" Then to Yardley, Aurora added, "Your timing could certainly be better, though."

"Mark my words. She'll end up pregnant and alone, just as you were." Turning on her heel, Lilith snatched up her purse and left with an obvious show of displeasure.

"Now you've done it," Yardley said to Mimi. "You opened the spigot and it all came pouring out."

Shrugging, Mimi said, "Same old, same old. Besides, there's no way I could have resisted. Look, even your mom is fighting a smile."

"Absurd," Aurora said, quickly tightening her mouth. "We have larger issues we should be handling than my sister's unfortunate choice of words, and Yardley's obvious distraction with a man who could be using her to get a bargain."

Outrage ran like an electric current through Mimi's entire frame. Anger would only appease Aurora, so instead, she forced herself to a calm she didn't feel.

Yardley, bless her, continued to sip tea. Mimi knew her, and she knew those damned barbs took their toll.

"A bargain?" Mimi pretended to like the idea. "Hey Yardley, maybe if you offered, say, a twenty percent discount—"

"Shush it," Yardley said.

Doing her best to regain control of the conversation, Aurora loudly cleared her throat. "We can't afford a discount, no matter the reward, because if Betty blackballs us—"

"Betty-freaking-Cemetery" Mimi murmured with a chuckle.

"—we're ruined."

Yardley looked to the heavens with a big sigh. "I've told you. She wouldn't dare, and if by some preposterous scenario she takes it that far, I'll handle it."

Aurora sniffed. "It would put Lilith's mind at ease, and mine as well, if you would handle it now, before it gets any uglier."

"Fine. I'll see Betty soon."

"No later than Monday," Aurora decreed. Then she, too, left the kitchen.

Sammy, who'd been avidly listening to the dispute, began to fuss now that the room had grown so quiet. Honestly, Mimi couldn't think of a single thing to say. She knew the evil duo would never see Yardley the way others did, but would it kill them to support her just once?

"Bleh," Yardley said, as if that whole distasteful thing hadn't just happened. "Guess I'm going to see Betty."

And now she was giving up? *Damn it.*

"What?" Yardley asked innocently. "You look like lightning might shoot out your ears."

"They infuriate me, that's what." Mimi darted around the island and headed to the sink to dampen some paper towels. "Why do you hold back with them, Yardley? Why don't you really blast them just once?" It was something she so desperately wanted to see.

Emotions contained, Yardley gathered up their empty

teacups and loaded them into the dishwasher. "I'm sorry they upset you."

"Don't you dare apologize for their bad manners."

"Shh… If they hear you, they'll just return and start all over again."

Mimi didn't want to be quiet. She wanted to defend Yardley the way she deserved. "What they said about me didn't bother me at all, because their opinions don't mean squat to me. It's the way they treat *you*, and the way you treat them, that makes me a little nuts." Using care, she swabbed Sammy's sticky face and hands…then even had to go over her ears and nose. "I know the real you, Yardley. When you let go, you're glorious."

Yardley choked on a laugh. "Glorious? When I let go I'm a babbling fool who no one can comprehend—other than you, of course."

"And Travis," she reminded her friend. "You said he kept up just fine."

"Yeah." Expression softening, Yardley leaned against the counter and smiled. "With you, I've always been myself. Just me. I don't use a single effort to be better or clearer and calmer."

"You don't need to."

"I know, and I love you for that. What's odd is that it was the same with Travis. It was like I'd stripped away a few layers and the very imperfect me was showing through—no, don't say it. I *am* imperfect, you know."

"We all are, silly." God knew her own flaws were immense.

"My imperfections usually turn people away."

Not even close to true, but it wasn't the point Mimi wanted to make right now. "Travis didn't turn away."

As if still confused by it, Yardley shook her head. "I

told you, I said the most outrageous things—*about my boobs*, Mimi. And instead of giving me funny looks, he seemed a little turned on. He even kissed me."

"And asked you to dinner." Mimi was still rejoicing over that.

"And he said he liked me."

"Well, of course he likes you. I knew right off that Travis wasn't an idiot—even if he wants to wait *two months* to do the nasty."

Yardley laughed. "He made it clear that he doesn't want to wait at all. He just thinks it's important for his sister's wedding success."

Mimi shrugged. "He thinks you're as hot as I do, and that makes you worth the wait." Blowing out a breath, she added, "Guess I'm more impatient than you. I want you to see just how awesome it all is with the right person." She had a gut instinct that Travis was that person, the right guy for her very special friend.

"I get his reasoning. If we found out we didn't suit at all, which is more likely than anything else, he might feel weird with me helping his sister with her wedding arrangements. The last thing I'd want is for Sheena to get hurt."

"Wouldn't happen. If anything, he's going to fall madly in love and want to make it a double wedding."

Yardley snorted. "You are so biased when it comes to me."

"What? It's true." She lifted Sammy from the chair and snagged up the diaper bag on her way to Yardley's room. It was the only place in the house she could change a diaper without Aurora or Lilith acting like she'd just nuked the place with toxic waste.

"I was just thinking." Falling into step behind Mimi,

Yardley asked, "Do you remember in second grade when I tried cutting my own hair and totally destroyed it?"

That was not one of her favorite memories. "Aurora gave you a ridiculously short pixie cut—" almost a burr cut "—supposedly to even it out." Personally, Mimi had always thought it was a mean, vindictive move meant to teach Yardley not to get out of line. As if the girl hadn't already been repressed enough. "With that short hair framing your face, you were all big eyes and wariness."

Yardley snickered. "Darren said my hair looked funny, and before I could even think of a comeback, there you were, saying his face looked funny."

"Almost made him cry," Mimi grumbled. The poor doofus. She'd always figured Darren had a crush on Yardley but was too chicken to say so. After Mimi had gotten nose to nose with him, mean-mugging him and dishing out the insults, he'd steered clear of them both.

To this day, she felt guilty about that.

"My point is that I'm not a backward little girl anymore. I can fight my own battles. Much as I love you for all the times you stood up for me, you don't need to do that anymore. I promise."

"I know." Yardley was the one who didn't seem to realize what a force she could be. "It's partly habit, left over from our school days." She finished fastening the dry diaper on Sammy, then kissed her pudgy little belly, her toes, and her perfect nose. "But it's also pure frustration because you never stand up to them the way I know that you can. I want you to do it for *you*. Unleash all the things you want to say. Don't think about it. Don't censor yourself. Just blurt it out and let them work to keep up—if they can."

Yardley waved that away. "You know I long ago got used to them slinging insults."

"But you shouldn't have! You are not their doormat." Holding Sammy against her shoulder, she hip-bumped Yardley. "You're amazing, girl. Phenomenal. A freaking gift to them. Please, I'm begging you to *realize* it."

Yardley blinked at the over-the-top emotion. As if soothing Mimi, she nodded. "I'll try. That's all I can promise right now."

"Good enough." Mimi grabbed her in for a rocking hug. That made it easy for Sammy to sink a tiny fist into Yardley's hair.

"Ouch, ouch, baby girl." Flinching, Yardley tried to free herself. "Let's not bald Aunt Yardley, okay? The pixie cut never really worked on me, regardless of what your mommy says."

"Oops, sorry." Mimi untangled her daughter's fingers, then smoothed down Yardley's hair. That led to her cupping her cheek, and to her feeling so much love. Being with Yardley was as comfortable as being in her own home. Even better, because Yardley fed her cookies and filled her cup with specialty teas—all caffeine-free, since she was nursing—and Yardley understood her, everything about her, the good, the bad and the hard to explain. "I am so damn glad to have you. So, so damn glad."

"Whoa." Yardley took Mimi's hand from her face and studied her expression. "What's that about? Are you projecting?" She took a step back to really look at Mimi. "You are, aren't you? What's happened? What's wrong?"

Mimi laughed. "Nothing, I promise. I just appreciate that I can hang here so often."

"Of course you can. Anytime, you know that."

"See, that attitude makes you super awesome. But now, as fun as this has been, I need to get Sammy home for her bath."

Though she still gave her curious looks, Yardley didn't argue. "I'll walk you out."

"Thanks." Mimi handed her the diaper bag. "Are you really going to see Betty-freaking-Cemetery?"

"That name is totally going to stick, isn't it?" A small smile curled one side of her mouth. "I'll have to concentrate on not calling her that."

"If you do, I want a blow-by-blow report of how she reacted to hearing it. It's bound to be good for some laughs."

"You play a mean game," Yardley accused with a grin, "but I know you wouldn't hurt Betty's feelings any more than I would."

"You're right, I wouldn't, not on purpose anyway. But you're the epitome of grace and tact so I'm sure you'll handle it perfectly."

"Keep complimenting me like that, and I'll know something is wrong."

As they went through the house, Mimi said, "I'm going to keep complimenting you until you believe it. Now, when do you plan to see Betty, and when do you see Travis again?" She knew Travis had called a few times just to chat over the past week, and she knew Yardley loved it. All the two of them needed was enough opportunity to get something going.

"Travis is taking me to see the house he's renovating this weekend. We'll probably do dinner after. That gives me a few days to figure out when I can see Betty. I have appointments the next couple of mornings, and one in the afternoon, but I should be able to make it work."

"Business has picked up, hasn't it?"

With a look of satisfaction, Yardley said, "I'm staying busy."

"But not too busy for Mr. Studly." Mimi bobbed her eyebrows, making Yardley laugh.

"No, definitely not too busy for him."

They stepped outside to an overcast sky with the scent of rain in the air. Mimi looked up to see dark clouds tumbling over one another. Knowing Yardley would follow, she headed for the car. "So what's the plan with Betty?" Hurrying so she wouldn't get caught in a storm, she secured Sammy in her car seat.

"What would you think of me offering Betty a compromise?"

"I don't like it."

Yardley laughed. "You haven't heard the compromise yet."

"You," she said, "compromise far too often."

Ignoring that, Yardley leaned against the front fender and stared up at the tree branches swaying from the wind. "I could volunteer to be her liaison with the business community. If I don't challenge Betty's position, maybe she'd be more inclined to listen to new ideas. I could pitch it in a way that it'd remain her final decision."

"See, that right there. Betty is power-hungry. She'll sense weakness and take advantage."

"Hmm." After giving it some thought, Yardley said, "You could be right."

"Let me get the air going, then we can finish this discussion." After giving Sammy her pacifier, Mimi sat behind the wheel, pressed the push-button ignition and… nothing.

Yardley said, "You have to press on the brake."

Duh. "I'm pressing it." She tried again, but still, the car was totally dead. Worse, the first sprinkling of rain started. "Well, damn."

"I'll get Sammy." Yardley quickly retrieved the baby and, bowing over her to protect her from the raindrops, hurried to the front door.

Mimi called Kevin as she darted up to the porch. He should be getting off work, so maybe he could swing by and...fix things. Man, she relied on him a lot. Sometimes too much.

He answered with, "Hey honey, what's up?"

"My car won't start and it's raining."

"You're at Yardley's?"

He knew her too well. "Yup."

"Good. At least it's not the grocery store or park. Go inside, okay? I'll be there in a few minutes."

"My hero."

Kevin paused. Then she heard the grin in his voice when he said, "I like the sound of that. Go stay dry, babe, and I'll rescue you soon."

He was always so upbeat, even when she'd be grumbling. She could count on one hand the number of times Kevin had been angry, and it had never really been at her. Once or twice when he'd been in a bad mood, he'd quickly apologized for taking it out on her. In so many remarkable ways, he *was* her hero.

But what was she to him? "I love you." Not giving him a chance to reply, she made a kissing sound and disconnected the phone.

DRIPPING WET, Kevin stood on the porch and spoke through the screen door. "It was just the key fob. Apparently the battery in it died. I'm glad I stopped by the house to get the spare."

Appearing relieved, Mimi asked, "You figured that was it, huh?"

"I maintain your car, so I knew it couldn't be anything serious."

"See," she said to Yardley. "A hero through and through."

"Totally agree," Yardley said with a smile.

Mimi and Sammy were his life. Of course he kept her car in top running condition. It was one small thing he could do to ensure their safety. "What's wrong, babe?" Whenever Mimi worried, she pursed her mouth. He found that just as cute today as he ever had, but he didn't want her worrying about anything serious.

"Nothing, now. I'm just sorry you got soaked."

"I won't melt," he promised.

"This one is so sweet, she might." Holding his daughter, Yardley continually nuzzled her cheek and stroked her hair. "You're pure sugar, aren't you, sweetheart? Yes, you are," she said in her version of baby talk. To Kevin, she added, "I'll grab you a towel."

"No need. We're just heading home." He looked up at the sky. "And I think it's blowing over now anyway."

"Still, for your seat…" Yardley wandered off with Sammy in her arms.

Propping a shoulder on the door frame, Mimi whispered, "She's been like that since Cruella and Maleficent got on her again. You should have heard them, talking about Yardley being a problem right in front of her."

"One of these days, they'll wise up." He'd been hearing about that particular problem since his and Mimi's first date. Yardley was special in many ways, and everyone knew it—except maybe Yardley. With the way Mimi constantly reminded her, eventually Yardley would get it. Until then…yeah, he had to agree that she put up with too much from her mother and aunt. "Does she ever give 'em hell?"

Mimi shook her head. "Only when they're rude to me."

Anger slowly had Kevin straightening. "They were rude to you?"

"Shh. I'll tell you all about it once we get home."

Yeah, he'd make sure of it.

Yardley reappeared with a big beach towel for him, a rain jacket for Mimi, and another towel to put over the baby's head.

Mimi gave Yardley a hug, took Sammy from her, and together they headed out to load up. The rain was only a very light sprinkle now. Using the towel to dry his hair, Kevin waited until Mimi got the baby in her seat, got behind the wheel and got the car started. Leaning down, he put his mouth to hers for a warm but too brief kiss. "Drive safe. I'll be right behind you."

Her brows lifted, and that sweet mouth pursed. "I know how to drive in the rain."

"Of course you do." She always got prickly when she was upset, and now he knew why. Yardley's mother and aunt had that effect on a lot of people, but none more so than Mimi. She and Yardley were closer than sisters.

He couldn't resist kissing her again.

With a sigh, she said, "Sorry. I'm grumpy but it's not your fault." She peeked up at the front door of the house, but Yardley had closed the door. "Aurora and Lilith seemed to draw some comparison between Yardley and Sammy. I swear, I wanted to blast them."

"But you didn't?" That wasn't like Mimi. She usually went after people—when they needed it.

"Yardley shut them down before I could." She glanced up at him. "Aurora suggested that I shouldn't eat so many cookies."

That miserable... "Aurora is a skinny rail with a stick up her ass. Ignore her."

Amusement switched Mimi's grumpy expression into a grin. "She is, right?" This time she kissed him, maybe a little too enthusiastically for Yardley's driveway, not that he'd complain. "Let's go before Yardley carries out a tray of snacks. You know she's a hostess at heart."

Feeling pretty damned good, Kevin closed her door and headed for his truck. Luckily, they didn't have far to go, but on the short drive behind Mimi, he thought of what she'd said. Comparisons between Yardley and Sammy couldn't be good, not with the way Aurora had always referred to Yardley as a disruption to her otherwise idyllic life.

His jaw tightened as he considered things. Did they think Sammy was a burden for Mimi? He could speak up for Mimi, no problem, but sometimes he worried that she might feel...stifled by motherhood. He knew she loved Sammy with all her heart, but did she wish for more free time? Did she miss seeing her past coworkers at Saul's restaurant?

Determining that he'd do more to help and would ensure she had more free time, he pulled into the driveway behind Mimi. With only a one-car garage, he always parked in the driveway and left the garage for her. He locked up and jogged to her car, but she was already getting Sammy from her car seat. The baby was sound asleep.

Feeling useless, he asked, "You're frustrated, aren't you?"

She shot him a look.

"About Yardley, I mean." What did she think he meant? Sexually frustrated? He figured she was too tired for that, but *he* sure as hell was on the ragged edge. "I know you like to tackle problems, not ignore them." It was one of the things he loved about her.

"True. Unfortunately, there's nothing I can do." Mimi lifted the baby to cuddle her in her arms. "Yardley is fiercely defensive of the witches."

"If there's ever anything I can do, just let me know." For Mimi, he'd confront the devil. Two rigid women didn't faze him.

Her expression softened. She brushed a kiss to Sammy's head, then went on tiptoe to kiss him lightly on the mouth. "That's sweet."

God, was there anything worse than having the woman you craved call you *sweet*? Mimi was his other half, his reason for breathing.

She was everything—and she considered him sweet.

But if that's how she wanted to look at him, he wouldn't argue the point. He wouldn't argue *anything*, not after almost losing her, not after seeing the flash of what his life would be without her. He'd come so close to that awful reality. Never again did he want to go through that particular hell.

Oblivious to his dark turmoil, Mimi started toward the door. "Even though I've been thinking the same thing, Yardley reminded me that she's a strong person who can protect herself. We just need to be there to support her."

"How do you think to do that?" He took Sammy from her, putting the baby against his shoulder, his free arm around Mimi.

"To start, I'm going to send a friend request to her hot new boyfriend." She bobbed her eyebrows. "I hate to sound disloyal, but I never imagined Yardley hooking up with a dude like him. You should see him, Kevin. He's walking testosterone, gorgeous enough to be a model or something but more rugged than that."

At the garage entry door, Kevin slowly turned to stare down at her. Damp blond curls framed her face, making her dark blue eyes more noticeable. "Are you trying to make me jealous?"

"Ha! Like that's even possible."

Trying to read the slight mockery in her expression, he stared harder. "I think it's possible for you to make me feel...everything." She had so much power over him, and judging by her surprise now, she didn't even know it. "I love you, babe. So damn much." He leaned down to take her parted lips in a longer, lingering kiss. Their tongues touched. He angled his head, liking the sound of her quickened breath. Her response made him want so much more, he knew he needed to cool it.

Fisting her hands into his shirt and tilting her head to deepen the kiss, Mimi didn't make it easy.

Much more of that and he'd be feeling her up against the garage wall, their daughter sleeping on his shoulder, and in plain view of any curious neighbors since the garage door was still up. Reluctantly, he lifted his head, easing away with a kiss to the corner of her mouth, her cheek, her temple.

She made him as hungry now as she had when they'd first started dating.

"That was..." Her tongue slipped out over her lips, almost making him groan. "Unexpected."

Why the hell would it be unexpected? He wanted her all the damn time and it took a lot of effort to temper that love-inspired lust. But while he had her undivided attention... "No more carrying on about another man."

"*Yardley's* man," she reminded him, her smile flickering into place. "I want her to be as happy as I am."

That appeased him…a little. "Let's get inside before someone reports us for a PDA."

"Public displays of affection are allowed for old married couples," she said, but she opened the door for him to enter with Sammy, and once he was inside, she pressed the button to close the garage.

Old married couple. Is that how she saw them? If so, it was an ego depressor because with Mimi, he still felt like a horny high school kid in a perpetual state of need. She talked about a bath and he wanted her. She held her nose while changing the baby's diaper and he wanted her. She called him over a dead key fob battery and he flat-out loved being her knight in shining armor.

Thinking of all the ways and reasons he wanted her put him on edge. He needed a distraction and fast. Touching her damp hair, he said, "While Sammy's sleeping, why don't you take a nice long soak?" Mimi loved her baths—or she used to, before her free time evaporated. "I'll get dinner started."

For the longest time, she just stared at him. Then her mouth flattened a little and she nodded. "Sure, I'll soak. That'll settle all my sparking nerve endings."

She suddenly seemed disgruntled, but he wasn't sure why. "Would you rather nap?"

"This late?" she asked on a strangled laugh. "I'd never be able to sleep tonight."

"You rarely get to sleep anyway." It killed him that she got so little rest. "If you'd let me get up more with Sammy—"

"News flash, Kevin, you can't breastfeed. Besides, you need to be up early for work."

Kevin had no illusions about the differences in their jobs. He got out in the world, sharing lunch with coworkers, working, yes, but also laughing, socializing. Other than her trips to visit Yardley or a pediatrician appointment or to do the grocery shopping, Mimi was cooped up much of the day.

No one could love a child more than she loved their daughter, but she had to miss being with other adults.

There was more he could do, and he'd damn well figure out how to do it. "Let's get back to that in a minute." After securing the door behind them, he headed for Sammy's room, where he gently placed the baby in her bed. He turned on the monitor, left the room, and found Mimi pouring some type of crystal-looking stuff into the bath as running water turned it all into fragrant bubbles.

God, she was beautiful bending over the bath like that, her cheeks flushed from the steam. He honestly couldn't imagine a woman with more overall appeal. He'd always adored her sassy way of dealing with people. He respected her allegiance to Yardley, and how she boldly defended her without concern for repercussions. She was dedicated to her mother, and so attentive to their daughter.

With her capacity for love and her lush body, Mimi was the whole package. She was it for him—always had been, always would be.

Soaking in the sight of her, he casually asked, "So why are you hooking up on social media with this Adonis who's interested in Yardley?"

"If I do, Yardley will," she said, standing and pulling off her shirt.

Pretty sure his heart skipped a few beats. Her body had always been his perfect vision of "sexy," but since giving birth her curves were even more pronounced. His nostrils flared, but by God, this was her time and he wouldn't infringe on it. She had little enough time to herself already. "So I have no reason to be jealous?" he asked mildly.

She snorted. "I have my own delicious hunk, thank you very much. No other guy could even come close to tempting me." She raised her eyebrows, doing a fine job of looking him over and making him go half hard.

"Are we talking about me?" he asked, just to have something to say.

"Damn right I'm talking about you." As she sauntered forward, she unsnapped her shorts and lowered the zipper.

He was only human, and Mimi in a teasing mood was impossible to resist. "I thought you wanted a bath."

"I can do that—after."

After… Hell yeah. He reached for her—and Sammy gave a loud cry. Tamping down his disappointment wasn't easy, especially when Mimi dropped against him, her forehead thumping into his sternum.

"The pip-squeak has miserable timing."

Kevin stroked a hand down her spine. If he was honest, he'd say Sammy's timing was perfect. Better to have her interrupt things before they could get started instead of waiting until they were in the middle of things. "I'm sorry."

Mimi looked up at him. "For what?"

He cupped her face and lightly kissed her mouth. "For missing out." Another kiss. "I love you, babe. Now soak and relax. Sammy and I will be in the kitchen putting a meal together."

He walked out before the baby got really worked up—or before his resistance became nonexistent.

7

AFTER A PRODUCTIVE few days, Yardley was just about to head out the door to visit Betty. She'd thought about making an appointment with her, but changed her mind. Odds were, Betty would have turned her down.

Pride could be a strong motivator.

More and more of those stupid signs had shown up around town, promoting Yardley for town council president. If she ever found the culprit producing them, she'd put an end to it. So far, no one seemed to have a clue.

Hoping to be gone before her mother and aunt returned, she hooked her purse strap over her shoulder, took one step toward the door—and her cell phone buzzed.

Digging it out as she walked, she saw it was Travis and was already smiling when she said, "Hello there."

"Hey. Am I catching you at a bad time?"

Hearing his voice brightened her day, giving her a focus other than the probable conflict with Betty. "Nope. I'm on my way out, but I can do hands-free in the car. What's up?"

"Okay if I pick you up at noon tomorrow?"

She'd freed up the entire day for him, but she asked, "Not two?" That's what he'd originally said. "If you have an issue in your schedule—"

"I don't." When he hesitated, she sensed his mental shrug before he said, "I have the day free and figured we could spend more of it together."

Well hallelujah! "Sounds great to me. Heck, I can be ready by nine." Too late, she realized that she probably shouldn't have sounded so eager.

"Done. Nine it is. We'll grab breakfast first, okay?"

Midway through locking the front door, Yardley paused. "For real?" A fresh breeze carried the scent of honeysuckle. A bee buzzed in a pot of pansies off to the side.

"No backing out now."

Happiness bubbled up inside her. "No, I wasn't. Nine it is."

"We'll have the whole day, so other than seeing the house I'm working on, what else would you like to do?"

Sex, she wanted to say, because that seemed to be on her mind an awful lot these days. For once, though, she was able to withhold the inappropriate words, substituting with, "I'm partial to long romantic walks…through antique stores."

He laughed. "I know just the place."

"Seriously? Another one? Is it as awesome as the one you already showed me?"

"It's a hodgepodge of quality stuff and junk, but that also makes it less pricey."

Enjoying the feel of the sun on her shoulders, Yardley moved on to her car. She'd worn her hair in a high, stubby ponytail to go with her casual white shorts and loose peach-colored T-shirt. "Sounds like my kind of place." When she opened her car door, a wave of sweltering air hit her. It was just like opening her oven.

"There's a park near there that has great trails." His voice dropped, went husky. "Want to wander the woods with me?"

It had to be a knack, saying something so simple but making it sound somehow sinful. "Heck, yeah." Even if that was a double entendre of sorts, she was still all in.

With a short laugh, he said, "You're making this too easy on me, Yardley."

"I'm not a difficult woman." Braving the heat, she sat in her car, started the ignition, and kicked on the air. "Not usually, anyway, but Betty might disagree."

"Betty, the president you're challenging?"

"I'm not challenging her. Someone else is using me to do that." Someone sly. A troublemaker. "It's nuts, Travis, but more of those blasted signs have shown up. At first I was tempted to steal them all, but now there are too many. They're on every street corner."

She could hear his smile when he asked, "What will you do?"

"For starters, I'm going to meet with Betty today. Depending on how that goes, I'll formulate the next step of my plan."

"I'll look forward to hearing all about it tomorrow. Good luck."

"Thanks." She almost blew him a kiss through the phone. She'd blame Mimi for that, since it was her signature signoff for phone conversations. Instead, she opted for softly admitting, "I'm looking forward to tomorrow."

"Yeah," he replied low. "Me, too."

Knowing she was pressing her luck because Aurora

and Lilith would be home any minute, she ended the call, dropped the phone in the slot on her console, and drove away from the curb…with a fat, anticipatory smile on her face.

She tried in vain to go over the conversation she hoped to have with Betty, but instead she kept hearing Travis's gravelly voice. *Me, too.*

Lord help her, the man was walking, talking enticement.

And he expects me to wait until after the wedding?

That bordered on cruel, especially to a woman starved for a really delicious experience.

At a stoplight, she called Mimi with her hands-free feature.

"Hey, babe," Mimi said.

Yardley could hear Sammy fussing in the background. "Got your hands full?"

"Sort of. I'm just about to mash potatoes. I made Italian breaded pork chops and asparagus because they're Kevin's favorites. I'm not the smooth chef you are, so I couldn't hold Sammy. She was content to be in her bouncer for a while, but now she's kicking up a fit. I sniffed her backside, but her diaper is still clean."

Yardley choked on a laugh. "You sniffed her backside?"

"Just wait. Someday when you're a mom, you'll do it, too."

When you're a mom. Her heart turned over in her chest.

Okay, yeah, she'd love children of her own.

Someday.

On the heels of that thought was the realization that any kid she had would also get Aurora for a…grandmother. Oh, God. She couldn't imagine.

"What?" Mimi asked. "Did you keel over? Is the idea of kids that terrifying? I mean, you're great with Sammy. A natural. I just figured—"

"My brain jumped ahead to the idea of Aurora as MeeMaw."

Mimi whooped a laugh. "Ohmigod, we have to do it! We have to teach the kid to call her that. Or maybe Granny. What a hoot that'd be!"

Yardley had her doubts. More likely it'd be catastrophic. "I'm on my way to Betty. These blasted signs are everywhere, Mimi. So many people have them, but no one will say where they got them."

"I have three in my own yard now."

Yardley's jaw dropped. Horror gripped her throat and she rasped, "No you don't."

"Do, too. They look great."

Umbrage filled her lungs. "Traitor!"

"Ha!" Far from insulted, Mimi said, "I'm doing it for your own good. If nothing else, the signs might help convince Betty to be open to change. The town is due."

Yardley couldn't disagree with that logic, and no way could she rein in Mimi, so she opted to change the subject. "I called for something else, too."

"Oh goody. Tell me quick before Sammy really gears up. You know I can't bear to hear her cry."

"I know," Yardley whispered with a smile. Mimi was everything a mother *should* be.

If Yardley ever had a baby of her own, Mimi would be a great example to follow. For now, she was content to work on her business and to help the town progress. "So," she said, getting to the point, "Travis called and guess what?" She didn't wait for Mimi to answer. Long ago she'd learned that Mimi would guess a hundred times before giving up. "Travis asked if he could pick me up earlier, not because of a conflict or anything, but just because he wants to spend more time with me."

Gleeful, Mimi said, "Bet he's rethinking that whole no-sex thing."

She wished. "We'll start the day with breakfast, then browse more antiques, meander through a park, and then I'll see the house he's working on. I think we're still doing dinner, too." It'd be a whole day together and she couldn't wait.

"Here's a hint. Do dinner before you see the house."

"Why?"

"Let it get as late as possible. Shadows are seductive. Wear something sexy. Maybe a short dress."

"For a walk in the park?"

"For easy access."

Yardley could practically see Mimi's eyebrows bobbing. "You've been a terrific distraction on my drive to see Betty, but I'm here now, so I guess I should park, hike up my big-girl panties, and handle business."

"I hope that's a joke and you're not wearing granny panties."

"Figure of speech." Though her choice of underwear would never be as sexy as Mimi's. Why should it? No one saw her undies so her sole focus was comfort.

"I know. Just teasing." Her voice faded for a moment, as if Mimi had moved away from the phone, and when it got closer again, Sammy's gurgle could also be heard. The baby now sounded very content. "You know, if you're at all nervous about this face-to-face with Betty, or if you'd just like backup, you can wait until tomorrow and then I'll go with you."

So she could irritate Betty more? Yardley smiled.

"Thanks, but I'm already geared up for it, and honestly, I just want it out of the way."

"That's what I figured. Seriously though, you've got this. Just be you and Betty-freaking-Cemetery won't stand a chance."

And…that was what she'd needed to hear. "I appreciate the confidence. Enjoy your special dinner."

"Update me after, okay?"

Nope, not okay. She knew Mimi was planning a date night with Kevin and the last thing Yardley wanted to do was interrupt. "I'll update you in the morning, before I leave with Travis. We're both up early anyway."

"That works—unless something major happens. Then you better call me, okay? Promise."

"Okay. Wish me luck."

"You don't need luck, babe. You've got this. *Mmm-whah.*"

Yardley laughed at the kissing sound, parked at the curb, and drew a few deep breaths.

Everyone knew that Betty spent Friday afternoons working on her garden—just as they knew she didn't like to be disturbed during that time. Still, Yardley figured they'd need privacy for this little chat. Better to talk here than at the board meeting with half the town listening in.

It was a beautiful day, so with her fingers figuratively crossed, Yardley left her car, strolled to the back of Betty's property, and found her sitting on a padded rolling chair, a small trowel in hand as she dug in an elevated bed. On a portable table beside her were numerous flowers ready to be planted.

At eighty-six, Betty still got around well. She made a pretty picture too, with her short cropped gray hair under a sky-blue visor, a ruffled apron over her casual floral dress. Pink gloves protected her fragile hands.

To Yardley's surprise, her feet were bare. She stared at Betty's toes for a moment, then noticed her house shoes off to the side. As she watched, Betty wiggled her toes in the sun-warmed grass.

Betty-freaking-Cemetery was a slightly eccentric, bossy, proud woman...but she was still just a woman, same as any other. How many real pleasures did Betty have in her life?

When she heard the humming, Yardley knew she'd encroached during a vulnerable moment. Betty would be doubly put out by her unannounced visit if she knew Yardley had seen her like this. For that reason, she quietly went back to the side of the house and, as if she'd just arrived, called out, "Ms. Cemetery? Yoo-hoo. Are you here?"

She took her time getting to the backyard, and when she stepped around the house, Betty was standing, her house shoes on her feet, stark suspicion on her face.

"Oh, there you are," Yardley said with a bright smile and a wave. "I'm sorry for dropping by like this, but I saw there were more of those silly signs around the town and I wanted to clear the air."

The suspicion sharpened more. "Silly signs?" Betty turned to stab the trowel into a bag of dirt. "Are you speaking of your campaign signs?"

"Those, yes, but they're not *mine*. I don't know where they're coming from."

Betty was not appeased. "No doubt you have the town stirred up with nonsense ideas and they're showing you support." Crossing her arms, she asked, "What will you do now?"

Inching closer—totally uninvited—Yardley said, "I will appeal to you for a compromise. That's why I'm here, you know." Seeing the animosity on Betty's set expression stole some of her courage, so she looked beyond her at the garden beds. "You've already done so much work. Everything is so organized and neat."

Three beats of silence passed… "I don't want a messy garden."

Oh, thank heavens. Yardley was terrible with silence. Her unruly tongue immediately wanted to fill it, even with nonsense. Thanks to Betty, she could actually say something coherent and to the point. "Will they all be flowers?"

For another moment or two, Betty waffled, but her need to boast obviously got the better of her and she began gesturing. "That bed is for zucchini, carrots, onions, and strawberries. I love strawberries."

"Yum, me too."

"What you get from the grocery isn't nearly as sweet as those you grow."

"I'm sure," she said, eagerly taking part in the more neutral conversation. "Unfortunately, I have just enough of a green thumb to keep potted plants alive for spring and summer. Anything beyond that is a disaster."

"It's all in the soil, sufficient watering, and tending to weeds." Betty indicated another area. "Over here are my climbers. Tomatoes, green beans and snow peas."

"Ah, I see the stakes." Neatly marked.

"Trellises for the beans." Glaring at a weed she'd just noticed, Betty carefully bent to remove it from the soil.

"That's so much work for one person." Seeing an opening, Yardley shared a truth. "I've always admired that about you. Please don't take this the wrong way—I know I stick my foot in my mouth a lot—but most people your age decide to relax. Not you. You dedicate so much time to the town, and then you do all this too. Dang, do you ever prop up your feet and just rest?"

The absurd mix of compliments left Betty floundering. Yes, Yardley had mentioned her age. She'd never understood why that was taboo anyway. All a person had to do was look at Betty with her papery skin lined from time, her heavier ankles, her loose jowls and fading eyes to know she was in her eighties. Not like it was a secret.

Thrusting up her wobbly chin, Betty glared at her. "Are you suggesting I should hand over the council to you, just because you're younger?"

It'd be grand if Betty retired, but Yardley had long since given up on that idea. Ten years from now, Betty would probably still be around, telling everyone what they could and couldn't do with their own businesses. "Heck no. I don't even want it. I was just saying I'm impressed, that's all. Most people have a clichéd image of the little old lady. You know, knitting scarves or something, several cats underfoot while watching game shows throughout the day."

Betty's gasp nearly knocked her over. With sharp affront, she repeated, "Little old lady?" as if it was the gravest insult.

"Clearly that's not you, right? Look at everything you've done." Yardley admired the garden, then moved closer to the bed Betty had been working on. "This is genius, by the way. You can garden without the backache."

More sounds of bluster came from behind Yardley.

"You're putting in flowers?"

Tense seconds ticked by and then Betty joined her. "Yes, I also grow flowers. I start them from seeds in my sunroom, and I pay close attention to the *Farmers' Almanac* so I know when it's safe to bring them outside. The forecast is pleasant, so I decided to start now."

"You've obviously been out here working for a while, though."

Betty gave her a look that more or less pronounced Yardley as a dunce. "There's a lot to be done in the spring to prep the soil. I start with clearing out any weeds. Everything gets compacted over the winter so I use a spade to loosen it up." She shot Yardley the side-eye. "You're correct that I'm no longer young, so it takes me a little longer to do all the beds. I don't want to overdo it."

A surprising dose of concern hit Yardley. "Your yard is so isolated." Woods bordered her quarter-acre property along the back and one side. Tall evergreens worked as a privacy fence on the other side. "If you got hurt or fell, no one would know." Not for a quite a while.

Betty considered her for far too long before admitting, "I have a medical alert that I keep on me." She fished in a pocket of her apron and lifted out the egg-sized device. "If I fell, I'd just push this button."

Relieved, Yardley teased, "But would you though? You're awfully proud, I know."

Betty shocked her with a grin. "I believe I'd prefer embarrassment to dying in my own backyard."

Just as surprising was Yardley's reaction. The truth hit her hard. "I'd prefer that for you, too."

The shared moment was nice. Peaceful. Friendly.

Then Betty caught herself. Wiping the smile from her face, she stuck the alert back in her pocket and picked up the gardening instruction in a brisk tone. "Next I mix in compost and test the pH and nutrient levels of the soil so I know if I need to add anything else."

"This is way more complicated than I realized."

Gaze sharpening, Betty said, "That's always the way with you young people. You think everything is easy and you're always looking for a shortcut. Well, it's the same for the town. You think you want change, but have you considered what kind of change you might get?"

"The good kind?" Heck, anything would be an improvement on the overuse of "Cemetery" in every single instance.

"We could hope. But what if Saul wanted to call his restaurant the Roadkill Café?"

Yardley laughed. "He wouldn't."

"What if, God forbid, something happened to him and a new owner moved in? Then what?"

"Hmm." Far-fetched as her example might be, she saw Betty's point. "That's a valid argument." She still thought the owner should be given more choices. No one had more hinging on the success of the business.

Compromise, Yardley reminded herself. "There are a lot of traditions here in Cemetery. We'd never want to forget them."

"No," Betty agreed firmly. "We wouldn't. My great-grandfather had a vision for this town. It was his sweat and blood that started it all."

Though Yardley had heard the story many times, she didn't interrupt, and she didn't look away. Now that she understood Betty a little better, the stories had new meaning.

"The lake drew everyone here, you know, but it was unsettled until my great-grandfather opened up a secondary boarding school. That's where Cemetery got its roots in education and tourism. You know, we've had quite a

few famous people through here, including Buffalo Bill."
On and on the history lesson went.

This time, though, Yardley heard a richness in the
words, a pride of history rather than accomplishment.

"I have photos from 1885 when the rail line first
reached us, passed down to me from my family."

"Hanging in your house?" Yardley asked with awe.

"Yes, indeed." More animated than Yardley had ever
seen her, Betty removed her gloves and lifted a hand toward the back door. "Come along. I'll show you."

"Awesome." Yardley matched her step to Betty's
slower stride. "Thank you."

"Did you know there used to be a floating dancing
pavilion? It was most popular in 1892. Then the tourism
picked up and the lake became too crowded, especially
with steamboats."

"I don't suppose you have any photos of that, do you?"

Betty slid her a glance. "Naturally, I do."

Oh wow, this was turning out to be a fun adventure.
"I've been to the historical society a dozen times." Half
those times during class trips when she was a kid. "I don't
recall seeing any photos like that."

"They're my own, and I don't want to part with them."

Hmm. Couldn't Betty have offered copies for display?
Maybe, Yardley thought with sudden insight, she kept
them to herself to lure visitors to her home.

Oh, how sad.

She'd never considered that in some ways, Betty would
be like many elderly people who were alone and lonely.
Yes, she had a position of power within the community,
and she often came off as cold and strict. Now, though?
Betty's attitudes seemed different.

Because Yardley saw her differently.

As they stepped into the kitchen, she was surprised again. "This is beautiful." Whitewashed shiplap covered the walls in a stunning accent to the white cabinets and black countertops. Massive decorative corbels supported the island top. The ceiling… "Wow. I love this tin ceiling."

"Thank you. It's reclaimed from my grandmother's kitchen."

"What? No way." In amazement, she craned her neck, searching out each imperfect tin tile. "This is fabulous," she breathed, earning another small smile from Betty. One long windowpane over the sink was stained glass, and above that, a large metal sign made a statement. "Are those antiques?"

"Two of them are. The sugar-curing sign and the drug-store sign. The others are reproductions."

Wicker baskets held napkins and large utensils. On the island, fresh flowers and a bowl of fruit looked inviting.

Everything was perfectly balanced…except for the roosters.

They were *everywhere*. Large colorful glass statues, smaller carved wood roosters, salt and pepper shakers, a canister set, and a wrought iron hook that held a few pot holders.

So… Betty liked cocks? Oh, she could just imagine the jokes Mimi would make. She'd have to be sure to stress how homey and welcoming it all looked together. "Ms. Cemetery, I'm blown away. Your kitchen is phenomenal."

"You're in my home. You may call me Betty."

Whoa. That was a real shocker. The quick shift was almost too easy, and Yardley started to wonder if this was a ploy so Betty could push her down the basement steps, never to be heard from again.

"Lemonade?"

Shaking her head to clear it, Yardley said, "Thank you."

Betty frowned. "That was a bit confusing."

"Right. My thoughts wandered. Yes, I'd love some lemonade. It's awfully warm today."

"Summer is coming early." She got ice from the freezer and filled two cups. "The almanac is rarely wrong, you know. It bodes well for our summer tourism."

That brought Yardley right back to the reason for her visit. "So, Betty." Ugh, that sounded incredibly awkward. "Those campaign signs around town. I want you to know that I respect your position in our community too much to rock the boat."

"I suppose your mother and aunt shared my ultimatum?"

Yardley waved that off. "They did, but I don't put any stock in that. If you tried it, there'd be pushback, and not just from me."

Stiffening, Betty paused in the act of pouring the lemonade. "Are you threatening me, young lady?"

"Nope. Wouldn't dream of it." Because Betty needed to understand, she added, "But I don't take kindly to threats either." Feeling as if she'd hit her stride, Yardley added, "That's why I'd like to work with you, instead of against you."

Distrustful, Betty studied her expression, then returned to pouring the lemonade. She handed a glass, with a small napkin, to Yardley before leading the way into the living room.

This, too, was a nice room. Done in a vintage style in shades of pale dusky blue and buttery yellow, it suited Betty. Over one arm of the small yellow-striped couch hung a beautiful throw blanket with a perfectly arranged fringe. Each toss pillow had been plumped and arranged. The tables were eclectic with a round, glass-topped coffee table in dark wood, a painted antique dresser refurbished to be a credenza, and mismatched white wood end tables.

"I love how everything is different, and yet it all co-ordinates so well."

"Thank you." Betty took a soft padded chair and carefully set her drink on a coaster.

Doilies were everywhere. Not cheap ones, either. Nope, these looked as if they too had stood the test of time—maybe a century or more. Yardley sipped her lemonade, then set it on a different table with a coaster before wandering to the wall of framed photos.

"That largest photo is the dancing pavilion," Betty said.

It was in sepia, but Yardley could still see that it was on the lake. "The shoreline looked so different then." Huge tufts of grass grew all along the water's edge. There were trees in the image that had since been removed.

"Yes, it was wild and a little overgrown with weeds except for the paths."

Yardley moved on to the next photo of a steamboat. Betty didn't leave her chair, and she wondered if she was tired. "Is this your grandfather?"

"Yes, and beside him is my grandmother. Such strong people," she said wistfully. "You know they opened the boarding school without any assurances that they'd succeed."

"And yet they did. A testament to their determination."

"Yes." Betty patiently allowed her to peruse each of the photos, answering questions when she had them, offering commentary on occasion. Finally, she said, "I have albums of photos if you'd ever like to go through them, but I know you sought me out today for a reason."

With a small wince, Yardley knew her time was up. "True. I suppose I should get to it."

"Yes."

She hurried over to take her seat. Then decided a few sips of lemonade were in order. When no other delay tactics came to mind, she cleared her throat. "I don't want your position."

"Excellent. If that's all, then?" Betty started to rise.

"Not quite." Yardley watched her sink back into the chair again. "Obviously, more than a few people support the idea of loosening up on the name, right? Otherwise those signs wouldn't have popped up everywhere."

"Your point?"

They were back to Betty being rigid. "My point is that with a little effort, we could appease everyone, including ourselves. I propose I work—" she almost said *for you*, but at the last second she adjusted to "—*with* you as a liaison for the local business owners. I think you know you've intimidated quite a few of them. Deliberately, I'm sure."

It was subtle, but the corners of Betty's mouth tilted up the tiniest bit.

So she liked that, did she? She enjoyed lording her power over others? Too bad, because Yardley was more determined than ever to end Betty's reign of domination, not only to benefit the business owners, but to help Betty, too. The woman was literally hungry for company but would never admit it. She'd been standoffish and inflexible for so many years that she'd probably forgotten how to bend.

Yardley was up to the task of showing her the way.

Slowly, carefully, with the hope that everyone would end up better for it.

Right. Like I'm a superhero or something. At least I'm trying. If she owned a cape, she'd wear it.

"So." Guzzling down the rest of her lemonade, Yardley stood. "Why don't you think about that, okay? No, no reason to give me an answer now. How about I visit again... I think I have next Wednesday open. I'll confirm that when I get home and then I'll... I dunno. Do you have Facebook?"

"I do not." Betty seemed highly affronted by the idea.

"Huh. I'll hook you up. You'll love it, I promise. Just think, you'll be able to keep up with everyone in Cemetery." As Yardley suspected, that lure drew Betty's interest. "If I'm not free Wednesday, I'll email you at the town council address."

"I have my own private email." Betty stood, went to a basket on the credenza and removed a beautiful linen business card.

"Awesome." After accepting the card, Yardley headed for the kitchen with her glass. "Assuming Wednesday works, I'll bring muffins. Do you prefer buttermilk cranberry, blueberry cream, or cinnamon-topped muffins?"

Dazed, Betty hurried to keep up with her. "I don't—"

"Let's do the cranberry ones." She rinsed her glass and put it in the dishwasher. It didn't surprise her that Betty had not a single dirty dish in there. "I have a feeling you'll like them. I have a specialty tea that's really good too. Should I bring that or will you have more lemonade?"

"I always have lemonade."

"Excellent." She thrust out her hand—and waited. "Thank you so much for showing me part of your house, Betty, and the living room photos, too. If you don't mind,

I'd love to see the albums you mentioned on my next visit."

"I...of course." Betty hesitated, her fingers toying with the short hair at her nape. "I could also show you the rest of the house then."

"Yes!" Man, she wanted to high-five Betty, but somehow that didn't seem appropriate. Instead, as Betty accepted her hand, Yardley gave it a gentle squeeze and said, "Thanks again," and made a hasty getaway out the kitchen door while she still could. If she gave Betty even five seconds to get her bearings, she might revert back to being unfriendly, and then her entire effort would be wasted.

From behind her, Betty called out, "You could have used the front door!"

Ha! Yeah, she probably should have. "I will when I return." Practically trotting, Yardley got to her car—which had been sitting in the sun all that time—and plopped down behind the wheel.

The seat burned her butt and the enclosed air was sweltering, but she cranked on the blower and quickly drove away. Whew. She felt like she'd robbed a bank and escaped unscathed.

Honestly though, robbing a bank might be easier than reforming Betty-freaking-Cemetery, but it was a task worth doing.

Now that Yardley knew the elder lady a little better, she didn't want Mimi to make fun of her.

She didn't want anyone to give her grief. Betty deserved a lot...

Maybe all of it good.

WHEN YARDLEY DIDN'T CALL, Mimi figured the trip had been a no-go. Odds were, Betty had refused to speak to her. Poor old Betty. It'd be her loss. Yardley brought the sunshine anywhere she went, and Betty could have used some of that, for sure.

Whatever, she'd get all the details in the morning. For now, she darted around the kitchen one last time, making sure everything was perfect before Kevin got home.

She finished, and then just had to wait.

And wait.

Worriedly, Mimi watched the clock. Thirty minutes passed. Then fifty.

What the hell? Where is he?

She was just about to blow a gasket when she heard his truck in the driveway. The urge to race to the door, to demand answers, surged through her bloodstream, but resentment kept her standing by the already set table. She'd gone to so much trouble, and now the food was cold.

Sammy, bless her heart, was occupied in the playpen with a few toys, leaving Mimi free to stand there, arms crossed, a belligerent scowl on her face.

"Mimi?" he called softly. He always came into the house quietly in case Sammy was napping.

"In here." Hoping he had a good excuse for not calling her, she tapped her foot—until he stepped through the dining room doorway.

Shock punted her heart to her feet. "Oh my God, *what happened?*" Rushing forward, she took in the blood on his shirt and the white bandage around his hand. "Kevin?"

With his left hand, he caught her shoulder and kept her from getting too close. "I'm okay, babe." He bent to steal a kiss, saying, "Stupid accident at work. I'm sorry I couldn't call you. I thought I'd get out of the hospital sooner, but the doc was busy giving me instructions." He laid a printed sheet of paper on the table. "Then I had to concentrate on driving one-handed."

Of all the... "I should have picked you up!" In the next breath, what he said sank in, and she lost it. "How *dare* you go to the hospital and not tell me?"

For an answer, he lifted one shoulder. "My bad. At first I didn't want to worry you because it wasn't serious. I thought I'd be home on time." Another kiss. "But damn, the waiting room was packed, and I ended up with ten stitches—"

"Ten stitches!" Her heart shot back into her chest to pound furiously against her ribs.

"Shh. Honey, I swear I'm okay." He lifted the bandaged hand. "Looks like I'll be off work a few days though. Unfortunately, I'm not sure how much help I'll be, and that pisses me off. I wanted to do more for you, not leave you with a bigger load."

Since he already did so much, she waved that off. "What happened?"

"Freak accident, really. I was working on a broken conveyor belt and—"

Blood rushed from her head. "Someone turned it on?"

"No. There are safety measures that keep that from happening."

She'd already imagined it, and now she couldn't breathe.

"Babe, hey. Calm down, okay? I swear I'm fine."

She nodded, trying to get it together. "So what did happen?"

Humor kicked up the corner of his mouth. "I'm trying to tell you." He softened that rebuke by stroking her hair. "A new guy was putting away a floor polisher, it got away from him and ran into me, and..." He shrugged.

"My hand jammed into the back of the machine against some gears."

"Sharp enough to cut you?"

"Yeah, sliced all the way across my knuckles. The good news is that there wasn't any ligament or tendon damage, but no flexing my fingers for a while."

Her heart continued to thud heavily. "God, I'm so sorry." She gently lifted his hand, pressing a light kiss to the bandages. "Does it hurt?"

"At the moment, not so much."

"Here, let me help you with your bloody shirt." Because she'd had a few years of practice with her hunk of a husband, she had the buttons opened and was pushing it off his shoulders before he got out a single objection. Carefully, she eased the material over his hand. "Do you need any aspirin or anything?"

"I told you, I'm fine. Stop fussing, okay?"

At least his undershirt wasn't too badly stained. "Want me to get you a different shirt?"

He gave her a look, then sniffed the air. "Damn, that smells good. Is dinner ready?"

Mimi stood there, shaken from seeing him hurt, still ridiculously irritated by her worry, and a little heartbroken that he hadn't asked her for help, that he didn't seem to want or need her help at all.

If the situation had been reversed, she'd have called him first thing. He was always her go-to for…everything.

Her attitude was ridiculous. She knew that. Kevin had always been that way. Other women complained that their husbands were wimps when they got colds, but Kevin would never admit he had a cold. He always pushed on. Women complained that their husbands didn't help out, and Kevin helped out so much that she often felt useless.

He always took care of her.

She wanted her turn, damn it. Trying not to sound pitiful, she said, "I made your favorites."

"You don't know how awesome that is, babe. I'm starved."

Clearly, she'd have to resign herself to no sex tonight, which wasn't easy since she'd been stewing all day on the ways she'd planned to drive him wild.

With a sigh, she ordered her unruly hormones to cool down, told her thoughts to quit the pity party, and pulled out the chair for Kevin.

He shot her another look of exasperation. "I can handle the chair. You don't have to—"

That did it. Hands on her hips, she snapped, "I'm going to help you and if you don't like it, too bad."

Eyeing her, Kevin said, "Okkaaaay."

Great. Now she sounded grumpy—which she was, but she didn't want to be. "You'd do the same for me, right?"

"That's different," he mumbled.

"Baloney. I love you just as much as you love me, so park your ass in the chair. I'll put your food on your plate, and I'm even going to cut your meat." She pointed at him. "I don't want to hear a single complaint. Got it?"

His mouth hitched on one side. "Okay, sure. Will you put Sammy in her high chair next to me so I can give her some loving, too? I missed you both."

Course he did. She exhaled as much frustration as she could and forced her stiff lips to smile. "Yes, I can do that." Feeling better now that he wasn't turning her away, Mimi decided her lecture could wait a bit—but he would hear it eventually.

They were in this together, and it was past time she

gave her fair share. And thinking of that… "When do you see the doctor again?"

"I'll need to set an appointment with our guy, but the ER doc said I should have the stitches checked in twelve days. Have to watch it for signs of infection, too." Once she got Sammy in her chair, he leaned in to kiss the baby's cheek, her nose, her forehead. "She doesn't understand why I'm not holding her."

True. Sammy kept reaching for him. He always cuddled the baby first thing when he got home—after he'd given Mimi a kiss and a hug. She gave it quick thought, then came up with a solution. "After dinner, we'll sit together and I'll help you." She waited for a complaint.

He only said, "Thanks." With his left hand, he played with the baby.

Glad that he wasn't arguing, Mimi got the food on the table.

"Wow, Italian breaded pork chops? Awesome."

Smug, she grinned while putting two chops on his plate along with a pile of buttery mashed potatoes and several asparagus spears. Instead of sitting across from him, as she'd originally intended, she moved to the chair beside him.

Before she could cut the meat as she planned, he stabbed one chop with a fork and lifted it for a big bite.

"Mmm, heaven." Leaving the fork stuck in the meat, he stole her fork to use for his vegetables.

Loving his gusto, Mimi laughed. She might not have Yardley's talent in the kitchen, but Kevin had never complained over her efforts. "Be right back." In the kitchen, she got together food for Sammy, grabbed another fork for herself, and rejoined him.

It wasn't the seductive date she'd envisioned, but as

she watched him devour his food, their thighs touching, she decided it was even better. Well, except for the missing sex part. But the closeness, the teasing…this was the special stuff that made up her marriage.

The type of special she'd missed lately.

Maybe she could use Kevin's downtime to her advantage. To *their* advantage.

They'd be together 24/7.

Good things were bound to happen.

BEFORE HEADING TO YARDLEY'S, Travis dropped in to see his sister. He wanted her to know his plans, and then he'd reassure her that nothing would interfere with her wedding. He and Yardley were taking it slow. She needed to understand that.

At her apartment door, he knocked.

Todd answered, looking harried and worried.

"Bad timing, dude," Todd said.

A second later, Travis heard Sheena retching. "What's happened?"

"Morning sickness," Todd lamented. "One minute she was showing me some of the choices she'd made with the wedding organizer, and then, bam! She turned green." Scrubbing a hand over his face, Todd said, "That was an hour ago. I don't know what to do, man."

Striding forward into the apartment, Travis tapped on the bathroom door. "Sheena? You okay?"

"Go away," she moaned.

"Not happening, sis. What can I do?"

The door opened, and there she stood. Travis took a step back. God, she looked like hell.

In a voice weak and rough, she whispered, "Call Yardley's friend, Mimi, will you? Her number is in my phone."

She swallowed heavily, covered her mouth, then drew a slow breath. "She's had a baby, so maybe she has advice."

"Right." Glad for something to do, Travis turned to Todd, who'd followed him to the bathroom door. "Where's her phone?"

Todd, too, looked thrilled to have a purpose. He literally jogged to the bedroom and grabbed her phone off the nightstand. He put in the passcode then scrolled through her contacts.

"I can do it," Travis said. After all, she'd asked him.

"Todd?" Sheena whispered. "Could you get me a damp rag?"

Instantly alert, Todd thrust the phone at Travis and ran off for the bathroom.

Travis stared after him, partly amused to see him so stressed over a little puking, but equally appreciative to see how much he cared.

When more retching followed, he started to worry, too.

He hit Mimi's number, waiting impatiently while it rang three times. A male voice answered with, "Hello?"

"Hey, is Mimi around?"

"She's changing a diaper." Then, with suspicion, "Who's calling?"

"Travis."

"The Travis who is Yardley's hot new boyfriend?"

Um… *Hot new boyfriend?* "Yes?"

"And you're calling my wife…why?"

A whole lot of possessiveness sounded in the tone. "My sister is suffering morning sickness as we speak. She said Mimi might have a suggestion that'll help."

"Ah. Okay then." The call was muffled as if the guy had covered the phone. Travis heard, "Hey babe, it's Yardley's guy."

Yardley's guy. He liked the sound of that. Then he heard, *"What?"* and a second later, Mimi demanded, "Is Yardley okay?"

"I assume she's fine. On my way to pick her up I stopped to see Sheena, who has some pretty hideous morning sickness. She thought you might have an idea on how to help her."

"Oh, whew. Way to scare a body. Here, I'll let you talk to Kevin. He handled all my morning sickness cures and right now, I have a naked baby trying to escape her blanket. Tell Yardley I said hi, and I hope Sheena feels better!"

"Thanks," he said, but Mimi had already left.

The guy came back, and this time he didn't sound so accusing. "I'm Kevin, Mimi's husband. I'm assuming you don't have Yardley preggers, but since my wife didn't fill me in, why don't you tell me what's up?"

Despite worrying for his sister, Travis smiled. "My sister is carrying, and she's currently puking her guts up."

From the bathroom, Sheena wailed, *"Travis,"* followed by a groan.

"Sucks. Morning sickness is the pits. She has a guy of her own?"

"Marrying soon, which is how I met Yardley. But yeah, they live together."

"Great. Here's what he'll want to do, though it might not help right away. First, tell him to try to keep all the smells out of the house. If he's cooking for her—and he should be—tell him to leave a window open or a fan going. Might not bother your sister, but Mimi chucked every time she smelled food cooking. Get your sis whatever kind of crackers she likes. She should eat a few in the morning before she even gets out of bed. Even before she gets up to pee. Got it?"

"Yeah." Travis felt like he should be taking notes. When he spotted a notepad and pen on the kitchen counter, he headed that way. After tearing off a growing grocery list, he added crackers, and then said, "Go on," while jotting down the pointers.

"Sniffing lemons and sipping lemonade helped Mimi. Half hour before a meal, and a half hour after, but not during the meal. Oh, and tell her guy that she needs to be napping. He should make that possible."

From the background, he heard Mimi call out, "See why I love him?"

Yeah, he did. Travis pictured her with her daughter, her husband nearby, probably smiling at her... It was a nice image and it put to mind things he hadn't considered before. Things to do with his future, a wife and kid of his own... "Anything else?"

"We found that Mimi could eat some things and not others. Try to figure out what she ate yesterday and if the morning sickness is worse today. It's trial and error, but I figured out Mimi couldn't eat Italian or anything spicy. She went from loving all things chocolate, like pies or candies, to favoring fruit stuff like Yardley's blueberry muffins. Oh, and the tea! Yardley got her this awesome cinnamon tea that helped a lot. Mimi loves it still, but she doesn't buy it for herself." Louder, maybe to make sure his wife heard, Kevin said, "She likes to use it as an excuse to visit Yardley."

Mimi's laughter told Travis that she wasn't offended by the accusation.

"Got a pen handy?"

Travis said, "Yeah. I've been writing all this down."

"Take my number and give it to your future brother-in-law. If he has any questions, he can give me a call."

Did all men form this rapport when taking care of pregnant women? He was pretty sure Todd would love any and all advice. "Sure thing." He wrote the number Kevin gave him onto a separate piece of paper. "By the way, I think you two work together."

They chatted a few minutes more, and by the time Travis was done, Todd had helped Sheena settle on the couch, her feet propped on the coffee table. He pressed a damp cloth to her head.

After taking in that scene, Travis explained what he'd just learned.

"We have lemonade!" Todd started to stand, then hesitated as he turned to Sheena. In a buttery-soft voice, he asked, "How does that sound, baby? Want some icy lemonade or will that just make things worse?"

"Actually…make it warm instead of icy, lots of sugar."

"You've got it." Todd pressed a careful kiss to her forehead. "Be right back." He moved around Travis in long, hurried strides to the kitchen.

Taking the seat Todd had just vacated, Travis lifted Sheena's hand. "You okay, sis?"

"I'm gross and limp. Todd is a saint to put up with me."

"Todd is in love. All that matters to him is making you feel better."

Her eyes, dark like his own and now smudged with exhaustion, gave him an assessing look. "He does, you know."

"What's that?"

"Love me." Her pale lips smiled. "I know you worry, but he's so good to me. He's good *for* me."

That was starting to become crystal clear. "Because you love him, too." Travis still had some misgivings, but little by little, they were fading away. Hearing Todd in the kitchen frantically fixing Sheena her lemonade helped.

"I love him more than I can explain."

"Don't even try. For now, just rest." Travis squeezed her hand, and then noticed a small framed black-and-white...something, on the end table. "What's this?"

"That's your niece or nephew in the making."

"No way." He turned the photo sideways.

Sheena took it from him. "This is the head. An arm, legs... You see the little stinker has its legs closed, so we couldn't tell the sex yet."

"Wow." A lump the size of a cantaloupe lodged in his chest. "I can see it now."

"The next one we get should be clearer. Pretty exciting, huh?"

"Yeah." Exciting, except for when Sheena was throwing up. He hated to admit it, but that was a little alarming. "You feel better now?" *Please let her say yes.*

"I do," she promised around a yawn, but she still had one arm across her middle. "I might drink my lemonade and then crash."

"I should get going, anyway." He tucked back her hair and stood. "If you think of anything you need—"

Todd hurried in with her drink and a napkin. "It's pretty warm, so be careful." As if unaware of Travis, he crowded into his seat, close to Sheena—edging Travis farther away in the process. Not deliberately—Travis wasn't offended, not when Todd was so focused on Sheena.

But it did give him something else to think about. Had part of his resentment toward Todd been because he didn't like sharing his sister? That made him seem like a selfish ass, but for the longest time it had been just the two of them. Sheena had come to him for everything from advice to support. He sometimes dated, she sometimes dated, but there hadn't been anyone serious for either of them, so they'd never expanded their family.

Taking on the role of parent as well as sibling had definitely changed him. Now that he analyzed it, though, it felt nice to know he could leave for his date with Yardley without having to worry.

He clasped Todd's shoulder. "Kevin suggested you two keep track of what she eats and whether or not it made her sicker the next day."

"We had fried chicken last night," Todd started to say—until Sheena moaned and covered her mouth. He winced. "I'm sorry."

Travis shook his head. "Just keep track, okay? Then you'll know what to avoid. Kevin's number is on there, but you also work with him."

"Different departments," Todd said. "We don't pass each other, but I can look him up during lunch." He lifted the notepad. "Thanks for this. I'm glad to know she has you when I'm working."

A magnanimous opinion, given Travis hadn't been all that subtle about his disapproval. "You both have me. Any problems, let me know." He glanced at Sheena. "I'll be out with Yardley today. Anything wedding-related you want me to ask her?"

She froze in the middle of sipping her lemonade. Eyes wide, she slowly lowered the cup. "You're seeing Yardley?"

He could soften the reality, say they were looking at antiques again, but he wasn't in the habit of lying to Sheena, not even lies of omission. "Will that be a problem?"

An impish smile went a long way to making her look less miserable. "It'll only be a problem if you screw it up."

She didn't have much faith in him. "Not my plan. Plus, we're taking it slow until after the wedding."

Todd's eyebrows shot up. "Slow as in…like friends? Dude, that has to suck."

Yes, it did. He winked at Sheena. "I won't risk messing up her big day."

"Hey," she protested, already looking somewhat recovered. "Don't mess up your life either."

Travis shook his head. "I just told you things are casual." For now. "Don't worry about it, okay? You have enough to deal with."

"I already feel better." She finished off her lemonade, set the cup aside, and snuggled back into the couch. "Could you ask Yardley if she locked down that adorable Honeymoon Cottage? I totally loved it and I don't want to risk someone else reserving it."

"I'll see to it."

Sheena's not-so-innocent gaze met his. "Yardley really liked the place too."

"She highly recommends it."

"Because *she* loves it. But I get the feeling she doesn't expect to ever stay there."

Travis didn't want to discuss Yardley's obvious misconceptions about her own appeal, so he merely said again, "Rest up, okay?"

In a very sleepy, but knowing voice, Sheena said, "Thanks for helping out."

"Anytime." He glanced at Todd, gave him a nod of sincere appreciation, and finally left the apartment. He wanted to see Yardley even more now. Never before had he shared much of his day-to-day life with someone, but he wanted to do that with her. They could laugh over Mimi and Kevin…and he knew Yardley would understand his shifting stance on the wedding.

Could he keep things platonic until July? By the minute, it seemed more doubtful.

8

"IT'S SO FUNNY that as soon as I hung up with Mimi, your sister called. She sounded better, by the way, so Kevin's lemonade advice must've helped."

The way Travis's brows lifted, it was news to him. "My sister called you?"

Uh-oh. She had to go carefully here. "Actually, we talk often."

After a two-second pause, he said, "I guess I shouldn't be surprised. Sheena's made it clear how much she likes you."

"The feeling is mutual."

His smile brightened. "Yeah, she's pretty special."

So much pride infused the words. "She's like her big brother that way."

His hands tightened on the wheel. "I hated seeing her so sick today."

"I remember Mimi got really sick too, though not all women do. Oh, and Sheena said her doctor wasn't worried, so there's that."

"I saw the image of the baby." He flashed her a crooked smile. "Looks like a little alien, really."

Yardley laughed. "Those first ultrasounds do." She enjoyed Travis's profile, how affectionate he appeared while discussing his sister. "Sheena said she napped for a bit, and now she's going to watch a movie with Todd. I guess they don't get a lot of time off together." She'd also asked some pointed questions about Yardley seeing her brother. Because she knew it was important to Travis, Yardley had insisted things were casual.

To Travis, they were, but Yardley had left casual far behind.

Sheena had claimed she approved, just in case they got serious, but with the caveat that Yardley couldn't bail on her wedding if things ended badly.

She'd assured Sheena that she was far too professional for anything vindictive…but was she? If Travis suddenly lost interest and then, horror of horrors, he brought a *date* to the wedding, would she be able to keep her cool while still supervising everything—or would she be too distracted to concentrate?

Yes, she decided. She would absolutely fulfill her duties as the wedding planner. It wouldn't be the first time her pride had carried her through a difficult situation.

Pride, and Mimi.

Maybe she could get Sheena to invite Mimi and Kevin to the wedding, just in case she needed moral support? The two of them seemed to be getting closer.

Unaware of the turbulent path her thoughts had taken, Travis said, "Todd works whatever overtime he can," as he pulled into the park. "That used to bug me, too. I understand hard work and long hours, but the timing seemed suspicious, like he was just dodging wedding responsibilities."

"Until you saw them together today." Shaking off her reservations, she beamed at him, glad that he wasn't one of those stubborn people who dug in and stuck with an opinion. "Now you have a better impression of their relationship."

"Hard not to, with the way he dotes on her, and how she looks at him." He passed a few different areas of the park. "The apartment is still too damn small for both of them and a baby, but hopefully that'll be temporary."

"Travis Long. You should know it doesn't matter where someone lives when they truly love each other."

"In theory, I agree. But it's different when it's personal."

"How so?"

"Look at it this way. Would you be okay with Kevin moving Mimi and Sammy into a one-bedroom place?"

No, she wouldn't like it, but she shrugged. "That depends on why they moved. If Kevin lost his job but was still trying, then sure. It'd be fine." Though she'd also be looking for ways to help them. "What's important is that together, they can figure out anything."

Travis smiled. "Good answer." He pulled into a smaller lot away from all the others. "I agree, even though that's not what I had planned for Sheena."

"You can't plan her life." She glanced around as he parked. This location didn't have any marked trails or picnic tables, and it appeared largely overgrown. "You gave her the right tools—common sense, support, guidance and love—and the rest is up to her. She's an adult, you know."

"She's *twenty*."

Yardley lost the effort to hold back her smile. "Okay, yeah, she's young. And I know it stings that she dropped out of college."

"And that she's pregnant, living in a very cramped apartment in a less than upstanding part of town, with a man who's years older."

"All that." Reaching over, Yardley put a hand on his forearm. "But she's smart, Travis. She's in love, and you said yourself that Todd is totally committed to her. They can work toward a better future, right?"

"That seems to be the plan, but it's going to be a rough start."

The dusting of hair around his wrist drew her fingers downward. Not stroking him was impossible, but she tried to stay on track verbally while also feeding her senses with the different textures of his body. "You'll still be around, giving great advice and helping out on occasion, right?"

His gaze met hers. To Yardley, it felt like they shared a moment. A heated, interested moment.

"I can't seem to help myself."

Lost in that special moment, she blinked. "With what?"

The corner of his mouth quirked upward. "With helping my sister."

"Oh." And here she'd hoped he meant something else entirely. "Well, speaking of helping your sister, she wanted to make sure you didn't forget to lock down the Honeymoon Cottage for her. I promised her it was all taken care of."

"Thanks." Travis took a moment to watch her. "You know, you sparkle a little more when you talk about that place."

That place? What a terrible way to refer to something so wonderful, it was almost magic. Then the rest of what he'd said sank in. "I don't sparkle."

"You do. Often." His look turned warmer, more probing. "How do you not know that?"

She didn't mean to, but she gave a rude snort, murmuring, "Sparkle," which just plain sounded silly. She wasn't the sparkling type. Now Mimi, that girl knew how to sparkle. "The Honeymoon Cottage is a very special place, that's all."

"It's special to you, too, isn't it?"

What he said, and how he said it, made her feel exposed, as if he saw all her deepest secrets. She tried to laugh it off. "It's for newlyweds, so no matter how much I like it, I won't be staying there."

"Maybe the owner would rent it out to you."

Yardley shook her head. "Nope, sorry. If just anyone used it, it'd lose part of its appeal, don't you think? I mean, the tub would be a waste for one person, right? And it wouldn't really suit a family with kids. It's small and only set up for two, so—"

Leaning over, Travis pressed a quick kiss to her mouth. "I understand."

When his gaze held hers, it seemed that he really did. And she felt raw because of it.

After another quick kiss, he opened his door and headed around the truck.

Lips tingling, thoughts scattered, Yardley stepped out before he reached her. The late afternoon sunshine peeked through the leaves of tall trees. Heat rose off the blacktop lot and bees buzzed nearby. The air smelled incredibly fresh. "No one else is here."

"This is a pretty remote part of the park, but I like it

here." He held out his hand. "It can't compete with the cottage, but I'll show you a few secret places."

Anticipating the warmth of his touch, she put her hand in his. His fingertips were rough, calloused from work, his hand twice the size of her own. She liked the differences.

As he led her toward the wooded area, she said, "Mimi told me to wear a dress, but I'm glad I didn't listen."

"A sundress?"

She lifted a shoulder. "Something suggestive."

He gave her another of those super sexy smiles. "Let me guess. You shared our conversation?"

Belatedly realizing that she shouldn't have said anything, Yardley flushed. "Sorry. That's a bad habit of mine. I blab everything, well, almost everything, to Mimi."

He lifted her hand to his mouth and kissed her knuckles. "No worries. I sort of told Sheena and Todd, too."

Yardley would be willing to bet his "sort of told" left out a lot of details that she'd gleefully shared with Mimi. "She mentioned that you said things were casual."

"I didn't want her worrying about it, but I didn't want to keep things secret either. Sheena and I have always been honest with each other."

"Same with me and Mimi." She was so glad that he understood. After a lifetime of sharing with Mimi, keeping things private from her would be tough.

"Much as I like Mimi's suggestion, I'm glad you wore jeans." He led her right up to the edge of the woods. "It'll make our trek to a special spot a little easier."

"Um…" Yardley held back. "Hate to break it to you, but that doesn't look penetrable, even with me wearing jeans and sneakers."

"Trust me." He stepped ahead of her, lifted away a big

branch, and then she saw the narrow dirt trail that meandered in and around mature trees and shaggy shrubs.

"It's hidden!" Darting forward, she took the lead,
and it was like stepping into a green cave. A cacophony
of birdsong filled the air. Bees buzzed around a wild
rosebush flourishing in the sunshine of a small clearing. A chattering squirrel gave them hell from an overhead branch.

Everything grew in abundance, sometimes overlap-
ping the trail and snagging on her jeans and shirt, but
she didn't mind at all. She paused to listen. "Do I hear
water?"

"You do," he confirmed. "Keep going. We're almost
there."

After another minute or two of dodging thorny vines
and stepping around exposed roots, they reached a creek
that opened into a ten-foot pool before narrowing as it
rushed over a fall of rocks and continued on downstream.
"Wow." Yardley turned in a circle to take in all the beautiful sights. "This is amazing."

"Careful," he said, taking her elbow and stopping her
from getting closer. "Last time I was here I found a big
rat snake over th—"

"Ack!" She moved behind him so quickly, she almost
knocked him over. Hands fisted in the back of his T-
shirt, she used him as a shield. "You brought me to a
snake haven?"

Laughing as he turned—or tried to turn—Travis said,
"It's not a haven, and I don't see any snakes around here
now. I just didn't want you to trip over one."

Trip over... "Oh, God," she whispered. "Pretty sure I
would have died on the spot."

"Yardley?"

"Hmm?" She peered over his shoulder.

"Let me loose, okay?"

No, she wasn't sure if it was okay or not. "Why? What are you going to do?"

"Hug you first, then maybe kiss you."

Okay, then. Her fingers loosened.

As he edged around, he promised, "And then I'll take a quick look to make sure we're entirely alone."

"No snakes?"

"No snakes." His hands settled on her shoulders. "I'm sorry I scared you."

Feeling a bit like a coward, she avoided eye contact by looking at the water. It appeared almost magical—unless there were snakes. Then the whole thing looked like a giant wet nightmare.

His finger curled beneath her chin and urged her face up. "Hey."

Reluctantly, she met his gaze…and amazingly, everything else, even hideous snakes, faded away. His eyes were so dark, full of intent. The scent of his warm skin filled her head. Her hands just naturally opened on his chest.

Could she really wait until after the wedding to touch him without clothes in the way? Doubtful when right now she had a hard time not climbing his sturdy frame. It'd be so easy to wrap herself around him—arms around his neck, legs around his waist…mouth to mouth.

For the longest time, he just looked at her. Then his fingertips glided over her cheek before cupping her nape. "Usually, your eyes are a smoky blue with flecks of green in them, and sometimes you have a darker blue ring around your irises. When you do, your eyes look stormy."

"Really?" Since she'd never studied her eyes that closely, she'd have to take his word for it.

"They look like the sky before a torrential rain." His thumb brushed along her temple. "In this light, though, they're pale gray, like the dawn."

"Or...maybe like I'm horny?"

He slowly grinned. "Is that what happens? Your eyes turn light gray?"

Don't blush, don't blush. "I don't know. Can't say I've ever stared at myself in a mirror while...in that state." *Yeah, that is definitely a blush scalding my cheeks.* "Let's move on."

He didn't. "I suppose that could do it. And now I'm imagining it."

"Your eyes don't change," she blurted, hoping to get the focus off her. She curled her hands over his hard shoulders. *Man, I really want him out of that shirt.* "They're always dark and sort of mysterious."

"Mysterious, huh?" His left hand slid around her back, drawing her even closer.

Their pelvises bumped together, making her über aware of the incendiary moment. "Travis?" she breathed.

"Yeah?" He bent to open his mouth against her throat, to touch her skin with his hot tongue.

"I'm not getting carried away in the woods where there might be snakes." She levered back with great regret and glanced around him, saying with distraction, "You're hot and believe me, I'm incredibly tempted, but yeah...not here."

He squeezed her close again, his chin on top of her head. She felt the rumble in his chest.

"Are you laughing?" she asked.

"Just a little." He cupped her face, gave her a firm but brief kiss, and said, "Stay right here while I check it out."

"I have to be able to see you, okay?"

"I won't go far."

Yardley sighed and glanced around again. A funny-looking mushroom grew along the base of a tree, so she withdrew her cell phone for a pic. Next she noticed tiny purple flowers and took another photo of those, then the sunlight filtering through the trees overhead, and one of a colorful rock at the edge of the creek.

Travis had removed his shoes and rolled up his jeans to cross to the other side of the creek. That deserved a photo also. He used a stick to shake a bush and move a few branches. Yardley admired the flex of his arm when he lifted a rock to look beneath it.

Another pic.

He carefully returned the rock to the same spot, then checked beneath a few more. He circled the whole area, taking her fear seriously.

How awesome was that?

Finally, he crossed the creek again. "It's all clear."

Her attention centered on his feet, big and now wet. It seemed silly to even think it, but they were masculine feet. Actually…sexy feet.

Everything about him was sexy, his body, the way he kissed, the way he focused on her and cared what she said…

He held out his hand. "Come on. There's a nice big rock over there where we can sit. You'll like it."

Yardley peered across the creek. "The thing is, my jeans are too tight to roll up."

"Just take off your shoes. You can use the rocks and I'll walk beside you."

She eyed the water. "Is it cold?"

"Freezing, but I won't let you fall in. Trust me."

Mumbling, "My feet aren't as nice as yours," she braced one hand on his shoulder and removed her shoes, one at a time.

Travis took them from her. "Your feet are cute."

Yardley stared down at them, glad that she'd recently painted her toenails. Unlike her mother and aunt, she didn't do weekly pedicures, but she had to admit, her feet weren't hideous. Lifting her right foot and flexing her ankle, she admired the polish. "Not too bad, I guess."

Travis grinned. "You know what?" As if it was nothing at all, he scooped her up into his arms and said, "Hold on. I'll just carry you."

She squawked all the way to the other side. If he'd slipped, which seemed entirely possible, they'd both have been doused. Luckily, he didn't seem the least bit strained carrying her, and he was sure-footed enough that she didn't feel jostled.

When he lowered her to sit on the rock, she sighed. "You're like Indiana Jones or something."

"It's just a creek, Yardley."

"But the way you carried me? Very heroic. I'm not used to stuff like that."

Sitting beside her, his feet still in the icy water, he took her hand, lacing their fingers together. "Give me a little time and you can get used to it, okay?"

Did he plan to spend a lot of time in Cemetery even after the wedding? Oh, she hoped so. "Does that mean you'll be toting me around a lot?"

Though she'd been joking, he answered seriously. "It means I like doing things with you and for you." He tucked back her hair, and let his fingers linger at the side of her face. "You do so much for everyone else. The other businesses in town, your mother and aunt, and your clients. You deserve to be pampered, too."

"Aww." Mimi would love to know he'd said that. "Thank you, but I like to stay busy."

"You said you and Sheena talk often. That can't be part of a wedding planner's duties."

"Not usually, no." Sheena was different, though. "I enjoy talking with her."

"I'm sure she appreciates it. She's anxious about so many things right now."

That made sense considering how her life was about to change. Yardley held his hand a little tighter. "I don't want to freak you out, okay?"

He frowned. "Okay."

"Sheena and I are becoming friends. I like her a lot— but that doesn't obligate you in any way." With an affectionate shoulder bump, she said, "If whatever this is between us suddenly ends, I won't let it affect my relationship with your sister, and it definitely won't impact her wedding plans."

"No trash-talking us on social media?"

"I would never." Though she was hoping a breakup wouldn't happen, and privately she'd be pretty bummed. "I'll accept it and move on—same as you would." She lifted her nose comically. "I'm an adult like that."

"I think it's more about you being very special. You have a huge heart, and you seem to care about everyone."

Another nice compliment. She could really get used to this.

"The way you've organized everything," Travis said, "you make it look easy. That means a lot to Sheena, so it also means a lot to me. Now more than ever, I think she misses having a mom, or aunt, or even a sister."

"You're pretty good at filling in on all counts, so don't sell yourself short." She started to say more, but a noise behind her put her on alert.

"What is it?" Travis asked.

In a whisper, she said, "I heard something."

"You're liable to hear all sorts of things. Rabbits, squirrels, maybe even a fox or deer."

"What if it's a snake?"

"Snakes don't walk through the woods."

No, they *slithered*—and now she was doubly edgy.

"Hey." Putting his arm around her, Travis pulled her protectively against him. "I checked for snakes, remember? And with us here talking, they'll avoid the area until we're gone."

Being so close to him, snuggled against his chest, scattered her thoughts once more. Maybe he'd discovered a cure for fear? He could just hug people and they'd forget what scared them.

It was impossible not to look up at him. And when she did, he looked down. Suddenly they were nose to nose, lips oh so close…and praise be, he made a low, rough sound and took her mouth.

Yes, this was the type of kiss she'd been thinking about nonstop. Urgent, a little hungry. He shifted, tilting his head one way as she tilted another, crowding closer, their mouths open and his tongue…

She tunneled her fingers into his hair and deepened the kiss even more.

This time when he shifted, she ended up on his lap. One of his broad hands opened over her hip. She managed to get her hand under his T-shirt and onto the taut skin of his back.

The man was hard all over. How awesome was that?

Sudden whining startled her so badly, she lurched away, slid off his lap and slipped ankle-deep into the creek. Immediately, Travis on was his feet in front of her, protecting her from any danger.

Only, when she peeked around him, all she saw was a little dog. A very sad-looking dog. A *young* dog, with black-and-brown spots…and blood on one mangled ear.

"Oh my God." Desperate to reach the poor creature, she awkwardly lumbered out of the creek and started forward.

Travis put an arm out in front of her.

She almost brained him. "It's *hurt*."

"I know," he said softly. "And hurt dogs sometimes bite. Let's go slowly, okay?"

Him and his slow approach to everything! Her heart hammered so hard that it hurt her rib cage. Her throat squeezed tight, making it impossible to draw a breath, or to release one.

She *needed* to help the poor thing. Right now.

Knowing Travis was right, she reasoned, "It's small. A bite won't be so bad and if it runs off, we might not find it again."

After a slight hesitation, he nodded…and slowly pulled off his shirt.

Wait…*what*? Her gaze didn't know where to go! Injured pup. Half-naked Travis. Injured pup. "What are you doing?" *Besides making me cross-eyed?*

"Promise me you'll stay back."

Dragging her attention off his shoulders, she said succinctly, "No. You stay back." She moved around him.

"Yardley—"

"Come here, baby," she whispered, crouching down and inching forward. "Are you hurt? Let me help, okay?" Tears clouded her eyes, especially when she saw the rope around the dog's neck, connected to a heavy limb. Had someone tied it to a tree? How long had he been dragging that around? It looked terribly awkward for such a small dog.

Slowly, Travis handed her his shirt. "If you can get him, wrap him in this."

"He'll like the smell," she predicted. Briefly she touched her own nose to it, which helped to calm *her*.

"Yardley," he said with fond exasperation.

She held out the shirt. "Come here, sweetie. Take a sniff of this deliciousness. I bet you'll want Travis to hold you."

Behind her, she could feel Travis close, but he didn't move. Smart man. If he tried to be all macho and ended up scaring the dog off, she would not be happy.

The dog's ears twitched and he whimpered.

His poor ear…it looked badly injured. Bony ribs showed through his muddy fur. And that damn rope around his neck was far too tight. He needed medical care, he needed food, and he needed her.

She held out the shirt. "Come on, sugar. Come to Mama."

"Mama?" Travis comically whispered.

Not caring what he thought, not about this, she said, "Yes, I'm going to be his mama." She shifted closer.

The dog shifted back and to the side, as if preparing to bolt.

A sort of tragic calm settled over her, helping her to function. "Travis, do you see that rope?" It was at least three feet long. "Try to slowly scooch over there and when I get close enough to the dog, grab the rope or that branch and that'll give us a chance."

"Damn it," he grumbled as he inched forward. "I do not want you to get bit."

"I don't want to get bit either, but more than anything right now, I want to help this dog."

She heard his deep inhale and measured exhale. "I want that too, just so we're clear."

The dog looked worriedly back and forth between them. She didn't know a lot about animals, but he didn't seem mean, just hurt, abandoned and terrified.

Continually whispering, she edged her way nearer until finally he was within reach.

Cautiously, he sniffed the shirt. God, how she wished she had some food to offer him. She'd make that a priority, but first—she held out her hand.

His lips curled in a low growl.

"I know you're afraid, baby. I understand because I used to be afraid all the time, too. You just need a best friend." She could feel Travis looking at her, but she kept her attention on the dog. She *had* been afraid— until Mimi.

"Come on, little bit. You need to trust. You need *me*." She reached out her hand—and he dodged to the side, further away from Travis.

"Shoot." Even though Yardley never looked away from the dog, she was aware of Travis's careful step. They were both barefoot in the woods with twigs and rocks and prickly weeds everywhere.

Without making a sound, Travis took a few careful steps, then whispered, "Now."

Yardley launched forward at the same time Travis

grabbed for the rope. She caught the dog and the poor thing screamed like a cornered pig. It was the most pitiful thing she'd ever heard and as she struggled to subdue its frantic attempt to escape, she cried, unable to stop the fat tears rolling down her cheeks.

Over and over she murmured, "Shh, baby, shh. I've got you. It's okay. I swear I won't hurt you. Shh. Easy now. Shh."

Trembling, panting, the dog gave up and tucked his head against her. Her heart absolutely melted. She knew in that instant that she'd never let anyone or anything ever again hurt him.

"I've got you now." Careful not to hurt its already injured ear, she locked it in close to her chest.

"Here." Travis pulled a knife from his pocket, shocking her silly, and said, "Hold him still. This fucking rope is so tight, it's strangling him."

"Oh, God." She'd forgotten about the rope. Using her shoulder, she wiped her tears and continued to murmur to the dog. Now that Travis had pointed it out, she saw that the rope had worn away strips of fur from his neck.

"There you go, baby," Travis murmured to the dog.

At least, she assumed that was for the dog and not her.

"Easy now." He managed to get the blade under the skinny rope, and just like that, he sliced it and eased it away. "Good boy." He gently smoothed a hand over the dog's narrow back.

That was a mighty sharp knife he carried.

With loads of sympathy and without her excess of emotion, Travis bundled his shirt around the dog.

Using the same tone on her, he asked, "Okay if I carry him, honey?"

She nodded, swiped at her cheeks once more, and nodded again. "Yes, thank you."

"Come on." He held the dog securely. "It'll be okay now."

Yes it would. She'd make it so.

Together, they went across the creek, neither of them as careful this time. In fact, Yardley didn't care that she stepped more in the water than out of it, or that the rocks hurt her feet. She snagged up her shoes and tugged them on, but when she started to hand Travis's to him, he shook his head.

"Let me get him in the truck first, okay? Then I can put them on."

He was so calm and take-charge that she gladly followed his lead. They had the dog, he'd be okay now, and that's what mattered most.

THE SECOND YARDLEY got the front door open, Travis heard Aurora say, "Dear God. Where in the world have you been?"

Then Lilith stated, "Isn't it obvious? She's been rolling around in the mud with that man."

Yardley stopped so abruptly, he almost ran into her back. Dodger, held in his arms, gave a startled bark. And both women shifted their widened gazes to him.

Yes, after their trek across the creek, then the bath they'd given the dog, with a lot of care in between, they were both a little worse for wear. But to accuse Yardley of rolling in the mud? They weren't *that* messy.

"Oh no," Aurora said, making shooing motions as she approached. "Please don't bring that mutt in here. Out. Keep it in the yard or your car or whatever. Just not in my house."

Dodger's ears flattened and he sank against Travis.

Irked by the woman's obnoxious tone and treatment, Travis stroked the dog's back. "She doesn't mean that, buddy." After the amount of time he and Yardley had spent getting the dog patched up, washed, fed and reassured, he didn't want him cowering again. "You're not a mutt."

"Of course it is," Aurora said with a frown, still advancing. "Just look at it. It's pathetic."

That seemed to shake Yardley out of her daze. She stepped into her mother's path and said in a low tone Travis had never heard before, "Not. Another. Word."

Aurora and Lilith both froze. Even Dodger went still, his head tipped to the side, his bandaged ear twitching.

"This is my house, too," Yardley stated. "He is now *my* dog, and he *is* coming in. In fact, he's going to live here."

Hand to her heart, Aurora breathed, "No," in a genuinely horrified manner.

"As usual," Yardley continued, "I will be responsible for him."

Lilith narrowed her eyes. "What do you mean, 'as usual'?"

Knowing exactly what she meant, Travis stepped up close behind her and put a hand to her shoulder. It didn't require a lot of attention to see that Yardley was tired, emotionally spent, frazzled, messy and still worried about Dodger.

It was the absolute worst time for her mother or aunt to be so insensitive.

"I mean," Yardley said with a bite, "that the running and maintenance of this house is my responsibility, and the care of the dog will be no different. He doesn't concern you." She lifted her chin. "By the way, his name is Dodger."

Lilith charged forward. "Now wait just a minute—"

"He *stays*," Yardley said, cutting her off. "Period. End of discussion." She stepped to the side and swept her hand toward the hall. "This way, Travis."

Wishing he could cheer, but accepting it would be inappropriate, he moved around her and headed toward her bedroom. Dodger looked over Travis's shoulder, anxiously waiting for Yardley to follow.

"We haven't had dinner," Aurora complained.

"I ordered pizza." Yardley fell into step behind him. "You're welcome to share some when it arrives." She slipped into the bedroom and closed the door behind her with a near silent click. For a moment, she leaned back against it, eyes closed.

Travis set down Dodger with the admonishment, "Don't pee anywhere," and then he went to Yardley. "You okay?"

"Absolutely fine."

That clipped voice didn't bode well, and she definitely didn't look fine. She looked ready to sink into the floorboards. "You did great today, honey."

With a snort, she pushed away from the door, sat on the side of the bed and dropped back with a bounce, her arms flopping out to her sides. "I cried. A *lot*. My eyes are puffy and my cheeks are still blotchy."

"Yes." He sat beside her hip, liking the way it caused her to roll slightly toward him. Now they touched, and that suited him just fine. "You cried, and then you did what had to be done." They'd gone straight from the park to an emergency hospital for animals. As soon as Yardley released the dog inside the clinic, he took off and they had to catch him all over again. Thankfully there were no open doors, so he didn't get far. The problem was that he was fast, and he had fear on his side.

Yardley had cried then, too, doing everything in her power to reassure the poor animal.

The vet needed a name for the dog to start a file, and together they decided on Dodger. The little beast was a dodger, for sure.

The entire time the vet assessed Dodger's health and his injuries, Yardley had hovered close. It was fortunate that other than a slightly mangled ear, dehydration and hunger, and obvious neglect, Dodger was okay. No broken bones, no serious illnesses. While the vet worked on him, they explained how they'd found him. The vet was equally furious that the dog had likely been left in the woods to die. She was also grateful that they had rescued him. When she asked if they'd keep him, Yardley gave an immediate confirmation.

Travis accepted that he was falling fast and hard. He'd looked at Yardley with her wet jeans and muddy shirt, the tear tracks on her cheeks, her mussed hair, her gentleness and iron resolve to rescue an injured dog, and unfamiliar emotions collided in their rush to fill his heart. Tenderness, affection, pride and respect, but also possessiveness and need.

She made him feel everything, all at once, in a giant bombardment on his senses.

He knew right then, he wanted her in his life. Hell, given how she leveled him, he *needed* her in his life.

While he wrestled with that newfound knowledge, Dodger's ear was cleaned and bandaged. The rope burn around his neck was treated with a special oil. Luckily they were able to buy supplies right there, including a harness that wouldn't overlap the sore area of Dodger's neck. They'd also gotten a leash, more of the oil, special soap for giving him a bath, food and a flea treatment.

They hung out there for a few hours so the vet could feed him and see how he did. He finished an entire bowl of water and ate a serving of food. Then they took him out to an enclosed grassy area where he did his business like a champ. Three times, in between smelling every blade of grass, watering it all, and investigating every corner.

All the while, he kept his gaze on Yardley, as if he feared she might leave him.

As someone else had.

Dodger had bonded with her immediately. Even more touching was the fact that she'd bonded with the dog. Every time Travis had looked at her, she'd been quietly crying. He'd see her brush the tears away, swallow heavily, and then she'd love on Dodger.

There was something going on there, a shared sense of abandonment that wrecked his heart. Did Yardley know how the dog felt—because she felt it, too?

He wanted to wrap his arms around them both and promise they'd never be hurt again.

Instead, he'd pitched in to make Dodger comfortable, and to relieve Yardley of as much as he could. He looked at her now, sprawled on the bed, her body boneless.

Clearly she didn't realize it, and she was in no shape for him to come on to her, but she offered up some mighty temptation.

She also made his heart feel too big for his chest.

"Hey, are you falling asleep?" If she was, he'd take the dog home with him tonight so she could rest up.

"No." Yardley stirred with a big, expressive sigh. "I was just thinking of the house you're working on." Her sleepy eyes searched his. "I'd had a few plans for when I got you alone."

"Is that so?"

She gave a lazy nod with a slight curl of her lips. "Your virtue would have been safe, I promise."

He laughed.

"I'm serious," she said. "I would've respected your wishes to wait, but I'd planned to kiss you. A lot."

"So gallant," he teased, and then admitted, "I'd have liked it—a lot—but it's okay. Dodger took precedence."

"Yes." Her voice went low and gruff. "Thank you for the tour of the house, brief as it was, and for helping me give the dog his bath there."

Seeing her like this, in a sort of exhausted sensual mood, being in her bedroom—even with her mother and aunt in the house, even with her looking so spent and with the dog currently sniffing his foot—made Travis want her even more. Taking her home with him, to his real home, where he lived, would suit him just fine.

He could hold her all night while Dodger slept close, and maybe they'd both feel more secure. For sure, it would right something in his world.

But he had made that stupid rule about waiting. If he shouldn't have sex with her until after his sister's wedding, then he definitely shouldn't have overnight visits just for emotional connecting. So instead, he'd taken her to the house he was renovating, where they'd bathed Dodger—and where there were no beds to test him.

Only now they were on a bed anyway.

And he *was* sorely tested.

Regretting the decision to keep things platonic, he said, "It was the perfect place for it. Running water but without any furniture to be ruined."

She didn't move, but her eyes took on that smoky gray hue—the color he would now associate with her being "horny." Damn.

"It's a beautiful house," she said. "I love everything you're doing with it. All the upgraded finishes and how closely you've kept it to the original designs. When I'm not so distracted, I'd like to see it again."

"Deal." Somehow he'd survive that. Or maybe he'd just give in by then.

She put her hand over his, lacing their fingers together. "Seriously. I'm sorry about being so weepy. It's not like me."

He thought it was probably exactly like her; she was a very bighearted, compassionate person, after all. From what he'd learned so far, Yardley had grown used to hiding that soft, emotional side of herself.

He was glad she hadn't hidden it from him.

"There's nothing wrong with crying, Yardley, especially when it's in sympathy for a helpless animal that's been mistreated."

The dog bounded up onto the bed and army-crawled up near her face. Smiling, she released Travis to gently scratch beside Dodger's uninjured ear. As if the dog needed no more invite than that, he snuffled against her.

She let out a trembling breath, already near tears again. "I bet you don't start bawling over every little thing."

Seeing the dog hurt like that…it wasn't a little thing. "No, and clearly you don't either." His own throat felt thick with emotion, especially now, seeing how happy Dodger was with Yardley's love. "The last time I cried was when my parents died." *Well hell. I didn't mean to say that.* Uncomfortable now that the words were out, he kept his gaze on Dodger.

Yardley sat up, drawing the pup into her lap. "I can't imagine how difficult that must've been for you."

"I didn't want anyone to know," he admitted. "When the police told me what happened, it was like my world dropped out from under me and I fell into this big void of emptiness and panic. At first, I couldn't quite process it all, you know?"

"Understandable." Her soft gaze stayed on him. "That's a lot of devastating news for anyone to deal with."

He rubbed the back of his neck. At that age, he'd considered himself an independent adult for years…until real-world responsibilities had landed in his lap. "I remember being thankful that Sheena was asleep. The cops hung around, worried about me, offering all kinds of help." He cleared his throat. "As nice as they were, I just wanted them to leave."

"You needed privacy for your grief."

That was a huge part of it. "I was afraid they'd think I couldn't handle things if they saw me fall apart, that they might take Sheena away, too." He drew a tight breath. "I couldn't let that happen."

"Oh, Travis. What an awful worry for someone so young."

Yes, it had been. "I knew I needed time to think. To figure out what to do." How to tell his little sis that their lives had just been shattered. "I was up all night, alternately crying and raging, then completely…lost."

Yardley leaned into him, one of her arms going around his back. Dodger looked at him, then crawled over to his lap and licked his chin.

Christ, how could anyone have mistreated that dog so badly?

"Thanks, buddy." He rubbed his chin against Dodger's head, and then kissed Yardley's temple. "Sorry. I don't mean to—"

"Please don't do that. Don't think you have to shield me or anything dumb like that, just because I've been sobbing all day." She looked up at him with her soft eyes full of understanding and damn, it left him undone. "I'm strong, Travis."

"I know that." He'd seen it from the start, and especially today.

"I want you to feel free to talk to me, about anything."

And then maybe she'd start sharing, too? That seemed like a fair trade. "It took me all night to get my head on straight, but once I made the decision to do whatever was needed to keep Sheena's life from changing too much, the rest fell into place."

"That's a tall order for a twenty-year-old college student."

The same age his sister was now. Did she have all the same determination, the illusion of maturity? Likely. "It gave me a purpose. A goal. By the time Sheena got up the next morning, I'd withdrawn from college and had started searching for full-time job opportunities in construction. I'd found phone numbers for my parents' accountant and their life insurance company. I had everything for the house—utilities, maintenance, all that—stacked on the counter."

"Were you able to keep the house?"

"Yes. I live there still. So did Sheena until she moved in with Todd." The family home had been the least of his problems. "My folks had already paid off their mortgage, and they had great life insurance. Still, we struggled financially at first. I knew I had to make the money last, but we managed. It was the other stuff—Sheena crying all night, hating school, sometimes hating…me."

Expression stricken, Yardley cuddled closer. "She was a little kid and she had to be so hurt and confused."

No denying that. "She'd be squeezing me, holding on tight, while also crying that she didn't want me, she wanted her mommy and daddy."

"Oh, God, Travis." More tears filled her eyes. "I can't even imagine…"

"Ah, honey, I'm sorry. I didn't mean to upset you more." He kissed each cheek. "In some ways, it helped. Focusing on her kept me from wallowing in my own misery."

"Maybe you needed to wallow a little."

That made him smile. "I did, here and there." When he could find time to breathe.

And when he was alone.

Done talking about all that, he ran his fingers through her hair. "It's been a hell of a day, hasn't it?"

"It has." Again, she stroked Dodger. "It's also been one of the best days of my life."

Even through all the sadness, she amazed him. "How's that?"

"I have this remarkably beautiful dog now." She kissed Dodger on the head, giving him a hug. "And I had this incredibly sexy guy flaunting his chest and playing hero and showing me what a terrific, patient person he is. A person who doesn't get repulsed when I cry too much, sniff too loudly, and end up with puffy eyes and a red nose."

The smile reached his heart. "You are always beautiful—and I wasn't flaunting."

She lowered her brows to give him a level look of censure. "Don't you dare ruin my illusion. Though I had it in the wish basket, no guy has ever flaunted for me before. You stripped off your shirt, showing me your gorgeous back—"

Gorgeous back?

"—and those enticing abs... You even carried me!" She sighed dreamily. "I'll see the whole thing however I choose to, thank you very much."

"Wish basket?"

Her eyes searched his for several heartbeats. Then she nodded toward her open closet. "See that basket?"

On the floor, surrounded by shoes, a wicker basket held multiple shells of different sizes. "Yeah."

"Each shell is a wish." She said very seriously, "I do a lot of wishing."

No kidding. "What do you wish for?"

"Well, one of them was for a guy to flaunt." She flashed a grin that didn't quite reach her tired eyes. "A few of them were for a man to sweep me off my feet."

"Literally or figuratively?"

"I mean, either would work, right?" Then softer, she added, "I think you did both."

Even at a time like this, she tugged at his heart and made him smile. "Glad I could oblige." Needing to know, he asked, "The others?"

"Oh, silly things." Her gaze flinched away. For the longest time she didn't answer. Then she said on a sigh, "Even a wedding planner has dreams."

He imagined Yardley had more than most. "Like?"

"A beach wedding." She smiled at Dodger. "A pet of my own." She glanced at him appreciatively. "A hot dude in my bed."

Somehow he knew she omitted the biggest wish. "What else?"

"You might've already guessed."

"The Honeymoon Cottage?"

As if it didn't matter, she lifted a shoulder. "Like I said, silly."

He didn't think it was silly at all.

"I love the place, always have. You were right that I've given Daniel advice on how to make it better, how to keep it updated, stylish and comfortable."

"And romantic." He'd felt certain that the owner hadn't added all those personal touches to the cottage.

"I appreciate that he listens to me." Trying to hide her emotion, she smiled. "Anyway, thanks to you, a few of those wishes came true today. Let me enjoy them."

"Fair enough." Because he'd see the day how he chose to, as well.

It was the day he'd found the one for him.

Hell, the first time Yardley had spoken, he'd somehow recognized her as *the one*. Every minute with her since then had only shored up that belief.

She twisted to press a brief kiss to his mouth. "I think I heard a car pull up. Probably our pizza. I don't know about you, but I'm famished." She kissed him once more and stood. "I need to blow my nose and change my muddy clothes and—"

The sound of a car door closing shot Dodger off the bed with a round of maniacal barking.

"Good Lord." Yardley put a hand to her heart, watching as the dog ran in hysterical circles.

Travis could barely hear her over the noise. "Take your time," he told her. "Your ferocious guard dog and I will collect the pizza."

"Leash him," she instructed as she turned for the bathroom. "Just in case he's turned demonic."

Travis laughed, but of course he did just that. They didn't yet know enough about the dog, but he appreciated Dodger's instinct to protect Yardley.

In that, they felt the same.

9

DINNER WITH TRAVIS, her family and Dodger should have been uncomfortable, but it wasn't, because she wouldn't let it be. As they ate, her mother and aunt alternately stared at Travis, then at the dog. Yardley could practically see their imaginations going wild with questions.

Dodger stayed under the table by her feet. Given the way he loudly licked his chops every so often, he was probably hoping something would hit the floor. She'd given him more food and water in the corner of the kitchen, but he wouldn't leave her side. She accepted that he'd be clingy for a while, but she didn't mind.

In fact, she loved it.

"We're going to get dog hair in our food."

Yardley glanced at her aunt. "He's short-haired. Not much shedding."

"I can hear him panting," Aurora said.

"Oh? I thought that was you." Yardley's attempt to look genuine made Travis snort and had her mother glaring.

"More wine?" Aurora asked Lilith, who held up her glass.

Between the two of them, they'd nearly finished a bottle. She and Travis, on the other hand, each had a cola.

Yardley rubbed Dodger with her foot and concentrated on devouring another slice of pizza. Dealing with the turmoil of the day had really worked up her appetite.

"I can come by tomorrow and set up an enclosure in your backyard," Travis offered. "Eventually he'll get used to letting you out of his sight."

"What kind of enclosure?" Aurora asked. "Our yard is small enough already. We don't want it crowded with a pen."

"And Yardley has flowers planted everywhere." Lilith frowned under the table with accusation. "The dog is bound to trample them."

"You're never in the backyard," Yardley said, looking first at her mother and then her aunt. "You've never before mentioned the flowers."

Travis sat back in his chair. "Flowers everywhere—do you ever rest? Take a day off? Seems to me you're always working."

Aurora and Lilith shared a sheepish look of culpability.

Huh. Had they really heard Travis? Had they truly realized what he said? Overall, they rarely seemed to see or hear anything that had to do with her, unless it reflected unfavorably on them.

"She likes to stay busy," Aurora explained.

"That's what she tells us," Lilith added.

Mostly, Yardley thought, she liked to keep her mind occupied. Not that she'd say that here at the dinner table. "We can discuss an enclosure before you leave, if you have time. I'm sure Dodger would enjoy familiarizing himself with the yard."

He nodded. "I'm in no hurry to go."

No, he wasn't—and how bizarre was that? She'd always assumed most guys—anyone, actually—would run in the opposite direction the second her mother and aunt started scrutinizing them. Travis flat-out didn't seem to care. Or rather, his focus was on her and not on whatever insulting things they were thinking.

Mimi was going to *love* him after Yardley told her everything that had happened.

Lilith patted her mouth with a napkin. "Yardley isn't too busy to fit in time to run as town council president, regardless of the problems it'll cause our business."

Her eyes narrowed. "I already told you I wasn't running. Someone else is putting out the signs and pushing that rumor."

Aurora elevated her chin a notch. "My guess would be Mimi is behind this. That girl has always enjoyed stirring up trouble. I have no idea why you remain friends with her."

A slow breath didn't help to stem Yardley's growing annoyance. This was such an old argument, she wasn't sure how to reply.

Then Travis put his arm across the back of her chair, his large hand curving over her shoulder.

Dodger rested against her knees.

And she remembered that she wasn't alone. Not anymore.

They were both backing her up.

During every battle she'd ever fought, with her mother and aunt, the school, even with Betty, only Mimi had stood beside her. What an odd feeling it was to have her world expand like this. Odd, but absolutely liberating.

"Why are you smiling like that?" Aurora asked with suspicion. "You *are* running, aren't you?"

Some evil bug got to her, and she said, "I'm considering it."

Lilith gasped with great fanfare. "You swore you wouldn't!"

"So? If you believed me, why are you still harassing me about it?"

"I'm not *harassing* you. I was only…" Lilith floundered.

Aurora came to her rescue, saying, "Why haven't you put a stop to it?"

Waving a hand, Yardley said, "As Travis just pointed out, I'm always working." The way their eyes flared proved she'd hit a sore spot. But hey, they were her family so she couldn't torment them for long.

"Actually," she said, stressing the word to obnoxious proportions, "I saw Betty just the other day. I believe she and I might have come to an understanding." At least, she hoped that was true.

Their suspicion only sharpened. "What agreement?" Lilith asked.

She was about to answer, but Dodger licked her fingers, and Travis caressed her shoulder, and she totally forgot what she was going to say. "I, ah…" Right. Betty. "I'm seeing her again soon. We're discussing things." She didn't want her mother or aunt to know that she had a specific date with Betty on Wednesday, or what her overall plans were in that regard, because she didn't trust them not to interfere. They'd sabotaged her before.

And now that she realized it, it seemed so damned awful.

Why had she ever put up with it?

Mimi was right. In her effort to stop being the weird

girl who always spoke without a filter, she'd become something of a doormat.

Mimi loved her, weirdness and all. Dodger obviously adored her. And Travis…he was here now, having dinner with her dysfunctional family and acting like it was the most normal thing in the world.

Could she be herself…with everyone?

Definitely not a decision to make after a long, emotionally draining and physically exhausting day.

With a pat to Travis's hand and a stroke of Dodger's good ear, she pushed back her chair. "Not to rush either of you," she said to Lilith and Aurora, "but I'm beat. I can either put up the mess now, or you can do it when you're finished eating."

Both women got to their feet.

"I'm all done," Aurora announced.

"I am as well," Lilith agreed, even though she still held a pizza slice.

That is, she held the slice until Dodger jumped up and snatched it straight out of her hand.

"Ack!" Jerking her hand away, Lilith stumbled back.

Dodger shot under the table with his stolen booty and finished it in two big bites.

Aurora snapped, "Bad dog!"

"Don't yell at him." Yardley wasn't sure what the right reaction should be for a pizza-thieving dog, but she wouldn't allow anyone else to mistreat him.

"He might have bitten me," Lilith gasped.

"No, he just wanted your food." At least, she didn't think he would bite. She bent to look under the table. Dodger's tongue lolled out and he wagged his tail. "I'll work on his manners."

Travis snickered.

"What?" Aurora and Lilith said together.

With a shrug and a widened grin, Travis said, "Yardley is so good at everything she does, I imagine she'll have Dodger saying 'please' and 'thank you' the next time he steals his meal."

Yardley imagined it as well, and that did it. Biting her lip didn't help. Once she started chuckling, it was all over and the next thing she knew, she was slumped against Travis, laughing her ass off.

THE SUN SETTLED low over the horizon, sending wide streaks of magenta across the sky. Hands in his pockets, Travis admired the way Yardley patiently showed Dodger around the yard. The little beast was happy now that he'd gotten his share of the pizza.

His smile crept back as he thought about Yardley's laughter. Her Aunt Lilith had fled the room with a red face and compressed lips.

Yeah, Aurora had wanted that pizza for herself.

She had used the excuse of checking on her sister's "overset nerves," though Travis figured they'd both just wanted to dodge out of cleanup duty. He hadn't minded helping. With Yardley and her unexpected reactions to situations, every moment, no matter how mundane, was made more enjoyable.

A short time later, sitting on a bench positioned under a flowering tree with potted plants at either side, Yardley tipped back her head and closed her eyes. "Wow, it was a busy day."

Dodger, held loosely with the leash, finished investigating a flower, then hopped up on the bench and licked her cheek.

"Oh." Smiling, she hugged the dog while wiping her cheek on her shoulder.

"I think I want in on that action." Sitting beside her, Travis turned her face toward him and pressed a lingering kiss to her lips.

"You're not nearly as slobbery as Dodger." She leaned into him.

"Good to know." The night had cooled down and she looked ready to nod off. "Are you sure you don't want me to take him home with me?"

"I'm sure. Dodger stays with me." As if in approval, the dog wagged his tail and sprawled out over her lap. Obviously, he was tired, too. "If you can come by tomorrow to help set up something, that'd be great." She glanced around the small yard. "Ideas?"

Not really. There was very little open space in the yard. "We could maybe put a runner between those two trees. Then he could go from one end to the other without trampling anything." Travis already knew how that would go, though. "He's going to bark." And probably freak out a little. "He was tied at the park, and then abandoned—"

"I won't tie him, not unless I'm right there with him." She chewed her lower lip. "I have meetings in the afternoon."

"On a Saturday?"

"On any day that's convenient for the clients." She stifled a yawn with the back of her hand. "I'll see if Mimi can come over to visit with Dodger while I review some paperwork with the client."

"Or," he said, making a leap without thinking it through, "I could pick him up for a few hours. He could go to the house with me, hang out there while I work."

He scratched the dog's head. "He likes me, and I assume you know I'll give him plenty of attention."

Half smiling, Yardley shook her head. He wasn't sure if that was a rejection of his offer or amusement that he'd made it. "You know you won't get anything done with him there."

"I'll get him a big chew to work on." He took in the dog's watchful eyes and added optimistically, "Should be fine."

Yardley put her head on his shoulder, which prompted him to ease his other arm around her.

Damn, but he enjoyed holding her like this. He loved the scent of her skin and the comfortable way she fit against him. She was a small woman with proud shoulders that carried a big load as if it were her right, her privilege to do so. In so many ways, he understood that.

He was the type of person who'd rather be in charge, even knowing it'd mean more work, than to have to rely on others.

Cupping her cheek, he tipped up her face. "What do you say?" Not giving her a chance to answer, he brushed his lips over hers for another light kiss.

"It'll give me an excuse to see you more, and it'll help Dodger to learn to trust." Travis saw in her eyes, which looked silver in the night, that she didn't want to. "You can't do it all, honey. No one can. Let me help. Please."

"Only for a few hours."

Her agreement felt like a gift. "You can call me when you're done and I'll bring him back over."

"Or," she said, "I can pick up food and we can share a meal before I bring him home." She nudged him. "You're not the only one who appreciates a good excuse to spend more time together."

Travis smiled. "I like making deals with you, Yardley Belanger."

"I like doing everything with you, Travis Long." This time she kissed him, and typical of Yardley, she went all out. By the time she and Dodger walked him to his truck, he knew he wouldn't last a month. Hell, he wasn't sure he'd last a week.

He needed Yardley—and soon.

"WE'VE FALLEN INTO such a wonderful pattern," Yardley told Mimi on Wednesday morning. "I have to say, seeing Travis every day has been awesome."

For once, Mimi was able to wait on Yardley instead of the other way around. Now that they'd finished the chicken salad on croissants that she'd prepared for lunch, Mimi handed her a cup of dark roast coffee, which paired perfectly with the sweet cranberry muffins Yardley had brought along. "It's been helpful, too, right?"

"Very. Dodger loves him as much as he loves me. He's gotten to where he's excited when Travis shows up, and he's happy to jump into his truck." She grinned. "He bribes the dog with treats, you know."

What Mimi knew was that her girl positively glowed. Her relationship with Travis wasn't what she had expected, but it sure was good for Yardley. She looked more relaxed, happier, and for that she owed Travis a debt.

They were on the back porch, shaded by a large umbrella attached to the table, watching Kevin toss a stick for Dodger. So far she'd been able to figure out meals that were easy for Kevin to eat one-handed—like the chicken salad. Having him around was great, but he was getting grumbly with too much time on his hands. Kevin was used to working forty-plus hours, then pitching in around the house too.

She'd suggested that he go fishing with his buddies, but he'd nixed that idea. He said there wasn't any way in hell he'd let the guys bait his hook, and he wasn't yet allowed to flex his injured hand.

The minute he was cleared, Mimi planned to make her moves on him.

Not that the extra snuggles hadn't been nice. Having him around all day, getting additional random kisses and extra affectionate hugs was pretty sweet. And she did enjoy the bonus freedom she had for simple things like, oh, running to the restroom without worrying that Sammy would choose that moment to start wailing.

"I think Kevin likes that dog as much as you do." Mimi put a few more pieces of dry cereal on the tray of Sammy's high chair. The baby was fascinated with Dodger, kicking her pudgy legs anytime he ran close, then watching wide-eyed when he dashed after a stick.

"Who wouldn't love Dodger? He's so sweet."

"Oh, I don't know. Cruella and Maleficent?"

Yardley curled her lip. "Yeah, they're not happy about having an energetic dog around, but overall they just ignore him."

In between bitching a lot, Mimi would bet. "Don't let them bother you."

Yardley smiled. "I'm not."

No, she really wasn't. Pleased, Mimi reclaimed her own seat. "I can't believe you two still haven't done the deed."

With a double take, Yardley asked, "What?"

"You and Travis. Obviously, you're falling in love."

"Yeah." Dropping back in her seat, Yardley sighed. "Pretty sure I am."

Awesome! Yardley deserved to find her forever love. Mimi wouldn't have cared if he was an unemployed clown, as long as he made her happy, but Travis was an all-around great guy. "So remind me again, why are we waiting?"

"*We* aren't. You're welcome to get busy anytime you want. I'm waiting because I don't want to pressure Travis."

"This is some weird alternate reality. You realize that, right?"

"Because guys are usually all about sex?" She eyed Mimi meaningfully. "And women aren't?"

"Okay, so yeah. Most people are all about sex, especially when with someone special. And he's special, right? I know you want it. Him. Whatever." She flapped a hand. "The whole shebang."

Yardley groaned. "Don't talk about it. I'm already on the ragged edge."

Mimi glanced out at the yard, seeing Kevin sit with his back to a tree to let Dodger crawl all over him. She shot to her feet to call out, "Be careful! Don't let him hurt your hand."

"No," Kevin said. "I'm going to be reckless. I like being a man of leisure."

She snorted, saying in an aside to Yardley, "No, he doesn't. It's making him nuts." Then louder, for Kevin, she yelled, "I mean it!"

"Yes, ma'am." Kevin blew her a kiss.

"He is such a smart-ass," Mimi said around her smile.

"I like seeing you like this." Yardley reached across the table for her hand. "You look so happy."

"I am." Lowering her voice, Mimi ensured Kevin wouldn't hear. "For once, I get to take care of him, and I'm enjoying it."

"Pretty sure he feels the same." Yardley shook her head. "You two are still dancing around things."

"Well, I was going to discuss stuff with him, but then he came home hurt, and now everything is different."

"No it isn't." Yardley gave her a stern look. "It might be on hold, but it isn't different."

Okay, so she was right. "I will, soon. I promise." Maybe after he was cleared for full use of his hand again. "For now, I just want to enjoy the way it is."

Yardley laughed. "With your husband maimed?"

"With my husband a little less independent." Mimi wanted him to need her—the same way she needed him.

Kevin started toward them, his hand elevated and resting against his chest.

It had to be thumping with discomfort, not that Kevin would complain. Elevating his hand helped, but he probably needed to sit somewhere comfortable and ice it again. It was still badly swollen, and horribly bruised. She knew because she helped him rewrap it each day.

Jumping up, Mimi pulled out a patio chair for him. "You want some coffee?"

He stepped past the chair, bent to give her a sound kiss, then kissed Sammy too, and even pressed a quick kiss to Yardley's cheek. "I'll get my own, babe. Relax and visit." He went on past them to the patio door, heading for the kitchen. "C'mon, Dodger." The dog trotted after him.

Mimi threw up her hands. "I could have gotten that for you," she tossed at him.

"Love you," he volleyed back, and disappeared into the house.

Eyes narrowing, she dropped into her chair. "See what I mean? If you looked up the definition of *stubborn*, I bet there'd be a big ole pic of Kevin wearing a smug grin."

Yardley shook her head. "I'm starting to think you just like to complain."

Struck by that observation, Mimi put her head in her hands and groaned. "You're right. I'm becoming a bitch."

"Not even close to what I said! But if you want my opinion—"

Fingers parting, she peeked at Yardley. "Do I?"

"Yes, because you know I love you with all my heart and would only tell you what you need to hear."

After a two-second hesitation, Mimi said, "Yeah, I do." She dropped her hands and sat up straight. "Okay, lay it on me, but be fast. Kevin will be back any second."

"It's *you* making yourself unhappy, not Kevin. First you think it's the body changes from carrying Sammy—"

"My body is different."

"—and then you say he's not attentive enough, that he wants to fish all the time—"

"He does! You know how he loves fishing."

"And now you complain because he won't let you baby him."

"Not *baby* him," Mimi grumbled. "But I should be an equal partner in this marriage, right?" Only she knew things were not equal. Not even close. "And that means he should lean on me occasionally." *The same way I lean on him.*

Yardley rolled her eyes. "If you just remember that he loves you and you love him, everything else should be easier. Not perfect, because no relationship ever is."

Very true. Her girl was full of wisdom.

"He loves your body, baby changes or not. Anyone

can see that. And he does lean on you." Yardley raised one brow. "Obviously in more ways than you realize."

"Say it," Mimi said. "You're holding back again. I can tell." She made a gesture toward herself. "Give it to me. I can handle it."

Since Yardley always gave her total honesty, she said, "All right, fine. If you weren't so determined to be critical of yourself, you'd see what everyone sees. Kevin is worried about you."

"About me? Why?"

Another eye roll. "If I know your hubby—and I do—he's probably picking up on a few things, same as me. I can tell you're stressed, so you better believe Kevin has noticed. The difference is that you're not talking to him about it, so he has no clue what's going on, which I'm sure makes it worse."

"Damn," Mimi said as realization sank in. "You're right. On top of his physical discomfort, and frustration over not working, I'm worrying him."

"Exactly. And you know how Kevin is. If he thinks you're struggling in any way, he could lose his hand completely and he wouldn't burden you more." She ran her finger in a circle. "See how this is all coming back around to you?"

"Yeah." That really did make sense. "Kevin is so in-tune to me, he'd pick up on even the smallest thing."

"Yup."

"Obviously, this is why I keep you around."

Kevin opened the patio door. "Because of her muffins? They really are great." He and Dodger rejoined them at the table, Kevin in a chair, Dodger under the table, where he rested against Yardley's feet.

"Hey," Yardley said in mock affront. "I'm more than tasty muffins, you know."

He grinned. "That sounded seriously sexual. Try that line on your new guy and see what he thinks."

Mimi laughed. "Guys always have sex on the brain."

"Especially guys who are married to hot babes," Kevin said with such a heated look, it made her lady parts perk up.

"Annnd, that's my cue." Yardley gulped back the last of her coffee and stood, which prompted Dodger to go on the alert, poised and ready to follow if Yardley moved.

Mimi thought he was the cutest dog ever.

"No cue," Kevin promised. "Not that I wouldn't be totally on board for some afternoon delight." He bobbed his eyebrows. "But the pip-squeak is wide awake, and even if she wasn't, my bum hand is a problem."

Yardley sent her an *I-told-you-so* grin. "I have to head out anyway, but hey, anytime I can be of assistance, let me know. I'll take Sammy to the park."

"And that," Kevin said, "is even better than your muffins."

Mimi sat there, surprised by it all and wondering if Kevin had overheard their conversation. She tried to recall exactly what she'd said but wasn't sure.

Yardley picked up on her silence and filled in. "Thinking of my new guy and your hot babe reminds me, I want to do a dinner party."

"Dinner party?" Mimi asked, pulled from her thoughts by the cautious way Yardley announced that.

"You and Kevin, Travis, Sheena and her fiancé, Todd, if he can make it."

Mimi pursed her mouth. "And your mother and aunt?"

"If they'll attend." She shrugged. "If they don't want to, though, they can skip it."

"Hmm." Mimi knew she was leaving something out. If not an issue with her mother and aunt, then what? "What aren't you telling me?"

"I'm working up to it."

Kevin looked back and forth between them. "How do you know she's leaving something out?"

Both women glanced at him.

"She knows me well," Yardley said.

"There are benefits to being friends for life," Mimi boasted. "Loyalty, love, support—and the ability to mind read."

Yardley laughed. "True. The thing is… I want Betty to attend." As if she thought Mimi might argue against the idea, she rushed on with, "She's actually very nice."

"Uh-huh."

"Nic*er* than what we thought, anyway. And I'm sure she's lonely."

Mimi nudged Kevin. "Not that you'll ever repeat that, okay? Anything Yardley says to me is in total confidence."

Kevin pretended to lock his lips—then immediately opened his mouth and bit off half a muffin.

Satisfied, Mimi turned back to Yardley. "You don't have to convince me, hon. I'm all in. especially if it'll help you in your current campaign." Again, she turned to Kevin. "She's going to be Betty's liaison with the town businesses."

"Nice," Kevin said, distracted with his food. "Go, Yardley. I'm rooting for you."

She laughed.

Mimi said, "Yeah, he's rooting for his food, but whatever." Kevin was a big guy with a robust appetite, and no one was immune to Yardley's baked goods. "So, a dinner party."

"Doesn't that sound fun?"

It sounded like another of Yardley's do-gooder efforts. Clearly, Betty was the benefactor this time. Mimi had already gotten an earful about how misunderstood Betty was. Or maybe Yardley was hoping to give Sheena a little R & R since the poor girl was so stressed about her big day.

Mimi had spoken with Sheena a few times now. She liked her. Sheena was open and friendly and, unfortunately, suffering some hideous morning sickness that didn't have the decency to stick to mornings.

"I haven't asked anyone else yet. I wanted to make sure you didn't have other plans the second weekend of next month."

Mimi explained to Kevin, "This will be Yardley's way of expanding Betty's world."

Yardley started to object, but then she said with a shrug, "Close enough."

"Count us in." He looked at Mimi. "I assume you want to go?"

"If your mom will sit with Sammy."

"If she can't," Yardley said, "bring her along. I'm sure Sheena would love to meet her."

Mimi agreed. It'd probably do Sheena good, if she was feeling up to it, to get some exposure to a baby. She claimed she knew nothing about kids. "I assume Dodger will be there, too?"

"Naturally." Yardley grinned down at the dog. "He's less needy now since he's been spending time with Travis also, but he still likes to stick close to me whenever possible."

"So your new guy." Kevin reached over to pet Dodger. "Things are moving right along?"

"I've seen him nearly every day since we got the dog. You'll like him. He's terrific."

"Already do," said Kevin. "He listened when I gave him advice for his sister, and I figure if you two approve of him, he must pass muster."

"I can't fault your logic." Yardley glanced at the time on her phone. "And now I really do have to go or I'll be late getting to Betty's." She reattached Dodger's leash to his harness.

"Go on," Kevin told Mimi. "Sammy and I will entertain ourselves while you walk her out to her car."

"Thanks." She stepped around the table and they left together. "You're taking Dodger with you to Betty's?"

"Yes, and I hope Betty doesn't mind."

Mimi wished she could be a fly on the wall. No one in town would count on Betty befriending Yardley, attending a dinner party, agreeing to a liaison, or being taken with a stray dog. Yardley had a gift, though, so Mimi would never bet against her. "Let me know what I can do to help with the dinner party, or with anything, really."

"Will do." She opened the back door for Dodger and got him in his doggy seat, then turned back to Mimi. "Now you."

Knowing exactly what Yardley would say, she smiled. "You made your point, hon. I promise I'll clear the air with Kevin."

"Thank you." Yardley gave her a very big hug. "I'd love to talk more, but I have to go. I want to get the rest of these muffins to Betty before she locks me out for being late."

Mimi laughed. Yup, that sounded like Betty. "Have fun—and thank you."

"That's the plan." With that parting comment, Yardley got in the car and left.

Mimi hustled back to Kevin. He was in the process of kissing Sammy's toes and making her laugh.

Pausing, her heart full of love, Mimi watched them for a while before coming closer and drawing his attention, just as she intended.

He said, "Yardley seems like a woman on a mission."

"To conquer the entire town, I know." Mimi kept walking. "She'll do it too. One way or another, she's going to make a difference."

"I meant with her guy."

"Travis? I think she's so busy falling in love, she can't plan ahead." She reached Kevin and took his face in her hands. "I love you."

Looping an arm around her waist, he opened his un-injured hand over her backside. "I love you, too."

"Even though I look dumpy now?"

"What the hell?" His hand stilled, then delivered a light swat as he frowned at her. "You're gorgeous, Mimi."

"I've gained weight and my stomach…" She dropped her gaze, wishing it didn't bother her so much. "I should try working out or something, but—"

"But you're busy being the most amazing mother in the world." With his bandaged hand, he touched her chin, bringing her face back up so he could look into her eyes. "You had a baby. *Our* baby." He held her gaze, his expression somber and deep, searching hers. "Your body is different now, but I swear to you, it's only made you sexier."

Tears clouded her eyes even as she laughed. She felt eons away from sexy. "You love me, so you're biased."

"I love you, yes, so damned much. But I'm also a man, and I know a hot chick when I see one." He grinned his rascal's grin. "And babe, you're smokin' hot."

Mimi glanced at Sammy, but her daughter was in the zone, caught between being awake and napping. Two more minutes and she'd be out. Normally, Mimi would have quickly cleaned her face and hands, checked her diaper, and gotten her into her bed.

This time, she straddled her husband's lap instead. "If that's true, why haven't we had sex like we used to?"

Startled surprise widened his eyes, and then emotion narrowed them. "Jesus, Mimi. I almost lost you." He gathered her close. So close. To a place she loved to be.

"Don't hurt your hand!"

He hugged her tighter. "Forget my hand."

"No, I will not." She pushed back to scowl at him. "You love me, I get that. Well, I love you, too." To make a point, she kissed him hard and fast. "You're my high school sweetheart, my one real love, my better half, my... *everything*." Breathing a little heavier, she whispered, "When you hurt, I hurt, too."

"Aw, Mimi." He smoothed her curls, his large hand so gentle, so wonderfully familiar. "That's exactly how I feel. Except I saw you almost die." His voice thickened, his nostrils flared. "I saw you go pale and I thought I was going to lose you."

Seeing his agony, really understanding it for the first time, she whispered, "I'm sorry." She'd known, and yet... she hadn't.

"I can't ever go through that again. You think it hurts you to see my hand cut? A *hand*? Imagine..." He choked off the words, cursing low in a voice gone raw. "No, don't imagine it. I don't want you to. Just promise me that you'll never leave me."

"I won't." Overcome with love, she kissed his face all over. "I swear I won't."

"While you're in an agreeable mood, don't ever put yourself down either. You're *it* for me, Mimi. The best of everything. You're funny and sometimes mean."

She gave a tearful laugh—because it was true.

"You somehow manage to make the 'frazzled mom look' super hot."

"It's a knack," she teased, already feeling like her old self.

"You're mine. Whether you're in mom mode, daughter mode, friend mode or wife mode. I admire the hell out of all of it. And FYI, I want you all the time. Like, seriously, all the freaking time. When I wake up before you and you're snoring with your mouth open and your face smooshed—"

"I don't snore!" Such an awful image.

"—or when you're covered in baby food and spit-up and God knows what else—"

She wrinkled her nose.

"—and now." He kissed her neck, nuzzling against her in all those awesome, sensitive spots that he knew so well. "When you're sitting on me," he growled. "And getting me hard."

"Am I?" she teased, rocking the tiniest bit. "Maybe we should—"

"No way. I won't perform under par. Now that my lady has demanded the whole show, she's going to get the whole show…if she can wait until they take these stupid stitches out."

"That sounds wonderful." Mimi removed herself from him and began gathering dishes.

"Just like that?" Extreme disappointment colored his tone.

"I'm an agreeable wife. I can wait for the main event." She headed for the patio door, but then looked back at him over her shoulder. "As long as I can get some preliminary bouts before then."

He inhaled sharply and quickly said, "That can be arranged."

"Good. Because honey, you might be down a hand, but both of mine are working just fine and dandy." She laughed at his expression, at the flare of heat in his eyes and how quickly he stood from his chair. *Bless you, Yardley.* She should have opened up to Kevin a long time ago. Luckily, she had a friend who wasn't afraid to tell her when she was being a total dumbass.

Well, tonight this dumbass was going to have a very good time…with the man of her dreams. She could hardly wait!

10

Yardley got to Betty's five minutes late, and she was horribly afraid she'd lose the progress she'd already made. As she knew from the town council meetings, Betty was big on punctuality. Holding a covered dish of muffins in one hand, she led Dodger from the car on his leash, lecturing him about behaving. "We're already late, so do not pee anywhere inside. That would be catastrophic. Do you understand?"

Dodger wagged his tail while staring at her adoringly. His good ear twitched, perking up to listen.

His poor injured ear remained bandaged.

"And try not to slobber on her. I know it's difficult for you. Slobbering seems to come naturally." Oh, his big brown eyes just melted her heart, and she had to lean down to give him some affection. "Somehow, it'll be okay, baby. I promise."

Dodger turned once, getting tangled in the leash, and she took a moment to right things. "There, that's better.

Don't want you tripping, do we?" Finally, she got them on their way.

Before she reached the front door, it opened and Betty stepped out. She stared at Dodger, her gaze fixed, her expression oddly absorbed.

Ready to bluster her way through things, Yardley breezily said, "So sorry we're late. I stopped by to see Mimi. Her husband injured his hand at work, you know. I figured we could spare a few muffins, so I gave them half. Kevin loved them, and I hope you will too." Drawing a breath, she waited.

Nothing. Not even a blink.

With a wan smile, Yardley added, "I wasn't held up too long." After all, she was only a few minutes behind.

Betty never diverted her attention from the dog.

With no choice but to stop on the walkway, which put her slightly below the covered stoop where Betty stood, she said, "So...this is Dodger." Dodger chose that moment to sprinkle a flower. *Shoot.* "He's, ah, my new dog."

To her surprise, Betty sat on the stoop and said, "Come here, sweetheart," in total, high-pitched baby talk.

Dodger, the big softie, kicked a little grass over where he'd just gone, then rushed to her, his tail, his butt, his whole body wagging!

No lie, it was like love at first sight.

Yardley stood there, caught between bemusement and hilarity. *Good boy, Dodger.* Thanks to the dog, Betty didn't even seem aware of her tardiness.

"Mind if I sit, too?"

Betty and Dodger ignored her, so Yardley stepped past them to set the container of muffins on a wicker chair and lowered herself—uninvited—to the party. "He's a cutie, isn't he?"

"You're beautiful, aren't you, sweetheart? Yes, you are," Betty gushed in a tone that made Yardley choke. She'd never seen Betty like this. She knew Dodger had a lot of charm, that was undeniable, but clearly she'd underestimated his influence.

"If I'd known you had a dog, I'd have bought him a few treats." Betty glanced at her. "What happened to his ear?"

"It's such a terrible thing. My heart breaks all over again just thinking about it." Yardley explained to Betty about her date with Travis, the trip to the park, his secret spot hidden in the woods...and how they'd found Dodger there. "We're pretty sure someone left him there tied to a tree so he'd..." She couldn't say it. "Did you see his neck? That's where the rope rubbed him as he tried to escape."

Betty went red-faced with anger.

"We took him to an emergency vet clinic and got him checked out first. Part of his ear is gone. We're not sure how that happened." It devastated her anew, so she added, as much for herself as for Betty, "He's overall okay, though, and he's the most lovable dog ever."

When she finished the story, Betty huffed out a breath. "Despicable! The park rangers there used to be lackluster at best, but I thought they'd improved over the years. How did they not find him?"

"Well, it was a very out-of-the-way spot, which I guess was the point." Her heart clenched. Poor Dodger. "Travis went back the next day to make certain Dodger didn't have any siblings, but he didn't find anything. It didn't even occur to us at first."

"Cemetery should form a committee to search those woods regularly for animals."

Yardley blinked in surprise—and agreement. "That's a wonderful idea." Betty was most comfortable in a committee setting, so naturally that's where her thoughts had gone. Yardley thought it was unlikely they'd find another dog in Dodger's predicament—surely there weren't that many unfeeling people around—but her heart was in the right place. "Wouldn't a shelter here in Cemetery be amazing, too? A place for homeless pets?"

Betty shot her a look. *"What?"*

Now that she'd said it, Yardley loved the idea. "It'd be especially nice if we could offer assistance to other, busier areas."

Full of umbrage, Betty stiffened her back and glared. "Are you thinking of giving up this fine dog?"

The demand took her by surprise, and Yardley gave a light push to Betty's shoulder for even thinking such a thing. "Absolutely not!" Then she realized what she'd done and panicked—which equated to her speaking loud and fast while patting Betty's shoulder in apology. "I was thinking of sparing any *other* dogs from the same fate. If people who don't want their animals—which is most definitely not me—knew there was a safe place where they could take them, then maybe they wouldn't get dumped in the woods, or worse, tied up somewhere to die as Dodger was."

Betty put her hands over the dog's ears and replied in a whisper, "Whoever did that needs to be left tied in the woods!"

Yardley grinned.

"Well, it's true." Oh so gently, Betty petted Dodger. "I have no tolerance for cruelty."

This time Yardley only rested her hand on Betty's shoulder. "I love that about you, how fierce you are in defending this town, and now homeless animals, too. If only we could be in charge of that, right?"

"We can. One way or another, I'll get the council and the citizens of Cemetery to approve the expenditure for a shelter." She reached up to pat Yardley's hand. "Perhaps it would help if you did take over as a liaison. It would free up some of my time so I could form the new committee. It's no easy feat, you know, putting together all the details we'll need."

Holy smokes, did she hear that correctly? Yardley stilled, shocked senseless but also pleased that Betty would use their discussion to give in gracefully on other matters. She schooled her features and attempted to look thoughtful instead of thrilled. "I believe you're right. It would certainly help me out."

"How so?"

"Well, if we announce that I'll be a liaison to give you time for other pursuits, whoever keeps sticking those candidacy signs around town will have to accept defeat. They'll know we're a united team, not competitors."

"Yes, that makes sense." Betty stood, and then held out her hand. "We have an agreement?"

"Yes, ma'am." She tried to keep her expression impassive, but a grin got the better of her as she took Betty's hand. "You know what I consider the best part of this whole thing?"

Betty gave her attention back to Dodger. "What's that?"

"Our new friendship." Yardley wanted to hug it to her chest and cherish it. "Thank you for that, Betty. It means a lot."

"Oh, stop." Betty turned and opened the door, patting her hip so Dodger would follow, then waiting for Yardley to grab the muffins before she entered as well. "You know it's nice for an old lady, too."

"Old lady?" Yardley made a point of looking around. "Where? I don't see her."

Betty laughed. *Laughed.* And it was absolutely magical, something she wanted to hear more often.

Yardley could hardly believe everything had happened so quickly, so easily. Half afraid to push her luck, she asked, "Should we announce our plans at the next council meeting?"

"Yes. And given that this little boy is so attached to you, feel free to bring him along." Betty turned, her weathered face lit with excitement. "I know! We could make him a Cemetery mascot."

Yardley winced. "Okay, first order of business." She took Betty's hand in both of hers and softened her tone. "Please, *please* don't make me tag my beautiful dog with…that name. He and I would both be honored for him to be a mascot, but for a place where they keep dead people?"

"Pfft. For our lovely town."

"Which is called *Cemetery.*"

Betty's mouth firmed, sending a web of little wrinkles into her papery cheeks. But it was her twinkling eyes that gave her away.

The old fraud was more amused than offended.

"Betty?" Yardley leaned down to stare her right in the eyes. "How about we just call him the *town* mascot. What do you say? Pretty please?"

Several more seconds passed where Betty kept her waiting, and then… "Fine. But don't get used to getting your way, young lady. I won't just roll over every time we—"

Dodger stopped sniffing the carpet to do a perfect roll, then sat up to look at them with expectation.

Speechless, they both stared.

"He rolled over," Betty whispered.

And Dodger, having heard her, did it again.

Delighted, Yardley clapped her hands. "Oh my gosh, and look. I think he wants a treat now!"

"I have just the thing." Betty hurried into the kitchen, so Yardley went with her.

Issuing a bark, Dodger raced after them.

Betty gifted the dog with a cocktail wiener, and because he loved it, and she had more, they went through several commands until they learned all his tricks. He could sit, roll over, and bark, but he utterly failed at staying. If Yardley moved, he was right on her heels.

Both she and Betty understood that reaction.

"He's so smart. I had no idea. I mean, he's young, and whoever had him clearly didn't love him."

"Maybe one person loved him, but someone else didn't."

Like Mimi loved her, but her mother... No. She wasn't going down that path. "Do you mind if I give him some water?" Yardley withdrew a special water bottle/bowl contraption that unfolded.

"Of course. I should have thought of that." Betty put a dish towel on the floor. "Put it there in case he splashes."

Dodger most definitely splashed. And since he left the bowl while water still dripped from his furry chin, his spills didn't stay on the dish towel.

Rather than be offended, Betty was amused. She got some paper towels and started to clean up the mess.

"Here, let me." Yardley couldn't imagine Betty bending down to the floor. Yes, she moved well for someone tipping toward ninety, but age showed in how stiffly she moved. Taking the towels from her, Yardley wiped up the water, then Dodger's chin, too.

"He's an exuberant drinker," Betty said as she poured them each a lemonade and sat at the table. "I imagine he eats the same way."

"Like he's starving," Yardley confirmed. "Which, at first, I guess he was."

"Poor thing. It'll take him time to get over being so cruelly abandoned. I'm glad he has you."

Touched by that sentiment, Yardley washed her hands, then joined Betty at the table. "You're so patient with him."

"Of course, I am." When Betty opened the container, the scent of fresh cranberry muffins and sweetness filled the air. "These smell delicious."

Yardley hoped she liked them. She'd taken extra care with her baking since it would be her first time sharing with Betty. "I wish my mother and aunt were the same. Every day, they make it clear that they resent Dodger being there." Much as they'd always seemed to resent her. "Not that I'll let it sway me. He's my dog and I'm keeping him."

Betty went quiet as she broke a muffin in half and took a bite. "They taste delicious as well." Another stretch of silence while they both ate, and then Betty said, "I tried, but I can't hold back."

"Hold back?"

"It's not in my nature. When something needs to be said, I say it."

Bracing herself, Yardley nodded. "Please, feel free." Honestly, it had all been too good to be true anyway.

Betty didn't hesitate. "You're intelligent and observant enough to realize that Aurora and Lilith are incapable of appreciating anything or anyone. There's something missing in them. They've been that way from the day I met them."

So…not at all what Yardley had expected. "Um…"

"Now, that's not an outright insult, so don't go defending them."

Had she been about to do that? Probably. Defending her family seemed like the thing to do—even when Yardley knew they didn't deserve it. With Betty, she wouldn't bother. She told herself it would be disrespectful to argue with an elder.

Yeah, that excuse worked just fine.

"It's who they are," Betty said. "I'm not sure at this point they can change, but it's for certain that they don't want to." She stared at Yardley from under lowered brows. "You've made it too easy for them to stay the same."

Was that true? Mimi had often said something similar. "I guess I just fell into the habit of making it all work." And that usually meant doing things herself. At least that way she knew it got done. Their livelihood depended on it.

Betty shocked her stupid when she put a frail veined hand to Yardley's cheek. "I know they've never appreciated *you*, so why would they care about a dog? No, it's better that you don't expect too much from them. I admire you for your loyalty, always have, but I've often wondered why you didn't walk away from them."

"They're family."

After a brief scrutiny, Betty smiled and dropped her hand. "That attitude is what makes you so admirable. And your tenacity, of course." She took another small nibble of the muffin, chewed and swallowed, then pinned Yardley again with her direct gaze. "I shouldn't admit this, but every time I would see you in the audience at the town council meeting, it would energize me. I'd know I was in for a rousing discussion."

Fairly certain that her jaw had just dropped, Yardley asked, "You did?"

"Oh yes. Made my blood sing—and at my age, that doesn't happen very often. Many a night, instead of feeling lonely, I'd ponder how I was going to deal with you."

Huh. That didn't sound…all that bad. Yardley fought a grin.

Betty finished off the muffin and drank some of her lemonade. "In fact, this, having a friendly visit and eating such a tasty treat, never crossed my mind. I was too busy figuring out ways to best you."

The laugh just bubbled out. "I think those are some of the sweetest compliments I've ever gotten." Compliments, compliments, everywhere these days.

How nice to know she had filled Betty's evenings and eased her loneliness. That made Yardley feel…important. Special. Not just to Mimi, who loved her always, but now Betty appreciated her, too.

"Don't get all sappy," Betty chided. "I'm sure the entire town feels the same way. You bring life to everything. Surely, even with your depressing mother and aunt, you've realized that by now."

The insults to Aurora and Lilith were gaining steam and making her uncomfortable. Old habits were hard to break, and Yardley had the terrible urge to "explain" her mother and aunt, as if such a thing were even possible.

She cleared her throat and changed the topic. "Why did you never marry, Betty?"

"Oh, I had my romances," she admitted with a sly smile. "But I'm an independent sort and I didn't want a man interfering with that. I'm sure you're too young to remember, but twenty years ago, I was still visiting my Edgar in another town." She leaned in to whisper, "I won't say where, and I won't give you his last name, but oh my, he was a handsome rascal."

"You sly dog," Yardley teased, thrilled for her new friend. "Carrying on a torrid love affair."

"That it was." Betty sighed. "So very torrid."

Yardley tried to remember Betty twenty years ago. The woman would have been sixty-six! "I was only eleven or so back then. Not real observant about romances, I guess."

"You and Mimi were always up to something," Betty said with a grin. "It amused me back then, watching Aurora fret over you."

"Over how I embarrassed her, you mean." Yardley remembered it well.

"That too. You were a very backward child, and no wonder, with the examples you had. It amazed me how your mother would style your hair and match your clothes and somehow within an hour it was all in disarray."

Things hadn't changed much in the last twenty years—except that she was learning to accept her faults and move on.

"I always thought your mother needed to find herself another man so that she wasn't so focused on you. After all, you needed time to just…be."

Time she'd never really gotten. Back then. But now? Now she could be herself with Mimi and Travis and Dodger…and Betty.

Betty shook her head. "A romance would have softened Aurora, but I'm not sure what man would have her."

"Betty!" Yardley barely held back her laugh.

"Unkind of me, I know, but it's still true." When a rooster crowed, Betty looked up at the clock on the wall. "It's getting late and I'm sure you have other places to be."

She did, actually. They'd spent far more time on learning Dodger's tricks than she'd realized. "I've enjoyed this so much. Can we do it again? I know Dodger would love another visit."

"I'd be pleased to have you stop by anytime. I'm always here, other than the town council meetings on Thursday evenings, and my hair appointments each month. Let me know what works for you and next time, I'll cook dinner for us."

What an amazing and unexpected offer. "That'd be great, but I don't want to put you to any trouble."

"Nonsense. It'll be nice to fix food enough for two."

That statement struck Yardley's heart. How sad would it be to always cook for one, to eat all alone, night after night? Yes, her mother and aunt were oftentimes difficult, but they were company. Steadfast. Reliable. "Thank you. I think that sounds wonderful."

The mention of dinner might have been a perfect segue to the dinner party she wanted to plan, but she didn't say anything to Betty yet. First, she'd see if Travis was available, and then Sheena and Todd.

The party would give Betty a chance to get to know the others better.

And it would show her mother and aunt, heck, the entire town that she and Betty were getting along just fine. Better than fine.

Now they were special friends.

For once, his sister seemed to be her old self. She wasn't green, gagging, or looking washed out. Instead, she was full of excitement as he drove them to Yardley's house for a pre-wedding meeting. Apparently, Yardley wanted to show her the samples of the flower displays for the wedding, and since Todd finally had some time off, they'd tour Wilson's barn again and go over the layout.

He wondered if Todd had arranged the time away because of Sheena's sick stomach. Surely, he'd noticed her barely banked anticipation at having him involved. She desperately wanted Todd's feedback. Travis only hoped Todd wouldn't disappoint her.

They'd now had the dog for two weeks, and Travis had enjoyed every evening with Yardley. Twice she'd been to his house. He couldn't deny how much he liked her compliments of his design choices. She'd also—very casually—made a few suggestions that had been perfect.

In fact, he was starting to like the house so much that the idea of selling it to strangers didn't suit him. To family, though...

He cast a sideways glance at his sister and Todd on the bench seat of his truck beside him. It had been Sheena's idea for them to ride together, and Travis had to wonder if her plan was for him and Todd to get to know each other better.

Fine by him. He'd met Todd many times, of course. They weren't strangers, and yet, they weren't really friends either. Given the circumstances, he wouldn't mind building on that relationship. Already his views on Todd had altered.

Like young people in love, Todd and Sheena held hands. Only Todd wasn't so young. Oddly, the age difference didn't bother Travis as much as it usually did. Maybe it was seeing the frantic way Todd had cared for Sheena during her vicious bouts of morning sickness...

but actually, his attitude shift had started when Todd visited him, man to man, to say he'd pay back the wedding costs.

He'd seen Todd differently after that. And now? Now he knew that Todd made his sister happy, and as Yardley had said, that was the most important thing.

Every day Travis thought about a niece or nephew, and his anticipation grew. He couldn't wait to hold a tiny baby.

Even Todd's claim that Travis would inherit his whole family didn't seem like a problem. For so long it had just been him and Sheena. Knowing she'd have so many more people in her life felt comforting and, oddly enough, it relieved some of the pressure. He wouldn't have to be everything anymore—parents, guardian, sibling, confidant...

Soon he could just be a doting big brother, a loving uncle, a supportive brother-in-law... Travis almost laughed. As much as Sheena's life was changing, so was his own.

They only had another fifteen minutes before they'd reach Yardley's house, so he figured now was as good a time as any to address Todd's concern without mentioning his visit. He'd planned to continue the conversation they'd started, but then he and Yardley got involved, and got a dog...and this was the first good chance he'd had.

Hoping to ease into it the right way, he said, "I wanted to talk to the two of you about something."

Sheena immediately started grinning. In a loud, obvious whisper, she said to Todd, "This is where he confesses that things are getting serious with my wedding planner."

Todd appeared startled. "They are?" He leaned around Sheena to see Travis. "I thought you were in the friend zone?"

"I was...am." *Liar.* "By choice, we're keeping things

friendly." Another lie, because Yardley didn't make that choice. In fact, she'd been clear that she'd prefer something altogether different.

"He thinks I haven't noticed how it is." Sheena sent her pointy elbow into Travis's ribs. "But to me, it's been pretty obvious that you're falling for her."

Ready to play along, Todd said, "You're sharp like that."

Travis shook his head. "Not what I was going to talk about, but can I assume by your smile that you don't mind?"

Having her suspicion confirmed thrilled Sheena. "Why would I mind? I love Yardley. She's smart and kind, has a great business, and she's been so patient with me. I don't think I could have tackled all this without her."

"She told me you're friends now."

"We are, but don't worry. She's not the type to blame me if you screw things up."

Todd took a sudden interest in looking out the window. *Good choice, bud.* Travis fought it, but exasperation tightened his mouth. "You refer to me 'screwing up' far too often. You really think I'm that bad?"

Sheena immediately gave up her hold on Todd to hug Travis's arm instead. She put her head on his shoulder. "I think you're the best big brother in the entire universe, and no, I don't think anything about you is *bad*. But you have to admit, you've been pretty shallow with girls. Love 'em and leave 'em. Never serious."

With so many responsibilities, he hadn't been able to consider anything more. Since the death of his parents, he'd had a full plate. It was worse when Sheena was little, but then the teenage years were an extra unique challenge, and from there, college—and now this. When exactly was he supposed to get serious with someone? Not that anyone had tempted him anyway.

And none of that was Sheena's fault, so he didn't mention it. "I haven't been anything with *girls*." His tastes leaned toward women—mature, smart, motivated, honest women…like Yardley.

"Are you chiding me on sexism?"

"Just saying, I haven't dated anyone under twenty-three. Not since…" Not since they'd lost their parents. He didn't want to say that either, so he substituted, "College."

"Because you were busy raising me." She hugged his arm again. "And I love you for it."

Damn, she was in an emotional mood. Maybe the pregnancy did that to her. "We were there for each other, and I love you, too. But back to me screwing up—I have a feeling you're basing that opinion off your one-time friend, Julie, who ended up not being much of a friend at all."

"Ouch." Sheena's mouth turned down. "You're right, and that's on me."

"I didn't say that." None of this was what he wanted to talk about, damn it.

"It was my bad judgment," she explained to Todd. "I thought she was a nice person, but she didn't even like me. Not really. She just wanted to hit on Travis and saw me as easy access to him. When he was friendly, *only* friendly, because like I said, big brother didn't do involvement, she misunderstood big-time. Travis politely cleared up the mistake, and she made a *huge*, ugly fuss about it. Turned out she wasn't nice at all. She was a total—"

Todd interrupted to say, "You're usually a terrific judge of character."

Travis snorted. "You think so because she adores you."

"No, that's the one thing I can't figure out." With humble sincerity, Todd said, "I would've bet someone as special as Sheena wouldn't give me a second look."

Mentally, Travis gave an eye roll.

Sheena, however, rushed to Todd's defense. "You are *wonderful*! Don't let anyone tell you otherwise, and if they try, let me know."

Travis asked, "Will you battle for him, hon?"

"Damn right I would." Sheena shot him a glare. "I learned that from you, you know. You always had my back."

Yeah, because she was his baby sister and he loved her. "He is lucky to have you."

"Hey!" Sheena said.

"But you're lucky to have him, too," he finished. "I'm happy for you both, and I think you'll be good together."

Todd brightened. "Thanks, man. I swear I'll make her happy."

"I make myself happy," Sheena said absently. Obviously, she had other things on her mind. "But what about you and Yardley? You two are a confirmed thing now, right?"

A *thing*? Like…a couple? Exclusive? A difficult question to answer—or was it? He'd only known her a month, but he knew he was fast falling in love; no one had ever hit him this hard, and he liked how right it felt to be with her. Had to be love, he reasoned, because he never wanted the feelings to end.

He wasn't ready to discuss any of that with Sheena, and he definitely wasn't going to share with Todd. "We're taking it one step at a time, but I like her a lot." Enough that he hated the idea of her being with anyone else.

Enough that he was already thinking long-term. "She's unique." Wonderfully, beautifully unique.

"Yes, she is." Sheena grew serious. "I say go for it. You don't want someone like Yardley to get away."

No, he didn't. "Thanks, hon, but that's not what I wanted to talk about." Wedding first, he decided, and depending on how that went, he'd discuss the house with them later.

It was important for her and Todd both to know how the costs would be covered. Todd had said Sheena felt guilty about every little expenditure. He didn't want guilt from either of them. He wanted them to start their life together as unencumbered as possible—financially and emotionally.

Before Sheena finalized any more choices, he wanted to further explain. "We'll be at Yardley's in just a few more minutes, so I wanted you both to understand how the wedding is being covered."

"With your generosity," Sheena said.

"But I'd like to pay you back," Todd added.

Stunned, Sheena turned to him. "You do? But I thought—"

Travis forged ahead. "When Mom and Dad died, they already had things set up financially. The house had been paid off for a few years. They had a hefty life insurance policy, and a nice cushion in the bank. Even back then, I knew I had to plan for the future, so I did."

"Isn't he remarkable?" Sheena asked Todd.

"Sure," Todd agreed. "And I appreciate it, but the wedding should be on me."

Travis shook his head. "My point is that I set aside money each year for Sheena. For her education, and for things like this." Same as his folks would have done.

They were planners, that much had been clear, and they'd set a damn fine example for him.

Sheena frowned. "I still plan to do the education."

"I know, and I'm not touching that money. It'll be there for you, whenever you're ready." And if she never used it, he'd give it to her as a gift, to do with as she pleased—or maybe she'd put it in an account for her son or daughter's education. He pulled up to the curb at Yardley's house and parked. "The thing is, I'm still living in the family house. If we were really going to be fair, I'd sell it and split the profits with you. That'd more than cover a wedding."

"No!" Stricken, Sheena pushed back to show him her displeasure. "Please don't tell me you're thinking of doing that."

"No." He loved that big old house and had planned to be there for the rest of his life. Ignoring Todd's attention, he cupped his sister's cheek. "That house is a part of us, Sheena. We have a lot of memories there, it's a great school district still, and..." It was his last connection to his parents. "I'd like to stay."

"I want that, too." She covered his hand with her own. "I want you happy, Travis, so if you needed to move, I'd support your decision. But honestly, it'd break my heart to think of other people living in *our* home. Todd and I can't afford the upkeep on a place that big, so I'd already been counting on you having us over for holidays and stuff."

"I'd love that, especially since I'll soon have a niece or nephew."

"I want to show my baby the tree we played in and the places where Daddy marked our heights on the basement wall. There's so much personal history there—history that I want to pass on to my kids, and someday to your kids, too."

Someday to my kids... Funny that he hadn't thought much about having kids until recently. Between Sheena expecting and Yardley's remarkable effect on him, the idea had a lot of merit.

Sheena's attitude would make his house discussion easier—when he was ready to have it. There wasn't enough time to go into all that right now, though. He imagined Dodger was already going nuts, barking and racing in circles, knowing he had company. The little dude adored him, and vice versa. "Then I'll keep it," Travis announced, "and you two will graciously accept that the wedding is paid for."

Sheena shrugged. "I thought we'd already covered all that." She glanced at Todd.

He ran a hand over his face, explaining to Sheena, "This is probably because I went to see him."

"You did? When?"

"I didn't want you worrying about the wedding. I know you were stressing over the costs, but baby, I want you to have the wedding of your dreams. You deserve it. You deserve...everything."

Travis saw her smile go crooked before she fully turned to face Todd. "I've told you, marrying you is what makes it my dream wedding. Everything else is just for fun."

Atta girl, Travis wanted to say. His sis wasn't superficial fluff. She had her priorities locked down and she knew her own mind. He should have remembered that sooner and maybe he wouldn't have worried about her so much.

When Yardley stepped into the open doorway of the Victorian house, Travis grabbed the excuse to exit from the mushy love talk. "I'll give you two some privacy. Come on in whenever you're ready. No rush."

As he left the truck, Yardley stepped out and a furry missile shot forward. Dodger yapped with joy, racing to him, twisting and jumping, until Travis caught him and lifted him to his chest. "Hey, buddy." Dodger planted several excited licks to his face before settling down and snuggling close in contentment. "Looks like you missed me."

Yardley said, "He's not the only one," but she spoke low so his sister and Todd wouldn't hear.

It struck him that his sister was right—he was screwing up by not boldly claiming his attraction for everyone to see. He cared about Yardley. A lot. She deserved to know it. Beyond that, there was no reason to hide it, especially since his sister understood.

In ways no one ever had, Yardley drew him in, making him happy and relaxed, causing him to think about things he hadn't considered before.

Like settling down with a family of his own.

She fit into his life, or more importantly, she complemented it. Made it better. Each day felt fuller with Yardley in it.

It wasn't that he'd been discontent before her, just that he'd focused on other things. Being there for Sheena. His business. The houses he flipped. He went day to day by rote...much as he had since the death of his parents. Things hadn't been bad; he loved his sister too much to ever feel that way.

It was just that now, with Yardley, he had more laughter, more contentment—and a hell of a lot more lust.

Seeing her smile and the warmth in her eyes, he wondered how he'd held out so long.

No more.

Walking right up to her, Travis took her mouth in a kiss almost as enthusiastic as Dodger's. She was startled at first, but quickly took part, her lips parting, her breath coming faster, leaning into him—at least until the dog excitedly stuck his wet snout between them.

Pulling back, Travis laughed.

Flustered, Yardley made a show of fanning her face before asking, "Does that mean you missed me, too?"

"Always." The shadows of the front porch turned her beautiful eyes a darker shade as she stared at him with uncertainty. An uncertainty that he'd needlessly caused. "Every single minute of every single day."

"Oh." She looked beyond him at the others, then to him again. "It's okay for your sister to see?"

"Why not? She knows we're involved." *She knows I'm in deep already.* Accepting that led his thoughts in a clear direction, so he asked, "How do you feel about being exclusive?"

At first Yardley went blank, followed by a tentative and curious smile. "Do you mean exclusive, as in only me and only you?"

"I don't want anyone but you." He drew his fingers along her glossy brown hair. "Your hair is so soft."

"I used a deep conditioner."

That was such a Yardley thing to say, he wanted to kiss her again. Instead, he traced one fingertip over her mouth. "I don't like the idea of some other guy admiring your hair, or any other part of you." He watched those kissable lips lift with pleasure. *Damn, but I want those smiles for my own.*

She gave a brief laugh. "There are no other guys. You know that."

He still had such a hard time bending his brain around that. Her energy level must intimidate most men. That, or her mother's and aunt's attitudes scared them off. "There are no other women either." There'd never been anyone like her. "So, what do you say?"

She nodded fast. "Works for me."

"Good." Satisfied, he glanced back in time to see Todd helping his sister out of the truck. The two of them were still talking, lingering, so Travis kissed Yardley once more—and this time, he managed to keep Dodger from interrupting.

But it was her front porch, and others might intrude, so he finally got himself together. With their lips still close, he said, "There are so many things I want to tell you." Now that they were more committed, he was anxious to share...everything. "Like the house I'm working on? Wouldn't it be nice for Sheena, Todd and the baby? I've been thinking about it and I could make it totally affordable for them. Probably the same as what he pays in rent on his apartment."

Her mouth dropped open, then snapped shut with a grin. "Ohmigod, *yes*! It would be perfect—"

"Shh. I haven't said anything to them yet."

"A surprise?" In a sincere show of emotion, she flattened a hand over her heart. "And you shared with me? Oh Travis, that's so sweet. Thank you."

"Sweet" didn't adequately describe his current mood. To make that point, he shifted Dodger to his other arm, leaned closer and lowered his voice. "I can't wait to get you alone."

Her eyes flared. "For?"

"For all the things I've been denying myself."

Her eyes locked desperately to his. "You've been denying me too, you know."

"Because I'm an idiot."

"No you're not. I understood." She considered things, then offered, "I'm free tonight. Actually, right after this meeting will work."

Laughing, Travis put his arm over her shoulders and turned them both so he could keep his eye on Sheena's approach. "Love your enthusiasm, Yardley, I really do." Actually, there were many things he loved about her, and every day he discovered more.

That particular word—*love*—had her beaming at him, and reciprocating. "I love that you care so much about your sister's happiness. I love that you're so generous and thoughtful." Leaning into him, she rubbed her nose against his neck. "I love that you smell so good."

"Maybe that's Dodger you're smelling," he teased.

"No, it's you—though I bathed Dodger again, so he is rather sweet right now." She stroked the dog while they waited together for Sheena and Todd.

Holding them both so close felt right in more ways than Travis had ever thought possible. He could see his life rolling out like this. Greeting Yardley with kisses. Hugging their dog. Maybe a kid or two as well.

He needed to ask Yardley what she thought about kids of her own. She was phenomenal with Mimi's daughter, and God knew she'd been exactly what Dodger needed.

"By the way," she said, looking up at him and interrupting his thoughts, "I want to share some stuff too."

"Anything wrong?"

"Nope. Everything is grand." Her face glowed with happiness. Yardley's particular brand of sunshine was addictive and he definitely wanted more. "I had my meeting with Betty, and I want to do a dinner party."

"Dinner party?" He looked back at the big Victorian house. "You mean here?" With the way the sitting room, her office, and the kitchen flowed together, the house would be perfect.

Her family, not so much.

He couldn't imagine how Aurora and Lilith would react, but he figured they'd find numerous ways to be snarky.

"Yes, here, with you, Sheena and Todd, Mimi and Kevin." She smiled. "And Betty. Everyone will like her once they get to know her."

"I take it you do?" Not that he was surprised. Yardley didn't have it in her to dislike anyone for long.

"I really do. She's so interesting, and she knows so much history about the town. Heck, at eighty-six, she's lived a lot of the history. We talked and shared muffins…" Suddenly her cheeks flushed.

"What's this?" he asked, brushing his fingertips over her heated cheeks. "Blushing?"

Her color increased. "Because of Mimi's husband. He teased me, that's all."

Having spoken with Kevin, and knowing how guys in general could be, Travis was already imagining a lot. "C'mon. Let's hear it."

Sheepish, she explained, "He and Mimi were going on about my baking skills, and I said I was more than tasty muffins."

Travis cracked a grin. "You realize that sounds—"

"Sexual, I know." She rolled her eyes. "Kevin told me so, and he suggested I should share that line on my new guy."

New guy. Old guy. *I need to be the only guy.* Near her ear, he whispered, "How about I try the muffins tonight?"

"Tonight?"

"Yeah." Already, he imagined a lot. Too much—especially with his sister and Todd closing in. "What do you think?"

She covered her mouth, but a silly laugh escaped. "I think I'm not sure what you mean and it's making me a little nuts."

God, he adored her quirkiness. "I'll explain tonight. How's that?"

"Dirty pool," she complained, still laughing. "Your sister will be with us in just a moment and now I'm thinking…about finally sharing my muffins with you."

He enjoyed seeing this flirty side of her. "To be fair, that's all I think about."

She snickered. "Never thought baked goods could pass as foreplay."

He hugged her. Luckily, Sheena and Todd were still talking, so they took their own sweet time reaching them. "That's because you're sexier than you realize."

Going serious on him, Yardley rested her hand on his chest. "Until you, I never thought of myself as sexy, or even sexual. I was just me, getting through each day with a purpose, dealing with my mother and aunt, trying to find ways to grow the business, assisting other residents when I could—"

"Leading a very busy life."

She shrugged. "And that was enough."

He didn't buy it. For someone with so much love to share, it had to be stifling to be caught in such a grind, especially the grind of her aunt and mother's nonstop negativity. That capacity for love likely explained her adoration of the Honeymoon Cottage. She saw it as an unattainable goal, always meant for someone else.

Yardley deserved someone special, someone who would prove to her just how amazing she was. He wanted that person to be him.

"But now there's you," she continued, "and it's like you really see me, a different me." She paused to consider that. "Or maybe every part of me, not just my clumsy exterior."

It astounded him that someone so attuned to others, someone who always saw the best in people, could so easily overlook all the amazing ways she stood out— physically and emotionally. "There's nothing clumsy about you, Yardley. How can you not know how pretty you are?"

"You see?" Touching his jaw, she whispered, "It's those type of comments that have me thinking about my dusty sexuality far too often."

There was no way Travis could resist kissing her again. He brushed his mouth over her forehead, the bridge of her nose, the corner of her irresistible lips. There were times when she broke his heart without realizing it.

Maybe it was because of her aunt and mother's constant criticism that she was always so positive and upbeat. A means of self-defense to deflect the hurt. He thought she employed it more than she realized.

To lighten the mood, he whispered, "No worries. I have a feather duster at home."

At that, she burst out laughing, which made Dodger bark.

"You tell her, bud," he said to the dog. "She's hot, isn't she?"

Obligingly, the dog barked again.

"See? You're as tempting as they come, Yardley Belanger, and you've tempted me from day one."

Though she looked unconvinced, she still grinned. "If you say so."

"Not just me. You heard Dodger."

Switching gears on him, she said, "That was the other awesome thing about Betty. She loved Dodger."

"Smart lady." He rubbed the dog's neck, which had finally healed. "I like her already."

Having heard the dog bark, Sheena called out, "If you two are done smooching, I'd love to see the puppy!" and started dragging Todd along at a faster clip.

"So, the dinner party?" Yardley asked. "Is a Saturday good for you?"

His Saturdays were hers to claim. "Sure. Count me in."

"Awesome. Mimi and Kevin are in, too." She turned to face his approaching sister and his soon-to-be brother-in-law. Even though Sheena wasn't showing much yet, she rested a hand over her stomach. "Sheena, it's good to see you again. And Todd." Yardley stepped forward, hand extended. "It's so nice that you could join us."

Ignoring her hand, Todd enthusiastically hauled her in for a rocking bear hug. "I feel like I know you already! Sheena goes on about you all the time. Yardley this and Yardley that. All of it great, I swear. She adores you."

"I do," Sheena agreed, while lavishing love on Dodger—who soaked it up as his due.

Travis gently freed her from the embrace. Little by little, he got used to Todd's over-the-top personality, but he didn't yet know how Yardley felt about it.

Laughing, she smoothed down her shirt and hair. "Hello to you, too."

Realizing he'd overstepped, Todd retreated with an

abashed grin. "My bad. Didn't mean to maul you. I'm just so glad to meet you finally."

"The feeling is mutual," Yardley assured him.

"Sheena's kept me up on everything. It all sounds so great. And it being so casual, man, that's a relief. Can't imagine myself all trussed up in a tux, ya know? Makes my feet hurt to think about it. And my mom in a fancy dress? Wow, that would've been something. Don't think I've ever seen her dressed up. She's usually in jeans and a loose shirt. But hey, she owns cowboy boots, so she's halfway there, right?"

When he drew a breath to continue, Yardley interjected, "I aim to please."

Another comment that Travis's body chose to take as sexual. *Get it together, man.* To keep Todd from launching into another round of gratitude, he said, "Yardley was just talking about a dinner party."

"I hope you'll both be able to make it." She shared the details while Travis released Dodger so he could dance around Sheena's feet.

"That sounds so fun!" Stooping down, Sheena showered love on the dog.

"Shouldn't be a problem," Todd said. "Thanks for inviting us. Seriously. Sheena's been cooped up so long with me working all the time."

Travis could feel him gaining momentum again. "And you've been nonstop working. A night out will be good for both of you."

Yardley quickly held open the front door. "I have something for you, Sheena. Let's go inside."

"What is it?" Sheena asked as she straightened with Todd's probably unneeded assistance.

"You have to wait and see. It's silly really. Sort of a gag gift for your wedding."

"Now I'm doubly curious!" Taking Todd with her, she hurried up the porch steps and through the door.

Dodger ran in after them.

Pausing a few steps back, Yardley turned to Travis to softly say, "They look so happy."

"They are," he confirmed. "And I'm happy for them."

She took his hand. "I knew you would be."

As she led him along, he felt like his life was moving forward in all the best ways—and he knew it was because of Yardley.

TODD WAS...BOISTEROUS. He had a booming voice and a zest for life that Sheena obviously adored. When Todd laughed, Sheena did, too, and Yardley couldn't help but join in. They were fun.

And they both thought the T-shirt she'd given Sheena was hilarious. It said, I had a Cemetery wedding and I liked it.

Seeing Travis grin as well really boosted Yardley's confidence that the shirts would be a hit.

"This is so awesome," Todd said for the fifth time. "Where can I buy one for myself?"

"Oh, I should have gotten one for you." She hadn't been sure if Todd would attend, and she didn't want it to seem like she was pushing the shirts on them.

"No way. You need to sell these." He hugged Sheena. "They'll be great for our anniversaries, right honey?"

In complete agreement, Sheena said, "We'll make it an annual photo! Oh, and we can start with the first pic at the Honeymoon Cottage."

"If you really mean that," Yardley said, "I'd love a

copy for my brochures. That is, if it's the type of photo I can share."

Travis groaned. "Please don't put ideas in my sister's head." Then, with playful insistence, he added, "Only PG-rated photos, sis. Got that?"

Todd cracked up again.

Yardley wasn't at all surprised when the laughter brought her mother and aunt down the stairs. Wearing identical disapproving expressions, they stepped into the room.

And…there went the fun. Whoosh. Like a deflating balloon.

No. Blast it, her enjoyment didn't hinge on their approval. If it did, she'd be a miserable, depressed mess already. Letting a genuine smile free, she said, "Mother, Aunt Lilith, you remember Sheena Long, Travis's sister."

"And a satisfied client," Sheena added with a big smile toward Yardley.

Appreciating the endorsement, Yardley's determination grew. "This is her fiancé, Todd Borden. Todd, my mother, Aurora, and my aunt, Lilith."

In a flat tone, Lilith said, "We heard shouting."

"Just laughter." Yardley hoped Todd wouldn't be offended. "I gave Sheena one of my new T-shirts and as you can tell, it was a hit."

"You're handing those out now?" Aurora gave an exaggerated shudder. "I thought you were joking about them."

"Nope." She stood her ground. "Todd wants one, too."

Travis came to stand beside her. "I need one that says, 'I attended a Cemetery wedding and I liked it,' so I can wear one, as well." He slipped his arm around her waist, his hand open on her hip—something both her mother and Lilith noted. "I'd prefer black with white print."

With her heart beating a little faster, Yardley said, "That's an awesome idea." She was so pleased with the reception of the shirt design that she didn't even mind her mother and aunt's sour attitudes about them.

"We're going to get photos wearing our shirts at the Honeymoon Cottage," Sheena bragged. "Yardley will use them in a brochure."

Aurora's eyes went wide. "That little shack? Surely not."

"It could do with some updates," Lilith said.

"They'd need to make it bigger first," Aurora insisted. "Perhaps with a separate bedroom, a bigger bathroom. And that ridiculous tub would have to go—"

Yardley's jaw locked. "If someone wanted all that, they can look outside Cemetery to get it. But the cottage stays rented because it's beautiful—"

Sheena added, "Charming and cozy."

And Travis said, "Perfectly located and private."

"Sold," Todd said. "I can't wait to see it."

The happy and vehement defenses of the cottage left Aurora and Lilith silent for several seconds, until finally Aurora said, "To each her own."

Oblivious to the tense undercurrents, Todd interjected, "So, your dinner party, it's not fancy, right?"

Since she hadn't yet mentioned it to the frowning duo, she had to choke back a groan. *They had to know sooner or later.* "It's as comfortable as you want to make it. Jeans are fine. Shorts even, since we might be outside some if the weather stays so nice."

"What's this?" Lilith's attention sharpened.

"A dinner party." Refusing to allow her smile to slip, Yardley was deliberately vague. "Not until next month."

Aurora's brows climbed high. "A dinner party? *Here?*"

"Yes, here." She'd worked hard on making the house special and she wanted to show it off. Was that such a terrible idea? She wanted to be around her friends, because she *had* friends, whether her mother and aunt acknowledged it or not. She wanted Travis to get to know Mimi and Kevin more, she wanted Sheena to relax, and she wanted everyone to like and respect Betty as much as she did.

Surely none of that was asking too much?

Crossing her arms, Aurora asked, "Why didn't we know about this?"

Yardley waved that off. "I was going to tell you once everyone confirmed."

"Tell us now," Lilith suggested, her brows together, her mouth tight.

Holding her smile became more difficult, but by God, she did it. "It'll be a small gathering. Mimi and Kevin are attending, Travis, Sheena and Todd." She hesitated. "And I have one other guest to invite." So that they wouldn't ask any questions, she plowed right into another statement. "I hope you both can make it, but of course I'll understand if you have other plans."

"I'll need a new dress," Aurora mused.

"As will I," Lilith agreed.

Great, added expenses, but whatever. Acceptance was better than outrage. "We should get going." Yardley grabbed up her purse and slung the strap over her shoulder, then hastily clipped Dodger's leash to his harness. "We're heading into town to see examples of the flower arrangements Emily's put together for Sheena, and Wilson has some tablecloths and candle selections for the barn."

"You're taking that dog with you?" Lilith asked.

I'm sure not leaving him here with you two. "Of course. Dodger has received open invitations from everyone." Her smile was starting to feel more like a snarl. "Everyone loves him."

Lilith looked dubious.

I don't care. "C'mon, Dodger. You want to go, right?"

With a happy yap, the dog took the lead toward the door.

Travis caught on quick and started ushering his sister and Todd along, too. Sheena understood, but Todd clearly didn't.

He paused near the ladies to say, "It was nice to meet you both. Great house you've got. Been here long?"

Before either of them could reply, Travis said, "Don't want to be late," and more or less rushed Todd out.

Sighing in relief, Yardley closed the door…but she'd gone only three steps when it opened again. Resigned, she met Travis's gaze. "Go ahead. I'll be right behind you."

She could tell he didn't want to, and in fact he handed his keys to Sheena, saying something that Yardley couldn't hear as she turned to face her mother and aunt. Dodger plopped down, confused but willing to wait.

"Will you be home for dinner?" Aurora asked.

"I don't know, but I left a chicken casserole in the refrigerator." Now that Travis had other plans, she definitely wouldn't be home until much, much later. *Yay for me!* "It's already been cooked. Just microwave your serving."

"Perfect." Travis surprised her by being *right there*,

close enough to put his arm around her again. "I was hoping to steal her for a meal at Saul's. Todd hasn't eaten there yet."

A meal at Saul's…and then hopefully dessert in his bed. Yardley was already counting down the minutes.

Eyes bright with an odd intensity that Yardley couldn't decipher, Aurora studied them. She didn't exactly seem annoyed anymore, but the look was well beyond mere curiosity.

"At least you're dressed for the Pit Stop," Lilith said, giving a dismissive glance to her skinny jeans and loose-fit coral pullover.

"Comfort first," Yardley sang, already turning away. "Enjoy the meal."

"Microwaving the food always dries it out," Lilith complained.

Aurora patted her sister's arm. "Let's allow the young people to get on their way. The casserole will be fine." She sent a smile and a wink over her shoulder to Yardley. "After all, Yardley's already made it. The rest is simple."

Lilith's shock matched Yardley's. Understanding? *From her mother?*

"What just happened?" Yardley whispered, staring in disbelief as the women retreated to the house.

"Past due appreciation," Travis murmured.

"Did I dream that?" She blew out a breath. "I dreamed it, didn't I?" Putting the back of her hand to her forehead, she asked, "Am I delirious?"

"You're taken for granted far too often, that's all."

Yeah, but being taken for granted was her shtick. It's what she was used to. This…this other thing, she didn't know what to do with it.

As if he'd read her mind, Travis gave her a hug. "I say

you should accept your due, let them work out dinner, and let's go have some fun."

"Right. Good plan." When the front door closed, she forced her feet to unglue from the sidewalk and allowed Travis to lead her and Dodger to her car. "Where's your truck?"

"Sheena's driven it before. I told her I'd ride with you." He secured the dog in the back seat, and then opened the driver's door for Yardley. "Want me to drive?" he asked. "You still look…rattled."

"No, it's fine." If he drove, he'd have to adjust everything to fit his larger size. Shaking off the feeling that something monumental had just happened, Yardley got behind the wheel.

Her mother was up to something, she just didn't know what.

Once Travis was seated, he reached over and took her hand. "Is it so unusual for your mother to have a kind word?"

"You've met her. What do you think?"

"If you want the truth, I think she speaks without thinking and is more unfeeling than she means to be. It's like you've put up with it for so long, she's gotten used to it and doesn't even realize that she's doing it anymore."

Holy smokes, that was a lot of insight. "You could be right. Mimi wants me to blast them both, but I'm not sure I could."

"Mimi strikes me as a natural-born hell-raiser. It fits her, but it's not really you." His fingers toyed with a lock of her hair. "I have a hunch if you did that, you'd only feel worse afterward, and in the end, nothing much would be accomplished except hard feelings that you'd all have to deal with."

For several long moments, Yardley stared at him. How was it possible that Travis understood her even better than Mimi did? Equal parts excitement and relief sent her heart beating in a harder, heavier rhythm. It left her awed that someone—that *Travis*—knew her so well. Staring into his dark eyes, knowing there'd never be another guy like him, she breathed, "You are nothing short of amazing. You know that, right?"

A wicked smile quirked his mouth. "I'll believe it if you kiss me."

"My mother and aunt are probably spying on us."

"So? Does that bother you?"

Yesterday her answer would have been yes. Heck, even ten minutes ago she'd have shied away from the idea. But now? "Nope. Doesn't bother me at all." Twisting half over the console, she clasped his face in her hands and took his mouth with all the wonder, all the escalating emotion she felt every time she was near him.

Breathless now, she said against his lips, "I'm so glad you're finally giving in."

"It's a wonder that I lasted this long."

Growing impatient, Dodger gave a bark. They had a full day ahead of them, so it'd be a while until she got Travis alone. Already imagining how they'd get from start to finish, her skin warmed.

As she backed out of the driveway, she decided her loose pullover top was perfect for easy access, but blast it, why had she chosen her skinniest skinny jeans?

11

To say she'd been distracted all afternoon would have been an understatement. Every time she looked at Travis, she thought about what was to come and suffered equal parts excitement, impatience, and…yeah, uncertainty. Never mind that she was an independent woman who knew her own mind.

She hadn't had sex in *years*. She really might be dusty!

Now here she was, kissing Travis goodbye at the restaurant and promising she and Dodger would be right along to his house. He had to drop off Sheena and Todd first, but that was on the way, so it wasn't like she had time to stop at the store and hastily purchase a different outfit.

Glancing in the rearview mirror at the dog, she mumbled, "You're going to be fine, right? Travis swears you like to nap in the sun at his house. I'm frazzled enough without you getting extra clingy."

For an answer, the dog yawned widely.

Good, she thought. Be sleepy. That worked perfectly.

With her options limited, Yardley did the next best thing: she sent a hands-free call to Mimi.

The second her friend answered, Yardley blurted, "I'm having sex!"

To which Mimi replied, "Like, right now? This second?" And then with accusation, "You aren't calling me in the middle of things, are you? That's bad form, Yardley."

Mimi's nonsense was exactly what she needed to shake off the nerves. Laughing, Yardley drove out of the Pit Stop parking lot and followed along behind Travis's truck. "Of course not," she said, then briefly explained everything.

"Go Travis! Glad to hear it." Knowing Yardley as she did, Mimi softened her tone and asked, "So what's the problem, hon?"

"I'm wearing super-skinny jeans. Like, the ultra-tight kind with the really small ankles that make me struggle to get out of them. And—oh, God—it just occurred to me that I had a loaded burger at the Pit Stop."

"Onions?" Mimi asked.

Yardley wilted. "You know how I love them."

"Okay, this is fine. We can handle this."

Knowing Mimi was on it, Yardley already felt better. "It's only going to take fifteen minutes to get to his place. I can't exactly stop to change, so what am I going to do? Without anyone watching, it takes me a good five minutes to peel off these jeans—and Mimi, it's not a graceful show." It was the opposite of graceful. Clumsy, ungainly, hilariously awkward. "What am I going to do?"

"Easy peasy," she said. "When you get to his place, give him a seductive smile, say you need a minute, and duck into his bathroom. Put a little toothpaste on your finger and clean your teeth so you don't smell like onions and Saul's special burger sauce, then wrestle those jeans off and voilà! Open the door and announce that you're ready. Travis will drop his eyeballs."

"But…" Trying to imagine such a thing, Yardley swallowed. "I wanted our first time to be romantic. I wanted to go the natural route. Kissing, touching, clothes melting away…"

"Pfft. Clothes don't melt away and you know it. That's fairy tale BS. Trust your bestie. Pants off. Top off would be good too, but if you—"

"No way."

"Right. Pants off. Strike a pose. He'll *love* it."

Inhaling and exhaling, Yardley whispered, "I can do this."

"Course you can." With more seriousness, Mimi said, "Girl, you can do anything. I can't tell you how many times you've amazed me. And oh, by the by, Kevin and I are getting ready for some hot and heavy stuff, so can we wrap up the pep talk?"

Luckily, Yardley had to stop for a red light because that gave her an opportunity to concentrate fully on Mimi. *"Hot and heavy?"* She grinned hugely. "When did that happen?"

"After your muffin visit. I took your advice and put things to him point-blank. You are so smart, Yardley, and I love you so, so much."

Wow. Just…wow. Her heart seemed to completely fill her chest, making it difficult to whisper, "I am so happy for you." Now Mimi could go back to being her usual confident, sassy self.

"Me, too. I was acting like such a whiny dope and you knew it. Better still, you called me on it."

From the background, Yardley heard Kevin say, "I'm working with one hand so if you ladies are going to gossip, I want that little detail front and center."

Mimi laughed, but Yardley's whole body flushed. *Good God, Kevin is listening.*

Softer, in a barely-there whisper, Mimi said, "He just came into the room, hon, I promise. Your secrets are always safe with me."

Whew. Yes, she knew that, but still, she was glad to have it confirmed again. "I want to make sure I don't flub the whole thing before anyone else knows."

"You're going to do great. Trust me, and trust Travis."

It was nice that Mimi didn't tease her about being a thirty-one-year-old almost-virgin with a case of performance anxiety. "I do."

"I'm crazy excited for you. I just know this time is going to show you how awesome sex can be."

Though Mimi couldn't see her, Yardley nodded. She was counting on it. She had very high expectations for this. Poor Travis. "Thank you for listening, and the advice. Now go have some fun before Sammy wakes up."

"Oh believe me, I'm on it." Mimi sent several kisses through the phone, then disconnected.

For the rest of the drive, Yardley thought about the plan Mimi had described. Get into the house. Be casual. Hit up the bathroom, clean her teeth, and…*gulp*…peel off her clingy, extra-skinny jeans.

Wearing only her loose top, step out, strike a pose, and smile.

Surely, Travis would take it from there. Not that she planned to be a passive participant, but it'd be pretty romantic if he swept her up and carried her to bed.

She liked that image a lot and kept it close—right up

until she pulled into Travis's driveway. At that point, she almost forgot to be nervous.

His family home.

That he'd brought her here had to be significant, right? She glanced back at Dodger, who'd come awake and was now busy looking around. "We're here, boy," she whispered. "Time to be on your best behavior."

Dodger gave her a skeptical look. True, he was still working on the good behavior gig.

"It's fine," she promised him. "Don't stress yourself." She tended to fret enough for the both of them.

When Travis opened her door, she jumped as if guilty. And she was—guilty of talking to her dog. Guilty of high expectations. Guilty of telling Mimi everything…

He'd pulled into his garage to park and she hadn't realized he'd already walked back to her. Could he be anxious, too? Oh, she hoped so.

"I'll get the dog," he said, waiting until she'd stepped out and he'd closed her door before retrieving Dodger, then taking her hand in his. "We'll go in through the garage if that's okay with you."

"Sure." Following along, they went through the two-car garage with Travis's truck on one side, a riding mower in the other space, and tool cabinets arranged around the walls in orderly fashion. "This is big." She wished she had the convenience of parking in the garage, but her mother and aunt had that honor.

In answer, Travis lifted her hand and kissed her knuckles, then opened a door that led into a mudroom.

Yardley stepped inside with a swirling sense of anticipation and excitement. It wasn't like her first time a decade ago.

A decade. Sheesh, she really was a clichéd old maid.

Dodger ran in ahead of them, his nose to the ground as he sniffed everywhere. Though it was Yardley's first time, the dog had been here before. "Does he know where he's going?"

"Probably the kitchen for a drink and a snack."

As they stepped through the foyer, she took in the large living room that opened to a formal dining room with a big kitchen to the side. A beautiful, wide staircase led up to the second floor. Not waiting for an invitation, she started prowling around the comfortable beige furniture in the sitting area, into the dining room with a dark wood table big enough for six, and then into a kitchen that had been updated but still fit the style of the home. Dodger had his own sunny spot all set up with a plump cozy bed, a few toys, and water and food dishes on a special mat. The window over the sink gave a view of the heavily treed backyard…and a tire swing. "Wow. I love this. All of it."

"Me, too," he said, joining her at the sink. "It's my family home. Sheena and I grew up here." He ran a hand over an aged set of coffee cups hanging from hooks on the wall in a niche. "There are some things I couldn't change, even when I did updates."

"I'm glad. It feels so cozy." She wrapped her arms around herself. "It feels…well-loved."

"It was." He drew her against him, and she ended up hugging him instead of herself. Much, much nicer. "There are still times when I see something and memories swamp me. Like this set of mugs. In the winter after playing in the snow, Mom, Dad and I would have hot chocolate in them. We'd sit around the fireplace and talk. Even after Mom had Sheena, it was like a tradition whenever I was home."

"The fireplace is beautiful." It was easy to picture the family scene in her mind.

He nodded to a corner of the living room. "The furniture has all changed, of course, but that's where Dad sat—across from the TV. Mom would sit at one end of the couch, usually with her feet up on the coffee table. Once Sheena was here, she'd lie on the couch with her head in Mom's lap."

"Where did you sit?"

"When I was younger, I had Sheena's spot. By the time she came along, I was usually sprawled in the other chair talking to Dad. I was at that age where I stuck around for those special moments, but otherwise I was up in my room for privacy. Talking to girls, planning a night out with my friends." He looked around the house. "I never want to give up the place. In every sense of the word, this is home."

"I completely understand." Though she'd tried to make her house the same, the warmth was missing, the friendly memories, the family bond, and the…love. "Could I see your room?" Hopefully there'd be a bathroom nearby. Then she could do her prep work and get the show on the road.

He gave her a slow grin. "It's totally different now. The twin bed got donated and I have a king. Sheena's room is now my office." He steered her toward the stairs.

Dodger looked at them quizzically, then went back into the kitchen and dropped into his bed with a lazy huff.

Near her ear, Travis said, "He thinks I'm going to work. Don't tell him otherwise and he'll probably nap the whole time."

That would be convenient. She watched the dog a second more, saw he was content, and allowed Travis to lead her away. "So, you're still in your old room?"

"Yes."

Quietly, worried about overstepping, she asked, "You didn't move into your parents' room?"

"Don't look like that." He kissed her knuckles again. "I can talk about anything with you, okay?"

That made her feel so special, especially since she felt the same with him. "Okay."

"I could move into their room. It wouldn't bother me. I just…haven't." He gave a shrug. "I changed everything, though. The floors, the bedding, got rid of the wallpaper and painted instead. Furniture rearranged. Their bathroom has been updated. It's all different now."

"So someday—" when he married and had a family of his own "—you might move into it?" The idea felt abhorrent. Not that he'd take the room, but that he'd move on…from her.

"Maybe. The bedrooms are about the same size, minus the connecting bathroom." He opened a door. "This was Sheena's room. It used to be nauseating shades of lavender. Sheena was all about the girly stuff as a kid."

Yes, Yardley could almost picture that. "Even though she likes snakes."

He laughed. "Let's just say as a little kid, she liked unicorns more."

Now the room was nice and neutral, with plenty of storage, a big heavy desk, and a wall of shelving. "This is all for your construction company?"

"And the houses I flip." He led her to another door. "Hall bathroom. Since it was always white, I didn't change much. Just put in a shower door and updated towels and rugs."

"I like it. The white is so bright and you can literally do any color scheme you want."

He skipped the next door and opened the one at the end of the hall. "This was my parents' room." With a hand at the small of her back, he urged her inside. "The windows let in a lot of light during the day. Mom had long dramatic drapes, but I switched them out for more modern blinds."

"This was their furniture?"

"Yeah. Still sturdy."

"It's beautiful." Dark, glossy mahogany in a traditional design. The hardwood floors were really nice too. She peeked into the bathroom and admired the updated tile design and faucets. The white tub and toilet looked older but were still in great shape. "You do amazing work."

Looping his arms around her waist, his gaze intent, he asked, "How are you feeling?"

"Feeling?" Now that he asked, she felt all sorts of things.

"Still nervous?"

Rather than fib, she shrugged. At this point she was more anxious. Bursting with anticipation. And yes, a wee bit nervous still.

He smiled as he led her to the last remaining door. "It's okay, you know. I'm not going to rush you."

She sort of wished he would. The wait was grueling. "I was just thinking how long it's been for me, and how much better it is this time."

Cockiness turned his smile into a grin. "Giving me credit before I've done anything?"

"Before *we've* done anything." She was a mature, modern woman, after all. She wanted half the credit, and she'd accept half the blame. "I won't hold you solely responsible for…" She gestured lamely. "Performance." *Oh God, Yardley, shut up.* She cleared her throat and rushed on. "I just meant that back then, I was super stressed. Dreading it almost, you know? I totally should have backed out, but it seemed like the thing to do." She gave a self-conscious laugh. "Mimi definitely recommended it."

Tenderness warmed his expression, but he teased, "Lucky Kevin."

"Yeah, they're great together. My luck was missing though. All my clumsiness came out and he wasn't much better, and overall it was a massive flop." A disappointment that didn't inspire her to keep trying. She opened the door, stepped into Travis's room, and fought the urge to continue blathering.

Nothing sexy about a woman who talked too much before sex, especially when she used words like *performance* and *flop*.

Saying nothing more, Travis watched her with an alert expression that somehow managed to scorch her. Apparently her poor word choices hadn't turned him off.

Whew, crisis averted…so far.

She went to the simply designed bed with an off-white padded headboard and a quilt with neutral tan-and-black stripes. The bed wasn't exactly made, just smoothed out, as if he'd straightened things before leaving the room.

"This suits you," she said, wondering how to segue into things. She needed an exodus to the hall bathroom. She needed out of her skinny jeans.

She needed Travis—now.

TRAVIS TOLD HIMSELF not to stare. Yardley was perceptive and she'd pick up on his escalating need. He didn't want to make her more nervous than she already was.

That in itself was unique. Not since high school had he been with a woman who seemed so tentative. Leaning back against the dresser, he made himself say, "If you'd rather wait—"

Her startled blue gaze shot up to clash with his and she straightened with a scowl. "Are you backing out?"

Silly Yardley. "Not even close. Actually, it's taking all my control to give you some time."

"Give *me* time?" She pointed at him. "How long has it been already? You're the one who needed time, not me."

Even her show of umbrage was unique—and a little hilarious. "I'm sorry," he said around a grin. "No insult intended."

Issuing a groan, she charged forward. Travis braced himself, but she didn't even pause before him. "I'm running to the bathroom to…get ready. I'll be right back."

"Okay…" Already out of the room, she opened and shut the bathroom door with a quiet click. He rubbed the smile off his mouth. Even on the ragged edge with need, he felt pretty damned good—because he was here with Yardley.

He heard water run…and he heard Yardley muttering.

Oh, how he'd love to know what she was saying to herself. A pep talk? Or maybe she was grumbling about him. Not that he didn't deserve it, but he'd take the first opportunity to change her opinion.

Going to the bed, he pulled back the quilt.

Suddenly there was a loud thump from the bathroom, and Yardley cursed. Worried, he crossed the room and called through the shared wall between his bedroom and the hall bath, "Hey, you okay?"

"Fine," she sang back.

He wasn't convinced. "Yardley?"

"I fell," she explained. "Stupid jeans." And after a two-second pause, she added, "I'll be there in a minute."

She fell? He ran a hand over his hair, fighting the nearly overwhelming urge to barge in on her, to make sure she wasn't hurt. Pacing the bedroom, he decided he'd give her thirty seconds. Then he'd ask her if—

The bathroom door opened and a split second later, Yardley appeared in the bedroom doorway.

Limping.

In her panties.

She awkwardly struck a pose and smiled.

God, she had beautiful legs. His gaze drifted all over her, from the shapely thighs to her smooth calves and her bare feet. On his visual trip back up her legs, he noticed the darkening bruise on her right leg. "You're hurt?"

She waved that off. "Stupid skinny jeans."

Tucking in his chin, he growled, "You look sexy as hell in your skinny jeans." They fit her like a second skin, hugging the curves of her behind, her thighs and calves.

"Thank you." The smile turned sincere. "See, that's what makes them worthwhile."

Casually, he moved closer. "What does that mean?"

"They're hard to get off, so Mimi recommended I do it myself." She gestured down at her bare lower body.

"I love Mimi's plan."

That made her grin. "I'll tell her…later though. Anyway, they tripped me up, I stumbled and hit the corner of your vanity."

"Ouch." Very lightly, Travis opened his palm over the bruise. "I'm sorry."

"Hey, they're off," she said breathlessly, "so mission accomplished."

"I could have helped you with that." *Her skin is so*

damned soft. He'd have enjoyed wrestling the tight denim from her body, but he wouldn't complain about having her in nothing more than a light summer top, bra and panties.

The top definitely had to go.

She breathed a little deeper. "Now what?"

For an answer, he stepped back and kicked off his shoes, sending them toward the corner of the room. He reached back, grabbed a handful of material, and stripped away his shirt.

Yardley quickly did the same, nearly stopping his heart.

Her sensible white bra and cotton panties were about the sexiest things he'd ever seen—because they were on her. And thankfully, no cutlets. Just her sweet curves, and nothing more. "Why the hell did you ever think these—" he gestured at her breasts "—were less than perfect?"

"I don't know," she murmured, stepping into him and reaching for the snap on his jeans. "I'm small with very little cleavage, but right now, here with you, it doesn't seem to matter."

"Because it doesn't." He cupped her face and took her mouth in a kiss that distracted them both. It was a different kind of kiss, the kind that said they both knew where it'd end up.

In bed.

Needing her to be closer, but mindful of her hurt leg, he opened his hands over her plump backside and drew her in.

With a sound of approval, she wiggled against him. "See," she whispered. "This is already much better."

"Nope." Travis nipped her bottom lip, then soothed it with his tongue. "No references to other times or other guys. No comparisons. No running tally."

"Is that a rule? Because I'm not up on the rules."

He absolutely loved how she teased him, no matter the situation. "It's just us, and we're good—together." *From now on*, if he had his way. "Agreed?"

Her small hand trailed over the fly of his jeans. "At this moment, pretty sure I'd agree to anything."

"I like the sound of that." He drew his fingers up one smooth cheek to her hip, then up along her spine until he reached the back closure of her bra. Watching her, ready to hold her to that promise of being agreeable, he flicked it open.

She looked down in surprise as the cups fell free. "Wow, that was slick," she said, and without a single sign of hesitation she lowered her arms so the bra could drop away.

Clasping her shoulders, Travis held her away, drinking in the sight of her, stunned that she'd somehow managed to go unattached for so long. "Yardley…"

"Hmm?" She tipped her head, her silky dark brown hair drifting over her shoulder, that plush mouth twitchy with a curious smile.

He didn't have the right words to tell her just how stunning she was, but he gave it a shot. "Sexy," he whispered, kissing the bridge of her nose. "Beautiful." He kissed her forehead—and cupped her breasts. "Sweet. Soft." He brushed his mouth over the top of each cheekbone.

Big blue eyes went heavy with need. "I like 'sexy' the best."

"*So* damned sexy," he reiterated, letting his thumbs tease her nipples.

"That's…" She labored for breath.

"Tempting?"

"Yeah, it is. But jeans off so we're even, okay? It's been a long time for me and I'm not going to last."

No problem at all. He stripped off his jeans, taking his boxers off at the same time, and when he straightened, she sailed her panties past his head.

Only Yardley could make him both combustible with lust and happy enough to laugh. There couldn't be another woman like her anywhere on the planet.

In his heart, he knew there was no other woman for him.

Now that she was naked, he couldn't keep his hands to himself. "Come here." He scooped her up, loving the feel of her body in his arms as he carried her to the bed.

"Be still my heart. You're a romantic."

More like he was desperate to have her, but if it seemed romantic to her, he'd count it as a win.

She kissed his throat, lightly bit his shoulder, and asked, "Do you have protection?"

"I do." He was always careful, and he'd be especially so with Yardley.

When he lowered her, she wrapped her arms around his neck and drew him down on top of her. After that, there was no more conversation. Yardley's nervousness was gone, replaced with instinct and need. No shyness or uncertainty. When he touched her, she made her preferences known with the way she moved, the husky sounds she made.

The way she touched him in return.

He explored every part of her body—with his hands, and his mouth. She tensed with pleasure when he licked her nipples, then melted when he leisurely suckled her. Pressing a hand between her legs, he found her wet and hot. He loved the way she opened her thighs, how her neck arched and her lips parted.

Knowing she had high expectations, he reveled in the pleasure that began coiling through her. Wanting her release as much as she likely wanted it, he amplified his efforts. When she came apart, he groaned with her.

Luckily, Dodger slept on. He wasn't sure how Yardley would react if the dog got anxious about being alone. Good thing Dodger was familiar with the house because Travis knew he couldn't handle an interruption, not when it felt like he'd been waiting his whole life for her.

"Travis," she whispered raggedly. "That was—"

"How it should be. Always." And in case she misunderstood, or made a wrong assumption, he added, "Between us."

Her beautiful eyes looked smoky now, lazy and sated but still very interested as he rolled on the condom and settled over her again.

He held her face in his hands, nudged her legs wider, and slowly entered her.

Her eyes grew brighter, and she breathed deeper. "Between us."

That soft agreement pushed him over the edge. He sealed his mouth to hers and began moving, deeper, stronger…faster.

Locking her legs around his hips, her hands behind his neck, Yardley encouraged him, meeting every thrust with the rise of her hips. Just when he knew he wouldn't last a second more, she clenched around him and climaxed again. He gave in to his own powerful release, holding her close to his heart.

Before this, before *her*, sex was just…sex. Satisfying, hot, and purely physical.

Not any longer. Now he knew it could be so much more.

Resting against her, his body numb, his thoughts buzzing, his heart full, Travis smiled.

She kissed his shoulder, her fingers lazily moving over his back as she hummed with satisfaction.

A mere minute later, Dodger was at the closed door, barking.

Yardley kissed his shoulder again. "It's not perfect timing, but it's better than if he'd shown up five minutes ago."

"I disagree." Raising himself up on his elbows, Travis looked at her, saw her—the beautiful person she was—and smoothed back her hair. "With you, everything *is* perfect, even a visit from an impatient dog when I'd rather keep touching you."

When she snickered, she got him grinning, too.

AFTER SPENDING MUCH of the evening with Travis, Yardley carried Dodger, hoping to keep him very quiet as she crept up to her front door.

When he suddenly snarled, she jumped—and spotted Kathleen, the mannequin, in a wicker chair on the front porch.

Wearing a nightgown. With curlers in her hair.

And holding a handwritten sign that said, "You're out late, young lady." Beneath that, in a very nice scrawl, was, "It's about time! :)"

OMG. It stopped her cold, her breath strangling as Dodger fought to get free.

"Shh, shh," she urged him, stepping forward so he could see it wasn't a live person, just… Kathleen. *What is she doing here?*

When she set Dodger down, he ran to the end of his

leash to suspiciously sniff the mannequin's foot. Deciding she wasn't a threat after all, he looked at Yardley expectantly.

"Sorry, bud," she whispered. "I don't have a clue." Surely her mother wouldn't…and no way would Aunt Lilith…but oh, Mimi most definitely would! It would serve her right if Yardley called her right now and woke her. She even considered it. After all, she had much to share, all of it wonderful.

But a call might also wake Sammy, and Yardley wasn't about to do that. Besides, talking on the phone, even in whispers, might wake the others, too. Of course, she couldn't leave Kathleen on the porch. She didn't want her mother and aunt to spot her in the morning.

What to do?

Well, she really had no choice but to sneak Kathleen into her car and hope no one noticed before she could drive off tomorrow. She tied Dodger's leash to the chair, whispered, "I'll only be a second," and hefted the cumbersome mannequin into her arms.

Dodger barked, misunderstanding when she opened the door to her back seat. "Shhh," she said again, and quickly jammed the dummy into the car.

Or at least, she tried to be quick about it. Only Kathleen didn't fit.

Not sure what else to do, Yardley turned her to her stomach, then bent her at the thigh joints, so she'd be on her knees and her legs would be in.

Ack. That left the mannequin's backside stuck up, visible through the window.

If anyone saw that butt, they could easily draw very wrong conclusions, and it would be entirely possible they'd mistake Kathleen for Yardley herself!

Nooky in the back seat of a car parked in the driveway wasn't done in Cemetery, at least not that Yardley had ever heard. Certainly, she hadn't partaken in any such activity. Until Travis, her life had never been that daring or exciting.

Best to rearrange her again, but it took her far too long to get Kathleen situated to her satisfaction. By then, Dodger had stretched out on the porch with his chin on his front paws, merely watching her.

She had to agree—humans were often weird.

While giving a quick glance around the quiet neighborhood, she let Dodger do his business one last time, then lifted him back into her arms and crept into the house. It was going on midnight and only the outside lights were on. Her mother and Lilith were sound asleep, and Yardley wanted to keep it that way.

After such an amazing, eye-opening experience with Travis, she didn't want anyone to burst her bubble of happiness. She wanted to take it to bed with her, hug it all night long, and dream impossible things…like a night in the Honeymoon Cottage together where they could re-enact every moment, again and again.

Yes, she was a romantic at heart. Unapologetically so.

Dodger was too tired to fuss as she locked up the entrance and did a cursory check of the other doors, careful to avoid the floorboards that squeaked. Cuddling him, she headed down the hall to her bedroom. She closed her door with the quietest of clicks, and moved toward the bed.

Just as she sat him on the mattress, he went into berserk mode, leaping to the floor in a fury, barking and snarling as if facing a rabid cow.

Rabid cow? Okay, that was a bizarre thought even for her, but her blasted heart, which had been floating seconds ago, had shot into a tailspin, stealing all her breath—until the bedroom light flipped on, momentarily blinding her—and then she saw it was only her mother standing in the doorway.

Yeah, she wouldn't mention the rabid cow thought. Somehow she knew Aurora wouldn't be amused, especially since she was without makeup or jewelry, wearing only a floral cotton duster that no one would ever consider sexy, with well-worn flat slippers on her feet.

To Dodger, Aurora whispered, "Silly dog. Quiet down or you'll wake Lilith."

Abashed, Dodger pivoted, gave an agile leap up to the bed, turned in a circle, and with one last grumbling growl toward Aurora, tucked his nose close to his butt to sleep.

Abandoned by her traitorous dog.

With a hand still splayed over her flipping heart, Yardley said, "Dear God, you nearly scared me to death."

Half smiling, Aurora stepped into the room to sit on the chair. "You realize you were supposed to do your sneaking around in your teens, not in your early thirties. You were always such a reliable child."

"I wasn't sneaking." *Liar.* "I didn't want to disturb you or Aunt Lilith."

Aurora waved that off. "Lilith sleeps like a hibernating bear. You could pound on her bedroom door and she still might not wake up. If you listen, you can hear her snoring."

Funny, because Lilith usually had that same complaint about Aurora. "Um…is there a reason you're here?" Yardley gave a theatrical yawn…that turned into a very real yawn. "I was just about to turn in."

Ignoring that, Aurora sat back and crossed her legs,

one slipper dangling from her toes. "You impressed me today."

There went her heart again. Surely she'd misheard. "What do you mean?"

"The way you left with your company, chin up and your dog beside you."

Had she lifted her chin? Maybe. "Everyone likes Dodger. No one minds that he goes where I go."

"Hmm. You have everyone around your little finger, don't you?"

Was that an insult? Hard to tell, given her mother's mood. Before Yardley could deny that as pure nonsense, Aurora continued.

"And that handsome man of yours. It's obvious, you know."

Yardley couldn't deny the handsome part. "Erm… what's obvious?"

"That you've slept with him."

Oxygen stuck in her windpipe and she made a revolting wheezing sound as she tried to recover.

"Oh, stop. It's perfectly fine. Better than fine. I'm thrilled that you're finally exploring a little. And what a prime specimen to start with."

Start with? Her mother made it sound like she'd soon tire of Travis and move on to other…specimens. Whatever the future held for the two of them, Yardley knew he would always be in her heart. "Travis is—" *Irreplaceable*. She didn't finish the thought; anything she said now would give away too much.

"He's very sexy. And when you're looking at him, you look sexy as well. It thrilled me. Everyone who sees you two together knows it, I'm sure."

"Knows…?"

"That you finally have a sexual relationship."

Did one time equal a sexual relationship? And seriously, everyone could tell? How was that even possible?

Aurora preened. "Proves that you inherited a few things from me as well, not just from your father."

Since her mother seemed so pleased by that, Yardley said, "Um…okay."

"I have an important piece of advice though." Aurora sat forward with purpose. "Do not lose your heart to him."

It was way too late for that. Pretty sure she'd lost her heart to him the moment he smiled. Not that she'd tell her mother so. "Because…?"

"Men like Travis Long—men who are gorgeous and confident—they don't settle down. They take what they want and then move on. You're a smart girl, Yardley, you've proven that. Beat him at his own game."

What game? "As you just pointed out, I'm thirty-one. Hardly a girl." Though having this chat in her bedroom with a mother who rarely visited her here did feel like the quintessential parent-to-wayward-child "talk."

"Oh, honey, in so many ways you're as inexperienced now as you were at thirteen."

Yardley plopped onto the end of the bed, disturbing Dodger, who gave her an accusing look before curling tighter and huffing. "Did you *want* me to be experienced at thirteen?"

Spreading her hands, Aurora said with feeling, "I wanted you to do *something*. Flirt, sneak a kiss…" In a statement that summed up her entire childhood, her mother added, "I wanted you to be the average child."

What a disappointment she'd been. *I will not apologize.*

Aurora sighed. "Instead you were so…" Dissatisfaction darkened her tone. "Studious."

"Yeah, having a kid who excelled academically had to be such a grind for you."

Totally missing the facetious snark, Aurora denied, "Not at all. You were such an *easy* child in so many ways, I could never find any of my own influence."

Ha! Much of Yardley's personality had been shaped by her mother's criticism, emotional distance, and unrealistic expectations. But again, Yardley kept that to herself. At thirty-one, airing old grievances would solve nothing.

"It occurred to me recently," Aurora mused, "that even Mimi's bad habits—and she has many—never rubbed off on you."

Far as Yardley was concerned, Mimi was awesome, but she'd had that conversation with her mother too many times to count, too, so she only asked, "I suppose you hoped they would?"

"Well, until she got married and gave birth." Putting her hands to her knees, Aurora straightened with an air of seriousness. "And that's why I'm here. You're making moves in the right direction with this new boyfriend."

Her mother made it sound so juvenile. "Hate to break it to you, Mother, but he's not my boyfriend." Such a dumb term for a guy like Travis. "It was a date, that's all."

"Nonsense. I saw how he looks at you." Smiling, Aurora opened her arms. "I'll happily pitch in more around here if it means you'll experience some of the thrills life has to offer."

Whoa. Her mother was offering to help out? "Okay, so…?" There had to be a catch.

With a long, serious look, Aurora stated, "It scares me that you'll jump on the first man who's interested."

Jumping on Travis was a pretty accurate description of her behavior, and she didn't regret a single second of it. On the contrary, she hoped she had the opportunity to jump him again. Multiple times.

"Feel free to explore with him. You *should*. It's wonderful that you are." Somber now, Aurora said, "But don't let him convince you that he's important, because he is not."

"No?" He felt pretty important to her. Not *vital*— she could get by without him, if, or likely when, things ended. She got by without a lot of stuff—like affection from her mother and aunt.

When it came to Travis, though…her romantic heart was already hoping for impossible things.

"There are a lot of men out there and now that you're showing your sensual side, more of them will be interested. Spread your wings, Yardley. Gain some experience with men. Learn more about *you* before you give your heart to some man who won't be around long enough to deserve it."

Wow. What a way to deflate her confidence. "You're pretty darned sure Travis won't want to stick around."

Her mother's particular look of pity hurt her more than a slap would have. "You're a realist, Yardley. You see things that I never did. Don't let a man, any man, trample your heart."

Was it so unbelievable that Travis might be interested in *her*, for *her*? Regardless of her quirky nature? Despite her awkwardness and uncensored comments?

Apparently her mother thought so.

No. Yardley would not let her mother drag her down, not even with good intentions.

She was likeable. She was *loveable*.

And she was done emoting so dramatically in her own head. "You know what, Aurora?"

A shadow passed over her mother's features, almost a flinch, before it was concealed. "What's that, dear?"

"People do like me. A lot of people."

"Of course they do! Oh Yardley, you are a very, very likeable person."

Hmm... "But you don't think Travis likes me? You think he's just looking for a good time while he gets his sister married off, and then he'll forget all about me?" If that was the case, he'd gone about it all wrong. One, she was a long shot for a good time, since she knew nada about sexual escapades and had gone a decade without practice. Two, he was the one who'd kept putting off the sex.

In her aching heart, Yardley knew her mother's assumptions weren't true. She trusted Travis, believed in him. She *knew* him. He hadn't made promises, but neither was he just passing the time. And that was okay.

"What I'm saying is that I want you to enjoy your time with him, but protect yourself along the way." Pressing a fist to her heart, Aurora said, "Don't build up romantic expectations..." Dramatic seconds passed, and then, in a whisper, "Not the way I did."

Yardley was ready to have this night end...but then something else occurred to her. Her mother, her usually chic, aloof mother, appeared tired. Worried and worn. As if this chat pained her.

In her head, Yardley started trying to formulate the words—but then she stopped herself and simply asked, "Who was my father?"

Alarm obliterated every other emotion on Aurora's face. "We don't need to talk about him."

"I think maybe we do. I think we should have long ago." After all, he was likely the man who inspired this little chat, the man who'd broken her mother's heart.

The man who'd left her alone and pregnant...with an unwanted child.

Pushing to her feet, Aurora paced to the door, but to Yardley's surprise, she didn't leave. She turned and paced back. "He was a handsome boy. Fun and easygoing. He made me feel so special."

Seeing things she'd never seen before, Yardley asked gently, "Until he got you pregnant and left you?"

With one firm nod, her mother said, "I'd just turned eighteen. My parents were horrified." Aurora's upper lip trembled before she stiffened it in a forbearing expression all too familiar. "Lilith almost took it worse than I did."

Interesting. "Why? Was she embarrassed?" They were sisters, in some ways very close, in other ways—at least for all of Yardley's life—always at odds.

"I don't know. She wouldn't talk about it. Wouldn't talk to me." Aurora drew a strained breath and admitted, "I was so alone."

Wow. Always before, her mother had made it out to be a dramatic, wild escapade. That she'd been devastated by it all seemed unlikely—until now.

Aurora's gaze met Yardley's. "I don't want to see you hurt, but if it happens, you won't be alone. You have me. You have Lilith. We will never abandon you." Her lip quivered again. "Not like I was abandoned."

Sympathy brought Yardley to her feet, and she did something she'd rarely done with Aurora. She embraced her. Even more rare, Aurora not only accepted the affection, she returned it, tightly.

How odd to have her mother cling to her. To feel her usually rigid shoulders trembling. To have her want comfort.

Aurora wasn't a fragile woman, but in this moment, it seemed that she needed Yardley's strength. "We don't have to talk about him, Mother. It's not important. Not right now." One day, soon, she'd need answers. Tonight though, what she needed most was sleep. With a final pat to her mother's shoulder, Yardley eased her away.

In the low light of Yardley's bedroom, unshed tears glistened in Aurora's eyes. "It's been a long day." Sniffling, her mother drew a breath. "I think we're both tired."

"Yes." Curious about this new persona, Yardley tipped her head. "You'll be okay?"

"Of course." Aurora curved her stiffened lips into a familiar staged smile. "I have you and Lilith and our wonderful business here. My life is full."

Yardley couldn't tell if she was being flippant or not. "I feel the same, but with Mimi added in." And Kevin, Sammy… Betty…so many wonderful people she cared about.

And Travis. He really rounded out the happiness.

Not that she'd tell her mother that, considering her concerns. "Thank you for the chat." Tentatively, Yardley suggested, "We should do this more often."

Aurora shook her head. "It'd give me wrinkles." Back to her usual self, she winked, went to the bed to give Dodger a light, affectionate pat on the butt, which badly startled the dog, causing him to jump up in alarm. With Dodger and Yardley both watching her in surprise, Aurora walked out and closed the door softly behind her.

Yardley and Dodger stared at each other, both wearing expressions of disbelief. "Yeah, that was weird."

Tomorrow, Yardley decided, she'd tell Mimi all about her fantastic time with Travis.

But she wouldn't tell her about this odd exchange with Aurora. It felt far, far too personal—for the mother who'd never seemed to care about her.

A mother that she now realized hid a lot of hurt.

12

OVER THE LAST few days, Mimi had watched Yardley falling in love. Oh, she'd been halfway there before sex, but now that Travis was showing her such a good time on the regular—as in every night—her girl was totally hooked. Emotionally and sexually. Go Yardley!

It wasn't that Yardley was different. She'd always been amazingly kind, open, funny and…yeah, Mimi could throw in every positive attribute known to mankind. All despite the difficulty from her family. But now Yardley was *more*. Mimi understood, because she was more, too. More in love with her husband. More blissful with her life. More inspired and more prepared to deal with the down days.

Like her weight? The extra jiggly pounds sucked, but she didn't need a body from her twenties when *this* body was so damned happy. After all, *this* body made her husband lose his train of thought. *This* body got to share delicious cookies and muffins with her bestie. *This* body had brought an amazing baby girl into the world, and now provided a soft cushion for Sammy to snuggle.

This body was strong, healthy, and it was very well-loved.

She didn't want to be an insecure woman who looked for flaws, so instead she started taking long walks with Sammy each day and counted it as exercise.

See, proactive. Empowered.

A win all the way around.

If the floor didn't get vacuumed, who cared? No one.

Mimi liked that reasoning since it gave her what she wanted. Currently, she was very into pleasing herself, and wonder of wonders, doing so seemed to please everyone else that she cared about, too.

Maybe, after having Sammy, she'd lost a little bit of herself. She knew she'd floundered and sometimes felt inadequate, but thanks to Yardley's encouragement, and Kevin's love, she'd found herself again. Had her hormones been off a little? Possibly.

Mostly though, she believed she'd suffered the age-old struggle of trying to be super mom. She'd wanted to maintain all her old chores, like cleaning the house, doing the laundry—looking sexy for her husband—on top of everything that came with caring for a baby. She hadn't wanted to look any different, regardless of what her body had gone through and how tired she might be.

Pfft. What a dope she'd been.

As Kevin kept insisting, they were in this together and he was more than happy to help carry the load.

Happiness kept a small smile on her mouth and left her heart soft and full. Oh sure, she'd still push herself a little too hard sometimes, but that was part of her nature. Just as it was Kevin's nature to protect and Yardley's to nurture.

After parking in the lot of the town council building, she sent a text to Kevin. Sammy sleeping?

Yup. Relax & have fun

Of course she would. After all, she was here to cheer on Yardley and offer moral support. With another fat smile, she texted: Luv u [kissy-face emoji]

Luv u more

That wasn't possible, but she sent him another kissy face anyway, stowed her phone, and headed into the building where Yardley was about to have her big day.

The place was packed. It seemed every business owner had shown up—and there was Kathleen!

Yardley had accused her of putting the mannequin on her front porch after her first night with Travis, but hey, Mimi had been indulging her own wild romance with her über hot hubby, so she couldn't take the credit.

Now they were both stumped.

The day after the mannequin's appearance, Mimi had helped Yardley change the dummy's clothes and hair, putting her in one of Mimi's old outfits that included cute pink shorts and a skimpy halter. Getting into the theme, Mimi had even given her pigtails and then insisted on buying a giant lollipop to put in the mannequin's hand before sneaking her to the front stoop of M.J.'s candy shop. Since then, they'd pondered the question of who had put the mannequin at Yardley's house. More importantly, was it meant to tease or embarrass?

Neither of them could believe Aurora or Lilith would do such a thing; they had nothing but disdain for the dummy.

So who?

Today, the mannequin sat poised in the front row, wearing a Yardley for President T-shirt that made Mimi chuckle. Someone had gone to a lot of trouble, including the customized T-shirt. It all amused her, or at least it did until she saw Yardley's face.

Sitting on the stage behind a long table with some of the council members, her expression was a cross between "deer in the headlights" at all the suspense in the audience, and barely banked excitement for what she would announce. Sitting prettily beside her at the end of his leash, Dodger drew loads of attention. He, at least, seemed to enjoy being front and center.

To let Yardley know she hadn't done this, Mimi caught her eye and shrugged. Someone was supporting Yardley with Kathleen, but neither of them had any idea who it might be.

Yardley blew out a breath and rolled her eyes, her way of saying it was fine. But was it? Poor Yardley looked incredibly tense. Odd, but Betty didn't look fazed. In fact, she had a rather placid smile on her face. Yardley's influence, no doubt.

Mimi turned…and spotted Travis in the back row.

Interesting that he'd come to support her as well! That made Mimi like him even more. She'd wanted to get to know him better, and Yardley was on board with that, except that when given a choice between socializing or sex, Yardley chose sex every time, and Mimi couldn't blame her. Her friend was no dummy.

It was obvious that Travis and Yardley had set the

sheets on fire. It was all Yardley could talk about. Heck, they'd celebrated over triple chocolate brownies the day after her first time. Mimi was thrilled for her. Now the only thing missing was for Travis to declare how much he cared, because everyone could see that he did.

Was Yardley really supposed to wait until after Sheena's wedding? Dumb.

Determined to get some answers, and maybe offer a nudge or two, Mimi switched direction to take a seat beside him toward the back. "Hey."

He gave her a half grin. "Hello, Mimi."

"It's nice that you're here."

"Wouldn't miss it. I'm glad you could make it too." He nodded at the crowd. "I take it this is a little more packed than usual?"

"A lot more." They were close to full capacity. "Most of these people are business owners, so decisions will affect their livelihoods, but I think they're here for Yardley, too."

"Probably," he agreed. "From what I've seen, she makes an impact on everyone she meets."

Obviously he included himself in that. "Okay if I ask you something?"

Cautiously, he eyed her. "I won't know until you ask it. How intrusive is it going to be?"

Oh…only about as intrusive as a body could get. Didn't stop her though. Now that she and Kevin were back on the right track, she wanted the same for Yardley. "You and Yardley?"

He lifted a brow.

"How's that going?"

A slow, wicked smile made him even more handsome. Looking at the stage where Yardley sat with the others, he zeroed in on her. "I figured you and Yardley had talked. That was my impression."

And knowing that, he looked pretty smug. Mimi didn't mind. From what Yardley had shared, the guy had reason. Except it wasn't satisfaction in the sack that concerned her now. "I know how she feels."

With renewed interest, he brought his gaze back to hers. "How's that?"

"Nuh-uh. You first."

"Ah. You're asking me about my intentions?"

Damn. She kind of was. When had she turned into a busybody? "Are your intentions a secret?"

"Nope."

What exactly did "nope" mean? He didn't expound on it. Leaning closer to ensure no one else could hear, Mimi asked, "Should I start guessing?"

His brows lifted. "That could be interesting."

He was laughing at her! Funny, but she didn't mind that too much. "Yardley doesn't seem to know it, but she's gorgeous, smart, sweet—"

"Yeah, she is." He frowned a little. "*Why* she doesn't realize it, that's what stumps me."

Since Travis obviously knew it, she wondered why he wasn't locking her down. "We agree Yardley is a catch, right?"

"Absolutely."

"So, is there anything wrong with you?" Damn, that didn't come out the right way.

Travis's brows gathered closer together, but not in annoyance—at least she didn't think so. His expression was something more like introspection. "I had a different focus for a lot of years."

"Raising Sheena, you mean?"

With a nod, he explained, "For the longest time, Sheena came first." He shot her another look. "But you didn't hear that from me, so don't repeat it to her. I won't have her feeling guilty about anything."

Mimi crossed her heart. Sheena was great and they'd quickly become friends. She would never say or do anything to hurt the younger woman. "So you were all about being the big brother, putting aside your own wants and needs to focus on her—"

"It was never that dramatic," he said with a grin.

Undaunted, she continued, "—and then *bam*! Yardley."

Repeatedly his gaze returned to Yardley, as it did now. He looked at her with such intensity, Mimi almost felt like blushing. "She threw me for such a loop," he murmured.

Now, that sounded promising. "Yardley has that effect on a lot of people."

"So how did the men in this town overlook her for so long?"

"The question of the decade, right?" Mimi glanced around. "There aren't a lot of eligible guys who own businesses, but business owners are Yardley's peers. Other than me, and now Betty, she doesn't really hang out with anyone else. Her work is all dudes getting married, so no help there, right? And when she's not working, she's playing Cinderella to her mother and aunt."

"It's not quite that bad."

Not the way Yardley told it, but Mimi had grown up alongside her, and she'd watched her friend take on more and more responsibility…instead of being a kid, living her own life, or doing anything fun, like dating.

"Don't get me wrong," Travis said. "I'm glad I don't have competition. I just don't understand it."

No, Mimi had never really gotten it either. "I think back in high school she convinced everybody that she was a goof, and for some dumb reason, the impression stuck."

He shook his head. "She didn't convince me."

Mimi smiled. Knowing Yardley, she'd probably tried, but thankfully, Travis hadn't bought it. "Now that we're chatting more, I get why Yardley is…" How should she put it?

Keen interest locked his gaze to hers. "She's what?"

With a shrug, Mimi said, "Hung up on you?" Yeah, that worked. "Definitely hung up."

Pure satisfaction curved his mouth. "Good to know."

"I mean, you look very fine. Even Kevin said so."

Travis laugh-coughed. "He did, huh? Wonder how that conversation went."

"Well, with me prompting him, but if you were an ogre, he wouldn't have hesitated to correct me. And FYI, I was saying how hunky you looked *for Yardley.* Don't ever think I'm flirting or anything. That'd just be weird."

He rubbed the bridge of his nose. "You and Yardley have a lot in common. I can see why you're best friends."

"I'll take that as a compliment."

"Exactly how I meant it." He nodded up at the raised stage. "I think they're about to begin."

"Soon. I've been to a few of these—"

"To support Yardley?"

"That's the *only* reason I'd attend." Overall, the town meetings bored her. "They'll do a reading of the minutes and go over budget stuff before my girl gets to share her big news." With any luck, they'd all be celebrating tonight.

Suddenly there was an expectant hush and everyone seemed to be looking at the doors. Mimi and Travis shared a *what now?* glance before they both twisted toward the entry to see who had caused such a reaction.

Mimi's jaw loosened. Dressed in their finest business attire, Aurora and Lilith not only came inside, but without pause they strode right up to the front. Distrust narrowed Mimi's eyes. If either of them did anything to embarrass Yardley, she'd... Well, she wasn't sure what she'd do because Yardley was absurdly protective of them. "They better not embarrass her," she muttered.

With ultimate confidence, Travis said, "Yardley can handle it."

"You think so?"

"I know so. Pretty sure she could handle anything. She's damned amazing that way."

Nice. Mimi nudged him with her shoulder. "You have a lot of faith in her. I like that."

A shocked inhalation filled the room when Aurora scooted in to sit on one side of Kathleen, while Lilith sat on the other. Together, as if choreographed, they took Kathleen by her rigid arms and...

Put her on the floor? Oh, poor Kathleen!

Now no one could see her wonderful shirt.

Yardley literally gaped at them. Not a good sign. She'd already been visibly nervous and now this? It was so unexpected that Mimi knew she had to do something.

She said to Travis, "Later, gator," and quickly sidled up the aisle to slide into the seat next to Aurora. She smiled at Yardley while out of the corner of her mouth she growled, "What are you doing here?"

Aurora said, "Supporting my daughter, of course."

Could that be true? Leaning to see around Aurora, she asked Lilith, "And you?"

Lilith kept her gaze forward. "The same."

Even though she didn't buy it, Mimi nodded. "Well, okay then."

Not amused, both women pinned her with their annoyance.

Concentrating on Yardley, Mimi gave her two thumbs up. A second later, Travis joined them, sitting beside Lilith. He smiled first at Mimi, then at Aurora and Lilith.

The two women, finding themselves sandwiched between Yardley's biggest supporters, looked surprised, but they rallied. Aurora even smiled.

Now see, how could Mimi not adore Travis? He'd just championed Yardley in a very public way. It was brilliant. "Look at Yardley's face," she whispered to Travis, even though Aurora and Lilith sat between them. "She doesn't know what to think."

"She'll do great," Travis assured her.

And surprise, surprise, Aurora said, "Of course she will. She's my daughter, after all. She has my poise."

Well, that was a new attitude!

"And my intelligence." Lilith smiled. "That's what'll carry her through."

Aurora scowled, Lilith smirked, and Mimi had visions of a catastrophe about to erupt.

"Whatever traits she's inherited," Travis said, interrupting the impending conflict, "she's made them uniquely her own. Just watch. She's going to wow the crowd."

Before anything else could be said, the meeting was called to order.

AS THE MEETING PROGRESSED, Yardley tried not to squirm. She'd been looking forward to making the announcement, but then she'd seen Kathleen in the audience with that bold shirt. Thank heavens Betty had dismissed it with only a slight show of exasperation.

She didn't want all her plans ruined by a dummy.

As if that wasn't enough, her mother and aunt had shown up too. Nervousness made her palms damp. She was used to dealing with all the business owners and the town council.

But not with her family watching.

Travis and Mimi, sure. She liked having them near.

Aurora and Lilith? Not so much, especially since she didn't know their motives.

Trying to look cool under pressure wasn't easy. Several times she'd met Travis's gaze, absorbing his confidence in her, his trust that she'd handle everything just fine. He believed in her, and that helped.

Mimi's smiles were also a boost. That particular curl of her mouth said *whatever happens, we'll deal with it together*. God love her, what would she do without Mimi?

Dodger, bless his heart, behaved. Though he stuck close to her, he'd greeted everyone with a wagging tail, doling out extra affection to Betty. Pretty sure that was the only time anyone on the board had ever heard the town matriarch use such a high-pitched, sugary voice.

Baby talk from Betty Cemetery had left everyone agog.

The dog was a total sweetheart—or so she thought— right up until Betty cleared her throat and accepted the microphone to begin her explanations. Then the little rascal decided it was the perfect time to lick himself.

On a stage.

With a full audience in attendance.

Right there, with everyone looking on, he lifted a leg and got to it. He sure was thorough, too.

Scorching heat crept into Yardley's cheeks, and she sort of hoped spontaneous combustion was imminent. She tried giving the leash a subtle tug, but that just caused Dodger to double his efforts. She could *hear* him.

No one looked at Betty now. Nope. They were all focused on Dodger's crude display.

What to do?

Betty surprised her by laughing—*into* the microphone.

That diverted attention real fast! People actually gasped. Hadn't anyone heard her laugh before? Wow. This was a meeting that'd go down in the history books.

"Our new town mascot," Betty announced with a fond smile directed at Dodger. "Clearly, he doesn't find these meetings nearly as fascinating as Yardley and I do."

And just like that, the gazes all jumped to Yardley. After all, by her wording alone, Betty had just united them.

Like a bug pinned down for inspection, Yardley went still. She could practically feel all that anticipation swelling. With a delicate clearing of her throat, she smiled. "Thank you, Betty, as always, for being so kind."

Betty snorted. As if they'd rehearsed a stage act, she said in an aside through the microphone, "I've got her fooled, huh?"

A chorus of uncertain titters filled the room.

Getting on board with the fun, Yardley replied, "I am ever an optimist."

"As well as tenacious and determined, and now a dear friend." Betty waited for the second round of gasps to die down. "That's why it's my pleasure to make several announcements."

With everyone holding their breath, the room grew incredibly quiet. Except for the sound of Dodger now grumbling as he wound his leash around a table leg.

Mimi's chuckle broke the tension, releasing everyone else so that they all laughed, too.

Standing, Travis approached her with his easy, long-legged stride. Leaning in, he said, "Why don't I take him for a few minutes so you can manage your business?"

Only too willing, Yardley practically threw him the leash, which he easily untangled from the table.

"Thank you," Betty announced, and darned if she didn't look Travis over in appreciation.

When he regained his seat, now holding Dodger, both Aurora and Lilith stared at the dog.

Betty, always a master at claiming an audience, declared, "We have three announcements. Obviously you've met our new town mascot, Dodger. Our own wonderful Yardley Belanger rescued Dodger from a park, where he'd been left to die."

Sounds of dismay and sympathy swelled in the room.

God, Yardley loved this town and the wonderful people in it.

"I know you'll all join me in welcoming him to Cemetery." Betty waited for the awkward applause for Dodger to subside before saying, "It's because of Dodger that Yardley and I have decided our town needs a loving, nurturing, no-kill animal shelter. Many of you might not know this, but I have a soft spot for animals." No one made a peep.

Most people didn't know Betty had a soft spot of any kind. Only because they didn't really know her.

Loud enough for all to hear, Yardley called out, "Dodger realized it as soon as he met you."

"He's obviously an excellent judge of character," Betty said with affection. "I want to spearhead that project, so it's with great relief that I make another announcement. Yardley will now be a very special liaison to help represent the local businesses here in Cemetery, which will afford me more time to dedicate to other pursuits, like the shelter." Though no one made a sound, Betty held up a stern hand as if to quiet them. "I'm not saying we'll make immediate changes. Nothing is going to happen overnight. However, Yardley and I will work closely together so that she can present your concerns to me and the other board members. Her position is official as of right now, so once the meeting ends, please feel free to approach her as you see fit."

At that, everyone surged to their feet with boisterous applause.

Oh, my.

Yardley put a hand to her heart. Through the bodies, she saw her mother and aunt glance at each other in surprise, then slowly stand as well. Dodger howled, he was so excited. Or maybe startled. Mimi let loose an ear-splitting whistle that had Betty huffing into the mic. Saul hugged Emily, and then they both cheered.

Deadpan, Betty said, "Please, don't hold back your enthusiasm," before she winked at Yardley and gestured for her to come take the mic. "Yardley will address you now."

Full of nervous excitement, her heart punching hard, Yardley approached the mic. As Betty started to retreat, Yardley took her hand and held on. This was Betty's show. In so many ways, it was Betty's town. She needed, she *deserved*, to stay front and center.

Quieter now, everyone started to sit. Yardley wanted them to remain on their feet. This part was important, because Betty was important—to Cemetery, to the history, and especially to Yardley.

"Just a moment, please." Shifting, she put her arm across Betty's proud but age-stooped shoulders. "Betty Cemetery has done so much for this town, for all of us really, and I know you're all as anxious to thank her as I am."

Crickets.

Yardley started to panic…

Until Mimi thrust a fist in the air and shouted, "To Betty!"

Travis yelled, "Hear, hear!"

Thank God, others quickly joined in. Soon the entire building shook with all the excitement. Unable to resist, Yardley turned to Betty and hugged her tight. "Thank you, Betty. So very much—for everything."

Swallowing heavily, Betty nodded, and Yardley was almost certain she saw a glassy sheen in her eyes.

As soon as the noise started to die down, Yardley leaned into the mic again. "It goes without saying that I am not running for town council president." Uneasy laughs ensued. "Whoever has been dressing Kathleen, I appreciate the faith you put in me, because Betty would be an incredibly hard act to follow, but we can all rest easy knowing she's still on the job. With that said, I'm anxious to get started as liaison. You all know me, so feel free to call on me anytime."

Betty crowded in next to her. "And I have a petition for the shelter that I hope you'll sign so that we, the board, can gauge community interest."

That started a round of interested questions, so Yardley returned to her seat, more than gratified in the outcome of the day.

Bursting with pleasure, she scanned the audience until her gaze collided with Travis's warm expression of pride. How nice was that?

Next she met Mimi's satisfied grin.

Last, she sought out her mother and aunt. They looked…gobsmacked. It was the only word Yardley could think of to describe their expressions of utter astonishment. Witnessing it almost made her laugh.

You see, she wanted to say, *I'm not so awkward after all*.

MIMI WATCHED YARDLEY glide from guest to guest, refilling drinks, bringing a smile or two, and basically making everyone feel special. She was in her element, and by God, Mimi hoped she realized just how much everyone adored her.

When her friend headed for the kitchen with an empty tray, Mimi followed. "You truly are a hostess extraordinaire."

"Pfft," Yardley said, making it look easy as she retrieved a fresh tray of tiny cakes and cookies from the fridge. "You know this is my jam. This is what I do for a living."

True, as a wedding organizer, Yardley knew her stuff. But that wasn't what she meant. "It's more than that, though." It was important for Yardley to realize it. "How you make everyone so comfortable, how warm you are—that's a gift. When people are with you, they feel…heard. Seen."

Turning away from the tray, Yardley studied Mimi. "You?"

Laughing, Mimi said, "You see? That right there."

"What?"

"How you just focused on me. That's what you always do. It's part of why the town loves you. And yes, it's one of the many reasons I love you."

Smiling, looking a little self-conscious, Yardley got back to work on her snack arrangement. "Thank you. I think it's gone well tonight. And these miniature cheesecakes have sure been a hit."

"The whole party has been a hit. There hasn't been a single dull moment because we're all too busy having fun."

"Not Betty," Yardley said, and it sounded like it bothered her. "She's still being standoffish—" Yardley gave Mimi a look "—and you aren't helping."

"Was I supposed to help with that?"

Pausing again, Yardley said, "You're supposed to help me with everything."

Yeah, she was. Softer now, Mimi said, "I'm working up to it. Taming dragons doesn't come as easily to me as it obviously does to you."

That had Yardley fighting a smile. "Thank you." Stepping back, she eyed the tray critically and must've decided it'd do. "It's been sort of a relief that Aurora and Lilith are absent."

Mimi wouldn't buy that for a single second. She moved closer, stopping Yardley before she could head out again. "I think," she whispered, "you wanted them to see this. Right?" This would have been Yardley's opportunity to show them that she wasn't awkward—just the opposite, in fact. She had real friends who found her to be incredibly kind, impressive and talented, and even the almighty Betty-freaking-Cemetery counted her as a friend.

Yardley wrinkled her nose. "Do I seem that desperate?"

"Not desperate, no. Never that." She bumped her

shoulder to Yardley's. "But you deserve their respect and if they don't give it, it's their loss."

It took a second, and then Yardley smiled brightly. "I agree. I've been so happy lately, I wanted to share it with all of you, and yes, a part of me wants to show them that they're just blind when it comes to me. I have talents, a good head for business, and I have amazing friends."

Mimi slowly smiled, too. "All that. I'm glad you know it."

Gently, Yardley took her hand. "I do now. If Aurora and Lilith choose not to be here…" She shrugged. "I'm still happy."

"And beautiful."

Yardley's lips twitched. "If you say so."

"And brilliant."

"Now you're just pushing your luck."

Laughing, Mimi glanced around the kitchen. Amazingly, it still looked tidy. "You've obviously got this down pat, but is there anything I can do?" As soon as she asked it, she winced. "Other than cozy up to Betty?"

That made Yardley grin. "Betty's fun. You'll see."

Already knowing she'd do it, Mimi rolled her eyes. "Uh-huh." She drew a resigned breath. "Wish me luck."

"You? Badass Mimi May? You don't need luck."

No, she didn't. She just needed a little of Yardley's sweet disposition.

Hoping for inspiration, she followed Yardley out of the kitchen, but paused as Yardley continued on to briefly engage with each guest while they chose another bite-size dessert. Betty declined more, so Yardley moved on to Travis—and there she stayed.

Wow, the way that man looked at Yardley, with admiration, pride, a whole lot of want, and—if Mimi wasn't mistaken—full-blown love. It was everything her best friend deserved.

As a win-win, she and Kevin both liked him a lot, too. Heck, everyone liked everyone else…

With one exception.

Throughout the dinner, people had tried to engage Betty, but while she'd been polite, she hadn't exactly opened up or taken part. Mostly she'd concentrated on her food, with the occasional compliment to Yardley on the marinated steak skewers, tender asparagus and potatoes roasted with Parmesan.

Easy foods, Yardley had told her, both to serve and to clear away. From the empty plates, it was evident the guests just knew it was all delicious.

As people left the table to mingle in groups, Betty chose to meander around the room alone, apparently intent on studying the renovations Yardley had made. Well, that wouldn't do.

Understanding what Yardley hoped to accomplish, Mimi walked up to Betty with a practiced smile in place. "Hey, Ms. Cemetery."

Expression guarded, perhaps a little dismissive, Betty eyed her. "Mimi."

"Having fun?"

After a slight hesitation, Betty narrowed her eyes. "The house is beautiful. I've admired the exterior, but this is the first time I've been inside."

"Drive past here often?" It wasn't along the strip of businesses, the beach or the town council.

"I've made a point to on occasion." She gave Mimi the side-eye. "Recently, in fact."

Hey, had she been spying on Yardley? Planning her defenses? Betty had always been so cantankerous, especially to Yardley. It didn't make it easy for Mimi to be-friend her now—except that she *had* made Yardley her liaison, and she *did* love animals. Plus…

It's what Yardley wants.

Reminding herself of that, Mimi nodded. "Yardley is a fantastic decorator. She makes awesome choices, right? Actually, my girl is good at everything she does."

"Including coercing her friends into approaching me with designs of making peace?"

A direct attack? Okay, fine. Mimi could work with that. "Yeah, she twisted my arm so hard, she damn near broke my elbow. But what can I say? I dragged my butt over here because she has a huge heart and a lot of love for this town."

"Yes, she does," Betty agreed. "The future of Cemetery is in good hands."

Surprise unclenched Mimi's teeth and lifted her brows. She recovered quickly. "Agree one hundred percent."

"It relieves my mind." Betty met her gaze squarely. "History is important."

Tentative, hoping she wouldn't set Betty off, Mimi said, "But maybe so is the present?"

This time Betty's look was longer and somewhat good-natured. "I like her new sweetheart."

They both glanced at Travis. "Me, too! He's great, right?"

Betty stepped closer. "Are we finding common ground, Mimi?"

Relief about took out her knees. "Sure, why not?" If Yardley could do it, Mimi could too.

"Because you don't like me?" Betty suggested.

Okay, maybe she'd celebrated too soon. "I was under the impression that went both ways."

Betty snorted. It was such a funny sound coming from her that Mimi had to fight a laugh. "What was that?" As if looking for the source of the sound, Mimi searched the floor. "I thought I heard some sort of wild animal grunting..."

"Oh, stop." Betty laughed.

Whoa. Enjoying herself, Mimi said with feigned shock, "A snort *and* a laugh? Damn, Betty—okay if I call you Betty?—if you're not careful you'll soon become part of the Mimi and Yardley club."

Betty leaned closer to confide, "I've always suspected the two of you had a lot of fun."

"Oh, for sure." Maybe Mimi's upfront honesty had softened Betty. Or more likely, Yardley was right and Betty was never as uppity as she'd let on. "We gossip, complain, share secrets and concerns. Sometimes we laugh like loons, but other times, on rarer occasions, we cry, too."

Sobering, Betty nodded. "True of most women, I suspect. I'm glad the two of you have each other." Betty's gaze went to Yardley, who chatted with Sheena, who was holding Sammy. "Yardley deserved a champion like you."

"She's always had me, but I've needed her just as much." Sometimes more. "And now she has Travis—and you, too, right?"

"I'm delighted to call her a friend."

When Betty spoke so softly, with so much reverence, it was easy to see what Yardley saw. "Something else Yardley and I do is swill delicious tea varieties and gorge ourselves on sweets. You look like a gal who could do some swilling."

"And gorging," Betty concurred.

Ha! Once she let out the starch, Betty had a wicked

sense of humor. "Awesome. So how about we take tea at your place one day? Yardley has the most phenomenal teas."

"It wouldn't be fair for her to always supply the refreshments."

Well, what do you know? She hadn't refused. Buoyed by that, Mimi nodded. "You're right. I think we should take turns. Heck, we could even form a tea club or something. I could handle that. Yardley, me, you, maybe the other ladies from the town businesses. Like Emily—she could bring some fresh flowers for us. And Sallie could bring pastries for us to eat. I could get M.J. to order the teas through her Sweets and Treats shop." Feeling it all come together, Mimi picked up steam. "It doesn't always have to be at your place. I could host too, and Yardley would, I'm sure, but for that first time, let's gather at your house. Yardley says you have some really gnarly historical photos. We could check 'em out, chat about old times. What do you say?"

Though Betty's mouth didn't move, her eyes smiled. "Old times, because I'm so ancient, I can remember them all?"

"Hey, we can't all stay spring chickens, right? I'm already a mom. God willing, I'll one day be in my eighties like you, and it'd be awesome if I could pass along some of the town history to my grandbabies."

"I had no idea you were interested in history. I thought you were more into mischief."

Betty's barbs no longer bothered her. In fact, Mimi realized she was enjoying herself. "I'm multi-talented, doncha know. I can handle both."

With that, Betty gave in to a grin. "Indeed." She folded her hands together. "I think I like your idea."

"Sweet." She held up a palm, Betty stared at it blankly, and Mimi laughed. "High five? No?"

"Oh, I see." Belatedly, Betty smacked her palm to Mimi's.

Success! Mimi smiled inside and out. Who knew befriending crotchety old Betty Cemetery could be so rewarding?

Obviously, Yardley did.

"Smile, you two." With her phone raised to take a photo, Yardley had moved nearer.

To Mimi's surprise, Betty slapped an arm around her and squeezed her in close with surprising strength, a big cheesy grin on her face. Huh. Betty wasn't as frail as she let on!

Mimi laughed—and Yardley took the shot. When Betty tried to move away, Mimi hooked her arm and kept her at her side.

Betty was so small, and in many ways she appeared fragile, but man, the lady had a will of iron and a quirky personality that she'd kept hidden behind steel pride. And that grip…hmm. It gave Mimi something to think about.

To Yardley, Mimi said, "Guess what? Betty and I are starting a tea club. How fun is that?" She ran through the details.

Cutting her off with a laugh, Yardley said, "I love it! This is going to be so fun."

"Naturally, you'll bring Dodger," Betty declared. "And I think little Sammy should join us as well, even though she can't yet have tea."

Sheena, still holding Sammy, sidled up to them with her hand raised. "Hey, didn't mean to eavesdrop, but could I take part too? I already love it here, and after the wedding, I plan to visit."

"Excellent," Betty said before anyone else could. "I think we should hand out flyers so all the women in town will know. I'll need more seating, of course. Perhaps a nice folding table like the one Yardley used tonight. Oh, and I might buy a new tea service."

Yardley shared a grateful smile with Mimi. Now that Betty was taking part, she just naturally took over. It was in her nature.

For the rest of the evening, they made plans. Eventually the men joined in, too. Mimi loved—literally, totally *loved*—seeing Yardley next to Travis, his arm resting over her shoulders, her arm around his waist. The happiness glowing in her eyes. The contentment on her face.

This, the dinner party, friends. Yardley was in her element.

Whatever happened between her and Travis, nothing would ever be the same. Yardley was out of her shell for real now. She hadn't needed Mimi to push her because she'd found her own way.

For the town.

In dealing with her mother and aunt.

And in finding love.

So often Yardley spoke of their friendship as if Mimi had helped her along. The truth was, Mimi didn't know what she would have done without Yardley.

They weren't sisters by blood, but they were so much more.

When Sammy fell asleep, Kevin eased her away from Sheena so that she could rest on his big solid shoulder, and be held safe in his strong arms. Dodger leaned against his foot; those two had become fast friends. She watched his mostly healed hand smooth gently over their daughter's small back. Saw him lightly kiss the top of her head.

If her heart got any bigger, it might not fit in her rib cage anymore.

"Mimi?" Yardley's hand curved over her shoulder in a gentle squeeze. "You okay?"

She realized Yardley had moved away from Travis and was now at her side, her eyes shadowed with concern. Mimi had been so busy with uplifting introspection, she hadn't even noticed. "I'm so incredibly great," she whispered, sending a smile to Kevin. "Look at all I have, Yardley. God, I am so, so blessed."

"Yes, you are. Blessed and beautiful."

"It makes me so happy I could cry."

"Don't," Yardley warned urgently. "If you cry, you know I'll be crying, too, and everyone will wonder what's wrong with us."

That made Mimi chuckle. "Most of the town has wondered that for years."

"Much better." Smiling with visible relief, Yardley drew her forward. "Come on. You can help me tidy up again."

Together, as they'd always been, they headed to the kitchen with empty glasses and crumb-filled napkins. Yup, Cemetery was in for some major changes, and it was all possible because of her unbelievably generous friend.

It wasn't only the town that was better with Yardley in it. The entire world benefited, Mimi most of all.

SHE'D DONE IT.

The dinner party was a huge success and she was high on the thrill of it all. Thanks to Mimi's help, everyone was now chatting with Betty, who basked in the limelight.

Even better, Travis made it obvious to one and all that they were now a couple.

Her life had changed in ways she'd never anticipated, mostly because it had all seemed far out of reach. Even though her mother and aunt were no-shows, who cared? She told herself that she hadn't truly expected them to join in anyway. It was enough that they'd come to the council meeting.

No sooner did she have that thought than both women stepped into the kitchen, Aurora first, followed by Lilith.

Oddly enough, her mother had a slightly panicked look on her face.

Mimi set down the tray she'd been holding and, as she'd so often done throughout the years, stationed herself at Yardley's side.

"Aurora," Mimi said. "How's it going?"

Her mother never looked away from Yardley's eyes. "I opened the door…" She drew a shuddering breath. "And your little dog ran out."

"We looked for him," Lilith promised in a rush, her hands clasped together in worry. "But it's dark and we can't find him."

Oh. Dear. God.

All her ebullience of moments ago sank like a stone into her gut.

Snacks forgotten, Yardley shot out of the kitchen at a run. As she raced through the house, Travis fell into step beside her. "What's wrong?"

"Dodger got out." Fear propelled her faster. *Oh please. Please, please, please let me find him.* Dodger was still so vulnerable, the memory of being hurt obvious in the way he sometimes ducked when people moved too quickly, and how he usually stuck close to a person.

They had that uncertainty in common, but she wanted to love him enough that he'd trust her to protect him always.

Behind her, she heard Mimi announcing the issue, organizing everyone to help.

Yardley pushed through the door, but Lilith was right. The night was dark, not a star in sight, and the porch light didn't travel far. "Dodger?" she called in her sweetest, albeit shaking voice. "Here, Dodger. Come here, sweetheart."

"I'll check the street," Travis said, jogging down the walkway.

Mimi rushed up beside her. "Kevin and Todd went out back. Sheena and I will take the side yards." She squeezed Yardley's shoulder. "We'll find him, hon." Then she ran off.

Her mother thrust a flashlight toward her. "Here, use this. Lilith and I will help, too." Aurora turned on her phone light. "Here, little doggy. Come here," her mother called in a high, urgent voice, moving off toward the cars parked along the curb.

Yardley spared a shocked glance at her mother.

"Please, Dodger," Aurora called. "Come on, baby."

Though astounded by her mother's and aunt's reactions, Yardley continued calling for the dog, and with every minute that passed, her fear grew more unbearable. This couldn't be happening. She would never accept that Dodger was gone. Never... She heard a bark!

She went still, listening hard.

"Found him," Travis called from across the street, though Yardley couldn't see him. "Over here!"

Her heart thundering wildly, only vaguely aware of her mother and aunt following, Yardley ran to him. "Is he okay?" He had to be okay. "Travis? Where are you?"

"Around here, Yardley." He stepped out from between

two houses. "Dodger's in your neighbor's backyard—
with another dog."

But that yard was fenced! How in the world... She
started forward in a sprint. Drawing breath wasn't easy.

And then Travis was there, pulling her close, his expression understanding. "It's okay, honey. Dodger's fine,
I swear. He just found a friend."

Relief nearly took out her knees.

With his protective arm around her, he led her to the
fenced-in backyard. Thankfully, it was well-lit, so she
immediately saw Dodger racing around, happily yapping
and playing with a big yellow Lab.

Oh my goodness. One hand covering her mouth, the
tears came, an overflow of emotion because the dogs
looked so happy.

Winded from running, Mimi braced her hands on her
knees and sucked air. "Dang, that dog needs a good talk-
ing-to."

"I'll handle that as soon as I stop shaking," Yardley
promised, which earned her another reassuring hug from
Travis.

Straightening, Mimi blew out one last breath and then
got down to business. "I'll knock on the front door, let
your neighbor know why we're all congregated out here
just so we don't spook anyone."

What in the world...? Yardley turned to find all her
guests—even her aunt and mother—gathered behind her.
Only one person was missing.

Mimi quickly explained, "Betty stayed in the house
with Sammy."

Sentiment made it hard to speak. Family, friends, Travis...they were all here, and she had to get it together.

"He's fine," she whispered, then cleared her throat and said louder, "He's okay. Travis found him."

Everyone exhaled a sigh of relief. Her mother even dabbed at her eyes, like maybe she'd been tearful. Marching up to the fence, Lilith shook her finger. "Naughty dog! Don't do things like that. You scared me half to death."

Yardley would have taken exception to her snapping at Dodger that way, except that she saw Lilith trembling. Besides, neither dog paid any attention to her.

Obviously her aunt had spoken through her own upset.

It struck Yardley that as a child, she'd heard that same sharp tone many times whenever Lilith had…worried about her? She hadn't realized it back then. She just knew she didn't like it when her aunt frowned and spoke so harshly.

Now though? Now she sort of understood.

With that understanding came emotional contentment. It was as if years of dark, troubled thoughts grew a tiny bit lighter.

Travis brushed his thumb over her cheek. "I think our boy has won over a lot of hearts already, including your aunt's."

Very true, though Lilith would likely deny it. "I keep saying, Dodger is a charmer…" And yet someone had mistreated him.

Oh, she knew exactly why that hit home for her, yet maybe she'd been misguided in her feelings. It was possible that her perception of her mother and aunt had been off. She'd started with a child's reaction of insecurity and disappointment…and she'd never veered from those hurt feelings. No, Aurora and Lilith weren't warm and openly affectionate, and they definitely criticized her far too often. Yet she'd put up with it. As an adult, she hadn't corrected them, or even really reacted.

Travis said much of it seemed out of habit—now she realized it was their habit, and her own.

"Yardley? You okay?"

Hearing the concern in his tone, she decided she didn't need to solve every problem tonight. She'd lived with those issues for decades, so she could hold on to them a while longer. "I am now." Her shoulders dropped with the release of tension. "I'm so glad you found him."

Trailing the backs of two fingers over her damp cheek, Travis whispered, "I'm so glad I found you." He pressed his mouth to hers in a warm caress. "So damn glad."

Yardley was about to make a profound statement— something that included the words *I* and *love* and *you*, but her neighbor, Mr. Hopper, chose that auspicious moment to step out his back door wearing a rumpled white T-shirt, baggy sleep pants and slippers. He was a retired schoolteacher, in his late seventies, and he loved his evening TV shows.

"Mr. Hopper, I'm so sorry. I hope we didn't wake you."

He stood there staring at the dogs. "Will you look at that? I haven't seen Stella so playful in years." He turned to Yardley, bushy brows down. "She's old, too, you know."

"She's not acting old." Yardley was so pleased to see Dodger enjoying himself. "My little guy got past the door—he's named Dodger for a reason—but I'm not sure how he got in your yard."

"I can guess." Mr. Hopper headed toward the back of his property. "Come have a look over here."

It didn't take long for Travis and Yardley to see the

path Stella had created along the fence line, and then near one post...a hole.

Travis knelt to examine it. "Sorry about this. I can repair it first thing tomorrow."

"Nah, your dog didn't do it. Stella likes to dig. I've refilled that spot more times than I can count." He nudged the bottom of the fence with the toe of his slipper. "Wonder how your Dodger kept from hurting himself though. Stella pushes the chain-link out when she's yapping at squirrels, and somehow he crawled under coming in. Seems like he would've gotten poked."

Both dogs finally decided to take notice of the humans. Side by side, they ran over. Being a sweetheart, Stella slowed before reaching Mr. Hopper. She sat beside him and looked up lovingly. Mr. Hopper rubbed her head.

Dodger jumped around without an ounce of manners before flattening himself and crawling under the fence toward Travis's feet.

"Huh," said Mr. Hopper. "He's a little Houdini for sure."

Travis scooped up the dog. "I can take care of the fence problem with some twelve-inch J hook rebar stakes. That'll secure it."

"Yeah, but then the dogs can't visit, and I can see my Stella won't like that."

Stella had her head tipped back, eyes closed and tongue out as she enjoyed the way Mr. Hopper gently rubbed her ears.

It struck Yardley that she had instant respect and affection for anyone who cared for animals. "Maybe we can set up playdates for the dogs. Dodger is obviously very taken with her, too."

"Playdates?" Considering that, Mr. Hopper said, "I'm here most every day. We could make it early evening.

When I have an appointment or have to go to the store, I'm always back by five."

"Wonderful! I'll come over tomorrow with my schedule and we can set up a few times for the dogs to visit." First Travis, then Betty and the town council, and now Mr. Hopper. Her social calendar was downright busy these days.

"We could also take them on walks together." Travis put his arm around Yardley's waist. "Do you think Stella would like that?"

"And you are?"

"Oh, I'm sorry. Mr. Hopper, this is my…" Yardley stalled. My *what*? "Travis Long." She blinked. *This is my Travis Long?* Gah. That didn't even make sense.

Travis smiled at her.

Mr. Hopper just waited.

Feeling the familiar burn of embarrassment in her face, she cleared her throat. "Travis and I were together when we found Dodger." She didn't go into the details of the sad story. No reason to burden her neighbor. "I've had him ever since."

Wearing a deliberately bland look, Mr. Hopper asked, "The man or the dog?"

Both? "Er, I meant the dog."

"But I've stuck around as well." Releasing her, Travis held out his hand.

Mr. Hopper accepted. "Nice to meet you, Travis. I always thought Yardley deserved a handsome young man. Guess you fit the bill."

"Thank you. I like to think I deserve her, too," said Travis with a totally straight face.

"She's a smart one." Mr. Hopper winked. "Wouldn't be with you otherwise."

Awk-ward. Yardley cleared her throat again. "Dodger, say your goodbyes. We need to return home, now." Thankfully everyone else had already migrated back to her house.

"And I need to finish my show. Enjoy the rest of your evening." Mr. Hopper turned, and Stella fell into step beside him.

Dodger watched, his uninjured ear perked high, his little furry face filled with anxiety. Poor baby! "It's okay, bud. You'll see Stella again." Obviously she hadn't been attentive enough during the party. And for sure she needed to better secure the dog when she had company coming and going.

Carrying Dodger with one arm, Travis reached for her hand, lacing their fingers together, palm to palm, as he started them back across the street. "You know it wasn't your fault that he got out, right?"

If not hers, then whose? "What if we hadn't found him? What if he'd gotten hit by a car, or someone took him?"

"It was a party, honey. Lots going on, and Dodger earned his name."

"By dodging out at the first opportunity?"

"Now we'll both know to keep a better eye on him. A notice on the door might help, too."

Not a bad idea. "Maybe I could stick a sign in a pretty flowerpot so people would know…" Her voice trailed off. Aurora and Aunt Lilith *had* known, and still he'd gotten by them.

"Your mother and aunt were sincerely concerned. They'll be more careful from now on. Everyone will."

"He's chipped, and he has his collar and rabies tag." They'd taken care of that soon after bringing him home.

"Maybe I need one of those identity tags for him too? Something that shares my phone number and address."

"Not a great idea." He stopped them beneath a tree, still several feet from the people who remained outside. "I know this is a small town and you're friendly with everyone, but giving out too much info is dangerous. If you need to list a contact, let it be me, okay?"

Staring up at him, Yardley felt so much love—but what if he didn't feel the same? She knew Dodger would be with her for all of his life.

She didn't know that about Travis.

He cupped her face, his thumb stroking oh so softly over her jaw. "What are you thinking?"

That I want you forever. She didn't want this to end. She wanted to marry Travis Long and have a beach wedding and spend a blissful week at the Honeymoon Cottage.

At the moment, here, now, with him, it seemed possible.

Heck, everything seemed possible. She opened her mouth, but caught herself before any words escaped.

It was too soon; at the very least Travis needed time enough to get to enjoy his sister's wedding. And then?

She'd always believed her life was right here, in a town with a name she disliked immensely, living in her beloved Victorian home with relatives she thought resented her existence. It had been easy to assume she'd spend that life as a single woman—after all, at thirty-one, she'd never had a serious boyfriend, much less a man who wanted to share her future.

Yet everything had changed lately. Now, the name Cemetery seemed important, because Betty Cemetery was so important. The house…well, she still loved it, but leaving it wouldn't break her heart.

Not if it meant spending her life with Travis.

Actually, even if Travis moved on, she'd still want a life separate from her mother and aunt. As a child, she'd adopted a weird effort to make herself important; she'd enabled them. In so many ways, she'd encouraged them to depend on her for everything.

The habits of the child had stuck with the adult. Familiarity was a comfortable thing.

Yet now that she recognized what she'd done and why, she wouldn't do it anymore. It was past time for some positive changes in her life.

Travis kissed her forehead. "I can see there's a lot going on in your head."

A lot, all of it insightful. A small fib seemed the way to go. "I was just thinking how much I like it when you're so touchy-feely. The little kisses and strokes and stuff." The signs of caring.

"My guess is that it was a whole lot more than that, and we'll need to talk about it soon."

From a fib to teasing, but hey, she could improvise. "Weighty conversation coming, check. But we could put that off for a bit, right? I have guests to entertain, and I've probably smeared my makeup with my panic-crying. At least it's dark out here so you can't see me with raccoon eyes."

Using only his baby finger, he eased a lock of hair away from her face. "I'd still want you, Yardley."

That husky voice gave the words meaning beyond physical need...or at least they did to her. "Is that so?"

With a nod, he murmured, "I love how protective you are of Dodger."

Love? Her stomach dipped. "Um..."

"I love how much you care, too." He shifted closer, so

close that she breathed him in and felt the heat of his big body. "About everyone and everything."

It left her unsettled, the casual way he tossed around that *L* word like confetti. It didn't sound like he had a pending brush-off planned, but she really needed to know. "So this conversation, is it about…"

"Get a room!" Mimi suddenly called out.

Yardley jumped back so quickly, she nearly stumbled. Luckily, Travis caught her arm and helped keep her upright. Since that jostled Dodger, he yapped in excitement.

Shaking his head, Travis again took her hand to lead her toward the others. "I *usually* like you, Mimi. Right now, not so much."

Mimi only laughed. "I didn't want you guys getting carried away out here, especially when Aurora and Lilith have joined the party."

Yeah, that could be problematic. Or not. Yardley wasn't sure anymore, not after the caring way they'd helped to look for Dodger.

Either way, it was a warm night with the scent of honeysuckle in the air. Everyone seemed to have enjoyed the party. Her mother and aunt had softened.

And Travis said he loved things about her.

Whatever their eventual conversation would entail, for right now she was pretty darned happy.

13

NEARLY A WEEK LATER, Yardley lounged in bed while perusing the list of businesses who'd contacted her in her new position as liaison. Dodger curled up against her side, and every so often he twitched, his legs pedaling as he ran in his sleep, little muffled "woofs" escaping. Hoping it was a good dream, maybe chasing a rabbit or a ball, Yardley stroked him until he quieted again.

She wanted all his dreams to be pleasant from now on.

She wanted the same for herself.

Over the last few days, with Travis's help, she'd installed a nifty retracting screen to the bottom half of each exterior door. Mimi had also surprised her with a new entry mat for the front porch that read, Don't Let the Dog Out, with paw prints and musical notes around it. Yardley loved it.

Currently, everything was just so wonderful that it sometimes scared her. Like, something had to go wrong…right?

She shook her head.

Fretting for no reason was a waste of time, so she concentrated on her meeting notes with Saul. He'd made a remarkable suggestion for his business sign. Saul's Pit Stop in large, bold print, with a smaller, more elegant font beneath that said, Remarkable Ribs from the Town of Cemetery. The sign would be created by one of their local artisans, which would please Betty a lot.

M.J. wanted to change her store name from Cemetery Sweets and Treats to just M.J.'s Sweets and Treats, reasoning that she wouldn't have to purchase a whole new sign, but could just paint over the first word, which to Yardley made perfect sense.

Stifling a yawn, Yardley checked the time. In another fifteen minutes it'd be midnight. Time for her to turn in. She stacked the papers together and put them in a folder.

It had been a long, busy day that started with an appointment with a newly engaged couple, then a visit with Mr. Hopper so Dodger and Stella could play. She'd met with Sheena to go over the program for her wedding, made dinner for her mother and aunt, and then spent a wonderful evening with Travis.

The only way her day could have been better was if she'd stayed with him after the amazing sex. Yardley sighed.

He hadn't asked her to leave. He never did. She knew he wouldn't. In subtle ways, but without pressure, he'd made it clear that he'd prefer for her to stay.

She always left anyway.

Luckily, Travis understood—but for how long?

It was past time for her to get her own place. That idea had merit. It was the only way to keep her mother and aunt from knowing her very personal business. Maybe it'd keep her from having another visit from Kathleen, too, since she hadn't yet figured out that mystery.

She was just about to turn out the light when a tap sounded on her door.

As if catapulted, Dodger sprang off the bed in his patented "attack beast mode" that including snarling and a lot of ferociousness. Amazing how he could do that, go from sound sleep to demented hellhound.

"Hush, baby. It's fine."

He looked skeptical, and he kept stiffly alert as he watched the door, but he did quiet down.

Assuming it'd be her mother for another late-night visit, Yardley opened the door a tiny bit. She planned to claim exhaustion—but she forgot to do that when she found Aunt Lilith standing there instead.

"I saw your light was on and I wanted to talk." Wearing practical but pretty—and no doubt pricey—pajamas, Lilith pressed the door wider. In her hands, she held a shoebox.

"I was, um, just about to turn in actually—" Yardley trailed off as Lilith let herself in. Mouth twisted to the side, she said, "Sure, let's talk."

With a friendly little pat to Dodger's head, Lilith sat in the same chair her mother had used during her evening visit, indicating this wouldn't be a short chat.

A sense of déjà vu sank into Yardley's tired brain. Deciding she might as well get the visit over, she dropped down on the end of the bed. "So…what's up?"

"I've been so proud of you lately."

A year ago, or actually, most of her life, Yardley would have cherished that statement. Now? Not so much. "Why's that?"

"Actually, I've always been proud of you. You know that."

Noooo, she didn't know any such thing. "Thanks," was the only reply to come to mind. Then she asked again, "Why?"

"Well, it's obvious, isn't it? You're smart and you've avoided the usual traps many young ladies fall into. Of course, I was disappointed that you'd settled for a business degree instead of pushing yourself for more."

Ah, there was the aunt she knew so well. Too many times to count, Yardley had explained why a business degree was necessary. One of them needed to turn around the wedding service. One of them had to be grounded in reality. One of them—always her—had to ensure they stayed afloat. Rehashing that argument would lead them to a longer visit, so instead she asked, "What kind of traps?"

"You didn't let boys affect your grades, for one thing. I've seen so many girls get distracted with flirting and dating to the detriment of everything else. Not you. You've always had a good head on your shoulders, always concentrated on the important things."

This was like the opposite of her mother's conversation. Finding that ironic, but not amusing, Yardley asked, "So, what's in the shoebox?" Her aunt held it clasped to her chest.

As if bracing herself, Lilith whispered, "You could have been my daughter, you know."

"I...what?" That was a new sentiment, and it left her confused.

"You're obviously intelligent, and you know how to use that intelligence to get what you want." Suddenly bristling, she looked away. "Unlike Aurora, you don't just rely on your good looks."

I have good looks? News to her, at least from her aunt's perspective. Mimi had certainly given her enough compliments, and now Travis, too.

Seeing the pinch of Lilith's mouth, the bowed shoulders, Yardley knew she had something more on her mind than old conflicts.

"I'm not sure I understand where this is going."

Pride had Lilith facing her again. "Your father was interested in me first."

One verbal blow after another. Her aunt said it like an accusation, but that couldn't be directed at Yardley. So... Aurora? "You mean—"

Lilith hugged the box tighter. "I've tried to deny it for years, but I loved him."

Holy cow. "You and my mom both..."

"We were happy." Her lip curled. "Then Aurora swept in and did what she always did."

Seeing her aunt's sadness made Yardley's heart heavy. "And that is?"

"She offered easy sex. And since I wasn't that way, well, men can't resist that, you know."

Oh, how awful. "Did Mother know how you felt?"

With a sniff of disdain, Lilith said, "We've never discussed it."

Of all the... "Maybe you should have." If Aurora had known, she might have acted differently.

And then I wouldn't be here.

Yeah, not a great thought.

"I was closer to his age," Lilith insisted. "He and I were twenty-two and Aurora had just turned eighteen. She shouldn't have been chasing after him, but once she met him, nothing else seemed to matter, not her age, not our parents' disapproval...certainly I didn't matter—to either of them."

How telling that Yardley didn't question the truth of that. The idea that Aurora would go after an older boy, one that Lilith was interested in, didn't surprise her at all. More than anything else, her mother cared about her appearance and what people thought. Her drive to be seen as an attractive, sexy woman bordered on...needy.

As did Lilith's drive to be seen as the smarter, savvier of the two.

Though her mother probably hadn't known the extent of Lilith's feelings, it was still wrong. If asked, she'd justify every action, or lack of action, she'd ever taken.

Just as Lilith would.

I'm different, Yardley reminded herself with conviction. Hadn't she been told that all her life? She wasn't like the Belanger women, she didn't have their refined features and flair for fashion. She said all the wrong things, at all the wrong times.

So what? She also didn't have their self-indulgent natures and lack of empathy, so score one for the awkward kid.

While her mother and aunt were often at odds, they'd aligned on one point—Yardley's need to know her father hadn't mattered, not when it might infringe on their own interests.

In their narrow ways, they loved her. In her more generous way, Yardley loved them back.

Being different was a blessing and right now, she genuinely pitied them both. "I'm sorry you went through that," Yardley said.

"Well, it wasn't your fault, now, was it?"

And yet, somehow Yardley knew she'd been blamed. By being born, she'd managed to negatively impact both their lives. "Not my fault, no, but I'm sorry all the same."

Lilith gave her a wan smile. "You've always been wiser and kinder than your mother."

Pretty sure she was wiser and kinder than her aunt, too.

"You've also been more levelheaded and responsible than me." A familiar look of censure settled over Lilith's features. "That's why I'm concerned with this new man of yours."

How did things always come back to Travis? "Don't be." Ready to put an end to this uncomfortable conversation, Yardley started to rise.

Lilith grabbed her hand. "I want you happy, Yardley."

That was something at least. "Awesome. Thanks."

"But I don't want you to lose your head over someone who isn't serious."

Here we go again. Maybe the sisters were more alike than they realized, because this all felt far too familiar. The urge to huff was there, but Lilith seemed too sincerely distraught for Yardley to add to it with attitude. "We're just dating—"

"Will he marry you?" Lilith demanded. "Has he mentioned a future?"

What a leap! "We, um…" *We're having wild, wonderful sex and for now, that's enough.* She cleared her throat. "No, Aunt Lilith. We're keeping things very casual until after Sheena's wedding."

Squeezing her hand, her expression pained, Lilith implored, "Don't let him use you, Yardley."

She tried a gentle smile. "Maybe I'm using him?" *And having the time of my life.*

"And now you sound like your mother." Derision firmed her mouth. "That's exactly what she said to me about your father when I tried to warn her away."

Yardley grimaced. "Sorry."

Accepting that, Lilith released her and sat back again. "You probably should have learned about your father long ago. I realize that now. It was wrong of Aurora and me to keep the information from you."

Since it had allowed ill feelings to fester, Yardley agreed. "I've never understood why it was such a secret anyway." As a kid, she hadn't even questioned it. As an adult, it didn't make sense but hadn't seemed worth the effort.

Chin elevated, Lilith admitted, "I was afraid—afraid you'd want to meet him, and that you'd bring him back into our lives."

And her wants trumped the need of a little girl? Yup. "I see."

"I'm sorry, but I would have been devastated all over again."

To Yardley, her father sounded like a grade-A dick. What type of jerk dated one sister, then slept with the other? *Total* dick move. The decision was sudden, but final all the same. "I don't care about meeting him." Not anymore.

Instead of being relieved, Lilith looked down at the shoebox. "You can't now anyway. He died years ago."

Well, that crumbled her convictions. Choosing not to, and knowing she never could, were two entirely different things. "Did he have any siblings?" Maybe there was an aunt or uncle who wasn't as much of a creep as her father.

"No. He was an only child."

"Parents?"

"I'm sorry, but his father died when he was just a boy, and his mother passed away when he was in his twenties."

Maybe losing his father helped to explain why he was such a jerk. "How did he die?"

"I don't know the details, but the obituary said he passed from a heart attack."

Interesting. "You kept up with him for all this time?"

In a rare show of humility, Lilith lowered her eyes. "That makes me sound rather pathetic, doesn't it?"

"It makes you sound human." It made her sound like a woman who'd been in love, a woman who still mourned the man she'd lost. So sad.

Did Aurora feel the same? It'd be the cruelest form of irony if one selfish man had twisted the fates of three women: her mother, her aunt…and herself.

"It's not like I kept daily tabs on him. Not even monthly tabs." This time Lilith looked toward Dodger, and her expression softened. "An entire year would pass, and then you'd do something, say something in your quirky way or affect a certain expression…and it would all come rushing back."

"Those were painful reminders for you." *She'd* been a painful reminder.

But Lilith shook her head. "Reminders, yes, but nothing about you pained me. It was just… I'd remember and end up checking online for information, and that, sometimes, did distress me."

Social media had probably made it easier for Lilith to hang on to the past. "Find anything interesting?"

"He married once. That lasted five years before she divorced him. No children, thank God." The second the words left her mouth, Lilith's eyes widened in appalled horror. "I didn't mean—"

"I know, and I agree." Yardley's entire outlook on her father was changing. "Not right now, but someday, would you show me his photo? I've been told all my life that I look like him."

"He was a very handsome man." Reaching out with uncharacteristic affection, Lilith stroked her cheek. "His hair was a little darker, almost black, but your eyes are definitely his. Beautiful eyes."

Her brows lifted. "I've never considered my eyes beautiful." Until Travis. He certainly commented on her eyes, always very favorably.

Lilith kept her hand on Yardley's cheek. "As a little girl, you had a way of looking at me that reminded me so much of him. As I said, you could have been mine... if things had gone differently."

That sounded almost...wistful.

"He was such a character. A real leader." Cracking a small smile, Lilith said, "After the way you handled the council meeting, and then how you organized your dinner party, I believe you inherited that from him as well."

A leader? Her? "I don't know about that." Yet she did know one thing for certain. "I like who I am, though."

"I like who you are, too. Very, very much. Even more than that, I love you—as if you *were* my own." With that momentous announcement, Lilith stood and pressed the box forward. "This is for you."

Curious, Yardley accepted it. "What is it?"

"Photos of your father. Newspaper clippings. Silly mementos that I know I shouldn't have kept, and yet now, I'm glad I can share them with you."

Holy smokes. Yardley stared down at the box, interest, excitement and dread waging an internal battle. In the end, love for her aunt won out and she offered the box back. "I don't need it."

Wearing a sad smile, Lilith took a step away. "Aurora and I discussed it and decided you should have had it years ago."

No way. Her aunt and her mother were in agreement?

"I know," Lilith said, her smile starting to curl with real humor. "Unheard of. Your mother and I have a great many differences, surely too many that have been shown to you, but we also share a bond. We both love you."

A tsunami of emotion battered her senses. Setting the box aside, she stood and grabbed her aunt in a tight hug. Lilith rocked with her, saying softly, "We are both so very proud of you, sweetheart."

Yardley strangled on a laugh. Funny, Lilith and Aurora were both proud of her, but for very different and opposing reasons.

"I should get going. I just wanted to add…please, protect your heart at all costs."

And they'd each issued similar warnings, but again, for different reasons.

She watched Lilith go, heard the door close very softly, and accepted the truth. It didn't matter what either of them said, because it was far too late to protect her heart.

Travis already owned it.

She glanced at the box, hesitated, but then scooped it up and got into bed, her back against the headboard. Dodger snuffled at the disruption, squirmed to get comfortable again, and went right back to sleep.

Carefully, telling herself that it didn't matter, Yardley opened the box. Right on top was a small photo of her father. For some reason, tears filled her eyes. Eyes that did indeed resemble his. When she turned over the photo, she found his name: Jeff Lloyd.

She waited to feel something beyond curiosity. Melancholy, yearning, a sense of loss. She didn't.

Her father was no longer faceless and nameless, but what she'd learned of him didn't inspire softer feelings.

Confused by her own lack of reaction, she lifted out an article cut from a local newspaper about his marriage. It was a short, formal and overall impersonal write-up without an image, and without flair. To Yardley, it sounded blah. If she'd been his wedding planner, she'd have... *what*? No. Definitely no. Pretty sure he didn't deserve her excellent wedding planner skills.

Pushing that thought aside, she next found a decade-old screenshot from his Facebook showing him sitting in a lawn chair, a can of beer in his hand. He wore a wrinkled T-shirt stretched taut over his bloated stomach, thin legs sprawled wide beneath loose shorts, and socks with black plastic sandals.

Clearly, he'd let himself go, though he wouldn't have been that old in the image. Maybe midforties. From what Lilith had said, that had to be close to the time he'd passed away.

Yardley tilted her head, studying his loose jowls and what appeared to be a beer gut. A drinker, apparently. In the earlier photo he had indeed been handsome. In this one, he was just shy of repulsive.

In another printed Facebook post, he mentioned his divorce, including a few obnoxious comments that made him seem very petty.

This was the man who'd done so much damage, the man Aurora and Lilith had allowed to make them bitter. The man who'd put the sisters forever at odds.

Oh, Yardley felt something now. Pity. Mostly for him, but a little for her mother and aunt also. As his only child, she might have made a positive impact on Jeff's life, but he'd chosen differently.

From all appearances, he hadn't been a happy man.

A half hour later, after going through the rest of the box, she came to another conclusion. Not knowing him was fine. Actually, the better choice.

Someday, maybe, she'd even thank her mother and aunt for that. For now, she simply put the lid on the box and shoved it under her bed. Tomorrow she'd share everything with Mimi, and later with Travis, too. Heck, she might even discuss it all with Betty.

With a smile, she turned out the light and snuggled into the bed, drifting off to the sounds of Dodger's doggy snores.

BECAUSE HE'D SPENT so much of his time with Yardley, it had taken Travis longer than expected to finish the renovations on the house, but he'd finally wrapped it up. Good thing, since the wedding was a little less than a month away.

Though he'd shown Yardley the house in progress many times, she still looked around with her usual interest and joy. Today, she looked really satisfied, too.

Funny that learning so much about her father seemed to lift a burden from her shoulders. Every day, she was busier with new responsibilities, with new friends like Betty, and with him and Dodger, but she was also more carefree. Travis liked to think he played a role in adding to her happiness. She'd certainly added to his.

"This is just amazing."

Yeah, he thought it had turned out great, ideal for his sister's first home.

They'd discussed telling Sheena and Todd about the offer he wanted to make them while he was still working on it, but together they'd decided it'd be more fun to surprise them with the finished project. "They have no idea why they're meeting us here."

Yardley grinned like a kid on Christmas morning. "Thank you so much for including me. I'm so excited to see their reactions."

"Hey." Tugging her closer, he looped his arms around her waist so that his hands rested on her spectacular rump. After a brief kiss, he gave her the simple truth. "It wouldn't be the same without you here." Now that she was in his life, he wanted her with him whenever possible.

Her eyes went smoky and her body melted against his. "That means something, right?"

It meant everything. How could she not realize that yet? It was past time for plain speaking. He needed to make a few declarations. "Yardley—"

"Knock, knock," Sheena said as she opened the front door and breezed in with Todd. Seeing the two of them hugged so closely together, she pulled up short. "Oops. Sorry if we're early and...interrupting?"

They were, but Travis only said, "It's fine."

Yardley's enormous grin returned. "I'm so glad you're here." Rushing forward, she took Sheena's hand and drew her to the center of the living room. "What do you think of the house?"

A little bewildered, Sheena looked around. "Wow, it's great. Travis is really good at flipping houses, always has been, but this is spectacular."

"You ain't kidding." Todd bounced his gaze everywhere. "I mean, it looked good when I saw it last, but now it's like brand-new, only better." Curious, he asked Yardley, "You buying this place or something? You already have such an awesome house—"

Looking ready to squeal in her excitement, Yardley said, "It's not for me."

Blank surprise fell over Sheena's features, as if she was starting to realize. "Travis," she whispered, her eyes already going tearful. "What did you do?"

"I can offer you a deal on it. Cost, basically." Since he'd been in the business for a while, Sheena knew what that meant. "What do you think, hon? You wouldn't be too far from me and the family home, and you'll have a lot more room for when the baby gets here."

Covering her mouth, she stared at Travis, then Yardley, then Todd and back to him. "You can't…you didn't…"

"He did!" Yardley's excitement bubbled over. "He saved it for you two."

Jaw loosening, Todd took a step back. "Wait, hold up. What's happening?" Unlike Sheena, he seemed more alarmed than happy. "Reality check, guys. I can't afford this place. Not that I wouldn't love it, because seriously, I would." He turned to Sheena. "I swear I'm going to get you a house. Soon, too. It won't be a house like this, but—"

Poor Sheena didn't know what to think.

Understanding Todd's reticence, Travis said, "Let's sit down and I'll explain, okay?" He led them all to the kitchen, where he had a few folding chairs and a worktable. Awakened from a snooze, Dodger abandoned the sunny spot on the floor and came over to greet Sheena. Going to her knees, she hugged the dog and waited.

"First," Travis said, "I got this house well under market value because it was such a wreck. Most of the interior had to be gutted, but by doing the labor myself, I saved a ton of money."

Todd didn't blink. He didn't look like he could, but he kept casting worried glances at Sheena.

His sister seemed confident that he'd make it work. She had enormous trust in him.

Glad that Yardley had sat beside him, Travis laced their fingers together. "I don't mean any offense."

"None taken," Sheena quickly said, which kept Todd from replying.

"I can sell you the house cheap—at cost. You'd start with instant equity since it's worth far more than that."

"But all your work…" Still flummoxed, Todd shook his head. "I know you want your sis in a better place. I get that cuz I want the same. Like I said, I'm working on it." Todd tried a laugh that lacked its usual boisterous volume.

Knowing Todd saw the offer as charity, Travis reminded him of a few important facts. "We're going to be family. Remember you told me that? Well, this is family helping family."

Rising from the floor, Sheena came to stand beside Todd's chair.

Ready to do her part to convince him, Yardley said, "If you've never flipped a house, you don't realize the difference it can make. I did the updates to my own house, and I couldn't have afforded any of it if I'd hired contractors."

"Usually my brother makes a killing off a job like this." Sheena cupped Todd's face, turning it up for a smacking kiss. "This is like a wedding gift, okay?"

"No one gives a gift like this!"

Sheena laughed. "He's not giving us the house, okay? We'll still be buying it." She grinned at Travis. "Tell us how it would work."

Glad to have the women on his side, Travis sat forward, forearms on his knees. "I'd sell it to you for what I'm out on the initial investment and materials, so I'm not losing money." He didn't want Todd to worry about that. "The nice part is that your payments to the bank would be no more than what you're now paying in rent."

When Todd gawked at everything this time, eagerness edged out trepidation. "For *this* place? Here in this neighborhood?"

"So you and Sheena would be close to Travis," Yardley said, encouraging him.

Wanting no misunderstandings, Travis pointed out, "Utilities will be higher, of course. Insurance and all that."

"I can handle that." Hugging Sheena a little tighter, Todd whispered, "Holy shit."

"Look at it this way. If you two bought a house that needed some work, I'd do it without charging." Travis held his gaze. "Just like you'll help me out whenever I need it. Right?"

Todd nodded. "Sure I would, but I couldn't do *this*."

"I can." Travis felt Yardley squeeze his hand. "This is what I can do. What I enjoy doing. And I'd love it if you two lived here."

Yardley said, "Long before he was done with this place, he told me he didn't want it to go to just anyone. It was so hard for me to keep it secret."

Sheena looked both giddy and hopeful.

"It'll make me feel better about staying in the family home." A home Travis hoped to share with Yardley, but first things first. "This evens things up a bit, so what do you say, Todd?"

Breathing harder, Todd stared at him. "Family helping family?"

"That's right."

"Dude." An enormous smile slowly spread over his face. *"Dude!"* Standing, his hands laced behind his neck, Todd turned in circles. "This place is freaking unbelievable."

Finally. Travis shared a smile with Yardley. "I left everything neutral so Sheena can change paint colors or decorate however she wants."

With that, Sheena sprang forward and Travis barely had time to stand before she landed against him.

Yardley started laughing. "I want to show you the whole house! It's all *so* beautiful."

Pulling Sheena into his own arms, Todd roughly rocked her side to side, but Sheena didn't seem to mind. In fact, she was bouncing in Todd's embrace and it all looked pretty chaotic—like Todd. Like love.

Like life.

With a final squeeze, Todd tucked her into his side. "Seriously, man. I have a really good down payment saved up. That's why I've been working my ass off. I wanted to let Sheena pick a house before we tied the knot, but then she was sick and I was so damned divided, wanting to be home more to take care of her, but wanting to rake in that overtime pay for the house…"

Sheena smacked his chest. "You didn't tell me that!"

He cupped her face. "I wanted to surprise you." He gave her a gentle kiss. "I want you and our baby in a home of our own. A real place. Like you had growing up."

Tears suddenly glimmered in Sheena's eyes. "I love you."

"I love you so damn much, too."

Yardley sighed happily, and Travis just naturally hugged her close.

"No more surprises," Sheena playfully ordered. "We have to share everything."

"Right. Share." Todd kissed her once more, this time hard and fast. "I'll do better, I swear."

Travis saw that Yardley was as amused as he was. Sharing seemed like a damn fine idea. In his head, he'd started a checklist of things to get done before adding to his commitments. Hell, for most of his life he'd lived by checklists, starting the night has parents had died.

His sister was right, though. He should have already told Yardley how much he cared.

Todd drew a breath, rubbed a hand over his mouth, and started looking around again. "I've packed away every penny, but I still couldn't have gotten a house like this."

Squeezing Todd tight, Sheena whispered, "I'd have lived with you forever in the apartment and we'd have made that a home."

With an emotional gulp, Todd said, "I know, because you're that amazing. But you've got to admit, having this place will be awesome."

She laughed. "Heck yeah, it will."

A reformed man, Todd straightened and said, "We'll go over finances tonight and if Sheena agrees, we'll give you what I had saved for a down payment to cover some of your labor."

"I'd rather you use it for any furniture you might need. Remember, you got my niece or nephew's nursery to set up."

Overwhelmed and undecided, Todd put his hands back on his head—until Travis reminded him, "Family helping family."

"Damn, man." In typical robust Todd fashion, he grabbed Travis in for a giant, bruising bear hug. "Damn."

Returning the tight embrace and clapping Todd on the back a few times, Travis suggested, "How about we look at everything now?"

"I'm leading the way!" Yardley caught Sheena's hand and started her down the hall. Todd hurried to catch up with them.

Family. *His* family.

And Yardley was part of it now.

He only had one more thing on his list.

KEVIN LAUGHED AS Travis stole a fry off Yardley's plate. She and Mimi were so busy talking, neither of them noticed. Wasn't like they didn't see each other through the week, but they always had plenty to whisper about. He heard something about an apartment and sex. Figured that had to do with Yardley and Travis, and that made him wonder.

They were having dinner at the Pit Stop, now renamed, thanks to Yardley, without Cemetery at the forefront. It was a warm evening for late June, perfect for sitting outside. On his leash, Dodger chewed on a dog treat under the table. Sammy was asleep in Kevin's arms.

With Yardley and Travis together, Saturday evenings like this had become the norm. Worked great for him, especially since Mimi was back in her element, being bubbly, bossy, and so upbeat that he finally felt like he had his wife back. She was safe, healthy, a beautiful mother, and a faithful friend.

The most phenomenal wife on the planet—and the sexiest.

Life couldn't be any better. In fact, without Mimi… no. Thinking that way, worrying about her too much, had stifled Mimi in awful ways. Never again would he hold back out of fear. He had her, she was here with him and Sammy, and from now on he planned to enjoy every single second with her.

Emily Lucretia, the florist, had stopped by the table earlier to ask Yardley if she'd had time to present her name change for her shop, too. Yardley had promised she was working on it and should have news soon, which made Emily beam and hug her tight—until her gaze snagged on Saul. She'd quickly gotten distracted, excused herself with another thank-you, and drifted closer to the bar.

Kevin nudged Travis, saying low, "I used to figure on Saul and Yardley hooking up."

Choking on the fry, Travis gave him a dirty look. "Don't remind me." His gaze went to Yardley, but she and Mimi had their heads together, laughing about something, propping each other up in their hilarity. "According to Saul, she never saw him that way. They were only ever friends."

"Yeah, sounds right. For a while there, Mimi was hopeful. Both women like Saul." Enjoying Travis's continued scowling, Kevin shrugged. "Now I figure Mimi prefers you."

That eased the ill humor. "I'm honored."

Using one of his wife's tactics of just tossing out a question, Kevin asked, "You around for the long haul?"

Instead of choking again, or being insulted, Travis gave a firm nod. "I'm not going anywhere."

Mimi would congratulate him on getting it confirmed. "I'm guessing you haven't told Yardley that yet, or she'd have told my wife." Kevin glanced at Mimi. "I don't like when she frets."

"Those two will always worry about each other." Pushing his now empty plate aside, Travis folded his arms on the table. "I'm glad they have each other. And I appreciate that they're including my sister in things."

"Sheena's a doll. Mimi likes sharing baby stuff with her."

Mimi stood and came around the table. "Did I hear my name?" She stroked the backs of her fingers over Sammy's hair.

"I was telling Travis how you're schooling his sister on changing diapers."

"Yeah." She gave a rascal's grin. "I keep telling her she almost has it down. With just a little more practice..."

Yardley laughed. "Don't tease Travis. He'll believe you." She stole a kiss from him, then asked, "You guys want any dessert?"

Mimi bobbed her eyebrows. "We're going to raid the dessert shelf."

"I'll take whatever you get." Kevin slid a hand around her waist and tugged her down so he could get a kiss, too. "And a coffee, if you can manage it."

"Are you kidding me? I used to work this place during the busiest hours. Of course I can handle it."

Travis said, "Same for me."

Soon as the women were gone, Kevin said, "I heard Yardley mention that she's found an apartment. What's that about?"

Going still, Travis gave him a blank stare.

Uh-oh. So Yardley hadn't clued in Travis. To clarify, Kevin said, "Just now, while they were whispering?"

"How did you hear with all this noise around us?"

True, music drifted out from the restaurant, diners sat around them, and plenty of people traveled back and forth to the beach. "I tune in when Mimi looks a certain way. Plus that word *sex* just kind of pops, you know? Makes a guy's ears perk up."

"Yardley mentioned an apartment *and* sex?"

It was Kevin's turn to scowl. "I guarantee you Mimi's not stepping out."

That amused Travis. "I wasn't accusing."

"You didn't know about it?"

"I have an idea." After casting a glance around to ensure no one could hear, Travis leaned closer. "She's probably hoping for added privacy, since apparently her mother and aunt have been inviting themselves to late-night chats. She doesn't want everyone knowing her business. Then there was that bit with Kathleen the mannequin. All fun and games, I'm sure, but since Yardley doesn't know who put Kathleen there…"

Kevin said with a grin, "Kathleen always shows up in unexpected places, sometimes with unexpected messages. Usually you know who's behind the prank because they share pics on Facebook. Other times, no one takes credit so it's a mystery."

"This was one of those mysterious incidents and it's driving Yardley nuts. Plus, I think she worries about having to answer more questions from Aurora and Lilith if she stays the night with me."

"Yardley should just tell them to butt out."

"Not Yardley's style. Here's the thing, though. I have a surprise planned that hopefully will solve that issue, and if I tell you, you'll tell Mimi and it won't be a surprise anymore."

"Is it a proposal?" Damn, Kevin hoped so. "If that's where you're going, I guarantee Mimi will be as surprised as Yardley. Just as happy, too. And I'll enjoy knowing something my wife doesn't, so count on me to keep it to myself."

Apparently Travis believed him. While they had time alone, Kevin heard it all and approved. "One suggestion, though. Don't wait until after your sister's wedding."

"I decided that on my own." With a satisfied smile, Travis said, "Yardley is too special to wait, but somehow you're going to have to talk her out of the apartment. I need one more week to finish getting things ready."

"No problem. I'll tell Mimi I overheard her talking about the apartment, I'll ask her about the place, then I'll make up some bullshit on why it won't do. Knowing my wife, she'll go directly to Yardley." Grinning, Kevin said, "Leave it to me."

IT WAS A cool evening, stars filling the sky when they arrived at Travis's house. He had a surprise for her, something special, he'd said. Yardley watched his profile as he parked, thinking whatever it was, it couldn't be more special than Travis himself.

His sister's wedding was rolling around quickly, probably in part because Yardley thoroughly enjoyed all the time she spent with Travis. The days had just flown by. In one more week, Sheena would marry Todd. They'd spend a week at the Honeymoon Cottage, and shortly after that, they'd move into the house.

She and Travis were planning to help them get set up. In so many ways, their lives were already intertwined.

It should have been enough, but each day she wanted more. Mostly because each day she loved him more.

That's why she'd been so busy trying to find a nearby apartment, something close to the Victorian home since she'd keep the wedding business there. That's where they were already established, and she didn't want her mother and aunt to feel abandoned. Unfortunately, there weren't many apartments convenient to Cemetery, and she couldn't see driving more than thirty minutes each way every day.

Somehow she'd work it out, because she wanted to be able to stay overnight with Travis. Thoughts of sleeping near him, waking in the night to his touch, drinking coffee with him in the morning… She'd added another shell to her basket. One more wish on top of many.

She had the guy for now. She had the awesome pet. Working on the independence from her mother and aunt. Beach wedding…maybe someday.

Honeymoon Cottage? She'd put a lot of shells on that one.

Now an apartment.

Sadly, the two she'd found had been disqualified by Kevin. He claimed to be looking out for her, something about her almost being Mimi's sister. She liked the sentiment.

Kevin swore the first apartment didn't have adequate security, which had also gotten Mimi worked up, so Yardley had passed on it. The second unit was supposedly a giant, costly repair waiting to happen. Plumbing, electrical, drywall… Kevin said it was all on the verge of falling apart, and since it was in an older building, she supposed it was possible.

She'd considered asking Travis to look at it, too, because seriously, she didn't think any of it was that bad. But she wanted the lease in hand when she told him her plan, so he wouldn't think she was hinting on moving in with him. If they ever took that big step, she wanted them to make the decision together, without either of them feeling coerced.

So her apartment surprise would have to wait, but tonight was Travis's surprise for her. "Will you give me a hint?"

Grinning, he got out of the truck and headed to her door, taking her by the waist to lift her down, then kissing her forehead before taking Dodger's leash. "Wait and see." He took her hand. "I hope you'll like it."

Of course she would—because she loved him.

With Dodger dancing around them, Travis led her through the front door and then up the stairs. Did the surprise have something to do with sex? Count her in. Anytime he made a beeline for the bed, she was more than ready.

Except…instead of Dodger napping, Travis brought him along.

So—boo hiss—probably not sex. "Where are we going?"

"You'll see." Walking past his room, which really stumped her, he paused outside the master bedroom door. "Ready?"

Now she wasn't sure. Biting her lip, she nodded.

He pushed open the door.

Though Dodger went right on in, Yardley drew up short. Everything was different.

The furniture that had belonged to his parents was now replaced with…wait. He'd moved in his *own* bedroom set, but with new bedding. Colorful bedding. *Beau-*

tiful bedding—exactly what she would have picked for her own room.

Her heart started a wild dance in her chest, stealing her breath in the process.

With a hand at the small of her back, Travis urged her into the room. "I did a little remodeling."

"How? When?" She'd been over nearly every day.

"This door has stayed shut, right? I've been working in here trying to get it all done…then yesterday Kevin and Todd helped me switch around the furniture."

"Mimi never said anything to me."

"Because Kevin kept it secret."

Though she wasn't sure why, elation expanded, leaving her giddy. "Mimi will give him hell about that." Taking in the room again, she said, "It's all… Well, it's exactly what I would have picked."

"Because I pay attention." With smiling impatience, he brought her forward through the room. "I remember you looked at a quilt just like this one."

Running her hand over it, Yardley felt the mixed textures, some silky, some velvety. "I love it so much." She glanced at the walls, now painted a gorgeous shade of blue, and the area rug, which was exactly the one she'd admired. "It's all so beautiful. Even better than I had imagined." These were *her* choices, only in a bedroom much bigger than her own…and in Travis's house, instead of the Victorian. "I don't understand, though."

He turned her toward the bathroom. "Come take a look and I think, I *hope*, it'll make sense." Watching her in an alert, almost anxious way, he opened the bathroom door, then stepped aside and waited.

Feeling as if she tiptoed on clouds, Yardley edged forward…and stalled at what she saw. "OMG."

He moved closer. "Is that a good OMG, or a horrified OMG?"

Shaking her head, she covered her mouth and blinked several times, but that was *her* tub, the one she'd admired at the antique show on one of their very first dates—though she hadn't known it was an actual date-date back then.

Needlessly, he offered, "It's the tub you wanted."

The tub she hadn't forgotten, but without enough funds to afford it, she'd tried.

When she still said nothing, he grew uneasy. "It wouldn't have fit in your attached bathroom. Not enough room."

"I know."

"It fits here, though."

"Travis," she breathed, gliding forward without being aware of her feet moving. In this room, with the other updates he'd done, the big copper tub was *stunning*. She spun around to face him. "I hope this means I'll get to use it."

He touched her cheek. "It's yours, Yardley."

The swirling elation left her dizzy. "Mine?" she squeaked.

His gaze softened. "I'd like to share it with you."

Pretty sure her stomach flipped. And yeah, her toes totally curled. "Yes, please. A grand plan. We could try it now? Or do we need to wait for Dodger to sleep?" She peeked out of the bathroom and saw Dodger up on the bed, circling for a good snooze. "I mean, it won't be a quick bath, right? That'd be a waste. But we could linger… Oh look! You have candles, too."

"Yardley." He took her hands, which effectively stifled

her overflow of words. "I know how much you love your Victorian home, but I was hoping—"

"I love you more," she blurted, then gasped at what she'd said, her eyes wide and her heart tripping. "Sorry. I opened my mouth and that just sort of fell out. Plop. Right there on the floor between us." *Plop? Words don't plop, especially not declarations of love.* "You know how I am. I get excited, and that makes me talkative, and I—"

"You love me?" A slow smile overtook him. "Is that what plopped on the floor between us?"

Again without thinking it through, she said, "Of course I love you. How could you not know that?"

He pulled her close. "Maybe because you seem to love everyone."

"Ha! Not like that. Not the way I do you."

He nuzzled her neck. "I love how you do me."

Finally catching on that this was it, the moment she'd wanted, and the man she wanted it with, Yardley snickered. "Ditto, but Travis, I said that I *love* you and if you don't say something romantic and memorable right now I'm going to—"

"I love you, Yardley." Throwing her own words back to her, he asked, "How could you not know that?"

Feeling smug, she said, "I think I sort of did." Despite her mother and aunt's warnings. Despite his hesitation and need to wait. Despite the obstacles ahead of them.

"No 'sort of' to it. I love you so damn much that sometimes I don't know how to deal with it."

Wow, that was exactly how she felt too! "We'll deal with it together. I'll even make it easy on you."

"You already do. Loving you is the easiest thing I've ever done." He cupped her face. "For years I put all my focus on filling in for my parents, on trying to ensure that Sheena grew up strong, feeling safe and secure. I didn't want her to miss our parents, but I didn't want her to forget them either. I stayed so intent on trying to balance her life that I forgot my own life for a while there."

Because he was an amazing and selfless man. "You did a great job," she promised quietly.

"I think so. She's a wonderful person, isn't she?"

Silly tears clouded Yardley's eyes. "Just like her big brother."

"She's all grown up now. I wanted to wait until after her wedding, but every day with you, it became more difficult to put it off."

Hopeful, thinking of all those shells she'd collected, she tentatively asked, "To put what off?"

"Asking you to stay with me."

"Yes," she immediately sang.

But he wasn't finished. "To marry me. To create a life with Dodger and me." He inhaled. "To live here with me."

"Yes, again and again!"

Surprise shot his brows high. "Yes?"

With no hesitation at all, she nodded fast and said impatiently, "Yes to all that. Everything. An unequivocal *yes*." And if he didn't wrap this up soon, she was going to tackle him to the floor and kiss him senseless.

This time his brows came down in confusion. "But your home, your mother and aunt—"

"They can't live with us."

His mouth quirked. "I wasn't asking for them to."

"Good. That would never work out." She shuddered with theatrical drama. "I love them, I don't want to disrupt their lives too much, but maybe a little disruption would be good for them. After all, they both thought you were using me."

His reaction to that bit of news was swift, and exactly what she expected.

Shoulders stiffening, mouth tight, he scowled. "They actually told you that?"

"Yup. Their lectures were nearly identical…except for one big difference. See, my mother was glad I was getting busy, since I'd always been too logical and strait-laced. But she didn't want me to lose my heart to you, since she was sure you wouldn't be around for the long haul. She thought I should take all this newfound sexuality and explore a little."

More annoyance clenched his jaw.

"Aunt Lilith was just the opposite. She liked how I'd always been smart and well-behaved, and she hoped I wouldn't lose my head over you because she, too, figured that once Sheena married, you'd move on." Holding her hands up like Lady Justice, she said, "Lose my head, lose my heart," as if weighing both. "Good thing I didn't listen."

"They don't know you at all, do they?"

Hey, nice reaction. Instead of questioning whether they knew *him* at all, he'd again focused on her. "Why do you say that?"

"Because you're smart enough to know what you're doing, every step of the way. You wouldn't easily lose your head or your heart."

"I did offer to jump your bones right off, though. Have to say, it was the best decision I ever made."

He grinned. "God, it was impossible to resist you."

"I'm glad you couldn't. So very, very glad. And hey, my talks with my mother and aunt were actually enlightening. I realized that how they are has almost nothing to do with me, and everything to do with them, which also meant that no matter what I did, they weren't likely to change."

His thumb brushed over her cheek. "They do love you, Yardley."

"I know. It's just different, not the way I love."

"Thank God."

Liking that attitude, she covered his hand with her own. "It's not how most people love." She had so many wonderful examples. Mimi, Kevin, and Sammy. Sheena and Todd. Betty. Even Mr. Hopper with his beloved Stella.

And Travis. He was the best example of all. "I think my father, that mythical sperm donor I never got to meet, did a real number on them." Never again would she dwell on him, or dream about what could have been. "The way he handled things, my aunt felt betrayed and my mother felt abandoned. In me, they both saw parts of him."

Travis kissed her forehead. "Aurora was reminded of the man who'd left her to face motherhood alone, and Lilith saw the man who didn't return her love."

"Pretty much." Yardley wrinkled her nose. "Not reminders you'd want to get on a daily basis."

"That's not a good excuse."

"There is no good excuse. Once I saw his photo, read his messages…it's just sad, don't you think?"

He tugged her closer, until she leaned against him. "Very sad. By hanging on to the past, they lost out on so much."

"Exactly. I see how Mimi and Kevin are with Sammy, and how much you love Sheena, and I know things should have been different. I was working on that, actually."

His warm brown gaze held hers. "Yardley, you have to know there are some things that aren't yours to fix."

"Very true, which is one of the reasons I'd decided to get an apartment." She looked at the beautiful tub, and was very glad she hadn't succeeded. "I wanted to stop being so convenient to them. I wanted them to finally accept more responsibility. Most of all, I wanted to stay the night with you. Yet here I am, a thirty-one-year-old woman who still answers to her mother and aunt. Not, like, for permission or anything."

"I know that. I've watched you create your own path numerous times."

Surprised, she asked, "Really?"

"With the remodels on your home, how you took over the wedding business, the town vendors, the town council, and most notably your friendship with Betty."

Yeah, she had done all that, and seeing the pride in his gaze made her feel proud, too. "The thing is, I didn't want my mother and aunt knowing my every move. Even though they've softened toward Dodger and might even like him now, I thought an apartment of my own seemed like a nice compromise. I was trying to figure out how to afford it, and then, pow."

"Pow," he agreed with obvious satisfaction.

"Here you are, surprising me with this—" she gestured at the bedroom remodel, and then toward the tub "—and saying all that—" she gestured at him, up and down his very fine self "—and making it okay for me to scream *yes* to everything, even before Sheena's wedding, which, by the way, is going to be a*maz*ing."

"With you, I haven't a single doubt."

Snuggling closer, she whispered, "Let's not say anything to anyone until after her wedding, okay? We don't want to step on her big day."

When Travis started grinning, Yardley knew something was up.

"Too late," he said, kissing the tip of her nose. "Remember, Todd helped me with stuff, and unlike Kevin, he can't keep a secret worth a damn. He told me he couldn't because Sheena made it clear they had to share everything."

"So he knew you were going to propose?"

"Yes, and my sister called with moral support, claiming all this—" it was his turn to gesture around "—was a wonderfully romantic gesture that you were sure to love."

Happiness made it impossible not to smile. "She is oh so right."

"Knowing my sister as I do, my bet is that she's already telling Mimi, now that she's given me time to 'seal the deal,' as she put it."

"No way. If Mimi knew—" The ringing of her phone cut her off. Laughing, Yardley pulled it from her pocket, and sure enough, it was Mimi. She answered with, "Yes he did, and you already know I said yes."

The excited scream made Dodger jump up and take notice. "When?" Mimi demanded. "On the beach? *The Honeymoon Cottage*. Oh, Yardley, we like Travis so much. This is going to be so spectacular."

"And," Yardley said, "you're on speaker."

Travis said, "Hi, Mimi."

"You sneaky stud! I've already swatted my husband— he liked that, by the way."

They both heard Kevin say, "One thing led to another, so yeah, I don't have any complaints."

Mimi chuckled. "But now I owe you one, too, that is, a very different type of swat than what Kevin got."

Travis laughed. "I'm relieved."

"Welcome to the family," Kevin called out, to ensure everyone heard him.

"Thank you." Pulling Yardley closer, Travis smiled down at her.

There was so much love in his dark eyes, Yardley wanted to melt. "We'll talk later, Mimi, okay?"

"Love you."

"Love you, too."

Travis took the phone from her and set it on the dresser. "We can get married however and whenever you want, but just so you know, I vote for soon."

She nodded. Far as she was concerned, the sooner the better. "Can we try out the tub now?"

In one of those wildly romantic gestures that she loved, he scooped her up into his arms. "I was counting on it."

THE DAY OF Sheena's wedding, even the weather cooperated, being sunny but not too humid, with the gentlest of breezes stirring the scent of wild honeysuckle. Because Sheena and Mimi had become good friends, Mimi was already on-site, helping Yardley to ensure that everything was exactly right.

Together in the parking lot, they checked each of the gauzy bows tied to lampposts and highlighted by rustic lanterns and baby's breath. Inside the barn, the band was tuning their instruments. Travis and Kevin stood just inside the wide double doors, chatting as they waited for further instructions from Yardley. Kevin held Sammy, and Travis held Dodger's leash, yet somehow they'd managed to rearrange chairs and adjust lanterns and were overall very handy in fine-tuning things.

Joining her, Mimi said, "They look great, don't they?"

Each man had dressed for the country theme—even Travis. He'd surprised Yardley by showing up in a white shirt with embroidered shoulders that his sister had chosen for the wedding party, and a really spiffy pair of new cowboy boots that he'd probably never wear again.

Kevin wore a similar shirt and jeans, but his boots were more broken in. "They're both gorgeous. And speaking of that…" She sighed again. "You look amazing, Mimi, and you definitely fill out your dress way better than I do mine."

The identical dresses, landing mid-thigh, were blush lace with a halter-style top, and where Mimi was stacked, Yardley was…not. She glanced at Travis and found him smiling toward her. Numerous times he'd told her how sexy she looked in her boots—which wasn't really the purpose of a bridesmaid's outfit, but she loved the compliment anyway. He certainly didn't find fault with her subtler curves, and no way did she feel lacking, so her complaint was more out of habit than any real concern.

Already knowing that, Mimi said, "You don't have to carry around my big butt, so be grateful." She tipped up the toe of one boot. "I do like how we coordinated boots, though."

Sheena had asked each of them to stand with her, along with Todd's sister, who would be her maid of honor. On Todd's side, he had his brother as best man, and Travis would serve two roles, first giving Sheena away and then standing with Kevin as a groomsman. A small party, but as Travis had said, family.

Sheena had at first worried that she wasn't doing things "right," but Yardley assured her that it was her wedding and she could set it up however she liked. Truly,

Yardley loved the end result. It was casual, comfortable, beautiful and cozy.

Guests weren't expected to arrive for another forty-five minutes, but as a car slowly drove into the lot, she recognized it as Betty's.

"Oh good," Mimi said. "I was starting to worry."

"Was Betty invited, too?" No one had told her!

"Yup. I made a promise to Sheena, but then couldn't deliver... Well, you'll see."

She and Mimi headed over to the designated parking area. When she got closer, she realized Aurora and Lilith were with Betty. "What in the world?"

Brows up, Mimi said, "I knew about Betty, but no idea about the plus two, sorry."

Betty stepped out—and like Yardley, she wore cowboy boots with a longer dress in a pretty blue floral.

"You look beautiful, Betty! I didn't know you'd be here," Yardley exclaimed.

"Well of course. Through those lovely tea parties Mimi arranged, Sheena and I have become quite chummy. She's like the granddaughter I never had." Saying that, Betty opened her back door, where Lilith sat beside a small wagon. Together, they struggled to get it out the door.

"Here, let me help you with that." Yardley maneuvered it out to the gravel drive.

Lilith stepped out and was immediately joined by Aurora, who'd been sitting next to Betty. Neither her mother nor her aunt wore boots, but they did sport wide-brimmed straw hats with their dresses, and they both wore eager smiles.

Taking in their expressions, Yardley said, "This is a surprise."

"I hope not an unpleasant one." Her mother nervously

glanced at Lilith, then back to Yardley. "Sheena agreed that we could attend since we assisted Betty."

To put them at ease, Yardley said, "I think it's great that you're here." She immediately shot Mimi a warning look to keep quiet. Dutifully, Mimi closed her mouth and grinned. "So, you're assisting Betty with what?"

"This," Mimi said, helping Betty to lift Kathleen from the trunk. The mannequin was all decked out and ready to attend the wedding. "I was supposed to bring Kathleen, but then I couldn't find her anywhere."

"Because I had her," Betty explained.

"And we dressed her," Lilith bragged. "Betty didn't own anything in the right size."

"Neither did we," Aurora added, before rushing on with, "We found this lovely outfit at the secondhand store. What do you think?"

"Wow." Her mother and aunt had shopped second-hand? Surprised, Yardley said, "It's perfect." Kathleen wore a long, ruffle-hemmed dress in a daisy pattern with a wide brown belt. "However did you get her feet in those boots?" The mannequin's feet were permanently arched for heels.

Being secretive, Aurora leaned forward. "We had to add a lot of stuffing to keep them in place. Shh."

Joining her in a whisper, Lilith said, "We had no idea dressing the dummy could be so fun."

"Very fun." Aurora grinned at Lilith.

Huh. Yardley imagined the sisters would have Kathleen up to no good all over the town in the coming weeks.

Drawing out a big poster board, Betty said, "By the way, on the drive over, we discussed your impending wedding."

"My…" Yardley hadn't yet told her mother or aunt

that she and Travis were marrying. She narrowed her eyes on Mimi.

Laughing, her friend shook her head. "Not me. Sheena. She's bragging to everyone that you'll soon be her sister through marriage. The girl is thrilled."

"Oh." Well, that was nice. She adored Sheena, too. "Sorry."

"Hey, I was looking forward to shouting it everywhere once you gave me the okay, but Betty beat me to it."

Betty harrumphed. "It should never have been a secret. You're the darling of this town. In many ways, the heart and soul. Did you really think your happiness wouldn't spread like wildfire?"

Half afraid to meet her mother's and aunt's gazes, Yardley gave a self-conscious shrug. "I didn't realize."

"Well, it has. And we're all very excited." Betty pinned Yardley with her shrewd gaze. "You'll have it on the beach, of course, so we can all attend."

Mimi raised a hand. "I might have shared that part once everyone knew."

Their excitement was contagious, and Yardley started to grin. "Who, specifically, is 'we all'?"

"Pretty much everyone. You've given the most beautiful weddings to so many. Now we want to give one to you."

She was used to Betty taking over—the woman was still a leader, after all—but this time Yardley didn't quite get it. "Who's giving me a wedding?"

"Cemetery is. The town council that you livened up. All the vendors that you've so faithfully represented. Basically, your family and friends."

Oh my. Again she glanced at Mimi, and her friend moved closer in automatic support.

"Sallie has already said she'll donate the cake." Mimi slipped her arm through Yardley's. "And Emily is super excited about doing the flowers."

"Saul is supplying the roast pig, but a lot of the residents are also donating food…" Betty grinned hugely. "And the part I know you'll love the most, Daniel is giving you a week at the Honeymoon Cottage, *plus* a yearly weekend until your tenth anniversary."

Staggered by the generosity, Yardley covered her mouth. "Every year?"

"He says you're great for business."

Oh my goodness. Overwhelmed, she turned to Mimi, who nodded happily. "Beautiful, inside and out."

"So very beautiful," Aurora agreed with pride.

That drew Yardley's gaze to her mother and aunt, and she found them leaning on each other, both wearing pleased, proud, ear-to-ear smiles.

"I, um…" No one seemed too upset about the idea of her moving on, so Yardley shared her plans…in her usual rush of convoluted words. "I'll be living with Travis, but I won't be that far away. And since the business is at home—that is, my current home, not where my home with Travis will be—but anyway, you'll see me often for business. I'm already set up there and everyone is familiar with it, and it's the perfect office, so—"

"You're keeping it where it is?" Aurora wilted with relief. "That's wonderful, Yardley. I'm so glad we'll still see you so often."

Lilith surprised her by saying, "We'd miss you terribly otherwise. And Dodger, of course."

Floored, Yardley stared at them. "I can still cook." When Mimi gave her a hard nudge, she added, "Sometimes."

Aurora beamed. "That would be wonderful. We're addicted to your meals, and especially all that delicious baking you do."

"But we can make do on our own. I promise we won't starve." Lilith dabbed at her eyes. "I'm so happy for you, Yardley. I knew you were smart enough to make the right choices."

"You'll always have us if you need us," Aurora said. "Though I suspect you're going to have a very long, very happy marriage to that young man. Anyone can see that he loves you."

"I really do." Travis stepped into the mix with Dodger. Kevin, holding Sammy, was right behind him. Travis smiled at one and all and draped his arm over Yardley's shoulders. "Should I take Kathleen in?"

"One moment." Betty turned around the poster board so Yardley could read it. "I came up with this. What do you think?"

Thank you for letting me share in your joyful day.
I love happy endings!

The sentiment was terrific, but it was the handwriting that struck a bell for Yardley. Her eyes widened, and she said to Betty, "You! You're the one who put Kathleen on my porch."

"Well of course it was me." Betty preened. "Everyone thinks I'm old and feeble, but with my little wagon, I can accomplish almost anything."

Travis laughed. "How often have you set up Kathleen?"

"Often enough to keep the tradition going." She winked at him. "She'll be at your wedding too, I guarantee."

"Yardley and I wondered about that forever!" When

Mimi offered Betty a high five, she readily smacked her palm.

Then, full of earnest intensity, Betty stepped up to Yardley and touched her cheek. "You've given this old heart new life. It's the truth. I care a great deal about you, young lady."

"Oh, Betty." Near tears, Yardley hugged her close.

"There now." Betty patted her back. "I knew you were falling in love, and I couldn't resist teasing you."

Not to be left out, Lilith caught Yardley next. "I'm so proud of you."

Then Aurora took a turn, her hug a little tighter. "I knew you had it in you," she whispered. "I'm the proudest of all."

"How do you know that?" Lilith demanded. "I'm terribly proud."

"Because she's my daughter," Aurora said, clutching Yardley even more.

"She could have been mine." Lilith took Yardley's arm, trying to tug her free.

"Whoa." Yardley stepped away from them both. "Let's not get carried away."

Travis tucked her protectively close to his side, but he was grinning.

"Much more of all that effusive emotion," Mimi complained, "and I'll be bawling, then Yardley will be bawling—"

"It's true," Yardley confirmed, sniffling and turning in to Travis's warm arms.

"—and we've still got a wedding to enjoy." Being the best of best friends, Mimi corralled everyone while Kevin caught the wagon handle, and together they all headed inside, giving Yardley a moment alone with Travis.

His hand smoothed down her back, and he kissed her temple. "It amazes me how surprised you always are."

That made no sense, so she pulled herself together and straightened away. "Surprised about what?"

"How special you are. How much this town loves you. How much *I* love you."

Deep contentment filled her. "I love you, too, so, so much. But you know, I think I like being surprised. I think I'll keep being surprised—for the rest of our lives. Now, let's go get Sheena happily married."

"And then," he murmured, "you can start planning the next perfect wedding."

"Apparently with the help of the entire town." She laughed. "I bet it'll be my best wedding yet."

* * * * *

Here's a sneak peek at New York Times *bestselling author Lori Foster's next all-new summer read,* The Little Flower Shop.

A BAREFOOT WEDDING on the beach. A novel idea that the tiny town of Cemetery, Indiana, had fully embraced. As Emily Lucretia looked around at all the naked feet on women, men and kids, as well as the bride and groom, she couldn't help but smile. After such a long day, it'd be so nice to do the same, to kick off her dress sandals and wiggle her toes in the summer-warm sand.

Of course, she didn't. For whatever reason, that type of carefree enjoyment wasn't in her DNA. Long ago she'd accepted being the proverbial stick-in-the-mud, as her ex-husband had claimed.

But, she told herself, she was also a perfectionist, and even after a day in the late-August heat, her flower arrangements still looked incredible. Yardley, the stunning bride, had been thrilled with them all.

Above the sound of music, conversation and laughter, Emily heard a group splash into the lake. Swimming at a wedding. How fun was that?

The day of celebration had, for many, turned into a

real party once the ceremony had concluded. The air was humid but fresh, the mood mellow and festive. Scents from the flowers mingled with sunscreen, roasted pork over an open spit and breezes across the water.

Nearly everyone from Cemetery had turned out for the wedding and the beach was full. It was an unfortunate name for the friendly town, yet the people were wonderful and Emily loved the quaint area with all her heart.

Carefully maneuvering from one stepping stone to another, Emily fluffed and straightened the various arrangements. From pink peonies and blue hydrangeas to freesia and gardenias, anemones and daisies to rosebuds and baby's breath, it was a beautifully colorful wedding, ideal for the setting and exactly what the bride had requested.

Emily heard laughter and looked up to see a group of women toasting Yardley as she and her new husband prepared to leave. Yardley made such a beautiful bride, and as the town's wedding planner, she was in her element. She'd known exactly what she wanted, and how she wanted it, yet she'd never expected the area businesses to make the wedding a gift.

The entire town loved Yardley—with good reason. Thanks to her, the matriarch and great granddaughter of the town founder had loosened up enough to remove the clarification of "Cemetery" from the different venues.

Before Yardley had won that particular argument, Emily had suffered the misfortune of running Cemetery Florals, which made it seem that she only supplied flowers for burials. Actually, the small town didn't even have a cemetery. Those who passed away were buried in Allbee, the next town over.

"You're still wearing shoes."

Jumping at the sound of that deep, rich voice coming

from right behind her, Emily turned too fast and almost stumbled off the stepping stone. Saul Culver reached out and caught her arm, his hand big and warm against her bare elbow as he steadied her.

She looked up, way up, into incredibly nice green eyes, then down to those broad shoulders and the open front of Saul's shirt.

"Careful," he said, releasing her and then pressing a wine cooler into her hand. "I didn't mean to startle you."

Emily took the frosty bottle automatically, realized what it was and tried to hand it back. "I can't have this," she protested. At forty-one, she was well past the age of drinking on the beach, especially during a job. "I'm working."

"Em, *no one* is working."

Saul was the only one who shortened her name… and from him, she liked it. "Says the man who only just stepped away from the fire pit." She breathed in the scent of wood laced with his sun-warmed hair and skin—such a pleasant mix.

HARLEQUIN
PLUS

Try the best multimedia
subscription service for romance
readers like you!

Read, Watch and Play.

Experience the easiest way to get
the romance content you crave.

Start your **FREE TRIAL** at
<u>www.harlequinplus.com/freetrial</u>.